MW01002185

THE LOEB CLASSICAL LIBRARY

FOUNDED BY JAMES LOEB

EDITED BY

G. P. GOOLD

PREVIOUS EDITORS

T. E. PAGE   E. CAPPS

W. H. D. ROUSE   L. A. POST

E. H. WARMINGTON

ARISTOPHANES

I

LCL 178

ARISTOPHANES

ACHARNIANS · KNIGHTS

EDITED AND TRANSLATED BY
JEFFREY HENDERSON

HARVARD UNIVERSITY PRESS
CAMBRIDGE, MASSACHUSETTS
LONDON, ENGLAND
1998

Copyright © 1998 by the President and Fellows
of Harvard College
All rights reserved

LOEB CLASSICAL LIBRARY® is a registered trademark
of the President and Fellows of Harvard College

Library of Congress Cataloging-in-Publication Data

Aristophanes.
[Works. English & Greek. 1998]
Aristophanes / edited and translated by Jeffrey Henderson.
p.   cm.—(Loeb classical library ; 178)
Includes bibliographical references and index.
Contents: 1. Acharnians ; Knights
ISBN 0-674-99567-8 (v. 1)
1. Aristophanes—Translations into English.   2. Greek drama
(Comedy)—Translations into English.   I. Henderson, Jeffrey.
II. Title.   III. Series.
PA3877.A1H46   1998
882'.01—dc21   97-24063
CIP

CONTENTS

For Patricia J. Johnson

PREFACE

The original Loeb Aristophanes, first published in 1924, adopted its Greek text and verse translation from the scholarly editions by Benjamin Bickley Rogers (1828-1919), and over the years it has served its purpose well. Rogers' translation, with its rollicking Gilbert and Sullivan rhythms, captures something of Aristophanes' poetic form, and its sparkling vitality something of his unique comic flavor. But it is only as Aristophanic as the Victorian era would allow, so that its utility as a guide to the Greek is limited, and it now seems dated. Meanwhile, Aristophanic scholarship has considerably advanced our knowledge of the transmission and formal features of the text, and has also deepened our understanding of the comedies and the society they so intimately portray. For these reasons a replacement edition is justified.

I have edited the Greek text afresh. My translation is intended to assist readers of the Greek text and so has no literary pretensions, though within this constraint I have tried to make it as lively as possible. Since a Loeb edition is not the place for a commentary, my introductions and explanatory notes fall short of what non-specialist readers ideally need in reading an author as densely topical as Aristophanes. But I have tried to supply at least some help where readers might otherwise be baffled. My notes gen-

PREFACE

erally cite ancient sources rather than modern scholarship, but interested readers will be able to pursue questions by consulting the works cited in the Select Bibliography. The Index of Personal Names is designed both for general reference and to reduce the need to multiply footnotes in the case of persons mentioned more than once in the plays.

I wish to express my thanks to Margaretta Fulton of the Harvard University Press for her technical advice and good suggestions; to the Editor of the Loeb Classical Library, George P. Goold, for his generous and bracing criticism; and to Zeph Stewart, Trustee of the Library, both for his encouragement and assistance in this project and for his mentorship and friendship over the past thirty years.

This volume is dedicated with love and gratitude to my wife and colleague, Patricia J. Johnson.

Jeffrey Henderson

INTRODUCTION

Aristophanes of Athens was judged in antiquity to be the foremost poet of Old Attic Comedy,[1] a theatrical genre of which he was one of the last practitioners and of which his eleven surviving plays are our only complete examples.[2] Since antiquity his comedies have been valued principally for their iridescent wit and beguiling fantasy, for the exuberance and elegance of their language, and for their brilliant satire of the social, intellectual, and political life of Athens in an important era of its history. Legend has it that when the Syracusan leader Dionysius wanted to study "the polity of the Athenians," Plato sent him Aristophanes' comedies (T 1.42-45).

Little is known about Aristophanes' life apart from his theatrical career. According to the ancient *Life* (T 1), he

---

[1] Already in Plato's *Symposium* (c. 380) Aristophanes represents comedy; cf. also Aristotle's *Poetics,* 1448a24-27; see further T 52-95. [Numerals preceded by T refer to the ancient and medieval testimonia about Aristophanes, as collected by R. Kassel and C. Austin, eds., *Poetae Comici Graeci,* vol. III.2 (Berlin and New York, 1984), pp. 1-33].

[2] The era of Old Comedy is conventionally dated from 486, when comedy became an official event at the City or Greater Dionysia, until roughly the end of the fifth century. Comedy at the Lenaea began in 440.

was the son of one Philippus and belonged to the urban deme Cydathenaeum in the tribe Pandionis. The exact date of his birth is unknown,[3] but probably fell within a few years of mid-century, for *Clouds* 528-532 imply that he was young and inexperienced when he produced his first play in 427, and by 424 people were wondering why he had yet to produce a play on his own (*Knights* 512-513). By his twenties his hair had thinned or receded enough that his rivals could call him bald (T 46-50). *Acharnians* 642-644 show that he had a residence on the island of Aegina, and the context suggests that detractors had tried to use this connection to question his loyalty to Athens or even his Athenian citizenship.[4] Four comic poets of the fourth century are reputed in ancient sources to be his sons (T 7-8). For Nicostratus and Philetaerus we lack supporting evidence, but for Araros and Philippus we are on firmer ground: Araros launched his career in 387 by producing one of Aristophanes' plays, probably *Cocalus,* and subsequently produced a revised version of another, *Aeolosicon;* and a son of one Philippus of Cydathenaeum served as Councillor *c.* 360 (*IG* ii² 2370).[5] Aristophanes was prob-

---

[3] The date of 444/3 found in ancient sources (T 2, Schol. *Frogs* 501) is unsubstantiated.

[4] Cf. T 2. Cleon seems to have charged Aristophanes with foreign birth (Schol. *Acharnians* 378, 503, T 1.19-21, 24), and perhaps rival comic poets did as well (cf. Eupolis 392.3–8). Statements in ancient sources (T 1.21-24; 2.1-2; 9-12) that Aristophanes was Aeginetan by birth or that his family had settled there after Athens expelled the natives in 431 are mere inferences from this text, and his assignment to other cities is the result of confusion with other poets.

[5] In addition to his deme membership, Philippus will have

ably dead when Plato made him a character in *Symposium* (written *c.* 380).

Although we do not know how wealthy Aristophanes was, what evidence we do have suggests that he belonged to a prospering family and moved in elite circles. Early in the fourth century he represented his tribe in the prestigious office of Councillor (T 9). In *Acharnians* (6-8, 299-302) and *Knights,* he aligns himself with the upperclass cavalry corps; one of his Chorus of Knights is named Simon (*Knights* 242, 351), possibly portraying the dedicator of a bronze horse at the Eleusinion and author of a treatise on horsemanship,[6] and another Panaetius (243), possibly the Panaetius later condemned in the scandal of the Mysteries in 415.[7] This Simon may also have been the priest of a private cult of Heracles in Cydathenaeum (typically these were upperclass fraternities[8]), whose members are listed in an inscription datable to *c.* 400 (*IG* ii² 2343); they include Amphitheus, the name of the demi-divine fetcher of peace treaties in *Acharnians,* and Philonides, the producer of at least three of Aristophanes' plays (*Proagon, Amphiaraus,* and *Frogs*). Throughout his career Aristophanes promotes the views and policies of men on the conservative right and assails their opponents. Finally, in *Symposium* Plato portrays Aristophanes as being at home among the social and intellectual elite of Athens, and as a man of old-fashioned ethical values (190b-d, 193a-d). Whether or

inherited his paternal grandfather's name, as often in Athenian families.

[6] Cf. Xenophon, *On Horsemanship* 1.1.

[7] See Andocides 1.13, 52, 67.

[8] See, for example, Demosthenes 57.46.

not such a symposium ever actually took place, there is no reason to doubt its historical plausibility.

There is a graceful epitaph attributed to Plato (T 130):

αἱ Χάριτες, τέμενός τι λαβεῖν ὅπερ οὐχὶ πεσεῖται
    ζητοῦσαι, ψυχὴν εὗρον Ἀριστοφάνους
The Graces, looking for an imperishable shrine,
    found the soul of Aristophanes.

Aristophanes' career as a comic poet spanned some forty years, from his debut in 427 until *c.* 386. Forty-four comedies ascribed to him were known in antiquity; four of these ancient scholars considered spurious, for reasons now obscure.[9] Eleven comedies have survived intact, and of the lost comedies we have nearly a thousand fragments, a few of them on papyrus, the rest quotations by ancient scholars, most consisting of a word, a phrase, or a line or so.

Aristophanes' comedies, together with the known or conjectured circumstances of their production, are as follows:[10]

427 L?   *Banqueters* (2nd prize); produced by
               Callistratus[11]

[9] These are *Dionysus Shipwrecked, Dramas or Niobus, Islands,* and *Poesy.*

[10] The extant plays are asterisked; L = Lenaea and D = Dionysia.

[11] It was not uncommon for a poet to employ someone else as the producer (*didaskalos*) of his play, nor were such collaborations confined to inexperienced poets, as the production of *Frogs* by Philonides shows. Nevertheless, Aristophanes' delay in producing in his own name seems to have been controversial (*Knights* 512-

4

426 D	*Babylonians* (1st prize?[12]); produced by Callistratus
425 L	**Acharnians* (1st prize); produced by Callistratus
424 L	**Knights* (1st prize); produced by Aristophanes
424? D	*Farmers*
423? L	*Merchant Ships*
423 D	*Clouds I* (3rd prize or lower[13]); produced by Aristophanes
422 L	*Proagon* (1st prize); produced by Philonides[14]
422 L	**Wasps* (2nd prize); produced by Aristophanes
421 D	**Peace I* (2nd prize); produced by Aristophanes
421-12	*Seasons*
after *c.* 420	*Women Claiming Tent Sites*
419-7	*Anagyrus*
c. 418	**Clouds II*; never produced, incomplete revision of *Clouds I*
after *c.* 415	*Polyidus*

546, *Wasps* 1015-50, T 1.7-10, 3.9-10), perhaps because of his feud with Cleon.

[12] Suggested not only by Aristophanes' pride in this comedy (cf. *Acharnians* 628-64) and by its political impact, but also by its position in the victory list (*IG* i² 2325).

[13] The number of competing comedies was five before the Peloponnesian War (431-404); whether and at what point during the war the number was reduced to three is unknown.

[14] See the Introduction to *Wasps*.

414 L	*Amphiaraus*; produced by Philonides
414 D	**Birds* (2nd prize); produced by Callistratus
c. 413-11	*Heroes*
413-406?	*Daedalus*
after 412	*Peace II*
411 L	**Lysistrata;* produced by Callistratus
411 D	**Women at the Thesmophoria I*
c. 410-9	*Triphales*
c. 410-5	*Women at the Thesmophoria II*
after 410	*Lemnian Women*
after 409	*Old Age*
after 409	*Phoenician Women*
408	*Wealth I*
c. 408	*Gerytades*
before 406	*Dramas or Centaur*
405 L	**Frogs* (1st prize); produced by Philonides; reperformed by civic decree, probably 404 L
c. 402	*Telemessians*
before 400	*Fry Cooks (Tagenistai)*
before 395?	*Aeolosicon I*
c. 398r-389	*Storks*
c. 392	**Assemblywomen*
388	**Wealth II* (1st prize?)
387 D	*Cocalus* (1st prize); produced by Araros
after 387	*Aeolosicon II;* produced by Araros
?	*Danaids*

Aristophanes was from the start remarkably successful in national competition, winning at least six first prizes and four second prizes, with only one or two lower rankings

attested.[15] At least once he produced a comedy in the deme
theater at Eleusis (T 21), and *Clouds* 522-23 suggest that
a first production of that play outside Athens had been an
option. Perhaps the highpoint of his theatrical career fol-
lowed his victory with *Frogs* in 405, when the Athenians
voted him an honorific crown of sacred olive for the advice
he had given them in the *parabasis* of that play, and de-
creed that the play should have the unique honor of being
performed a second time (T 1.35-39), probably at the Le-
naea of 404.

Aristophanes often boasts of the superior quality and
originality of his work. The lack of complete comedies by
other poets limits our ability to evaluate Aristophanes'
claims, but the ancient critics who could still read much of
the Old Comic corpus do not contradict him, and the criti-
cisms of his rivals are few and comparatively mild.[16] A few
large-scale contributions to the genre can be identified
with some confidence. *Knights* was the first comedy en-
tirely devoted to the vilification of a single individual, and
seems to have established the main features of the dema-
gogue figure, which Aristophanes did not use again but
which proved fruitful for other poets until the end of the
century. In plays like *Banqueters, Clouds,* and *Lysistrata*
Aristophanes seems to have amalgamated the comedy of
political satire, pioneered by Cratinus in the 450s and Her-

[15] The first *Clouds* in 423, and perhaps the otherwise unat-
tested play *Odom]antopres[beis* listed in *IG* i[2] 2321.87-89.

[16] Cratinus 342 (as modishly clever as Euripides); Eupolis 60,
89 (plagiarism); Eupolis 62 and Plato Comicus 86 (the statue in
Peace); Ameipsias 27, Aristonymus 3, and Sannyrion 5 (that, like
Heracles, he spent his career working for others).

mippus in the 430s, with the domestic and ethical comedy of Crates and Pherecrates, which resembled Sicilian comedy and drew on tragedy to develop tighter plots and more complex characters.[17] Aristophanes is the only comic poet recorded as claiming intellectual sophistication as a virtue. Under this heading we may place his tendency to enrich his language with allusions to many genres of poetry; his intimate satire of sophistic ideas; and his frequent use of tragedy, especially Euripides, both for incidental parody and large-scale usurpation (most notably the virtual recreation of *Telephus* in *Acharnians* and *Women at the Thesmophoria);* Cratinus coined the verb "to euripidaristophanize" (fr. 342). In *Lysistrata* Aristophanes apparently introduced the first comic heroine; in previous comedies, female roles seem to have been confined to such disreputable types as market women, prostitutes, and the wives or mothers of demagogues. Finally, Aristophanes seems to have played a role in the transition from Old to Middle and New Comedy: *Wealth* was perhaps the first comedy to dispense with an integral chorus (T 1.51-54), and *Cocalus* "introduced rape and recognition and all the other motifs that Menander emulated" (T 1.49-51).

Aristophanes is best known as a political satirist. Although not all of his plays dealt primarily with politics—after 415 he seems to have broadened his scope to include more domestic, literary, and mythological subjects—it was his political comedies that most impressed contemporaries and fascinated posterity, and that during his career problematized the distinction between citizen and artist.

[17] Cf. Aristotle, *Poetics* 1449b.

Audience and Festival

As institutions the Athenian theatrical festivals were primarily civic: patriotic showcases for the democracy sponsored and administered by the demos (sovereign people) and funded on a grand scale by its wealthiest liturgists, the chorus masters (*choregoi*), who, along with poets selected by the appropriate officeholder, competed for prizes and civic prestige in dithyramb, tragedy and satyr drama, and comedy. The dancers, numbering some 1165 per festival, could be compelled to perform and were exempted from military service to do so. Front-row seating (*prohedria*) was a reward that the demos bestowed upon its most distinguished citizens and guests.

The distinctness of the dramatic festivals from other venues of civic assembly is also significant. The theater, which accommodated at least 17,000 spectators, concentrated much more of the Attic populace in one place at the same time than any other public event; the Assembly could house only 6,000. And the dramatic festivals were not exclusive; we hear of no attempt to restrict attendance by any class of residents or even foreigners.[18] Alongside the demos sat as many of those people who were otherwise debarred from civic assemblies as could get seats: women,[19] children, even slaves, metics (who could also perform at the Lenaea) and visiting foreigners. Moreover, all these

[18] Foreigners did not attend the Lenaea (*Acharnians* 504-6) because it was held in winter, not because they were barred.

[19] No ancient evidence supports the modern notion that women must have been excluded, and Plato twice explicitly mentions them among the spectators (*Gorgias* 502b-d, *Laws* 658a-d).

categories of people, normally invisible from the vantage point of civic deliberation, were standard characters in drama. As for the poets, they were elite competitors in a democratically organized contest, but unlike purely civic speakers, who could appeal only to democratic laws and procedures, the poets could appeal to much older cultic and poetic traditions, and to a more universal ethical code.

The dramatic festivals might thus be called supracivic: public meetings that encompassed the whole of society, not just its political subset. The concerns expressed in the dramas included but significantly transcended the set of problems specific to the executive worlds of lawcourt and Assembly, for they treated the ethics of family and private life; the lives of people as individuals as opposed to civic categories; the very discontinuity between the political and the larger society; and the wider world beyond Athens. And so drama became the principal communal outlet for portraying the polis in all its diversity and social hierarchies; for reconsidering traditions and norms, airing concerns, examining problems and testing solutions that affected the democratic culture as a whole but that had no other public outlet. As theatergoers, people debarred from all other venues of civic discourse could here experience the role of democratic audience. Community knowledge, from popular gossip to the concerns of the political class, could be aired and diffused. And people whose suggestions, concerns, or complaints had not been, or could not be, presented to the executive demos might expect them to be raised by one of the poets, not least the comic poets. Such people would include civic minorities like the "quiet" members of the elite and the "little people" who were rarely able to attend civic meetings, let alone likely to rise in the Assembly or to litigate, e.g. farmers from distant demes, or the poor. In these ways the dramatic festivals served to mend, or at least to paper over, generally perceived rifts in the body politic.

One important difference between the theater and other public assemblies, festive or political, was that attendees had to pay: two obols per person per day, roughly equivalent to the cost of attending a major concert today. The cost to a family of four who wished to attend all four days of a dramatic festival would have been significant: about a week's wages for a laborer, or ten days in court for a juror. This cost may well have deterred the poorer classes from attending, as the creation of the *theorikon* (a spectator fund to subsidize tickets for poorer citizens) perhaps implies, though it is only first attested in 343.[20] On the other hand, the dramatic festivals were held only twice a year, so that even a laborer or a juror who wanted to participate would have had no great difficulty saving up the cost of attendance.

Drama and democracy were closely related historically. Although the dramatic genres had ancient roots, their fifth-century forms were the product of festivals revamped for, and in some respects created by the emerging democracy, and they developed in step with democratic institutions. Significantly, both *choregia* and *theorikon* were abolished by the oligarchy of 322-17. The history of comedy in par-

[20] Other explanations for the Theoric Fund include mere demagogic egalitarianism and a decline in attendance at the national festivals due to competition from local theaters. In any case, Pericles and Cleon, both sponsors of jury payments, apparently saw no reason to institute such a fund in their own era.

ticular reveals an especially close synchrony with the history of democracy at Athens, and perhaps elsewhere too.[21] Comedy became part of the Dionysia in the reform year 487/6, when archons were first allotted and could be drawn from the second as well as the first census class, and when ostracism was introduced. Its most intensely political phase—pioneered by Cratinus in the 450s, continued by Hermippus in the 430s, and blossoming in the work of Aristophanes, Eupolis, Plato Comicus, and others during the "demagogic" era of the Peloponnesian War—coincided with the era of full popular sovereignty that was inaugurated by the reforms of Ephialtes in 461 and nurtured during the long ascendancy of his protégé Pericles. This phase tapered off after the reforms of 403, disappeared entirely during the oligarchic period of 322-307 (the era of the entirely apolitical New Comedy), but reappeared during two democratic restorations.[22] By contrast, the contemporary West Greek court comedy of Epicharmus and Sophron was entirely apolitical. Conversely, writers critical of democracy, for example Plato, were hostile toward all dramatic festivity and explicitly link it to democratic practice.

Aristophanes and Athenian Politics

Aristophanes, who stresses more often than any of his rivals the comic poet's duty to chastise and advise the city, early adopted the political style of comedy and did so in spectacular fashion, becoming embroiled in a legal and

[21] Cf. Aristotle, *Poetics* 1448a28-40 on 6th-century Megara.
[22] The fragments of Timocles are especially instructive.

political feud with his fellow demesman Cleon, the most
powerful politician in Athens at the time. The feud lasted
for nearly five years and inspired some of Aristophanes'
sharpest satire and most exuberant comedy. *Babylonians*
evidently criticized Athenian imperial policies, and at-
tacked Cleon personally,[23] prompting the politician to in-
dict the poet (less likely the producer Callistratus[24]) on
charges of having slandered the magistrates, Councillors,
and people of Athens in the presence of foreign allies.[25]
This round went to the poet, for the Council dismissed the
charges. At the following year's Lenaea, in *Acharnians*
(again produced by Callistratus), Aristophanes presented
a vigorous defence of himself and his art, and announced
his intention to launch a more thoroughgoing attack on
Cleon soon.

Aristophanes carried out his threat with *Knights,* the
first play produced in his own name and the play he was
subsequently to recall more often, and with more pride,
than any of his others, on grounds both of artistic original-
ity and political courage. Its production was in fact coura-
geous, even if the character Paphlagon is never explicitly
identified as representing Cleon: Cleon's stunning victory

[23] *Acharnians* 377-382, 502-508, with Schol.; T 1.21-29.

[24] *Knights* 512 shows that the identity of an author was known
even if someone else was the producer, and *IG* i² 2318, a list of
victorious poets, credits Aristophanes, not Callistratus, with a vic-
tory at the Dionysia in 426 or 425. Aristophanes' own references,
in the plays of the 420s, to his battles with Cleon also make it clear
that he and no one else was involved.

[25] The allies made their annual tribute payments at the City
Dionysia.

at Pylos had made him a popular hero, who was to be elected to the board of generals a few weeks after the production. Cleon again retaliated by indicting, or threatening to indict, the poet. The winner of this round is less clear, to judge from Aristophanes' cryptic recollection in *Wasps*: evidently Cleon violently abused and menaced Aristophanes (1285-1286), who, receiving little support from the public (1287-1289), decided to issue some sort of public apology (1290), which some considered sincere (1284) but which was in fact a trick (1291), since Aristophanes attacked Cleon again in the following year (*Clouds* 581-594) and again in *Wasps*, where he is caricatured as a vicious dog.

Aristophanes' hostility to Cleon was but one element of his consistent tendency to espouse the social, moral, and political sentiments of contemporary upperclass conservatives, a tendency that corroborates the picture of his social position as sketched above. The wealthy as a class are never criticised, whereas the poor often are.[26] There is nostalgia for the good old days of the early democracy, before the reforms of Ephialtes in 461 established its "radical" phase, and before Pericles eclipsed Cimon. In those days the people were still united and still deferred to "the best" (meaning men from the traditional ruling families), and so had been able to repel the Persian invaders, win a great empire, and lift Athens to unprecedented heights of prosperity. There is disapproval of the popular intellectual movements associated with the "sophists" (including Socrates),

---

[26] In his postwar plays *Assemblywomen* and *Wealth*, however, Aristophanes seems to have mitigated his attitude toward the poor.

and of such "vulgar" novelties in poetry and music as those of Euripides (never Sophocles) and the new dithyrambists.[27] There is hostility to the populist policies of Pericles and the new breed of leaders (like Cleon) who had emerged after his death in 429, such as the subsidy that enabled the poor to serve on juries (but not the equipment subsidies paid to the wealthy Knights). There is criticism of the way the Council, the Assembly, and the courts exercised their authority, particularly when private wealth in Athens and the empire was thereby threatened. And there is disagreement with the rationale behind, and the leadership of, the Peloponnesian War (431-404), because it had ended the Cimonian dream of joint Athenian-Spartan hegemony and pitted Greek against Greek; because it encouraged renewed barbarian aggression; and because it furthered the selfish and dangerous ambitions of leaders like Cleon. But significantly, we hear such disagreement only when current policy exposed the Attic countryside, and thus the landowners, to enemy invasion and devastation; at other times the plays either say nothing about the war or positively support it, for example *Birds* 186, 640, 813-816, 1360-1369.

Aristophanes shows the same consistent bias in his choice of political figures to vilify and not to vilify. All of his political targets were on what may be called the left, that is to say radical democrats like Pericles and his successors, whereas men like Nicias, Laches, Alcibiades, those implicated in the scandals of 415, and the oligarchs disenfranchised after the coup d'état of 411—potential targets

[27] Even though Aristophanes' satire reveals his own intimate familiarity with, and some artistic dependence on these targets.

15

at least as obvious as Pericles and Cleon—are entirely spared, and occasionally even defended. This bias cannot be satisfactorily explained as merely an automatic response to the political predominance of the left during Aristophanes' career, on the theory that political comedy tends to attack the powers that be whatever their political stripe, for these reasons: Aristophanes also mentions some political figures favorably, all of them opponents of leftists; he not only ridicules leftist policies but also champions rightist policies on their merits; and during periods when the leftists were in eclipse, he continues to attack them and to spare the currently ascendant rightists.[28]

The partisan character of the criticism, advice, and advocacy expressed in Aristophanes' plays, and apparently in the political comedy of his rivals as well, supports the poets' frequently expressed claim to be serious advisers as well as comedians: "even comedy knows about what's right" (*Acharnians* 500); "let the prize go to him who gives the best advice to this city" (Cratinus 52). And there is evidence that such comic politics could indeed have an impact on Athenian public opinion. In addition to the *Frogs* decree and the prosecutions by Cleon mentioned above, there was the prosecution of Socrates in 399, which Plato attributes in large part to prejudices popularized by comedy;[29] a proposal to reduce the honoraria of comic poets, which Aristophanes attributes to the proposer's re-

[28] For example, he continues to attack Cleon in *Clouds,* during the truce won by Cleon's enemy Laches, and in *Peace,* when Cleon was dead and his opponent Nicias was predominant.

[29] See *Apology* 18b-19c, 23c-d.

16

sentment at having been ridiculed;[30] and at least two well-attested decrees that somehow limited the scope of comic satire: the decree of Morychides, in force from 440/39 until 437/6, during the politically divisive Samian War,[31] and the decree of Syracosius, in force from 415-*c.* 410, years that saw the scandals of the Mysteries and the Herms and the political and military disasters precipitated by the Sicilian Expedition.[32] Beyond these cases we cannot trace the precise impact of comic politics, but it would be surprising if, for example, the drumbeat of comic abuse that preceded the destruction of the popular leaders Hyperbolus and Cleophon did not materially strengthen their enemies' hand. Political comedy, unconstrained by the agenda of deliberative debate, could thus serve as a kind of experimental politics, freely revisiting or previewing matters of public interest that had no other public outlet.

If comic poets reveled in the privilege of "frank speech" (*parrhesia*) that was so proud a hallmark of Athenian democracy, they nevertheless show self-restraint in those areas where they might offend the public or expose themselves to legal or political sanctions. After all, they had been authorized by a magistrate representing the people to perform in a major national festival, and they were competing for prizes that would be awarded by judges representing the people. As the pamphleteer known as the Old Oligarch points out (*c.* 425), in part to question the reality of the Athenians' vaunted *parrhesia,* "they do not allow

[30] See *Frogs* 367-368, where Schol. identifies the proposer as Archinus or (less likely) Agyrrhius.

[31] See Schol. *Acharnians* 67.

[32] See *Birds* 1297 with Schol.; Phrynichus fr. 27.

comic ridicule and criticism of the demos, lest their reputation suffer, but they encourage this in the case of individuals ... For they are sure that the victim is generally not one of the demos or the crowd but a rich, well-born, or powerful person."[33]

Now Aristophanes does often criticize the shortcomings of the demos, but is always careful to blame them on bad leadership. He never criticizes the democratic constitution or the right of the demos to full sovereignty; he condemns both demagogic tyranny and elite oligarchy;[34] he does not foment class antagonism, as he accuses Cleon of doing; and he presents all his advice and criticisms as being in the best interests of the demos. Even in their abuse of individuals, comic poets avoid the *aporrheta* ("unspeakable allegations") that would, if true, interfere with the victim's right to participate in public life and so constitute actionable slander (except, of course, when such charges were unanswerable): they do not vilify acting magistrates or generals (though these could be abused as a class), charge people with murder, parent abuse, public debt, evasion of military duty, aspiration to tyranny, *asebeia* (offending the gods), shield throwing,[35] inheritance squandering, prostitution, foreign parentage.[36] Nor do they ridicule such popular figures as athletes or even mention such

[33] [Xenophon] *Constitution of the Athenians* 2.18; for the wording compare *Acharnians* 503 and 630-631.

[34] Cf. *Birds* 125-126, *Lysistrata* 577-578.

[35] For the unique case of Cleonymus see *Acharnians* 88 n.

[36] In each testable case, the individuals so abused were born near enough to 451 (when the citizenship law was enacted) that the charge was plausible and thus unlikely to be answered.

18

sensitive figures as unmarried citizen women. Save for their more indecent language, the comic poets frame their advice and criticisms by the same rules of engagement as the orators.

Like the orators, then, the comic poets were elite voices who were allowed, indeed expected, to speak frankly and honestly in the service of, or at any rate not to the detriment of, the people, and who could be held accountable for abuse of that privilege. After all, general moralizing, the offering of advice, criticism of the status quo, and abuse of one's competitors were standard ingredients of all public speech in fifth-century Athens, and had a traditional place in the Greek poetic tradition as well, from Hesiod onward.[37] In this respect comic drama was a festive extension of political debate. By contrast, private writers like Thucydides, the Old Oligarch, and Plato, who share many of Aristophanes' qualms about radical democracy and its leaders, could afford to be less guarded in their criticisms, and are decidedly less constructive in advancing solutions.

The comic poets' perennial success with plays that sharply satirized the demos and its leaders, that urged policies that only a minority of voters were prepared to accept, and that occasionally provoked legal or legislative sanctions does, however, raise the question whether the members of the demos who attended the theater were representative of the demos as a whole. If so, the success of plays like *Knights* is surprising, as is the poets' refusal to cater to majority opinion. Lack of documentary evidence pre-

---

[37] In *Frogs* Aristophanes, like Plato, assumes that poets are teachers of the people and should be held accountable for the effects of their work.

cludes a definitive answer, but on balance it seems unlikely that any subset of the politically active citizenry who shaped or enacted Athenian policy was significantly under-represented in theatrical audiences, or to put it another way, unlikely that theatrical audiences were dominated by disgruntled upperclass Athenians whose views were at odds with the majority of the executive demos.

Comic poets, orators, and litigators invariably treat their audiences as identical to the demos, but in neither case can this equation be literally true: just as not all members of the demos were present at a given Assembly meeting or court session, so the theatrical audiences included many who did not otherwise participate in democratic life. Thus the equation was only notionally true: official civic and festive assemblies were taken to represent the demos because the demos was in charge of them and because they represented the ideology, character, and authority of the democracy. But nowhere are we given to understand that a theatrical audience was in reality unrepresentative. For instance, if the audience of *Clouds* were largely composed of Cleon haters, we would expect the reproach at 587 "you elected him anyway" to be aimed rather at "those fools in the Assembly." And it was of course the actual demos that took the advice Aristophanes offered in *Frogs*.

Plato, who as a private writer had no motive for adopting the notional stance toward the demos, also takes it for granted that theatrical audiences constituted a representative cross section of the Athenian populace and included the same members of the demos who otherwise constituted assemblies and juries.[38] By contrast with Aris-

---

[38] See for example *Gorgias* 502b-d, *Laws* 817c, 658a-d.

tophanes, who often flatters his audience on their intelligence and discernment, Agathon in Plato's *Symposium* contrasts the company of his friends, "the few who have sense," with the theatrical audience, "the many who have no sense" (194b). And the charge in *Apology* is that the comic portrayal of Socrates created prejudice against him in the populace at large, including the jurors who heard his case.

Finally, the upperclass and conservative biases of Aristophanes and his rivals cannot by themselves be taken as evidence that their audiences largely shared these biases: orators and litigators, whose audiences did include the lower classes, often expressed the same sorts of biases, even when not championing conservative positions; and the New Comedy that flourished after the establishment of the *theorikon* subsidy largely depicts the life, and reflects the attitudes, of the upper classes. When Aristophanes is urging his views, attacking his victims, and defending himself to the demos, he does not sound like a man preaching to the converted; nor can we imagine him sparing Cleon and attacking Nicias even if his audience were composed entirely of Cleon's partisans.

It would thus appear that in their political moments the comic poets did commend to the demos, sitting among the other spectators, the views of their class, and did hope to persuade the demos to rethink or even change its mind about the way they were governing or about issues that had been decided but might be changed; to discard dangerous novelties; and to be more critical of its leaders. Nor was this effort as quixotic as we might imagine in long retrospect, since the comic poets were contributing to debates and divisions of opinion that were yet unresolved. Aristophanes' ongoing plea for a negotiated peace may have been a minority view at the time, but it was not a view entertained solely by Aristophanes nor an issue that was ever finally decided. As for Cleon, the people's discrepant responses in the theater and in the Assembly may well reflect real ambivalence: as Assemblymen the people wanted Cleon, and after Pylos they could hardly deny him a command, but as citizens they may have felt unhappy about giving him so much power; and for all we know *Knights* may have undermined his stature in ways not precisely measurable. The commendation for Aristophanes' advice in *Frogs* was the most salient, but surely not the only instance of political comedy affecting political life.

So perhaps the best explanation for the comic poets' conservative appeals is that they still retained some power: by urging rejection of radical novelties, the poets were trying to recall the demos to its past greatness in a period of political transition and evident decline, when the demos too must have been at least a bit nervous, for all its support of a Cleon. In addition, the soul of Aristophanic comedy was essentially popular: his hero(in)es and other sympathetic characters, always fictitious, exclusively represent ordinary or quiet people who in real life would have little or no power; he offers the city advice and criticism exclusively on their behalf; and he shows them winning out over individuals and groups that held power or celebrity. The comic vantage point is essentially that of the ordinary citizen looking into the arena of civic power and faulting those who dominate it, while they themselves, as the Old Oligarch noted, are righteously spared. The utopia constructed by a comic hero(ine) invariably appeals to the fantasies of the ordinary citizen.

But our fascination with Aristophanes' politics should not blinker our view of his overall artistry. Even political comedy was much more than a mere platform for criticism and advice: the award of the first prize to *Knights* was not so much a referendum on Cleon as the recognition of a superior drama in which the quality of the poetry, music, dancing, costumes, slapstick, humor, and wit were all relevant criteria of judgment.

The Form and Style of Aristophanic Comedy

Fifth century tragedy and satyr drama have a relatively simple structure: a number of episodes (dialogue among characters) each followed by a choral ode (stasimon) performed by a chorus of 12-15 dancers, who have little or no interaction with the characters on stage. The chorus of Old Comedy, by contrast, had 24 dancers—a legacy of the *komos* (band of revellers) from which comedy (*komoidia* "song of the *komos*") derives its name—who along with their leader (usually named) have a much more prominent role in the action, a role which moreover changes from play to play. To provide for its complex chorus-stage interactions, comedy developed an elaborate structural scheme that was highly formalized but flexible enough to allow for variation and novelty.[39] At the beginning of his career Aristophanes follows this scheme with little variation; by the time of *Lysistrata* he begins to show greater freedom in manipulating its elements; and by the early fourth century

---

[39] All of the elements of this structural scheme can be paralleled in the fragments of other comic poets.

the choral elements are largely abandoned, comedy having already reached its Middle period.

The elements of the traditional scheme are these:[40]

A *Prologue* in spoken iambic trimeters sometimes enlivened by a song, which warms up the audience, explains the initial situation (either in an expository speech or in dialogue), and sets the plot in motion.

The *Parodos* or entry of the Chorus, in a mixture of song (usually strophic) and recitative in "long-verse" tetrameters (iambic, trochaic, or anapaestic), which often end with a *pnigos* ("choker"), a series of dimeter verses not unlike a Gilbert and Sullivan patter song. In the Parodos the Chorus is introduced and characterized, engages in lively (often violent) interaction with the characters on stage, and after an easing of tension prepares for the next section, sometimes with an iambic trimeter scene.

The *Agon* is a formal debate between two contestants,[41] with interjections by a third party and presided over by the Chorus Leader. By convention, the first contestant ultimately loses the debate. The Agon regularly takes the form of an epirrhematic syzygy: a song by the Chorus followed by a speech (*epirrhema*) in a tetrameter meter (the number of verses is almost always divisible by four), then a responding song and a speech by the other contestant in the same meter and with the same number of lines as the

[40] Whether or with what permutations Aristophanes followed these structural features in his lost domestic and mythological comedies cannot be determined.

[41] In *Birds, Lysistrata,* and *Assemblywomen* we have less a debate than a news conference held by the hero(ine), with incredulous questions from an opponent.

first; the structure is thus ABAB. In *Acharnians, Peace,* and
Women at the Thesmophoria the Agon's epirrhematic
structure is replaced by a debate in iambic trimeters. The
Agon normally concludes the antagonistic phase of the
Chorus' involvement in the plot, and settles the motive
conflict in which the characters have been involved, but
some plays (like *Knights, Clouds,* and *Frogs*) have more
than one Agon.

The *Parabasis* (the "stepping forth" or self-revelation
of the Chorus), during which no characters appear on stage
and the plot of the play is not mentioned, consists of (1) a
speech in tetrameters (normally anapaestic) delivered by
the Chorus Leader *qua* Chorus Leader to the spectators,
followed by (2) an epirrhematic syzygy in which the Chorus
Leader speaks, and the Chorus sings, in character about
some topic of interest to them. In (1) the Chorus Leader
often speaks on behalf of the poet, praising his art, de-
nouncing his enemies, and offering advice to the city. In
(2) the speeches consist of sixteen verses, except for
Clouds, Wasps, and *Frogs,* where there are twenty, and
Peace, where there are no speeches at all. In some plays
there is a second parabasis consisting only of the syzygy. In
Lysistrata, whose Chorus is divided until late in the play,
there is only a brief epirrhematic syzygy for each of the two
Semichoruses.

A series of *Episodes* illustrating the hero(ine)'s success
and/or the consequences of the debate, punctuated by cho-
ral songs, usually strophic and usually consisting of free-
form abuse of individuals in the audience. These Episodes
allowed the poet scope for revue-like scenes which do not
advance the plot, which is often effectively concluded be-
fore the Parabasis, while in plays like *Clouds, Birds,* and

25

INTRODUCTION

Lysistrata the Episodes illustrate a plot that is not resolved until the end of the play.

The *Exodos* is the conclusion of the play, which has no fixed pattern (thus maximizing the poet's opportunity to spring surprises) but typically features feasting, wine, women (or boys), and song in a celebratory mode.

In its functional structure, an Aristophanic comedy typically depicts a character in the grip of an apparently intractable problem, usually one shared by a particular class of spectators: for example, misconceived warfare, bad political leaders, an unjust jury system, dangerous artistic or intellectual trends, turmoil in the family. This character, who becomes the play's hero, conceives of a fantastic but essentially plausible way to solve this problem and thus to achieve the sort of safety and success that everyone would envy—for him- or herself, family, city, or (as in *Peace* and *Lysistrata*) the whole Greek world. But before the hero succeeds he or she must face determined opposition from opposing characters and/or the Chorus, and overcome it by persuasion, guile, magic, or force.

Aristophanes' characters fall into two main categories: sympathetic and unsympathetic. The sympathetic characters—the hero and his or her supporters—are always fictitious creations embodying ideal civic types or representing idealized versions of ordinary, marginal, or powerless Athenians. The unsympathetic characters embody disapproved civic behavior (political, social, artistic, religious, or intellectual) and usually represent specific leaders or categories of leaders. The sympathetic characters typically advocate positions allegedly held by political or social minorities (e.g. women) or by ordinary, disempowered citizens (e.g. small farmers). But these are shown winning out against the unsympathetic characters, who represent the current social or political hegemony. Characters or choruses representing the demos as a whole are portrayed as initially sceptical or hostile to the sympathetic character(s), but in the end they are persuaded. Those who are responsible for the problem are exposed, then disgraced or expelled, and Athens is recalled to a sense of her true (traditional) ideals and thus renewed.[42]

The language (or better, literary dialect) of tragedy and satyr drama is loftily "poetic" in both dialogue and choral lyric (which has a traditional Doric color); any approach to the topical or colloquial could be criticized as vulgarization, with which Aristophanes taxes Euripides in *Frogs.* By contrast, the basic linguistic register of Old Comedy (both characters and choruses) was urbane, colloquial Attic. In addition, the conventions of the genre allowed, and evidently encouraged, a strong admixture of other registers both higher (e.g. parody of tragedy and other serious poetry) and lower (e.g. imitation of vulgar speech) than the colloquial norm, together with any other elements that the poet cared to toss into the rich linguistic farrago. Very prominent are puns and other types of word play; novel coinages; rabelaisian compound words; long accumulations and enumerations; and metaphors verbal, visual, or both. To a significant degree, the invective, obscenity, and colloquial styles of Old Comedy preserve the ethos of iambic poetry, which had flourished in the archaic period, and elaborate the carnivalesque festivity of the fertility cults,

---

[42] *Clouds,* with its misguided and unsuccessful "hero" Strepsiades, is the exception to this pattern, and that may well have contributed to its failure in competition.

particularly those of Demeter and Dionysus. Old Comedy also features the open (though grotesquely stylized) display of human sexual, excremental, and gustatory functions. In the classical period, iambus, comedy, and the fertility cults were the only permissible public outlets for this sort of language and display.

The rough, abusive language and uninhibited action of Old Comedy may strike some readers as being shockingly crude, sexist, homophobic, xenophobic, or the like. But we should bear in mind (1) that Aristophanes was writing not for us but for contemporaries living in a society at once very sophisticated and very different from our own, and (2) that outrageousness was a traditional ingredient of Old Comedy and one fully in keeping with comedy's tendency to expose, deflate, and provoke. Thus nothing that we hear or see in an Aristophanic comedy can automatically be assumed to reflect the norms and behavior of the average, or indeed any, Athenian. In my translation I have therefore made no attempt to spare the modern reader by censoring or circumventing potentially disturbing material; instead I have tried to render each of Aristophanes' linguistic registers by using the nearest English equivalent.

Production

The principal occasions for the production of comedy, as of tragedy and satyr drama, were the Dionysiac festivals of the Lenaea (January or February) and the City, or Greater Dionysia (March or April). At both festivals the dramatic competitions were held in the Theater of Dionysus on the south slope of the Acropolis, but we also hear of a special Lenaean theater (location unknown). Normally five comic poets competed at each festival, each with a single play, though during at least some of the Peloponnesian War the number of competitors may have been reduced to three.

Comedy, tragedy, and satyr drama were performed in the same theater and perhaps on the same day (if that is the import of *Birds* 786-789), but the requirements of comedy were more elaborate and quite various, suggesting that the performance areas could be rapidly and flexibly configured both during and between plays.

The chorus performed on a large circular *orchestra*, or dance floor, surrounded on three sides by the audience; the chorus entered and left the *orchestra* by walkways called *parodoi* by modern scholars but *eisodoi* by Aristophanes. Behind the *orchestra* and approached by a few steps was a slightly raised stage, where the actors performed. Behind the stage was a two story building called the *skene* ("tent," from which our word "scene"). It had two or three doors at stage level, windows at the second story, and a roof on which actors could appear. The variety of form and decor that we find in the comedies suggests that the *skene* was a temporary modular structure of wood. On the roof of the *skene* was a crane called the *mechane* ("machine"), on which actors could fly above the stage (as gods, for example, whence the Latin expression *deus ex machina*, "god from the machine"). Another piece of permanent equipment was a wheeled platform called the *eccyclema* ("device for rolling out"), on which actors and scenery could be wheeled onstage from the *skene* to reveal "interior" action. A painted or otherwise decorated plywood facade could be attached to the *skene* if a play (or scene) required it, and movable props (of which comedy used a great many) and other scenery were used as needed. Since plays were performed in daylight in a large outdoor amphitheater, all entrances and exits of performers and objects took place in full view of the spectators. All in all, more demand was made on the spectators' imagination than in modern illusionistic theater, so that performers must often tell the spectators what they are supposed to see.

The actors wore masks that covered the entire head. These were generic (young man, old woman, etc.), but in comedy they might occasionally be special, like a portrait mask of a prominent citizen (Socrates may well have been so caricatured in *Clouds*, for example). The costumes of tragic actors were grand, as befitted personages from heroic myth; comic costumes were contemporary and generically suited to the characters except that, wherever possible, they accommodated the traditional features of padded stomach and rump and (for men) the *phallos*, made of leather, either dangling or erect as appropriate, and circumcised in the case of outlandish barbarians.[43] All dramatic roles were played by men; the "naked" women who often appear were men wearing body stockings to which false breasts and genitalia were attached. The city supplied an equal number of actors to each competing poet, probably three, and these actors played all the speaking roles. In *Birds*, for example, there are 22 speaking roles, but the text's entrances and exits are so arranged that three actors can play them all. Some plays (like *Lysistrata*)

---

[43] The phallus, in addition to being a traditional element of comic and satyric costumes, symbolized fertility and masculine power, and it was especially associated with the worship of Dionysus.

do, however, require a fourth (or even a fifth) actor in small roles. Perhaps in given years the allotment changed, or novices were periodically allowed to take small parts, or poets or producers could add extra actors at their own expense. During Aristophanes' career, the actors (unlike the chorus) were professionals; at the Lenaea (though not at the Dionysia) they competed for a separate prize (Best Leading Actor, or *protagonist*).

That all female characters, from tragic heroines to the "naked women" of comedy, were played by men does not mean that Athenian drama was a drag show nor tell against the possibility that these portrayals of women were intended to be believable. After all, Shakespeare's women were also played by men (before audiences that included women), but no one finds them especially untrue to life: like the female characters of Athenian drama, they are now played by female actors without any need of adjustment. If male portrayal of females was not simply an Athenian theatrical convention but a drag show for men, we would expect to find the dramatists (especially the comic poets) calling attention to its artificiality. But there are no examples of this: male and female characters are at all times understood to be respectively men and women, and every character's gender was always obvious at least from the mask: pale for women, dark for men. Finally, the convention by which men played women's roles was less a strain on the imagination in the theater of Dionysus than it would be in today's theatrical media: the wearing of masks, together with the huge amphitheater setting, put a premium on the actor's voice and on broad, stylized gestures.

In the orchestra was a chorus of 24 men, amateurs recruited by the *choregos*, who sang and danced to the accompaniment of an *aulos,* a wind instrument that had two recorder-like pipes played simultaneously by a specially costumed player; and there could be other instruments as well. Like the actors, members of the chorus wore masks and costumes appropriate to their dramatic identity. There could be dialogue between the Chorus Leader and the actors on stage, but the chorus as a whole only sings and dances.[44] The choral songs of comedy were in music and language usually in a popular style, though serious styles were often parodied, and the dancing was expressive, adding a visual dimension to the words and music.

The History of the Text

The earliest text of a play of Aristophanes, being made not for readers or theater companies but for those who would perform it at a single festival, included only the words of the script; there were no lists of dramatis personae, notes, stage directions, or even assignments of lines to speakers. All performance aspects of a play had to be inferred from the script, so that editors ancient and modern differ to some degree in reconstructing them. The scripts themselves, as in all texts duplicated in handwritten copies, no doubt contained errors and omissions, and these inevitably multiplied in subsequent copies. In choosing among the readings in available manuscripts, and in emending the text where no manuscript reading seems right, editors differ in their restoration of the hypothetical original. Although some information about ancient copies

---

[44] There was no ancient counterpart to the "choral speaking" often heard in modern performances of Greek drama.

of the text survives indirectly—on a few papyri, through quotations in other authors, and in exegetical scholarship of the sort preserved in scholia (marginal annotations in manuscripts of the text)—our earliest copy of the text itself dates only from *c.* A.D. 950.

Very few copies of Old Comic texts circulated in the fourth century BC. Old Comedy was used as a source by historians like Theopompus, and from *c.* 335 Aristotle and other scholars of the Peripatos (e.g. Dicaearchus) did research on drama using official archival records and texts. Early in the third century Ptolemy I commissioned the collection of all classical Greek authors still extant, including the Old Comic dramatists, for deposit in the Library attached to the Museum in Alexandria. There scholars began the process of cataloguing comic texts and writing historical, literary, and exegetical studies of them. Principal among these scholars are Callimachus, Lycophron, Eratosthenes, Machon, and Dionysiades of Mallos.

Early in the second century, Aristophanes of Byzantium produced the first critical edition of his namesake's plays, including the first colometry of the lyric passages. His text became the vulgate as well as the standard Alexandrian text; all our copies descend ultimately from it. The first learned commentaries on this text were written by Callistratus and Euphronius for some of the plays; Aristarchus of Samothrace wrote the first major commentary, treating at least eight, and possibly all eleven of our extant plays.[45]

---

[45] Beyond our eleven plays, only three are known to have been commented on in antiquity (*Danaids, Merchant Ships,* and *Storks*).

At about the same time, scholars in the Library at Pergamum in Mysia also worked on Aristophanes (Crates of Mallos is the principal name), but very little of their work was absorbed by our tradition. Around the time of Augustus, Didymus of Alexandria compiled a variorum commentary that both collected a large amount of previous scholarship on comedy and added a considerable amount of new, particularly historical, information from a broad range of sources. Probably at the same time, Heliodorus and then Hephaestion reworked the lyrics; their systems superseded the Alexandrian colometry and were inherited by the medieval tradition.

Over the next three centuries, and especially during the Atticist revival of the second century, the plays of Aristophanes, Cratinus, and Eupolis were still widely read, and Didymus' commentary was excerpted and recompiled by Symmachus, Phaeinus, and perhaps others. Around A.D. 400, probably as a result of the suitability of the new commentaries for use in schools, our eleven extant plays became canonical, while all the rest of Old Comedy was gradually lost through neglect or as a result of the anti-pagan extremism of the period *c.* 650-850. By stages no longer precisely traceable, abridged and often dislocated versions of these commentaries, infused with grammatical and rhetorical matter from Byzantine schoolrooms, found their way into the margins of our medieval manuscripts and into reference works like the tenth century Suda. Meanwhile the text itself, protected from irremediable corruption by the learned commentaries and by its relatively restricted circulation in late antiquity,[46] survived to be copied and studied by scholars of the ninth century renaissance, in particular Photius and Arethas. Whether only one or more than one copy of a given play survived into their era cannot be determined with assurance.

We possess some three hundred manuscripts of Aristophanes dating from the tenth to the sixteenth century, most containing only the Byzantine triad of (in numerical order) *Wealth, Clouds,* and *Frogs,* with *Knights* the next best attested (31 manuscripts); at the other extreme are *Peace* (ten, only one complete), *Lysistrata* (eight, only one complete), *Assemblywomen* (seven), and *Women at the Thesmophoria* (one). Only two manuscripts, R (*c.* 950) and V (11th-12th c.), precede and thus are unaffected by the editorial interventions and conjectural activity of the scholars of the Palaeologan period (1261-1453), principally Maximus Planudes (*c.* 1255-1305), Manuel Moschopoulos (*c.* 1265-1316), Thomas Magister (*c.* 1275-*c.* 1350), and Demetrius Triclinius (*c.* 1280-*c.* 1335). Of these, Triclinius most heavily influenced the subsequent tradition: he made full-scale editions of eight, perhaps nine, of the plays (omitting *Lysistrata* and *Women at the Thesmophoria*); compiled his own massive corpus of scholia (including some ancient material otherwise unattested); and extensively emended the texts, especially the lyrics.

R is the only manuscript containing all eleven plays complete; V contains seven plays complete. Both R and V

[46] The some 35 papyrus fragments of Aristophanes that we possess reveal no substantial difference in quality between the ancient and the medieval text.

carry copious scholia derived from a common source, but those in V are fuller and more accurately preserved. The relative value of R and V for constituting the text varies from play to play. In addition to R and V, the Suda is an important early witness: it contains a great many quotations of Aristophanes' plays from lost pre-Palaeologan manuscripts and sometimes preserves readings unattested elsewhere.[47] Of the remaining significant manuscripts, none equals R and V in value, but collectively they provide a check on R in the four plays missing in V; often help us decide the inherited reading where RV are divided; and sometimes (singly or in groups) preserve the truth when both R and V are in error.

Since the transmission of the Aristophanic corpus was "open," with scribes often using more than one exemplar and drawing variants from sources different from their exemplar(s), any manuscript or group of manuscripts may in a given case preserve a good reading, and manuscripts may change their affiliations and thus their relative value from play to play, or even within a play. Therefore nothing that is said about the relative value of, or the relationship between the manuscripts in any one play of Aristophanes is necessarily valid for the same manuscripts in another play. Accordingly, in this edition the transmission of each play is separately described.

The first printed edition of Aristophanes was an Aldine (Venice, 1498), edited by Marcus Musurus and containing nine plays, the texts drawn from Triclinian manuscripts,

---

[47] The standard edition of the Suda is by Ada Adler (Leipzig, 1928-1938).

and the scholia (which formed the basis of all editions of the scholia until the late nineteenth century) mostly from the fourteenth-century manuscript E. The remaining two plays, *Lysistrata* and *Women at the Thesmophoria,* were published in a Juntine edition (Florence, 1515) when R, the only manuscript to preserve them both intact, was rediscovered in Urbino by Euphrosynus Boninus, who used it as printer's copy for the edition. A second Juntine edition (Florence, 1525) restored, again from R, the missing lines of *Peace* (948-1011). Subsequently R again disappeared from circulation until the late eighteenth century. The first editor to print all eleven plays together was Cratander (Basle, 1532).

Thereafter no major improvements were made to the text until the edition by L. Küster (Amsterdam, 1710), who used the Suda, which he also edited, and incorporated important conjectures by Richard Bentley.[48] The edition by R. P. F. Brunck (Strasbourg, 1783) incorporated the Paris manuscripts A, B, and C, and that of P. Invernizi (Leipzig, 1794) first incorporated R. The edition by I. Bekker (London, 1829) first systematically based the text on R and V. Of the subsequent nineteenth-century editions, the most important are those by W. Dindorf, A. Meineke, T. Kock, and A. von Velsen, who provided the first accurate collations of the principal manuscripts.

---

[48] Bentley's conjectures were entered in his copy of the Gelenius edition (Basle, 1547), now in the British Library (676. h. 13). They were first published in full by G. Burges in *Classical Journal* 11-14 (1815-1816), but should be republished, since Burges' report contains many errors and omissions.

Modern editions are cited in the introductions to each play.

Editorial Principles

For the special conditions affecting an editor of Aristophanes' plays, I refer the reader to the preceding discussion of the history of the text.

The present text is my own. For the most part I have relied on previous editions for manuscript readings, but in cases where previous editors differ in their reports, or where I or other editors suspect a textual problem, I have consulted my own microfilm copies of the relevant manuscripts.

Since this is a reader's text with facing translation, I have tried to make it continuously readable: where the text is lacunose but the meaning of the missing line(s) is clear enough in context, I print a suitable supplement in angle brackets and translate it, and where the text is irrecoverably corrupt, I print and translate a conjecture that answers the requirements of sense and style; only if no plausible conjecture can be found do I enclose corrupt text in daggers (obeli).

The notes to the text are not a critical apparatus, but alert the reader only to textual problems, variants, or conjectures that significantly affect the interpretation (and therefore the translation) of the Greek, and to conjectures that have not been published or adopted before. In describing the transmission of individual plays, I do not present a full analysis but only what the reader needs to grasp the essentials.

Two features of this edition break with usual practice: lines which I assign to the Chorus Leader in the translation are so assigned in the Greek text as well; and in the translation, sung passages are indented and follow the lineation of the Greek.

SELECT BIBLIOGRAPHY

Complete Critical Editions of Aristophanes

Blaydes, F. H. M., ed. *Aristophanis Comoediae.* Halle, 1880–1893.

Cantarella, R., ed. *Aristofane, le Commedie.* Milan, 1949–1964.

Coulon, V., ed. and H. van Daele, transl. *Aristophane.* Paris, 1923–1930.

Hall, F. W., and W. M. Geldart, eds. *Aristophanis Comoediae.* Oxford, 1900–1901.

Rogers, B. B., ed. and transl. *The Acharnians, etc. of Aristophanes.* London, 1902–1916.

Sommerstein, A. H., ed. and transl. *The Comedies of Aristophanes.* Warminster, 1980—.

Aristophanic Fragments

Austin, C., ed. *Comicorum Graecorum Fragmenta in Papyris Reperta.* Berlin and New York, 1973.

Demianczuk, I., ed. *Supplementum Comicum.* Krakow, 1912.

Edmonds, J. M., ed. and transl. *The Fragments of Attic Comedy.* Leiden, 1957–1961.

Kassel, R., and C. Austin, eds. *Poetae Comici Graeci.* Berlin and New York, 1983—.

Kock, T., ed. *Comicorum Atticorum Fragmenta.* Leipzig, 1880–1888.

Meineke, A., ed. *Fragmenta Comicorum Graecorum.* Berlin, 1839–1857.

Scholia

Dübner, F., ed. *Scholia Graeca in Aristophanem.* Paris, 1842.

Koster, W. J. W., et al., eds. *Scholia in Aristophanem.* Groningen and Amsterdam, 1960—.

Zuntz, G. *Die Aristophanes-Scholien der Papyri*, 2nd ed. Berlin, 1975.

Concordances

Dunbar, A. *A Complete Concordance for the Comedies and Fragments of Aristophanes* (Oxford, 1883), rev. B. Marzullo. Hildesheim, 1973.

Holden, H. A. *Onomasticon Aristophaneum*, 2nd ed. Cambridge, 1902.

Todd, O. J. *Index Aristophaneus.* Cambridge, Mass., 1932.

General Works

Bowie, A. M. *Aristophanes: Myth, Ritual and Comedy.* Cambridge, 1993.

Cartledge, P. A. *Aristophanes and His Theatre of the Absurd.* Bristol, 1990.

41

BIBLIOGRAPHY

de Ste. Croix, G. E. M. *The Origins of the Peloponnesian War*, Appendix XXIX. London, 1972.

Ehrenberg, V. *The People of Aristophanes*, 2nd ed. Oxford, 1951.

K. J. Dover, *Aristophanic Comedy*. Berkeley and Los Angeles, 1972.

Gelzer, T. *Aristophanes der Komiker*, in Pauly-Wissowa, Supplementband XII, columns 1391–1570. Munich, 1970.

Lind, H. *Der Gerber Kleon in den "Rittern" des Aristophanes. Studien zur Demagogenkomödie.* Studien zur klassischen Philologie 51. Frankfurt am Main, 1990.

MacDowell, D. M. *Aristophanes and Athens.* Oxford, 1995.

Mastromarco, G. *Introduzione a Aristofane.* Rome and Bari, 1994.

Newiger, H.-J. *Metapher und Allegorie. Studien zu Aristophanes.* Munich, 1957.

Reckford, K. J. *Aristophanes' Old-and-New Comedy.* Chapel Hill, 1987.

Schmid, W. "Aristophanes," in *Geschichte der griechischen Literatur*, vol. IV.1, pp.174- 470. Munich, 1946.

Whitman, C. H. *Aristophanes and the Comic Hero.* Cambridge, Mass., 1964.

Theater and Production

Csapo, E., and W. J. Slater, *The Context of Ancient Drama.* Ann Arbor, 1995.

Geissler, P. *Chronologie der altattische Komödie*, 2nd ed. Dublin and Zürich, 1969.

Green, J. R. "Theatre Production: 1971–1986," *Lustrum* 31 (1989): 7–95.

———— "On Seeing and Depicting the Theatre in Classical Athens," *Greek, Roman, and Byzantine Studies* 32 (1991): 15–50.

———— *Theatre in Ancient Greek Society.* London and New York, 1994.

Pickard-Cambridge, A. W. *The Dramatic Festivals of Athens*, 2nd ed., rev. J. Gould and D. M. Lewis. Oxford, 1988.

Russo, C. F. *Aristophanes, an Author for the Stage,* transl. K. Wren. London, 1994.

Simon, E. *The Ancient Theatre*, transl. C. E. Vafopoulo-Richardson. London, 1982.

Stone, L. M. *Costume in Aristophanic Comedy.* New York, 1984.

Taplin, O. *Comic Angels and Other Approaches to Greek Drama through Vase-Paintings.* Oxford, 1993.

Webster, T. B. L. *Monuments Illustrating Old and Middle Comedy*, 3rd ed., rev. J. R. Green. *Bulletin of the Institute for Classical Studies* Supplement 39: London, 1978.

Dramatic Form

Gelzer, T. *Der epirrhematische Agon bei Aristophanes.* Munich, 1960.

———— "Feste Strukturen in der Komödie des Aristophanes," in *Aristophane*, Entretiens sur l'Antiquité Classique, vol. XXXVIII, edd. J. M. Bremer and E. W. Handley. Fondation Hardt, Geneva, 1993, pp. 51–96.

Händel, P. *Formen und Darstellungsweisen in der aristophanischen Komödie.* Heidelberg, 1963.

Horn, W. *Gebet und Gebetsparodie in den Komödien des Aristophanes.* Nürnberg, 1970.

Hubbard, T. K. *The Mask of Comedy: Aristophanes and the Intertextual Parabasis.* Ithaca, 1991.

Kleinknecht, H. *Die Gebetsparodie in der Antike.* Stuttgart and Berlin, 1937.

Sifakis, G. M. *Parabasis and Animal Choruses.* London, 1971.

——— "The Structure of Aristophanic Comedy," *Journal of Hellenic Studies* 112 (1992): 123- 142.

Zimmermann, B. *Untersuchungen zur Form und dramatischen Technik der aristophanischen Komödien.* Königstein and Frankfurt, 1984–1987.

Language and Style

Dover, K. J. "The Style of Aristophanes," in *Greek and the Greeks*, pp. 224–236. Oxford, 1987.

——— "Language and Character in Aristophanes," ibid., pp. 237–248.

Henderson, J. *The Maculate Muse: Obscene Language in Attic Comedy*, 2nd ed. Oxford, 1991.

López Eire, A. *La lengua coloquial de la comedia aristofánica.* Murcia, 1996.

Olson, S. D. "Names and Naming in Aristophanic Comedy," *Classical Quarterly* 42 (1992): 304–319.

Rau, P. *Paratragodia. Untersuchung einer komischen Form des Aristophanes.* Munich, 1967.

Taillardat, J. *Les Images d' Aristophane*, 2nd ed. Paris, 1965.

BIBLIOGRAPHY

Meter

Dale, A. M. *The Lyric Metres of Greek Drama,* 2nd ed. Cambridge, 1968.

Parker, L. P. E. *The Songs of Aristophanes.* Oxford, 1997.

West, M. L. *Greek Metre.* Oxford, 1982.

White, J. W. *The Verse of Greek Comedy.* London, 1912.

Wilamowitz-Moellendorff, U. von. *Griechische Verskunst.* Berlin, 1921.

Zimmermann: see under Dramatic Form above.

Textual Transmission

Dover, K. J. "Explorations in the History of the Text of Aristophanes," in *The Greeks and Their Legacy* (Oxford, 1988), pp. 223–265.

Dunbar, N. *Aristophanes Birds* (Oxford, 1995), pp. 31–51.

Henderson, J. *Aristophanes Lysistrata* (Oxford 1987), pp. lvi-lxix.

Kassel, R. "Aus der Arbeit an den *Poetae Comici Graeci,*" *Zeitschrift für Papyrologie und Epigraphik* 27 (1977): 54–94 and 32 (1978): 23–33.

Kraus, W., ed. *Testimonia Aristophanea cum Scholiorum Lectionibus.* Vienna 1931.

White, J. W. "The Manuscripts of Aristophanes," *Classical Philology* 1 (1906): 1–20, 255- 278.

Bibliographical Aids

Periodic reports on Aristophanic scholarship appeared in *Bursians Jahresbericht über die Fortschritte der klassis-*

chen Altertumswissenschaft from 1877–1939; thereafter see the following:

Dover, K. J. "Aristophanes 1938–1955," *Lustrum* 2 (1957): 52–112.

———— "Greek Comedy," in *Fifty Years (and Twelve) of Classical Scholarship* (Oxford, 1968), pp. 123–158.

Gelzer, T. "Hinweise auf einige neuere Bücher zu Aristophanes," *Museum Helveticum* 21 (1964): 103–106.

Komornicka, A. M. "Aristofane negli ultimi decenni," *Cultura e Scuola* 23 (1967): 37–42.

Kraus, W. "Griechische Komödie: Alte Komödie und Epicharm," *Anzeiger für die Altertumswissenschaft* 24 (1971), columns 161–80.

Murphy, C. T. "A Survey of Recent Work on Aristophanes and Old Comedy (1957–1967)," *Classical World* 65 (1972): 261–273.

Storey, I. C. "Old Comedy 1975–1984," *Echos du Monde Classique* 31 (1987): 1–46.

———— "Δέκατον μὲν ἔτος τόδ'": Old Comedy 1982–1991," *Antichthon* 26 (1992): 1–29.

Zimmermann, B. "Griechische Komödie," *Anzeiger für die Altertumswissenschaft* 45 (1992), columns 161–184; and 47 (1994), columns 1–18.

Current listings can be found in the periodicals *Dioniso*, *Gnomon*, and *L'Année Philologique*.

ACHARNIANS

INTRODUCTORY NOTE

Acharnians, Aristophanes' third (and first extant) play, was produced by Callistratus at the Lenaea of 425 B.C. and won the first prize; Cratinus was second with *Stormtossed* and Eupolis third with *New Moons.* The war against the Peloponnesians and the Boeotians, begun nearly six years earlier on Pericles' assurance that the Athenians would quickly prevail, was effectively stalemated. During these years, the Athenian countryside had been devastated by annual invasions and its residents forced to take refuge within the city walls;[1] a debilitating plague had struck in 430 and was not yet in remission; and the Athenian financial reserves had run out by 428, so that the cost of the war was becoming an increasingly heavy burden on citizens and allies alike. At least some Athenians had begun to question the rationale for continued war. Nevertheless, a new breed of populist politicians, foremost among whom was Aristophanes' fellow demesman Cleon, successfully championed a more aggressive version of the Periclean policy, playing on the Athenians' pride and desire for revenge and questioning the patriotism of anyone inclined toward a negotiated peace.

[1] See Thucydides' poignant description of the evacuation (2.16).

The hero of *Acharnians,* an ordinary countryman who calls himself Dicaeopolis, embodies (as his name suggests) "what is right for the polis" on the question of the war. Being unable even to raise the subject of peace in the Assembly, Dicaeopolis secures a private truce for himself and his family and refuses to share its magical blessings with anyone except for a young bride, "since she's a woman and does not deserve to suffer from the war" (1062). Dicaeopolis' truce enables him to return to his farm, to trade freely with enemy states, and to enjoy the wholesome pleasures of good food, drink, and sex, which the war has disrupted for everyone else. In the end, Dicaeopolis wins the national drinking contest, while General Lamachus suffers ignominious wounds in a wintry action against Boeotian raiders.

To a large extent the play condemns the war simply by displaying the comforts and benefits that come to Dicaeopolis as a result of his truce and by contrasting these with the hardships and dangers faced by Lamachus. But there is more. In the prologue, the apathy of the Assembly and the arrogance of its officials are sharply criticized; in his confrontation with Lamachus, Dicaeopolis (rather like Achilles in *Iliad* 1) contrasts the hard work done by the rank and file with the profits enjoyed by commanders and politicians; and in Dicaeopolis' defence speech to the Acharnians (497 ff.) we are given arguments that are amusing, to be sure, but nonetheless trenchantly critical and clearly intended to be taken to heart.[2] An unusual feature of this speech is the poet's overt self-identification with his

[2] In its essentials, Dicaeopolis' speech jibes with Thucydides' account of the steps leading to war; cf. especially Th. 1.67, 139.

hero, referring to his own denunciation by Cleon for "slandering the city in the presence of foreigners" at the previous year's Dionysia (in *Babylonians*) and for being of non-Athenian birth.[3] In the parabasis the poet stresses the themes of freedom of speech and the value of listening even to unpopular views by boasting of his own courage in telling the Athenians unpleasant but important truths: for this he deserves not abuse but rich rewards (628 ff.).[4]

Dicaeopolis' confrontation with the Acharnians (lines 204-625) is modelled on Euripides' lost tragedy *Telephus* (produced in 438). Its hero, the son of Heracles and Auge, had become king of Mysia in the Troad and son-in-law of Priam. When the Greek expedition against Troy mistakenly attacked Mysia, Telephus was wounded by Achilles and then informed by an oracle that his wound could be healed only by its inflictor. So much Telephus probably explained in a prologue speech. As the action begins, Telephus is on his way to Argos, disguised as a Mysian beggar, to look for Achilles. In a speech he defends himself and the Mysians by arguing that the Greeks would have acted the same way had they suffered an unprovoked attack. He probably also questioned the Greeks' motive for the war against Troy (Paris' abduction of Helen) and urged them to consider matters from the Trojan/Mysian perspective.

[3] Whether we should understand "the poet" as indicating the producer Callistratus or the author Aristophanes has long been debated, but the details of Aristophanes' references to Cleon in this and subsequent plays suggest that it was the author whom Cleon had prosecuted for *Babylonians* (though Cleon may have attacked Callistratus too).

[4] Compare the attitude of Plato's Socrates (*Apology* 35a-37a).

The Greeks' reaction to Telephus' speech is hostile, though perhaps not unanimously so, for in several fragments Agamemnon and Menelaus argue about continuing the war. When Telephus' disguise is exposed and he is threatened with death, he takes refuge at an altar, with the baby Orestes as hostage, and convinces the Greeks that he too is in fact a Greek. Achilles arrives and agrees to cure Telephus' wound. In response to another oracle, which says that the Greeks can take Troy only if a Greek leads them, Telephus agrees to guide the Greeks to Troy.

Like Telephus, Dicaeopolis disguises himself in rags, pleads his cause before a hostile audience, and takes a hostage; and his argument against the Athenians' continuing the war against Sparta resembles Telephus' argument against the Greeks' continuing the war against the Mysians. Moreover, behind the comic hero Dicaeopolis-Telephus we are invited to see Aristophanes himself, who had been accused of treason and foreign birth by Cleon, defending his standing as an authentic and loyal Athenian (cf. esp. 366-82, 497-556, 628-64).[5]

Through this extensive usurpation of *Telephus* Aristophanes borrows the authority of tragedy, creates a play within a play, and constructs a complex layering of disguises that work on several levels simultaneously (Telephus vs. Greeks ~ Dicaeopolis vs. Acharnians ~ Aristophanes vs. Athenians). He also calls attention to what he is up to as a playwright, thus educating the spectators about the nature of theatrical illusion and persuasion generally. Further, by using the spectators themselves to represent

---

[5] In *Women at the Thesmophoria* (produced in 411) Aristophanes would again parody *Telephus* extensively (lines 466-764).

the Assembly and identifying his own case with that of his hero, Aristophanes establishes a connection between theatrical and political persuasion. In these ways Aristophanes, as dramatist and citizen, at once challenges the spectators to engage critically and reflectively with the theatrical event in which they are participants and invites them to be just as reflective and critical as assemblymen, when they must judge the arguments of a Cleon.

A salient feature of Aristophanic paratragedy is its incorporation (by quotation and pastiche) of tragic diction and style, whose archaic and elevated tone contrasts markedly with the colloquial registers of comic speech. I have tried to reproduce this feature by rendering paratragic lines in grandiloquent English.

Text

Two papyri preserve fragments of *Acharnians*.[6] There are ten independent medieval manuscripts, all descended from a common ancestor (z), which divide into two main families, one represented by R and the other by the ancestor of the other nine (*y*). From *y* descend two subfamilies, one represented by AΓE (*a*) and the other by Vp3 and the Triclinian manuscripts Vp2 H L Vv17 and B (*j*). In addition, many of the Suda's quotations of the play were drawn from a text or texts related to but distinct from z, and still another relative of z furnished the corrections found in Γ and E.

---

[6] *PBerlin.* 13231 + 21201/2 (V-VI) partially preserves lines 593-975 and *PMich.* inv. 5607a (IV) preserves lines 446-55 and 474-94. Another papyrus, *POxy.* 6.856 (III), contains fragmentary scholia on lines 108-671.

Sigla

R	Ravennas 429 (*c.* 950)
S	readings found in the Suda
A	Parisinus Regius 2712 (*c.* 1300)
Γ	Laurentianus 31.15 (*c.* 1325)
E	Estensis a.U.5.10 (XIV-XVin)
Vp3	Vaticanus Palatinus 128 (XV)
Vp2	Vaticanus Palatinus Graecus 67 (XV)
H	Havniensis 1980 (XV)
L	Holkhamensis 1980 (1400-1430)
Vv17	Vaticanus Graecus 2181 (XIVex)
B	Parisinus Graecus 2715 (XV)
z	the archetype of R*y*
y	the hyparchetype of *aj*
j	the hyparchetype of Vp3*t*
a	the hyparchetype of AΓE
t	Triclinian manuscripts (Vp2 H L Vv17 B)

Annotated Editions

F. H. M. Blaydes (Halle 1887).

J. van Leeuwen (Leiden 1901).

W. J. M. Starkie (London 1909), with English translation.

B. B. Rogers (London 1910), with English translation.

R. T. Elliott (Oxford 1914).

A. H. Sommerstein (Warminster 1980), with English translation.

P. Thiercy (Montpellier 1988), with French translation.

ΤΑ ΤΟΥ ΔΡΑΜΑΤΟΣ ΠΡΟΣΩΠΑ

<table>
<tr><td>ΔΙΚΑΙΟΠΟΛΙΣ</td><td>ΚΩΦΑ ΠΡΟΣΩΠΑ</td></tr>
<tr><td>ΚΗΡΥΞ</td><td>ΠΡΥΤΑΝΕΙΣ</td></tr>
<tr><td>ΑΜΦΙΘΕΟΣ</td><td>ΕΚΚΛΗΣΙΑΣΤΑΙ</td></tr>
<tr><td>ΠΡΕΣΒΕΤΤΗΣ</td><td>ΤΟΞΟΤΑΙ</td></tr>
<tr><td>ΨΕΤΔΑΡΤΑΒΑΣ</td><td>ΠΡΕΣΒΕΙΣ</td></tr>
<tr><td>ΘΕΩΡΟΣ</td><td>ΕΤΝΟΤΧΟΙ δύο</td></tr>
<tr><td>ΘΤΓΑΤΗΡ Δικαιοπόλιδος</td><td>ΟΔΟΜΑΝΤΩΝ στρατός</td></tr>
<tr><td>ΘΕΡΑΠΩΝ Εὐριπίδου</td><td>ΞΑΝΘΙΑΣ καὶ ἄλλοι</td></tr>
<tr><td>ΕΤΡΙΠΙΔΗΣ</td><td>οἰκέται Δικαιοπόλιδος</td></tr>
<tr><td>ΛΑΜΑΧΟΣ</td><td>ΓΤΝΗ Δικαιοπόλιδος</td></tr>
<tr><td>ΜΕΓΑΡΕΤΣ</td><td>ΠΑΙΔΙΑ Δικαιοπόλιδος</td></tr>
<tr><td>ΚΟΡΗ Α</td><td>ΛΟΧΙΤΑΙ Λαμάχου</td></tr>
<tr><td>ΚΟΡΗ Β</td><td>ΙΣΜΗΝΙΑΣ</td></tr>
<tr><td>ΣΤΚΟΦΑΝΤΗΣ</td><td>ΑΤΛΗΤΑΙ Θηβαῖοι</td></tr>
<tr><td>ΘΗΒΑΙΟΣ</td><td>ΝΥΜΦΕΤΤΡΙΑ</td></tr>
<tr><td>ΝΙΚΑΡΧΟΣ</td><td>ΟΡΧΗΣΤΡΙΔΕΣ δύο</td></tr>
<tr><td>ΟΙΚΕΤΗΣ Λαμάχου</td><td></td></tr>
<tr><td>ΔΕΡΚΕΤΗΣ</td><td></td></tr>
<tr><td>ΠΑΡΑΝΤΜΦΟΣ</td><td></td></tr>
<tr><td>ΑΓΓΕΛΟΣ Α</td><td></td></tr>
<tr><td>ΑΓΓΕΛΟΣ Β</td><td></td></tr>
<tr><td>ΑΓΓΕΛΟΣ Γ</td><td></td></tr>
</table>

ΧΟΡΟΣ Ἀχαρνέων

DRAMATIS PERSONAE

DICAEOPOLIS
HERALD
AMPHITHEUS
AMBASSADOR
PSEUDO-ARTABAS
THEORUS
DAUGHTER of Dicaeopolis
SLAVE of Euripides
EURIPIDES
LAMACHUS
MEGARIAN
FIRST GIRL
SECOND GIRL
INFORMER
THEBAN
NICARCHUS
SLAVE of Lamachus
DERCETES
BEST MAN
FIRST MESSENGER
SECOND MESSENGER
THIRD MESSENGER

CHORUS of Acharnians

SILENT CHARACTERS

PRESIDENTS (Prytaneis)
ASSEMBLYMEN
ARCHER POLICE
AMBASSADORS
TWO EUNUCHS
TROOP OF ODOMANTIANS
XANTHIAS and other
   SLAVES of Dicaeopolis
WIFE and other WOMEN-
   FOLK of Dicaeopolis
CHILDREN of Dicaeopolis
SOLDIERS with Lamachus
ISMENIAS
THEBAN PIPERS
BRIDESMAID
TWO DANCING GIRLS

ΑΧΑΡΝΗΣ

ΔΙΚΑΙΟΠΟΛΙΣ

Ὅσα δὴ δέδηγμαι τὴν ἐμαυτοῦ καρδίαν,
ἥσθην δὲ βαιά, πάνυ δὲ βαιά, τέτταρα·
ἃ δ' ὠδυνήθην, ψαμμακοσιογάργαρα.
φέρ' ἴδω, τί δ' ἥσθην ἄξιον χαιρηδόνος;
5   ἐγῷδ' ἐφ' ᾧ γε τὸ κέαρ εὐφράνθην ἰδών,
τοῖς πέντε ταλάντοις οἷς Κλέων ἐξήμεσεν.
ταῦθ' ὡς ἐγανώθην· καὶ φιλῶ τοὺς ἱππέας
διὰ τοῦτο τοὔργον· ἄξιον γὰρ Ἑλλάδι.
ἀλλ' ὠδυνήθην ἕτερον αὖ τραγῳδικόν,
10 ὅτε δὴ 'κεχήνη προσδοκῶν τὸν Αἰσχύλον,
ὁ δ' ἀνεῖπεν· "εἴσαγ', ὦ Θέογνι, τὸν χορόν".
πῶς τοῦτ' ἔσεισέ μου δοκεῖς τὴν καρδίαν;

---

[1] The hero's name (which we do not hear until line 406) suggests that he has "just" advice for the city; cf. 497-501.

[2] The nature of this incident, variously explained by ancient commentators, is obscure. Since we hear of no trial, Cleon may have "disgorged" the money by the settlement procedure called *probole*. Some think that the incident was not historical but happened in a comedy, but this is unlikely, since the Knights seem to have played no role in comedy before *Knights* in 424; cf. 377 ff., *Knights* 507 ff.

ACHARNIANS

The scene building has a roof on which actors can appear and three doors. Onstage is a rostrum, flanked by two benches and facing the spectators. In the orchestra is a chair just in front of the spectators and facing the stage. DICAEOPOLIS, a rustic older man with a walking stick and a large wallet, appears from the side and enters the orchestra.[1]

DICAEOPOLIS

How often I've been bitten to my very heart! My delights? Scant, quite scant—just four! My pains? Heaps by the umpteen million loads! Let's see, what delight have I had worthy of delectation? I know—it's something my heart rejoiced to see: those five talents Cleon had to disgorge. That made me sparkle! I love the Knights for that deed,[2] "a worthy thing for Greece"![3] But then I had another pain, quite tragic: when I was waiting open-mouthed for Aeschylus, the announcer cried, "Theognis, bring your chorus on!"[4] How do you think that made my heart quake?

---

[3] Quoting Euripides, *Telephus* (fr. 720), where the preceding words were "he would perish wretchedly."

[4] The comic poets called this "frigid" tragic poet "Snow," cf. 138-40.

ἀλλ' ἕτερον ἥσθην, ἡνίκ' ἐπὶ μόσχῳ ποτὲ
Δεξίθεος εἰσῆλθ' ᾀσόμενος Βοιώτιον.
15 τῆτες δ' ἀπέθανον καὶ διεστράφην ἰδών,
ὅτε δὴ παρέκυψε Χαῖρις ἐπὶ τὸν ὄρθιον.
ἀλλ' οὐδεπώποτ' ἐξ ὅτου 'γὼ ῥύπτομαι
οὕτως ἐδήχθην ὑπὸ κονίας τὰς ὀφρῦς
ὡς νῦν, ὁπότ' οὔσης κυρίας ἐκκλησίας
20 ἑωθινῆς ἔρημος ἡ πνὺξ αὑτηί,
οἱ δ' ἐν ἀγορᾷ λαλοῦσι κἄνω καὶ κάτω
τὸ σχοινίον φεύγουσι τὸ μεμιλτωμένον.
οὐδ' οἱ πρυτάνεις ἥκουσιν, ἀλλ' ἀωρίαν
ἥκοντες, εἶτα δ' ὠστιοῦνται πῶς δοκεῖς
25 ἐλθόντες ἀλλήλοισι περὶ πρώτου ξύλου,
ἀθρόοι καταρρέοντες· εἰρήνη δ' ὅπως
ἔσται προτιμῶσ' οὐδέν· ὦ πόλις πόλις.
ἐγὼ δ' ἀεὶ πρώτιστος εἰς ἐκκλησίαν
νοστῶν κάθημαι· κᾆτ' ἐπειδὰν ὦ μόνος,
30 στένω, κέχηνα, σκορδινῶμαι, πέρδομαι,
ἀπορῶ, γράφω, παρατίλλομαι, λογίζομαι,
ἀποβλέπων εἰς τὸν ἀγρόν, εἰρήνης ἐρῶν,
στυγῶν μὲν ἄστυ, τὸν δ' ἐμὸν δῆμον ποθῶν,
ὃς οὐδεπώποτ' εἶπεν· "ἄνθρακας πρίω",
35 οὐκ ὄξος, οὐκ ἔλαιον, οὐδ' ᾔδει πρίω,
ἀλλ' αὐτὸς ἔφερε πάντα χὠ πρίων ἀπῆν.
νῦν οὖν ἀτεχνῶς ἥκω παρεσκευασμένος
βοᾶν, ὑποκρούειν, λοιδορεῖν τοὺς ῥήτορας,
ἐάν τις ἄλλο πλὴν περὶ εἰρήνης λέγῃ.

But I had another delight, when "Once Upon A Calf"[5] Dexitheus[6] came on to sing Boeotian-style. But just this year I died on the rack when I saw Chaeris[7] creeping on to play the Orthian tune. But never since my first bath have my brows been as soap stung as they are now, when the Assembly's scheduled for a regular dawn meeting, and here's an empty Pnyx: everybody's gossiping in the market as up and down they dodge the ruddled rope.[8] The Presidents aren't even here. No, they'll come late, and when they do you can't imagine how they'll shove each other for the front row, streaming down en masse. But they don't care at all about making peace. O city, city! I am always the very first to come to Assembly and take my seat. Then, in my solitude, I sigh, I yawn, I stretch myself, I fart, I fiddle, scribble, pluck my beard, do sums, while I gaze off to the countryside and pine for peace, loathing the city and yearning for my own deme, that never cried "buy coal," "buy vinegar," "buy oil"; it didn't know the word "buy"; no, it produced everything itself, and the Buy Man was out of sight. So now I'm here, all set to shout, interrupt, revile the speakers, if anyone speaks of anything except peace.

Two Presidents, the HERALD, *some Archer Police, and Assemblymen enter through the* parodoi *and mount the stage.*

[5] Or (less likely) "after Moschus," taking *moschos* (calf) as a proper name.

[6] A lyre player known to have won a musical contest at the Pythian games.

[7] A lyre player and piper often ridiculed in comedy for poor technique.

[8] Citizens marked with the dye, as being late to enter or leave the Assembly, were liable to a fine.

ARISTOPHANES

40 ἀλλ᾽ οἱ πρυτάνεις γὰρ οὗτοὶ μεσημβρινοί.
οὐκ ἠγόρευον; τοῦτ᾽ ἐκεῖν᾽ οὑγὼ ᾽λεγον·
εἰς τὴν προεδρίαν πᾶς ἀνὴρ ὠστίζεται.

ΚΗΡΤΞ

πάριτ᾽ εἰς τὸ πρόσθεν,
πάριθ᾽, ὡς ἂν ἐντὸς ἦτε τοῦ καθάρματος.

ΑΜΦΙΘΕΟΣ

ἤδη τις εἶπε;

ΚΗΡΤΞ

45   τίς ἀγορεύειν βούλεται;

ΑΜΦΙΘΕΟΣ

ἐγώ.

ΚΗΡΤΞ

τίς ὤν;

ΑΜΦΙΘΕΟΣ

Ἀμφίθεος.

ΚΗΡΤΞ

οὐκ ἄνθρωπος;

ΑΜΦΙΘΕΟΣ

οὔ,

ἀλλ᾽ ἀθάνατος. ὁ γὰρ Ἀμφίθεος Δήμητρος ἦν
καὶ Τριπτολέμου· τούτου δὲ Κελεὸς γίγνεται·

---

9 The name, which appropriately means "divine on both sides
of the family," is attested only once in Attica, in a list of members

The Herald stands at the rostrum and the Presidents sit on the benches at either side of it.

Well, here are the Presidents—at noon! What did I tell you? It's just as I said: every man jostles for the front-row seats.

HERALD
Move forward! Move, inside the sacred precinct with you!

AMPHITHEUS *enters from one side, mounts the stage and addresses the Herald.*

AMPHITHEUS
Has anybody spoken?

HERALD
Who wishes to speak?

AMPHITHEUS
Me!

HERALD
Who are you?

AMPHITHEUS
Amphitheus.[9]

HERALD
Not a human being?

AMPHITHEUS
No. I'm immortal. For Amphitheus was son of Demeter and Triptolemus, and to him was born Celeus, and Celeus

of a private cult of Heracles in Cydathenaeum, Aristophanes' and Cleon's deme; see the General Introduction.

γαμεῖ δὲ Κελεὸς Φαιναρέτην τήθην ἐμήν,
50 ἐξ ἧς Λυκῖνος ἐγένετ'· ἐκ τούτου δ' ἐγώ.
ἀθάνατός εἰμ'· ἐμοὶ δ' ἐπέτρεψαν οἱ θεοὶ
σπονδὰς ποιεῖσθαι πρὸς Λακεδαιμονίους μόνῳ.
ἀλλ' ἀθάνατος ὤν, ἄνδρες, ἐφόδι' οὐκ ἔχω·
οὐ γὰρ διδόασιν οἱ πρυτάνεις.

ΚΗΡΥΞ
οἱ τοξόται.

ΑΜΦΙΘΕΟΣ
55 ὦ Τριπτόλεμε καὶ Κελεέ, περιόψεσθέ με;

ΔΙΚΑΙΟΠΟΛΙΣ
ὦνδρες πρυτάνεις, ἀδικεῖτε τὴν ἐκκλησίαν
τὸν ἄνδρ' ἀπάγοντες, ὅστις ἡμῖν ἤθελεν
σπονδὰς ποιῆσαι καὶ κρεμάσαι τὰς ἀσπίδας.

ΚΗΡΥΞ
κάθησο, σίγα.

ΔΙΚΑΙΟΠΟΛΙΣ
μὰ τὸν Ἀπόλλω 'γὼ μὲν οὔ,
60 ἢν μὴ περὶ εἰρήνης γε πρυτανεύσητέ μοι.

ΚΗΡΥΞ
οἱ πρέσβεις οἱ παρὰ βασιλέως.

ΔΙΚΑΙΟΠΟΛΙΣ
ποίου βασιλέως; ἄχθομαι 'γὼ πρέσβεσιν

---

10 Mangled Eleusinian genealogy to be taken as preposterous,

married Phaenarete my grandmother, of whom Lycinus
was born, and being his son I'm immortal.[10] To me have
the gods commissioned the making of a treaty with the
Spartans, and to me alone. But though immortal, gentle-
men, I have no travel money. The Presidents won't pro-
vide it.

HERALD

Police!

The Archers seize Amphitheus and march him to the wings.

AMPHITHEUS

Triptolemus and Celeus, will you look aside while I'm—

DICAEOPOLIS

Esteemed Presidents, you wrong the Assembly by remov-
ing the gentleman who offered to make a treaty for us and
let us hang up our shields!

HERALD

Sit down and be quiet!

DICAEOPOLIS

I most certainly will not, unless you call for a discussion
about peace!

HERALD

The ambassadors back from the King![11]

DICAEOPOLIS

The King indeed! I'm sick of ambassadors and their pea-

even deranged; but Phaenarete was (allegedly) the name of Soc-
rates' mother.   [11] Both Athens and Sparta sought money from
the Persian King, but old soldiers like Dicaeopolis will have de-
spised him as a barbarian and as their onetime enemy.

ARISTOPHANES

καὶ τοῖς ταῶσι τοῖς τ' ἀλαζονεύμασιν.

ΚΗΡΥΞ

σίγα.

ΔΙΚΑΙΟΠΟΛΙΣ

βαβαιάξ. ὦκβάτανα τοῦ σχήματος.

ΠΡΕΣΒΕΥΤΗΣ

65 ἐπέμψαθ' ἡμᾶς ὡς βασιλέα τὸν μέγαν
μισθὸν φέροντας δύο δραχμὰς τῆς ἡμέρας
ἐπ' Εὐθυμένους ἄρχοντος.

ΔΙΚΑΙΟΠΟΛΙΣ

οἴμοι τῶν δραχμῶν.

ΠΡΕΣΒΕΥΤΗΣ

καὶ δῆτ' ἐτρυχόμεσθα τῶν Καϋστρίων
πεδίων ὁδοιπλανοῦντες ἐσκηνημένοι,
70 ἐφ' ἁρμαμαξῶν μαλθακῶς κατακείμενοι,
ἀπολλύμενοι.

ΔΙΚΑΙΟΠΟΛΙΣ

σφόδρα γ' ἄρ' ἐσῳζόμην ἐγὼ
παρὰ τὴν ἔπαλξιν ἐν φορυτῷ κατακείμενος.

ΠΡΕΣΒΕΥΤΗΣ

ξενιζόμενοι δὲ πρὸς βίαν ἐπίνομεν
ἐξ ὑαλίνων ἐκπωμάτων καὶ χρυσίδων
ἄκρατον οἶνον ἡδύν.

---

[12] The capital of Media and summer home of the Great Kings of Persia; an "Eldorado" in the view of ordinary Athenians.

cocks and their empty bragging.

HERALD

Silence!

Two opulently dressed AMBASSADORS *enter by a* parodos *and mount the stage.*

DICAEOPOLIS

Wowee! Ecbatana,[12] what a getup!

AMBASSADOR

(*to the audience*) You sent us to the Great King, on a salary of two drachmas per diem, when Euthymenes was archon[13]—

DICAEOPOLIS

Oh dear, the drachmas!

AMBASSADOR

—and we truly wore ourselves out a-wayfaring through Caÿstrian plains, under canopies, reclining softly on litters, simply perishing!

DICAEOPOLIS

I must have been on easy street, then—reclining in the garbage by the ramparts![14]

AMBASSADOR

And when they regaled us they forced us to drink fine unmixed wine from goblets of crystal and gold.

---

[13] I.e., in 437/6 (eleven years earlier).

[14] Common soldiers stood watch at the walls (Thucydides 2.13), while refugees from the countryside "took up quarters in the towers along the walls or indeed wherever they could find space to live in" (2.17).

ΔΙΚΑΙΟΠΟΛΙΣ

75   ὦ Κραναὰ πόλις,
ἆρ᾽ αἰσθάνει τὸν κατάγελων τῶν πρέσβεων;

ΠΡΕΣΒΕΥΤΗΣ

οἱ βάρβαροι γὰρ ἄνδρας ἡγοῦνται μόνους
τοὺς πλεῖστα δυναμένους καταφαγεῖν καὶ πιεῖν.

ΔΙΚΑΙΟΠΟΛΙΣ

ἡμεῖς δὲ λαικαστάς τε καὶ καταπύγονας.

ΠΡΕΣΒΕΥΤΗΣ

80 ἔτει τετάρτῳ δ᾽ εἰς τὰ βασίλει᾽ ἤλθομεν·
ἀλλ᾽ εἰς ἀπόπατον ᾤχετο στρατιὰν λαβών,
κἄχεζεν ὀκτὼ μῆνας ἐπὶ χρυσῶν ὀρῶν.

ΔΙΚΑΙΟΠΟΛΙΣ

πόσου δὲ τὸν πρωκτὸν χρόνου ξυνήγαγεν;
τῇ πανσελήνῳ;

ΠΡΕΣΒΕΥΤΗΣ

        κᾆτ᾽ ἀπῆλθεν οἴκαδε.
85 εἶτ᾽ ἐξένιζε παρετίθει θ᾽ ἡμῖν ὅλους
ἐκ κριβάνου βοῦς.

ΔΙΚΑΙΟΠΟΛΙΣ

        καὶ τίς εἶδε πώποτε
βοῦς κριβανίτας; τῶν ἀλαζονευμάτων.

ΠΡΕΣΒΕΥΤΗΣ

καὶ ναὶ μὰ Δί᾽ ὄρνιν τριπλάσιον Κλεωνύμου

ACHARNIANS

DICAEOPOLIS
Ah, city of Cranaus![15] Do you see how these ambassadors laugh at you?

AMBASSADOR
Barbarians, you see, recognize as real men only those who can gobble and guzzle the most.

DICAEOPOLIS
While with us it's cock-suckers and arse-peddlers.[16]

AMBASSADOR
So, after three years we got to the royal palace, but the King had gone off with an army to a latrine, and he stayed shitting for eight months upon the Golden Hills—

DICAEOPOLIS
And when was it he closed up his arsehole? At the full moon?

AMBASSADOR
—and then he departed for home. Then he threw us a party and served us up whole ox *en casserole*—

DICAEOPOLIS
And who has ever seen ox casserole? What swaggering charlatanism![17]

AMBASSADOR
—and, I swear by Zeus, he served us up a bird three times

[15] A mythical king of Athens.

[16] Comic poets routinely assumed that political leaders had prostituted themselves for advancement.

[17] Though Herodotus 1.133 reports that on their birthdays rich Persians might be served an ox, horse, camel, or donkey baked whole.

ARISTOPHANES

παρέθηκεν ἡμῖν· ὄνομα δ' ἦν αὐτῷ φέναξ.

ΔΙΚΑΙΟΠΟΛΙΣ

90 ταῦτ' ἄρ' ἐφενάκιζες σὺ δύο δραχμὰς φέρων.

ΠΡΕΣΒΕΥΤΗΣ

καὶ νῦν ἄγοντες ἥκομεν Ψευδαρτάβαν,
τὸν βασιλέως Ὀφθαλμόν.

ΔΙΚΑΙΟΠΟΛΙΣ

                    ἐκκόψειέ γε
κόραξ πατάξας, τόν γε σὸν τοῦ πρέσβεως.

ΚΗΡΤΞ

ὁ βασιλέως Ὀφθαλμός.

ΔΙΚΑΙΟΠΟΛΙΣ

                    ὦναξ Ἡράκλεις.

95 πρὸς τῶν θεῶν, ἄνθρωπε, ναύφαρκτον βλέπεις,
ἢ περὶ ἄκραν κάμπτων νεώσοικον σκοπεῖς;
ἄσκωμ' ἔχεις που περὶ τὸν ὀφθαλμὸν κάτω;

ΠΡΕΣΒΕΥΤΗΣ

ἄγε δὴ σὺ βασιλεὺς ἄττα σ' ἀπέπεμψεν φράσον
λέξοντ' Ἀθηναίοισιν, ὦ Ψευδαρτάβα.

ΨΕΥΔΑΡΤΑΒΑΣ

100 ιαρτα ναμε ξαρξανα πισονα σατρα.

---

[18] A political crony of Cleon's, ridiculed by comic poets as a fat
glutton, a coward, and a shield thrower; the latter charge (unique

the size of Cleonymus;[18] he called it a gull.

DICAEOPOLIS
That figures, since *you* were gulling *us*, drawing your two drachmas.

AMBASSADOR
And now we're back, bringing Pseudo-Artabas, the King's Eye.

DICAEOPOLIS
May a crow peck it out, and yours too, the ambassador's!

PSEUDO-ARTABAS enters by a parodos *and mounts the stage. He has one huge eye in the center of his mask and a long scarf around his neck, and is attended by two Eunuchs.*

DICAEOPOLIS
Lord Heracles! Ye gods, fellow, you look like a man-o'-war in dangerous waters! Or are you rounding a point and looking for a berth? Is that a porthole-flap there under your eye?

AMBASSADOR
Come then, tell the Athenians what the King sent you to say, Pseudo-Artabas.

PSEUDO-ARTABAS
Iarta name xarxana pisona satra.[19]

in comedy) evidently refers to Cleonymus' behavior in the Athenian retreat at Delium in 424, when his fatness made him conspicuous and thus a suitable scapegoat.

[19] Comic Persian, suggesting King (Arta)xerxes and Pissuthnes, satrap of Sardis.

ΠΡΕΣΒΕΤΤΗΣ

ξυνήκαθ᾽ ὃ λέγει;

ΔΙΚΑΙΟΠΟΛΙΣ

μὰ τὸν Ἀπόλλω ᾽γὼ μὲν οὔ.

ΠΡΕΣΒΕΤΤΗΣ

πέμψειν βασιλέα φησὶν ὑμῖν χρυσίον.
λέγε δὴ σὺ μεῖζον καὶ σαφῶς τὸ χρυσίον.

ΨΕΤΔΑΡΤΑΒΑΣ

οὐ λῆψι χρυσό, χαυνόπρωκτ᾽ Ἰαοναῦ.

ΔΙΚΑΙΟΠΟΛΙΣ

οἴμοι κακοδαίμων ὡς σαφῶς.

ΠΡΕΣΒΕΤΤΗΣ

105   τί δαὶ λέγει;

ΔΙΚΑΙΟΠΟΛΙΣ

ὅ τι; χαυνοπρώκτους τοὺς Ἰάονας λέγει,
εἰ προσδοκῶσι χρυσίον ἐκ τῶν βαρβάρων.

ΠΡΕΣΒΕΤΤΗΣ

οὔκ, ἀλλ᾽ ἀχάνας ὅδε γε χρυσίου λέγει.

ΔΙΚΑΙΟΠΟΛΙΣ

ποίας ἀχάνας; σὺ μὲν ἀλαζὼν εἶ μέγας.
110 ἀλλ᾽ ἄπιθ᾽· ἐγὼ δὲ βασανιῶ τοῦτον μόνος.
ἄγε δὴ σὺ φράσον ἐμοὶ σαφῶς πρὸς τουτονί,
ἵνα μή σε βάψω βάμμα Σαρδιανικόν·
βασιλεὺς ὁ μέγας ἡμῖν ἀποπέμψει χρυσίον; —
ἄλλως ἄρ᾽ ἐξαπατώμεθ᾽ ὑπὸ τῶν πρέσβεων; —
115 ἑλληνικόν γ᾽ ἐπένευσαν ἄνδρες οὑτοί,

AMBASSADOR

You all understand what he says?

DICAEOPOLIS

By Apollo, *I* surely didn't.

AMBASSADOR

He says the King is going to send you gold. (*to Pseudo-Artabas*) Speak louder and clearer about the gold.

PSEUDO-ARTABAS

No gettum goldum, gapey-arse Ioni-o.

DICAEOPOLIS

I'll be damned, that's pretty clear!

AMBASSADOR

Eh? What's he saying?

DICAEOPOLIS

Why, he says the Ionians have gaping arseholes if they're expecting any gold from the barbarians.

AMBASSADOR

No, he says gobs of gold, no hassle.

DICAEOPOLIS

Gobs indeed! You are a giant phony. Away with you; I'll do the questioning myself.

The AMBASSADORS exit; DICAEOPOLIS mounts the stage.

All right you, tell me plainly, in the face of *this* (*he brandishes his walking stick*), so I won't have to dye you Sardian crimson: does the Great King intend to send us gold? Then we're simply being bamboozled by our ambassadors? These two men here have a distinctly Greek way of nod-

οὐκ ἔσθ᾽ ὅπως οὐκ εἰσὶν ἐνθένδ᾽ αὐτόθεν.
καὶ τοῖν μὲν εὐνούχοιν τὸν ἕτερον τουτονὶ
ἐγῷδ᾽ ὅς ἐστι, Κλεισθένης ὁ Σιβυρτίου.
ὦ θερμόβουλον πρωκτὸν ἐξυρημένε.

120 τοιόνδε δ᾽, ὦ πίθηκε, τὸν πώγων᾽ ἔχων
εὐνοῦχος ἡμῖν ἦλθες ἐσκευασμένος;
ὁδὶ δὲ τίς ποτ᾽ ἐστίν; οὐ δήπου Στράτων;

ΚΗΡΤΞ

σίγα, κάθιζε.
τὸν βασιλέως Ὀφθαλμὸν ἡ βουλὴ καλεῖ
εἰς τὸ πρυτανεῖον.

ΔΙΚΑΙΟΠΟΛΙΣ

125   ταῦτα δῆτ᾽ οὐκ ἀγχόνη;
κἄπειτ᾽ ἐγὼ δῆτ᾽ ἐνθαδὶ στραγγεύομαι,
τοὺς δὲ ξενίζειν οὐδέποτ᾽ ἴσχει γ᾽ ἡ θύρα;
ἀλλ᾽ ἐργάσομαί τι δεινὸν ἔργον καὶ μέγα.
ἀλλ᾽ Ἀμφίθεός μοι ποῦ ᾽στιν;

ΑΜΦΙΘΕΟΣ

                        οὑτοσὶ πάρα.

ΔΙΚΑΙΟΠΟΛΙΣ

130 ἐμοὶ σὺ ταυτασὶ λαβὼν ὀκτὼ δραχμὰς
σπονδὰς ποιῆσαι πρὸς Λακεδαιμονίους μόνῳ
καὶ τοῖσι παιδίοισι καὶ τῇ πλάτιδι·

---

²⁰Cleisthenes is ridiculed elsewhere as a beardless effemi-
nate, and Strato as his lover. If Sibyrtius, who ran a wrestling
school, was not really Cleisthenes' father, the joke may be sarcastic

ding; I'm convinced they hail from this very place! And one of the eunuchs, this one here, I recognize as Cleisthenes son of Sibyrtius![20] O shaver of a hot and horny arsehole, with such a beard, you monkey, do you come before us appareled as a eunuch?[21] And this one, who is he? Surely not Strato!

HERALD

Sit down and be quiet! The Council invites the King's Eye to the Prytaneum![22]

PSEUDO-ARTABAS and Eunuchs exit.

DICAEOPOLIS

Isn't that a killer? I'm supposed to cool my heels here, while for *their* entertainment the door is never closed. No, I'm going to do a great and dire deed. Where can I find Amphitheus?

AMPHITHEUS enters from the wing.

AMPHITHEUS

Over here!

DICAEOPOLIS

Look, take these eight drachmas and make a treaty with the Spartans for me alone and my children and the missus.

(wrestling being a manly activity) or may suggest that Sibyrtius had enjoyed Cleisthenes sexually.   [21] Line 120 parodies Archilochus fr. 187 West, substituting "beard" for "rump."

     [22] The Prytaneum, in the agora, was used to entertain, at public expense, foreign ambassadors and Athenians returning from embassies. Citizens could be rewarded for especially great services to the state with meals there for life.

ARISTOPHANES

ὑμεῖς δὲ πρεσβεύεσθε καὶ κεχήνατε.

ΚΗΡΤΞ

προσίτω Θέωρος ὁ παρὰ Σιτάλκους.

ΘΕΩΡΟΣ

ὁδί.

ΔΙΚΑΙΟΠΟΛΙΣ

135 ἕτερος ἀλαζὼν οὗτος εἰσκηρύττεται.

ΘΕΩΡΟΣ

χρόνον μὲν οὐκ ἂν ἦμεν ἐν Θρᾴκῃ πολύν, —

ΔΙΚΑΙΟΠΟΛΙΣ

μὰ Δί᾽ οὐκ ἄν, εἰ μισθόν γε μὴ ᾽φερες πολύν.

ΘΕΩΡΟΣ

εἰ μὴ κατένειψε χιόνι τὴν Θρᾴκην ὅλην
καὶ τοὺς ποταμοὺς ἔπηξ᾽, —

ΔΙΚΑΙΟΠΟΛΙΣ

ὑπ᾽ αὐτὸν τὸν χρόνον

140 ὅτ᾽ ἐνθαδὶ Θέογνις ἠγωνίζετο.

ΘΕΩΡΟΣ

τοῦτον μετὰ Σιτάλκους ἔπινον τὸν χρόνον.
καὶ δῆτα φιλαθήναιος ἦν ὑπερφυῶς
ὑμῶν τ᾽ ἐραστὴς ὡς ἀληθῶς, ὥστε καὶ

---

23 The King of the Odrysai in Thrace, who had aided the
Athenians in an abortive invasion of Macedonia four years ear-
lier (Thucydides 2.95-101). Theorus is mentioned elsewhere as a
crony of Cleon.

(*to the audience*) And you can carry on with your embassies and your gaping!

AMPHITHEUS exits.

HERALD
Let Theorus approach, back from the court of Sitalces![23]

THEORUS enters.

THEORUS
Present!

DICAEOPOLIS
Yet another phony is announced.

THEORUS
We wouldn't have stayed in Thrace so very long—

DICAEOPOLIS
Zeus no, if you hadn't been drawing hefty pay!

THEORUS
—if the whole of Thrace hadn't been snowed in and the rivers frozen.

DICAEOPOLIS
About the same time Theognis was competing here!

THEORUS
All the while I was drinking with Sitalces. He was exceedingly pro-Athenian, too, and your true lover.[24] Why, he

---

[24] Recalling, and taking literally, Pericles' famous exhortation (anticipated by Aeschylus, *Eum.* 852) that Athenians should "fall in love with Athens" (Thucydides 2.43).

ἐν τοῖσι τοίχοις ἔγραφ'· "Ἀθηναῖοι καλοί".
145 ὁ δ' υἱός, ὃν Ἀθηναῖον ἐπεποιήμεθα,
ἤρα φαγεῖν ἀλλᾶντας ἐξ Ἀπατουρίων,
καὶ τὸν πατέρ' ἠντεβόλει βοηθεῖν τῇ πάτρᾳ·
ὁ δ' ὤμοσε σπένδων βοηθήσειν ἔχων
στρατιὰν τοσαύτην ὥστ' Ἀθηναίους ἐρεῖν·
150 "ὅσον τὸ χρῆμα παρνόπων προσέρχεται".

ΔΙΚΑΙΟΠΟΛΙΣ
κάκιστ' ἀπολοίμην, εἴ τι τούτων πείθομαι
ὧν εἶπας ἐνταυθοῖ σὺ πλὴν τῶν παρνόπων.

ΘΕΩΡΟΣ
καὶ νῦν ὅπερ μαχιμώτατον Θρᾳκῶν ἔθνος
ἔπεμψεν ὑμῖν.

ΔΙΚΑΙΟΠΟΛΙΣ
τοῦτο μέν γ' ἤδη σαφές.

ΚΗΡΤΞ
155 οἱ Θρᾷκες ἴτε δεῦρ', οὓς Θέωρος ἤγαγεν.

ΔΙΚΑΙΟΠΟΛΙΣ
τουτὶ τί ἐστι τὸ κακόν;

ΘΕΩΡΟΣ
Ὀδομάντων στρατός.

---

²⁵ After the formula inscribed by lovers on courtship gifts to boys.   ²⁶ Sitalces' son Sadocus had been made a citizen in 431 (Thucydides 2.29).

²⁷ The festival where children and new citizens became members of Athenian kinship groups.

even wrote "Athenians are handsome" on the walls![25] And
his son, whom we'd made an Athenian citizen,[26] yearned
to eat sausages at the Apaturia[27] and kept begging his fa-
ther to help his fatherland. And Sitalces poured a libation
and swore he would help us by sending an army so large
that the Athenians would say, "What a giant swarm of lo-
custs heads our way!"[28]

DICAEOPOLIS
I'm damned if I believe a word of what you've said here,
except the part about the locusts!

THEORUS
And now he sends you the most bellicose tribe in Thrace.[29]

DICAEOPOLIS
Now that's clear enough, at least.

HERALD
You Thracians that Theorus brought, come forward!

Enter Soldiers.

DICAEOPOLIS
What the hell is this?

THEORUS
A troop of Odomantians.

[28] No cooperation of Sitalces with Athens is recorded after the
Macedonian operation (134 n.), and when he died later in this year
he was succeeded not by his son Sadocus but by his nephew
Seuthes, an ally of Macedonia.

[29] For the savagery of Thracian mercenaries, cf. Thucydides'
account of their attack on Mycalessus in 413 (7.29).

ΔΙΚΑΙΟΠΟΛΙΣ

ποίων Ὀδομάντων; εἰπέ μοι, τουτὶ τί ἦν;
τίς τῶν Ὀδομάντων τὸ πέος ἀποτεθρίακεν;

ΘΕΩΡΟΣ

τούτοις ἐάν τις δύο δραχμὰς μισθὸν διδῷ,
160 καταπελτάσονται τὴν Βοιωτίαν ὅλην.

ΔΙΚΑΙΟΠΟΛΙΣ

τοισδὶ δύο δραχμὰς τοῖς ἀπεψωλημένοις;
ὑποστένοι μένταν ὁ θρανίτης λεώς,
ὁ σωσίπολις. οἴμοι τάλας ἀπόλλυμαι,
ὑπὸ τῶν Ὀδομάντων τὰ σκόροδα πορθούμενος.
οὐ καταβαλεῖτε τὰ σκόροδ᾽;

ΘΕΩΡΟΣ

165   ὦ μόχθηρε σύ,
οὐ μὴ πρόσει τούτοισιν ἐσκοροδισμένοις;

ΔΙΚΑΙΟΠΟΛΙΣ

ταυτὶ περιείδεθ᾽ οἱ πρυτάνεις πάσχοντά με
ἐν τῇ πατρίδι καὶ ταῦθ᾽ ὑπ᾽ ἀνδρῶν βαρβάρων;
ἀλλ᾽ ἀπαγορεύω μὴ ποιεῖν ἐκκλησίαν
170 τοῖς Θρᾳξὶ περὶ μισθοῦ· λέγω δ᾽ ὑμῖν ὅτι
διοσημία ᾽στὶ καὶ ῥανὶς βέβληκέ με.

---

30 The Greeks, in contrast to barbarians, did not practice cir-
cumcision. Since actual Odomantians were also uncircumcised,
Dicaeopolis here exposes Theorus' troop as barbaric (and there-
fore cowardly) imposters. Evidently they wore the large, circum-

DICAEOPOLIS

Odomantians indeed! Pray tell me the meaning of this! (*he exposes their stage phalloi*) Who's pruned the Odomantians' cocks?[30]

THEORUS

Pay these fellows two drachmas and they'll swashbuckle all of Boeotia.

DICAEOPOLIS

Two drachmas for these docked cocks? The crowd who row our ships and defend our city would sure yell about that! (*the Odomantians rush Dicaeopolis and grab his wallet*) Hey, damn it! I'm getting killed! The Odomantians are plundering my garlic! Come on, drop that garlic!

THEORUS

You troublemaker! Don't approach them when they're garlic-primed![31]

DICAEOPOLIS

Presidents! Were you looking away as I was suffering this kind of treatment in my own country, and at the hands of barbarians to boot? I insist that the Assembly table the question of pay for the Thracians, and I declare to you that there is a sign from Zeus, and a raindrop has hit me.[32]

---

cised phallus that Aristophanes lists among trite ways to get a laugh in *Clouds* 537-39.

[31] Like fighting cocks.

[32] Although official business could be adjourned at a sign of divine displeasure, an individual's motion at a single drop of rain would in reality not suffice; apparently this Assembly is more eager to adjourn than it was to convene.

ARISTOPHANES

ΚΗΡΥΞ
τοὺς Θρᾷκας ἀπιέναι, παρεῖναι δ᾽ εἰς ἔνην·
οἱ γὰρ πρυτάνεις λύουσι τὴν ἐκκλησίαν.

ΔΙΚΑΙΟΠΟΛΙΣ
οἴμοι τάλας, μυττωτὸν ὅσον ἀπώλεσα.
175 ἀλλ᾽ ἐκ Λακεδαίμονος γὰρ Ἀμφίθεος ὁδί.
χαῖρ᾽ Ἀμφίθεε.

ΑΜΦΙΘΕΟΣ
          μήπω γε πρίν ‹γ᾽› ἂν στῶ τρέχων·
δεῖ γάρ με φεύγοντ᾽ ἐκφυγεῖν Ἀχαρνέας.

ΔΙΚΑΙΟΠΟΛΙΣ
τί δ᾽ ἔστ᾽;

ΑΜΦΙΘΕΟΣ
          ἐγὼ μὲν δεῦρό σοι σπονδὰς φέρων
ἔσπευδον· οἱ δ᾽ ὤσφροντο πρεσβῦταί τινες
180 Ἀχαρνικοί, στιπτοὶ γέροντες, πρίνινοι,
ἀτεράμονες, Μαραθωνομάχαι, σφενδάμνινοι.
ἔπειτ᾽ ἀνέκραγον πάντες· "ὦ μιαρώτατε,
σπονδὰς φέρεις τῶν ἀμπέλων τετμημένων;"
κἀς τοὺς τρίβωνας ξυνελέγοντο τῶν λίθων·
185 ἐγὼ δ᾽ ἔφευγον· οἱ δ᾽ ἐδίωκον κἀβόων.

HERALD

The Thracians are excused and will return in two days' time. The Presidents declare the Assembly adjourned.

All exit except DICAEOPOLIS.

DICAEOPOLIS

Damn it all, what a good salad I've lost.

AMPHITHEUS enters on the run, carrying three wineskins.

But here comes Amphitheus, back from Sparta! Welcome, Amphitheus!

AMPHITHEUS

No welcome yet, not till I've stopped running! I've got to run till I outrun the Acharnians!

DICAEOPOLIS

What's up?

AMPHITHEUS

I was hurrying back here with some treaties for you when some elders of Acharnae got wind of them, sturdy geezers, tough as hardwood, stubborn Marathon fighters,[33] men of maple. Then they all started yelling, "Traitor! Are you bringing treaties when our vines are slashed?" And they began to fill their cloaks with stones. I ran away; they kept chasing me and shouting.

---

[33] In reality, veterans of Marathon (490) would have been at least 82 years old, but "Marathon fighters" was a conventional comic way to refer to the oldest living generation—the generation that had repulsed the Persians, established the democracy, and acquired the empire.

ARISTOPHANES

ΔΙΚΑΙΟΠΟΛΙΣ
οἱ δ' οὖν βοώντων. ἀλλὰ τὰς σπονδὰς φέρεις;

ΑΜΦΙΘΕΟΣ
ἔγωγέ, φημι, τρία γε ταυτὶ γεύματα.
αὗται μέν εἰσι πεντέτεις. γεῦσαι λαβών.

ΔΙΚΑΙΟΠΟΛΙΣ
αἰβοῖ.

ΑΜΦΙΘΕΟΣ
   τί ἐστιν;

ΔΙΚΑΙΟΠΟΛΙΣ
      οὐκ ἀρέσκουσίν μ' ὅτι
190 ὄζουσι πίττης καὶ παρασκευῆς νεῶν.

ΑΜΦΙΘΕΟΣ
σὺ δ' ἀλλὰ τασδὶ τὰς δεκέτεις γεῦσαι λαβών.

ΔΙΚΑΙΟΠΟΛΙΣ
ὄζουσι χαὗται πρέσβεων εἰς τὰς πόλεις
ὀξύτατον ὥσπερ διατριβῆς τῶν ξυμμάχων.

ΑΜΦΙΘΕΟΣ
ἀλλ' αὑταὶ σπονδαὶ τριακοντούτιδες
κατὰ γῆν τε καὶ θάλατταν.

ΔΙΚΑΙΟΠΟΛΙΣ
195   ὦ Διονύσια,

---

[34] In this scene, Aristophanes combines the literal meaning of the word *spondai* ("libation of wine") with its metonymic meaning "treaty": libation was part of the ceremony by which treaties were ratified.

DICAEOPOLIS

Well, let them shout. Do you have the treaties?[34]

AMPHITHEUS

Yes indeed, I've three samples for sipping. This one's a
five-year treaty. Have a sip.

DICAEOPOLIS

Yuk!

AMPHITHEUS

What's the matter?

DICAEOPOLIS

I don't like this one; it stinks of pitch and battleship con-
struction.[35]

AMPHITHEUS

Well then, here's a ten-year treaty for you to sip.

DICAEOPOLIS

This one stinks too, of embassies to the allies, a sour smell,
like someone being bullied.[36]

AMPHITHEUS

Well, this one's a thirty-year treaty by land and sea.[37]

DICAEOPOLIS

Holy Dionysia! This treaty smells of nectar and ambrosia,

---

[35] Pitch was used to caulk ships and to flavor inferior wines;
retsina is still a popular table wine in Greece.

[36] Official delegations from Athens threatened allies tempted
to revolt from the empire with severe punishment, like that meted
out to the people of Mytilene in 427 (Thucydides 3.1-50).

[37] Like the one ratified with Sparta twenty years earlier; the
50-year treaty ratified in 421 lasted barely six years.

αὗται μὲν ὄζουσ᾽ ἀμβροσίας καὶ νέκταρος
καὶ μὴ 'πιτηρεῖν σιτί᾽ ἡμερῶν τριῶν,
κἂν τῷ στόματι λέγουσι· "βαῖν᾽ ὅπῃ 'θέλεις".
ταύτας δέχομαι καὶ σπένδομαι κἀκπίομαι,
200 χαίρειν κελεύων πολλὰ τοὺς Ἀχαρνέας.

ΑΜΦΙΘΕΟΣ

203 ἐγὼ δὲ φευξοῦμαί γε τοὺς Ἀχαρνέας.

ΔΙΚΑΙΟΠΟΛΙΣ

201 ἐγὼ δὲ πολέμου καὶ κακῶν ἀπαλλαγεὶς
202 ἄξω τὰ κατ᾽ ἀγροὺς εἰσιὼν Διονύσια.

ΚΟΡΥΦΑΙΟΣ

(στρ) τῇδε πᾶς ἕπου, δίωκε καὶ τὸν ἄνδρα πυνθάνου
205 τῶν ὁδοιπόρων ἁπάντων· τῇ πόλει γὰρ ἄξιον
ξυλλαβεῖν τὸν ἄνδρα τοῦτον. ἀλλά μοι μηνύσατε,
εἴ τις οἶδ᾽ ὅποι τέτραπται γῆς ὁ τὰς σπονδὰς
φέρων.

ΧΟΡΟΣ

ἐκπέφευγ᾽, οἴχεται
φροῦδος. οἴμοι τάλας
210 τῶν ἐτῶν τῶν ἐμῶν·
οὐκ ἂν ἐπ᾽ ἐμῆς γε νεό-
τητος, ὅτ᾽ ἐγὼ φέρων
ἀνθράκων φορτίον
ἠκολούθουν Φαύλλῳ τρέχων,

203 post 200 transposuit Elmsley

84

and never waiting to hear "time for three days' rations,"
and it says to my palate, "go wherever you like." I accept
it; I pour it in libation; I drink it off! And I tell the Acharni-
ans to go to hell!

AMPHITHEUS
As for me, I'll be getting clear of the Acharnians!

AMPHITHEUS runs off.

DICAEOPOLIS
And as for me, free now of war and hardships, I'm going
home to celebrate the Rural Dionysia!

*DICAEOPOLIS enters the central door of the scene building.
The* CHORUS *enters the orchestra.*

CHORUS LEADER
This way, everybody, chase him, and question every pas-
serby about the man! It'll be a worthy thing for the city
to arrest this man. (*to the audience*) Please inform me, if
anyone knows where on earth the man with the treaty has
headed.

CHORUS
He's fled, he's gone,
he's clean away. Damn and blast
these years of mine!
Never in my youth,
when I could carry
a load of coal
and run just behind Phaÿllus,[38]

[38] This famous athlete from Croton in southern Italy com-
manded a ship at the battle of Salamis in 480.

215   ὧδε φαύλως ἂν ὁ
     σπονδοφόρος οὗτος ὑπ' ἐ-
     μοῦ τότε διωκόμενος
     ἐξέφυγεν οὐδ' ἂν ἐλα-
     φρῶς ἂν ἀπεπλίξατο.

ΚΟΡΥΦΑΙΟΣ

(ἀντ) νῦν δ' ἐπειδὴ στερρὸν ἤδη τοὐμὸν ἀντικνήμιον
220   καὶ παλαιῷ Λακρατείδῃ τὸ σκέλος βαρύνεται,
    οἴχεται. διωκτέος δέ· μὴ γὰρ ἐγχάνοι ποτὲ
    μηδέ περ γέροντας ὄντας ἐκφυγὼν Ἀχαρνέας,

ΧΟΡΟΣ

    ὅστις, ὦ Ζεῦ πάτερ
     καὶ θεοί, τοῖσιν ἐχ-
225   θροῖσιν ἐσπείσατο,
    οἷσι παρ' ἐμοῦ πόλεμος
    ἐχθοδοπὸς αὔξεται
    τῶν ἐμῶν χωρίων·
    κοὐκ ἀνήσω πρὶν ἂν σχοῖνος αὐ-
230   τοῖσιν ἀντεμπαγῶ
    ⟨καὶ σκόλοψ⟩ ὀξύς, ὀδυνηρός, ἐπίκωπος, ἵνα
    μήποτε πατῶσιν ἔτι
    τὰς ἐμὰς ἀμπέλους.

ΚΟΡΥΦΑΙΟΣ

    ἀλλὰ δεῖ ζητεῖν τὸν ἄνδρα καὶ βλέπειν Βαλλήναδε

231 ⟨καὶ σκόλοψ⟩ Hermann cl. S σ 648
234 Βαλλήναδε v.l. Σ: Παλλήναδε z

86

would this treaty bearer,
pursued by me then,
have so easily
escaped or so
nimbly skipped off.

CHORUS LEADER

But now, because my shin's arthritic and old Lacrateides'[39]
legs weigh him down, he's gone. But we must chase him:
never let him boast that he gave us Acharnians the slip, old
though we be,

CHORUS

that man, Father Zeus
and ye gods, who's made a truce
with our foes,
though on my side malevolent war
waxes strong against them
on account of my lands.
Nor will I ease off, till like a reed
I impale them in revenge,
like a stake sharp and painful, up to the hilt,
so that never again
will they trample my vines.

CHORUS LEADER

We must hunt for the man, and look to Peltingham, and

[39] The name (meaning "son of great-strength") was borne by
a sixth-century archon and a political enemy of Pericles (Plutarch,
Pericles 35).

235 καὶ διώκειν γῆν πρὸ γῆς, ἕως ἂν εὑρεθῇ ποτέ·
ὡς ἐγὼ βάλλων ἐκεῖνον οὐκ ἂν ἐμπλήμην λίθοις.

ΔΙΚΑΙΟΠΟΛΙΣ

εὐφημεῖτε, εὐφημεῖτε.

ΚΟΡΥΦΑΙΟΣ

σῖγα πᾶς. ἠκούσατ᾽, ἄνδρες, ἆρα τῆς εὐφημίας;
οὗτος αὐτός ἐστιν ὃν ζητοῦμεν. ἀλλὰ δεῦρο πᾶς
240 ἐκποδών· θύσων γὰρ ἀνήρ, ὡς ἔοικ᾽, ἐξέρχεται.

ΔΙΚΑΙΟΠΟΛΙΣ

εὐφημεῖτε, εὐφημεῖτε.
πρόιθ᾽ εἰς τὸ πρόσθεν ὀλίγον, ἡ κανηφόρος.
ὁ Ξανθίας τὸν φαλλὸν ὀρθὸν στησάτω.
κατάθου τὸ κανοῦν, ὦ θύγατερ, ἵν᾽ ἀπαρξώμεθα.

ΘΥΓΑΤΗΡ

245 ὦ μῆτερ, ἀνάδος δεῦρο τὴν ἐτνήρυσιν,
ἵν᾽ ἔτνος καταχέω τοὐλατῆρος τουτουί.

ΔΙΚΑΙΟΠΟΛΙΣ

καὶ μὴν καλόν γ᾽ ἔστ᾽. ὦ Διόνυσε δέσποτα,
κεχαρισμένως σοι τήνδε τὴν πομπὴν ἐμὲ
πέμψαντα καὶ θύσαντα μετὰ τῶν οἰκετῶν
250 ἀγαγεῖν τυχηρῶς τὰ κατ᾽ ἀγροὺς Διονύσια,
στρατιᾶς ἀπαλλαχθέντα, τὰς σπονδὰς δέ μοι
καλῶς ξυνενεγκεῖν τὰς τριακοντούτιδας.
ἄγ᾽, ὦ θύγατερ, ὅπως τὸ κανοῦν καλὴ καλῶς
οἴσεις βλέπουσα θυμβροφάγον. ὡς μακάριος
255 ὅστις σ᾽ ὀπύσει κἀκποιήσεται γαλᾶς
σοῦ μηδὲν ἥττους βδεῖν, ἐπειδὰν ὄρθρος ᾖ.

88

chase him from land to land until he's found at last; for never shall I have my fill of pelting him with stones.

DICAEOPOLIS
Pray silence, silence!

CHORUS LEADER
Quiet, everyone! Didn't you hear the call for silence? This is the very man we're looking for! This way, everyone, out of the way; the man is coming out, apparently to make a sacrifice.

DICAEOPOLIS
Pray silence, silence!

DICAEOPOLIS *emerges from the central door with his Wife,* DAUGHTER, *and two Slaves who carry a large phallus.*

Basket Bearer, step forward a bit! Xanthias, hold that phallus up straight! Put the basket down, daughter, so I can perform the preliminaries.

DAUGHTER
Mother, hand me up the broth ladle, so I can pour broth over this cake.

DICAEOPOLIS
There, that's good. O Lord Dionysos, may my performance of this procession and this sacrifice be pleasing to you, and may I and my household with good fortune celebrate the Rural Dionysia, now that I'm released from campaigning; and may the Thirty Years' Peace turn out well for me. Come now, my pretty daughter, be sure you bear the basket prettily, and keep a lemon-sucking look on your face. Ah, blest the man who'll wed you and get upon you a litter of kittens as good as you are at farting when the dawn is nigh!

πρόβαινε, κἂν τὤχλῳ φυλάττεσθαι σφόδρα
μή τις λαθών σου περιτράγῃ τὰ χρυσία.
ὦ Ξανθία, σφῷν δ' ἐστὶν ὀρθὸς ἑκτέος
260   ὁ φαλλὸς ἐξόπισθε τῆς κανηφόρου·
ἐγὼ δ' ἀκολουθῶν ᾄσομαι τὸ φαλλικόν·
σὺ δ', ὦ γύναι, θεῶ μ' ἀπὸ τοῦ τέγους. πρόβα.

Φαλῆς, ἑταῖρε Βακχίου,
    ξύγκωμε, νυκτοπεριπλάνη–
265   τε, μοιχέ, παιδεραστά,
    ἕκτῳ σ' ἔτει προσεῖπον εἰς
    τὸν δῆμον ἐλθὼν ἄσμενος,
    σπονδὰς ποιησάμενος ἐμαυ–
    τῷ, πραγμάτων τε καὶ μαχῶν
270   καὶ Λαμάχων ἀπαλλαγείς.
    πολλῷ γάρ ἐσθ' ἥδιον, ὦ Φαλῆς Φαλῆς,
    κλέπτουσαν εὑρόνθ' ὡρικὴν ὑληφόρον,
    τὴν Στρυμοδώρου Θρᾷτταν ἐκ τοῦ φελλέως,
    μέσην λαβόντ', ἄραντα, κατα–
275   βαλόντα καταγιγαρτίσαι.
    Φαλῆς Φαλῆς,
    ἐὰν μεθ' ἡμῶν ξυμπίῃς, ἐκ κραιπάλης
    ἕωθεν εἰρήνης ῥοφήσει τρύβλιον·
    ἡ δ' ἀσπὶς ἐν τῷ φεψάλῳ κρεμήσεται.

ΧΟΡΟΣ
280   οὗτος αὐτός ἐστιν, οὗτος·

90

Forward march! And when in the crowd, take special care
that no one steals up and pinches your bangles. Xanthias,
you two must keep your phallus erect behind the Basket
Bearer! I'll bring up the rear and sing the Phallic Hymn.
And you, milady, watch me from the roof. Forward!

> Phales,[40] friend of Bacchus,
> revel mate, nocturnal rambler,
> fornicator, pederast:
> after six years I greet you,
> as gladly I return to my deme,
> with a peace I made for myself,
> released from bothers and battles
> and Lamachuses.[41]
> Yes, it's far more pleasant, Phales, Phales,
> to catch a budding maid with pilfered wood—
> Strymodorus' Thratta from the Rocky Bottom—
> and grab her waist, lift her up, throw her down
> and take her cherry.
> Phales, Phales,
> if you drink with us, after the carouse
> at dawn you shall quaff a cup of peace;
> and my shield shall be hung by the hearth.

CHORUS
That's the man! That one there!

All except DICAEOPOLIS *run inside.*

[40] The personification of the processional phallus.

[41] *Lamachon* (the name means "great battler") jingles with
machon "battles" but also alludes to the general Lamachus, later
to appear as Dicaeopolis' antagonist (cf. 566).

βάλλε, βάλλε, βάλλε, βάλλε,
παῖε παῖε τὸν μιαρόν.
οὐ βαλεῖς, οὐ βαλεῖς;

ΔΙΚΑΙΟΠΟΛΙΣ

(στρ) Ἡράκλεις τουτὶ τί ἐστι; τὴν χύτραν συντρίψετε.

ΧΟΡΟΣ

285 σὲ μὲν οὖν καταλεύσομεν, ὦ μιαρὰ κεφαλή.

ΔΙΚΑΙΟΠΟΛΙΣ

ἀντὶ ποίας αἰτίας, ὠχαρνέων γεραίτατοι;

ΧΟΡΟΣ

τοῦτ᾿ ἐρωτᾷς; ἀναί-
σχυντος εἶ καὶ βδελυρός,
ὦ προδότα τῆς πατρίδος,
290 ὅστις ἡμῶν μόνος
σπεισάμενος εἶτα δύνα-
σαι πρὸς ἔμ᾿ ἀποβλέπειν.

ΔΙΚΑΙΟΠΟΛΙΣ

ἀντὶ δ᾿ ὧν ἐσπεισάμην οὐκ ἰστέ; ἀλλ᾿ ἀκούσατε.

ΧΟΡΟΣ

295 σοῦ γ᾿ ἀκούσωμεν; ἀπολεῖ· κατά σε χώσομεν τοῖς
λίθοις.

ΔΙΚΑΙΟΠΟΛΙΣ

μηδαμῶς πρὶν ἄν γ᾿ ἀκούσητ᾿· ἀλλ᾿ ἀνάσχεσθ᾿,
ὦγαθοί.

ΧΟΡΟΣ

οὐκ ἀνασχήσομαι·

ACHARNIANS

Pelt him, pelt him, pelt him, pelt him!
Hit him! Hit the pariah!
Won't you pelt him? Won't you pelt him?

DICAEOPOLIS

Heracles! What's going on? You'll smash my bowl!

CHORUS

No, it's you we'll stone to death, foul fellow!

DICAEOPOLIS

On what grounds, venerable Acharnian elders?

CHORUS

You ask that? You're
shameless and disgusting,
you traitor to your country,
the only one among us
to make peace, and then
you've the nerve to look me in the eye!

DICAEOPOLIS

But shouldn't you know my reasons for making peace?
Please listen!

CHORUS

Listen to you? You're done for! We'll bury you under a
mound of stones!

DICAEOPOLIS

Don't do it, at least till you've heard me out! Come now,
hold off, good sirs.

CHORUS

I will not hold off!

μηδὲ λέγε μοι σὺ λόγον·
ὡς μεμίσηκά σε Κλέ-
300   ωνος ἔτι μᾶλλον, ὃν
κατατεμῶ τοῖσιν ἱπ-
πεῦσι καττύματα.

ΚΟΡΥΦΑΙΟΣ

σοῦ δ' ἐγὼ λόγους λέγοντος οὐκ ἀκούσομαι μακ-
ροὺς,
ὅστις ἐσπείσω Λάκωσιν, ἀλλὰ τιμωρήσομαι.

ΔΙΚΑΙΟΠΟΛΙΣ

305   ὦγαθοί, τοὺς μὲν Λάκωνας ἐκποδὼν ἐάσατε,
τῶν δ' ἐμῶν σπονδῶν ἀκούσατ', εἰ καλῶς
ἐσπεισάμην.

ΚΟΡΥΦΑΙΟΣ

πῶς δ' ἔτ' ἂν καλῶς λέγοις ἄν, εἴπερ ἐσπείσω γ'
ἅπαξ
οἷσιν οὔτε βωμὸς οὔτε πίστις οὔθ' ὅρκος μένει;

ΔΙΚΑΙΟΠΟΛΙΣ

οἶδ' ἐγὼ καὶ τοὺς Λάκωνας, οἷς ἄγαν ἐγκείμεθα,
310   οὐχ ἁπάντων ὄντας ἡμῖν αἰτίους τῶν πραγμάτων.

ΚΟΡΥΦΑΙΟΣ

οὐχ ἁπάντων, ὦ πανοῦργε; ταῦτα δὴ τολμᾷς λέγειν
ἐμφανῶς ἤδη πρὸς ἡμᾶς; εἶτ' ἐγώ σου φείσομαι;

ΔΙΚΑΙΟΠΟΛΙΣ

οὐχ ἁπάντων, οὐχ ἁπάντων· ἀλλ' ἐγὼ λέγων ὁδὶ
πόλλ' ἂν ἀποφήναιμ' ἐκείνους ἔσθ' ἃ κἀδικουμένους.

94

And don't you give me a speech;
for I hate you even more
than Cleon, whom
I intend to cut up
as shoeleather for the Knights.[42]

CHORUS LEADER

I'm not going to listen to long speeches from you; you've made peace with the Spartans! I'm going to punish you instead.

DICAEOPOLIS

Good sirs, forget the Spartans for a moment and hear about my treaty, whether I was right to make one.

CHORUS LEADER

How can you say it's right to have any dealings at all with people who abide by no altar, no agreement, no oath?

DICAEOPOLIS

I know that even the Spartans, whom we treat too ruthlessly, are not responsible for all our problems.

CHORUS LEADER

Not all of them? You criminal! You dare to say this right to our face, and then I'm to spare you?

DICAEOPOLIS

Not for all our problems, not all of them. Here and now, in fact, I could make a speech showing that in many respects they're the wronged party.

[42] Speaking not as Acharnians but as Aristophanes' own chorus, they advertise the following year's Lenaean play, *Knights*, with a jibe at Cleon's trade.

ΚΟΡΥΦΑΙΟΣ

315 τοῦτο τοὔπος δεινὸν ἤδη καὶ ταραξικάρδιον,
εἰ σὺ τολμήσεις ὑπὲρ τῶν πολεμίων ἡμῖν λέγειν.

ΔΙΚΑΙΟΠΟΛΙΣ

κἄν γε μὴ λέγω δίκαια μηδὲ τῷ πλήθει δοκῶ,
ὑπὲρ ἐπιξήνου ᾿θελήσω τὴν κεφαλὴν ἔχων λέγειν.

ΚΟΡΥΦΑΙΟΣ

εἰπέ μοι, τί φειδόμεσθα τῶν λίθων, ὦ δημόται,
320 μὴ οὐ καταξαίνειν τὸν ἄνδρα τοῦτον εἰς φοινικίδα;

ΔΙΚΑΙΟΠΟΛΙΣ

οἷον αὖ μέλας τις ὑμῖν θυμάλωψ ἐπέζεσεν.
οὐκ ἀκούσεσθ᾿, οὐκ ἀκούσεσθ᾿ ἐτεόν, ὦχαρνηΐδαι;

ΚΟΡΥΦΑΙΟΣ

οὐκ ἀκουσόμεσθα δῆτα.

ΔΙΚΑΙΟΠΟΛΙΣ

δεινά γ᾿ ἆρα πείσομαι.

ΚΟΡΥΦΑΙΟΣ

ἐξολοίμην, ἢν ἀκούσω.

ΔΙΚΑΙΟΠΟΛΙΣ

μηδαμῶς, ὦχαρνικοί.

ΚΟΡΥΦΑΙΟΣ

ὡς τεθνήξων ἴσθι νυνί.

ACHARNIANS

CHORUS LEADER

What you say is truly awful and stomach-turning, if you'll
dare to speak to us in defence of our enemies.

DICAEOPOLIS

And what's more, if what I say isn't right and doesn't seem
right to the people, I'll be happy to speak with my head on
a butcher's block![43]

CHORUS LEADER

Tell me, why are we sparing the stones, fellow demes-
men, instead of unraveling this man till he's red as a scarlet
cloak?[44]

DICAEOPOLIS

What a dark ember blazed up in you then! Won't you lis-
ten? Won't you really listen, sons of Acharneus?

CHORUS LEADER

Absolutely not.

DICAEOPOLIS

Then dire will be my suffering.

CHORUS LEADER

May I die if I listen to you!

DICAEOPOLIS

Don't say that, Acharnians!

CHORUS LEADER

Count on being an instant goner!

---

[43] Literalizing a metaphor from *Telephus*, where the hero tells
Agamemnon that he will not withhold a just reply "even if a man
with an axe were about to strike my neck" (fr. 706).

[44] Such as the Spartans wore on campaign.

ΔΙΚΑΙΟΠΟΛΙΣ

325 δήξομάρ᾽ ὑμᾶς ἐγώ.
ἀνταποκτενῶ γὰρ ὑμῶν τῶν φίλων τοὺς φιλτάτους·
ὡς ἔχω γ᾽ ὑμῶν ὁμήρους, οὓς ἀποσφάξω λαβών.

ΚΟΡΥΦΑΙΟΣ

εἰπέ μοι, τί τοῦτ᾽ ἀπειλεῖ τοὔπος, ἄνδρες δημόται,
τοῖς Ἀχαρνικοῖσιν ἡμῖν; μῶν ἔχει του παιδίον
330 τῶν παρόντων ἔνδον εἴρξας; ἢ ᾽πὶ τῷ θρασύνεται;

ΔΙΚΑΙΟΠΟΛΙΣ

βάλλετ᾽, εἰ βούλεσθ᾽· ἐγὼ γὰρ τουτονὶ διαφθερῶ.
εἴσομαι δ᾽ ὑμῶν τάχ᾽ ὅστις ἀνθράκων τι κήδεται.

ΚΟΡΥΦΑΙΟΣ

ὡς ἀπωλόμεσθ᾽· ὁ λάρκος δημότης ὅδ᾽ ἔστ᾽ ἐμός.
ἀλλὰ μὴ δράσῃς ὃ μέλλεις, μηδαμῶς, ὦ μηδαμῶς.

ΔΙΚΑΙΟΠΟΛΙΣ

(ἀντ) ὡς ἀποκτενῶ· κέκραχθ᾽· ἐγὼ γὰρ οὐκ ἀκούσομαι.

ΧΟΡΟΣ

336 ἀπολεῖς ἄρ᾽ ὁμήλικα τόνδε φιλανθρακέα;

ΔΙΚΑΙΟΠΟΛΙΣ

οὐδ᾽ ἐμοῦ λέγοντος ὑμεῖς ἀρτίως ἠκούσατε.

ΧΟΡΟΣ

ἀλλὰ νυνὶ λέγ᾽, ὅ τι
σοι δοκεῖ, τόν τε Λακε—

---

[45] Making charcoal was a characteristic Acharnian industry;
for the parody of *Telephus* see Introductory Note.

ACHARNIANS

DICAEOPOLIS
Then *I'll* bite *you!* I'll kill in return your nearest and dearest; for I've got hostages of yours; I'm going to fetch them and cut their throats!

DICAEOPOLIS goes inside.

CHORUS LEADER
Tell me, fellow demesmen, what does he mean by this threat against us Acharnians? He hasn't got somebody's child, one of ours, locked up in there, has he? Then why is he so cocky?

DICAEOPOLIS reappears with a large knife and a coal basket.

DICAEOPOLIS
Pelt me, if you like! And I'll murder this![45] I'll soon see which among you has a care for kith and kindling!

CHORUS LEADER
Now we're done for! That coal basket is from my deme! Don't do what you're set on doing! Don't, oh don't!

DICAEOPOLIS
Kill I will. Shout away; I don't intend to listen.

CHORUS
Then you'll kill this, my coeval, my coal-eague?

DICAEOPOLIS
You were deaf to *my* pleas a moment ago.

CHORUS
Very well, say your piece,
tell us here and now

99

δαιμόνιον αὐτόθεν ὅ-
τῳ τρόπῳ σούστὶ φίλος·
340   ὡς τόδε τὸ λαρκίδιον
οὐ προδώσω ποτέ.

ΔΙΚΑΙΟΠΟΛΙΣ
τοὺς λίθους νύν μοι χαμᾶζε πρῶτον ἐξεράσατε.

ΧΟΡΟΣ
οὑτοί σοι χαμαί, καὶ σὺ κατάθου πάλιν τὸ ξίφος.

ΔΙΚΑΙΟΠΟΛΙΣ
ἀλλ᾿ ὅπως μὴ 'ν τοῖς τρίβωσιν ἐγκάθηνταί που
λίθοι.

ΧΟΡΟΣ
ἐκσέσεισται χαμᾶζ᾿.
οὐχ ὁρᾷς σειόμενον;
345   ἀλλὰ μή μοι πρόφασιν,
ἀλλὰ κατάθου τὸ βέλος.
ὡς ὅδε γε σειστὸς ἅμα
τῇ στροφῇ γίγνεται.

ΔΙΚΑΙΟΠΟΛΙΣ
ἐμέλλετ᾿ ἄρ᾿ ἅπαντες ἀνασείσειν βοήν,
ὀλίγου τ᾿ ἀπέθανον ἄνθρακες Παρνάσιοι,
καὶ ταῦτα διὰ τὴν ἀτοπίαν τῶν δημοτῶν.
350   ὑπὸ τοῦ δέους δὲ τῆς μαρίλης μοι συχνὴν
ὁ λάρκος ἐπετίλησεν ὥσπερ σηπία.

in what way
the Spartan's your friend.
For this dear little basket
I'll never desert.

DICAEOPOLIS

Please begin by disgorging your stones on the ground.

CHORUS

There you are, they're on the ground. Now you lay
    down your sword.

DICAEOPOLIS

But maybe there are some stones lurking somewhere in
your cloaks.

CHORUS

It's shaken out to the ground.
Don't you see it being shaken?
Come, no excuses, please,
just lay down that weapon;
for this is getting shaken[46]
as I twirl in the dance.

DICAEOPOLIS

So you were all getting ready to shake your shouts at me,
and some Parnasian[47] coals were very nearly killed, and all
because of their fellow demesmen's eccentricity. And in its
fear this basket has dirtied me with a load of coal dust, like

[46] For Greeks ancient and modern, "shaking out" one's cloth-
ing expresses or reinforces a remonstration, curse, or threat.
[47] "Parnasian" seems to be a comic demotic, "of Parnes"; a
spur of this mountain extended into Acharnae and furnished the
wood burned to make Acharnian coal.

δεινὸν γὰρ οὕτως ὀμφακίαν πεφυκέναι
τὸν θυμὸν ἀνδρῶν ὥστε βάλλειν καὶ βοᾶν
ἐθέλειν τ᾽ ἀκοῦσαι μηδὲν ἴσον ἴσῳ φέρον,
355 ἐμοῦ ᾽θέλοντος ὑπὲρ ἐπιξήνου λέγειν
ὑπὲρ Λακεδαιμονίων ἅπανθ᾽ ὅσ᾽ ἂν λέγω·
καίτοι φιλῶ γε τὴν ἐμὴν ψυχὴν ἐγώ.

ΧΟΡΟΣ

(στρ) τί οὖν ⟨οὐ⟩ λέγεις, ἐπίξηνον ἐξενεγκὼν θύραζ᾽,
360 ὅ τι ποτ᾽, ὦ σχέτλιε, τὸ μέγα τοῦτ᾽ ἔχεις;
πάνυ γὰρ ἐμέ γε πόθος ὅ τι φρονεῖς ἔχει.

ΚΟΡΥΦΑΙΟΣ

ἀλλ᾽ ἧπερ αὐτὸς τὴν δίκην διωρίσω,
365 θεὶς δεῦρο τοὐπίξηνον ἐγχείρει λέγειν.

ΔΙΚΑΙΟΠΟΛΙΣ

ἰδοὺ θέασαι, τὸ μὲν ἐπίξηνον τοδί,
ὁ δ᾽ ἀνὴρ ὁ λέξων οὑτοσὶ τυννουτοσί.
ἀμέλει μὰ τὸν Δί᾽ οὐκ ἐνασπιδώσομαι,
λέξω δ᾽ ὑπὲρ Λακεδαιμονίων ἁμοὶ δοκεῖ.
370 καίτοι δέδοικα πολλά· τούς τε γὰρ τρόπους
τοὺς τῶν ἀγροίκων οἶδα χαίροντας σφόδρα,
ἐάν τις αὐτοὺς εὐλογῇ καὶ τὴν πόλιν
ἀνὴρ ἀλαζὼν καὶ δίκαια κἄδικα·
κἀνταῦθα λανθάνουσ᾽ ἀπεμπολώμενοι·
375 τῶν τ᾽ αὖ γερόντων οἶδα τὰς ψυχὰς ὅτι
οὐδὲν βλέπουσιν ἄλλο πλὴν ψήφῳ δακεῖν.

a squid. It's terrible that the temper of gentlemen should grow so vinegary that they throw stones, and shout, and are unwilling to listen to something evenly balanced, even when I'm ready to say over a butcher's block everything I have to say on behalf of the Spartans, though I value my life.

CHORUS

Then why don't you bring a butcher's block outside
 and state,
hard man, whatever this great piece is that you've got
 to say?
An avid longing grips me to know what's on your
 mind.

CHORUS LEADER

All right then, place the block here, the way you yourself prescribed for your ordeal, and begin your speech.

DICAEOPOLIS goes inside and produces a butcher's block.

DICAEOPOLIS

Look, now: here's the butcher's block, and here's the man who's ready to make a speech, such as he is. Don't worry: I swear to god I won't buckler myself, but will speak in defence of the Spartans just what I think. And yet I'm very apprehensive: I know the way country people act, deeply delighted when some fraudulent personage eulogizes them and the city, whether truly or falsely; that's how they can be bought and sold all unawares. And I know the hearts of the oldsters too, looking forward only to biting

αὐτός τ' ἐμαυτὸν ὑπὸ Κλέωνος ἄπαθον
ἐπίσταμαι διὰ τὴν πέρυσι κωμῳδίαν.
εἰσελκύσας γάρ μ' εἰς τὸ βουλευτήριον
380 διέβαλλε καὶ ψευδῆ κατεγλώττιζέ μου
κἀκυκλοβόρει κἄπλυνεν, ὥστ' ὀλίγου πάνυ
ἀπωλόμην μολυνοπραγμονούμενος.
νῦν οὖν με πρῶτον πρὶν λέγειν ἐάσατε
384 ἐνσκευάσασθαί μ' οἷον ἀθλιώτατον.

ΧΟΡΟΣ

(ἀντ) τί ταῦτα στρέφει τεχνάζεις τε καὶ πορίζεις τριβάς;
λαβὲ δ' ἐμοῦ γ' ἕνεκα παρ' Ἱερωνύμου
390 σκοτοδασυπυκνότριχά τιν' Ἄιδος κυνῆν,

ΚΟΡΥΦΑΙΟΣ

εἶτ' ἐξάνοιγε μηχανὰς τὰς Σισύφου·
ὡς σκῆψιν ἁγὼν οὗτος οὐκ εἰσδέξεται.

ΔΙΚΑΙΟΠΟΛΙΣ

ὥρα 'στὶν ἁρμοῖ καρτερὰν ψυχὴν λαβεῖν·
καί μοι βαδιστέ' ἐστὶν ὡς Εὐριπίδην.
παῖ παῖ.

ΘΕΡΑΠΩΝ

τίς οὗτος;

393 ἁρμοῖ Robertson et Lloyd-Jones: ἁρά μοι R: ἤδη y Suda

---

48 He refers to the popular courts, whose jurymen tended to
be elderly and poor and were often suspected by wealthy litigants
of voting vindictively from class bias; the jury system is satirized
in *Wasps*.

with their ballots.[48] And in my own case I know what Cleon did to me because of last year's comedy. He hauled me before the Council, and slandered me, and tongue-lashed me with lies, and roared like the Cycloborus,[49] and soaked me in abuse, so that I nearly died in a mephitic miasma of misadventure.[50] So now, before I make my speech, please let me array myself in guise most piteous.

CHORUS

Why this dodging and scheming and contriving
    delays?
For all I care you may get from Hieronymus[51]
a dim dense shaggy-maned cap of invisibility.

CHORUS LEADER

Come now, disclose your Sisyphean[52] ruses: this case will acknowledge no mitigating circumstances!

DICAEOPOLIS

Now's the time to gain a sturdy heart, and make a visit to Euripides. (*he knocks on Euripides' door*) Boy! Boy!

SLAVE

(*opening the door a crack*) Who's that?

---

[49] An Attic stream noted for its loudness when in spate.

[50] For Cleon's action against Aristophanes see Introductory Note.

[51] A tragic and dithyrambic poet with long hair who, according to ancient commentators, was fond of using frightening masks in his plays.

[52] Sisyphus, a mythical king of Corinth, was proverbial for cunning.

ΔΙΚΑΙΟΠΟΛΙΣ

395   ἔνδον ἔστ' Εὐριπίδης;

ΘΕΡΑΠΩΝ

οὐκ ἔνδον ἔνδον ἐστίν, εἰ γνώμην ἔχεις.

ΔΙΚΑΙΟΠΟΛΙΣ

πῶς ἔνδον, εἶτ' οὐκ ἔνδον;

ΘΕΡΑΠΩΝ

              ὀρθῶς, ὦ γέρον.

ὁ νοῦς μὲν ἔξω ξυλλέγων ἐπύλλια

οὐκ ἔνδον, αὐτὸς δ' ἔνδον ἀναβάδην ποιεῖ

τραγῳδίαν.

ΔΙΚΑΙΟΠΟΛΙΣ

400   ὦ τρισμακάρι' Εὐριπίδη,

ὅθ' ὁ δοῦλος οὑτωσὶ σοφῶς ὑποκρίνεται.

ἐκκάλεσον αὐτόν.

ΘΕΡΑΠΩΝ

         ἀλλ' ἀδύνατον.

ΔΙΚΑΙΟΠΟΛΙΣ

                ἀλλ' ὅμως·

οὐ γὰρ ἂν ἀπέλθοιμ', ἀλλὰ κόψω τὴν θύραν.

Εὐριπίδη, Εὐριπίδιον,

405 ὑπάκουσον, εἴπερ πώποτ' ἀνθρώπων τινί·

Δικαιόπολις καλῶ σ' ὁ Χολλῄδης ἐγώ.

ΕΥΡΙΠΙΔΗΣ

ἀλλ' οὐ σχολή.

DICAEOPOLIS

Is Euripides at home?

SLAVE

He's home and not at home, if you get my point.

DICAEOPOLIS

Home and not at home—how can that be?

SLAVE

It's straightforward, old sir. His mind, being outside collecting versicles, is not at home, while he himself is at home, with his feet up, composing tragedy.

DICAEOPOLIS

Thrice-blessed Euripides, that your slave renders you so convincingly! Ask him to come out.

SLAVE

Quite impossible. (*he shuts the door*)

DICAEOPOLIS

Do it anyway. Well, I won't leave; I'll keep knocking on the door. Euripides! Dear Euripides, answer, if ever you answered any mortal. Dicaeopolis of Cholleidai[53] calls you—'tis I.

EURIPIDES

(*from within*) I'm busy.

[53] Here the audience first learns the hero's name. The deme Cholleidai was not far from Acharnae; why Dicaeopolis is associated with it is unclear. It may simply pun on *cholos* "lame," though that theme has yet to be introduced (line 411).

---

[401] σοφῶς ὑποκρίνεται R: σαφῶς ἀπεκρίνατο y

ARISTOPHANES

ΔΙΚΑΙΟΠΟΛΙΣ

ἀλλ᾽ ἐκκυκλήθητ᾽.

ΕΤΡΙΠΙΔΗΣ

ἀλλ᾽ ἀδύνατον.

ΔΙΚΑΙΟΠΟΛΙΣ

ἀλλ᾽ ὅμως.

ΕΤΡΙΠΙΔΗΣ

ἀλλ᾽ ἐκκυκλήσομαι· καταβαίνειν δ᾽ οὐ σχολή.

ΔΙΚΑΙΟΠΟΛΙΣ

Εὐριπίδη.

ΕΤΡΙΠΙΔΗΣ

τί λέλακας;

ΔΙΚΑΙΟΠΟΛΙΣ

410   ἀναβάδην ποιεῖς,
ἐξὸν καταβάδην; οὐκ ἐτὸς χωλοὺς ποιεῖς.
ἀτὰρ τί τὰ ῥάκι᾽ ἐκ τραγῳδίας ἔχεις,
ἐσθῆτ᾽ ἐλεινήν; οὐκ ἐτὸς πτωχοὺς ποιεῖς.
ἀλλ᾽ ἀντιβολῶ πρὸς τῶν γονάτων σ᾽, Εὐριπίδη,
415 δός μοι ῥάκιόν τι τοῦ παλαιοῦ δράματος.
δεῖ γάρ με λέξαι τῷ χορῷ ῥῆσιν μακράν·
αὕτη δὲ θάνατον, ἢν κακῶς λέξω, φέρει.

ΕΤΡΙΠΙΔΗΣ

τὰ ποῖα τρύχη; μῶν ἐν οἷς Οἰνεὺς ὁδὶ

DICAEOPOLIS

Then have yourself wheeled out.[54]

EURIPIDES

Quite impossible.

DICAEOPOLIS

Do it anyway.

EURIPIDES

All right, I'll have myself wheeled out; I've no time to get up.

EURIPIDES is revealed reclining on a couch.

DICAEOPOLIS

Euripides?

EURIPIDES

Why this utterance?

DICAEOPOLIS

Do you compose with your feet up, when they could be down? No wonder you create cripples! And why do you wear those rags from tragedy, a raiment piteous? No wonder you create beggars! But come, I beg you by your knees, Euripides, give me a bit of rag from that old play. I've got to make a long speech to the chorus, and if I speak poorly, it means my death.

EURIPIDES

Which ragged garb? (*rummaging through his costumes*)

---

[54] I.e. on the *eccyclema,* a platform which could be wheeled out of the stage building to reveal interior space.

ὁ δύσποτμος γεραιὸς ἠγωνίζετο;

ΔΙΚΑΙΟΠΟΛΙΣ
420 οὐκ Οἰνέως ἦν, ἀλλ᾽ ἔτ᾽ ἀθλιωτέρου.

ΕΤΡΙΠΙΔΗΣ
τὰ τοῦ τυφλοῦ Φοίνικος;

ΔΙΚΑΙΟΠΟΛΙΣ
                οὐ Φοίνικος, οὔ·
ἀλλ᾽ ἕτερος ἦν Φοίνικος ἀθλιώτερος.

ΕΤΡΙΠΙΔΗΣ
ποίας ποθ᾽ ἀνὴρ λακίδας αἰτεῖται πέπλων;
ἀλλ᾽ ἦ Φιλοκτήτου τὰ τοῦ πτωχοῦ λέγεις;

ΔΙΚΑΙΟΠΟΛΙΣ
425 οὔκ, ἀλλὰ τούτου πολὺ πολὺ πτωχιστέρου.

ΕΤΡΙΠΙΔΗΣ
ἀλλ᾽ ἦ τὰ δυσπινῆ θέλεις πεπλώματα,
ἃ Βελλεροφόντης εἶχ᾽ ὁ χωλὸς οὑτοσί;

ΔΙΚΑΙΟΠΟΛΙΣ
οὐ Βελλεροφόντης· ἀλλὰ κἀκεῖνος μὲν ἦν
χωλός, προσαιτῶν, στωμύλος, δεινὸς λέγειν.

---

⁵⁵ Oeneus, King of Calydon, deposed by his nephews in fa-
vor of his brother Agrius, became an impoverished exile. In
Euripides' lost play, Oeneus is returned to power by his grandson
Diomedes.

Not that in which this Oeneus, the star-crossed ancient, did contend?[55]

DICAEOPOLIS

No, not from Oeneus, but someone even more wretched.

EURIPIDES

From Phoenix, who was blind?[56]

DICAEOPOLIS

Not Phoenix, no; someone else more wretched than Phoenix.

EURIPIDES

What tatters of robing does the man seek? Do you mean those of the beggar Philoctetes?[57]

DICAEOPOLIS

No, someone far, far more beggarly than he.

EURIPIDES

Then do you want the foul accouterment that this Bellerophon, the cripple, wore?[58]

DICAEOPOLIS

Not Bellerophon, though the man I want was also a cripple, a beggar, a smooth-talker, an impressive speaker.

[56] Phoenix was falsely accused by his father's concubine of trying to seduce her, made an unconvincing defence speech, and was blinded and exiled.

[57] Euripides had portrayed the castaway Philoctetes as living on the charity of the Lemnians.

[58] Bellerophon tried to scale Olympus on the winged horse, Pegasus, but was thrown and crippled when Zeus sent a gadfly to vex the horse.

111

ΕΥΡΙΠΙΔΗΣ

οἶδ' ἄνδρα, Μυσὸν Τήλεφον.

ΔΙΚΑΙΟΠΟΛΙΣ

430   ναί, Τήλεφον·
τούτου δός, ἀντιβολῶ σέ, μοι τὰ σπάργανα.

ΕΥΡΙΠΙΔΗΣ

ὦ παῖ, δὸς αὐτῷ Τηλέφου ῥακώματα.
κεῖται δ' ἄνωθεν τῶν Θυεστείων ῥακῶν
μεταξὺ τῶν Ἰνοῦς. ἰδού, ταυτὶ λαβέ.

ΔΙΚΑΙΟΠΟΛΙΣ

435 ὦ Ζεῦ διόπτα καὶ κατόπτα πανταχῇ.
"ἐνσκευάσασθαί μ' οἷον ἀθλιώτατον."
Εὐριπίδη, 'πειδήπερ ἐχαρίσω ταδί,
κἀκεῖνά μοι δὸς τἀκόλουθα τῶν ῥακῶν,
τὸ πιλίδιον περὶ τὴν κεφαλὴν τὸ Μύσιον.
440 δεῖ γάρ με δόξαι πτωχὸν εἶναι τήμερον,
εἶναι μὲν ὅσπερ εἰμί, φαίνεσθαι δὲ μή·
τοὺς μὲν θεατὰς εἰδέναι μ' ὅς εἰμ' ἐγώ,
τοὺς δ' αὖ χορευτὰς ἠλιθίους παρεστάναι,
ὅπως ἂν αὐτοὺς ῥηματίοις σκιμαλίσω.

ΕΥΡΙΠΙΔΗΣ

445 δώσω· πυκνῇ γὰρ λεπτὰ μηχανᾷ φρενί.

ΔΙΚΑΙΟΠΟΛΙΣ

εὐδαιμονοίης· Τηλέφῳ δ' ἁγὼ φρονῶ.
εὖ γ'· οἷον ἤδη ῥηματίων ἐμπίμπλαμαι.

---

436 (=384) del. Dobree

EURIPIDES

I know the man: Mysian Telephus![59]

DICAEOPOLIS

Yes, Telephus! Give me, I entreat you, his swaddlings!

EURIPIDES

Boy, give him the ragments of Telephus. They lie above the Thyestean[60] rags, 'tween them and Ino's.[61]

SLAVE

Here, take them.

DICAEOPOLIS

(*inspecting the rags*) O Zeus who sees everywhere, through and under! Euripides, since you've been so kind to me, please give me what goes along with the rags: that little Mysian beanie for my head. For the beggar must I seem to be today: to be who I am, yet seem not so. The audience must know me for who I am, but the chorus must stand there like simpletons, so that with my pointed phrases I can give them the finger.

EURIPIDES

I'll give it, for you contrive finely with your dense mind.

DICAEOPOLIS

God bless you, and as for Telephus—what's in my thoughts! Bravo! How I'm filling up with phraselets already! But I do

---

[59] See Introductory Note.

[60] Referring probably to *Thyestes,* in which the title character is banished for seducing the wife of his brother, Atreus.

[61] In *Ino,* the title character is imprisoned by her former husband, Athamas.

ἀτὰρ δέομαί γε πτωχικοῦ βακτηρίου.

ΕΤΡΙΠΙΔΗΣ

τουτὶ λαβὼν ἄπελθε λαΐνων σταθμῶν.

ΔΙΚΑΙΟΠΟΛΙΣ

450 ὦ θύμ᾽, ὁρᾷς γὰρ ὡς ἀπωθοῦμαι δόμων,
πολλῶν δεόμενος σκευαρίων, νῦν δὴ γενοῦ
γλίσχρος, προσαιτῶν λιπαρῶν τ᾽. Εὐριπίδη,
δός μοι σπυρίδιον διακεκαυμένον λύχνῳ.

ΕΤΡΙΠΙΔΗΣ

τί δ᾽, ὦ τάλας, σε τοῦδ᾽ ἔχει πλέκους χρέος;

ΔΙΚΑΙΟΠΟΛΙΣ

455 χρέος μὲν οὐδέν, βούλομαι δ᾽ ὅμως λαβεῖν.

ΕΤΡΙΠΙΔΗΣ

λυπηρὸς ἴσθ᾽ ὢν κἀποχώρησον δόμων.

ΔΙΚΑΙΟΠΟΛΙΣ

φεῦ. εὐδαιμονοίης, ὥσπερ ἡ μήτηρ ποτέ.

ΕΤΡΙΠΙΔΗΣ

ἄπελθέ νύν μοι.

ΔΙΚΑΙΟΠΟΛΙΣ

μἀλλά μοι δὸς ἓν μόνον,
κοτυλίσκιον τὸ χεῖλος ἀποκεκρουμένον.

ΕΤΡΙΠΙΔΗΣ

460 φθείρου λαβὼν τόδ᾽· ἴσθ᾽ ὀχληρὸς ὢν δόμοις.

ΔΙΚΑΙΟΠΟΛΙΣ

οὔπω μὰ Δί᾽ οἶσθ᾽ οἷ᾽ αὐτὸς ἐργάζει κακά.

need a beggar's cane.

EURIPIDES
Take this, and begone from these marble halls.

DICAEOPOLIS
My soul, you see how I'm driven from the halls still needing many props. So now be whiny, beggarly, and precatory! Euripides, give me a little basket burned through by a lamp!

EURIPIDES
What need have you, poor wretch, for this wickerwork?

DICAEOPOLIS
No need at all; I want to have it anyway.

EURIPIDES
Know you are irksome, and depart my halls!

DICAEOPOLIS
Whew! God's blessings on you—as once on your mother!

EURIPIDES
Now pray begone!

DICAEOPOLIS
No, but give me just one thing more, a little goblet with a broken lip.

EURIPIDES
Take this one—to blazes! Know you are troublesome to my halls!

DICAEOPOLIS
By Zeus, you don't yet realize how much trouble you make

ARISTOPHANES

ἀλλ᾽, ὦ γλυκύτατ᾽ Εὐριπίδη, τουτὶ μόνον
δός μοι χυτρίδιον σπογγίῳ βεβυσμένον.

ΕΤΡΙΠΙΔΗΣ
ἄνθρωπ᾽, ἀφαιρήσει με τὴν τραγῳδίαν.
ἄπελθε ταυτηνὶ λαβών.

ΔΙΚΑΙΟΠΟΛΙΣ
465   ἀπέρχομαι.
καίτοι τί δράσω; δεῖ γὰρ ἑνὸς οὗ μὴ τυχὼν
ἀπόλωλ᾽. ἄκουσον, ὦ γλυκύτατ᾽ Εὐριπίδη·
τουτὶ λαβὼν ἄπειμι κοὐ πρόσειμ᾽ ἔτι·
εἰς τὸ σπυρίδιον ἰσχνά μοι φυλλεῖα δός.

ΕΤΡΙΠΙΔΗΣ
470 ἀπολεῖς μ᾽. ἰδού σοι. φροῦδά μοι τὰ δράματα.

ΔΙΚΑΙΟΠΟΛΙΣ
ἀλλ᾽ οὐκέτ᾽, ἀλλ᾽ ἄπειμι. καὶ γὰρ εἰμ᾽ ἄγαν
ὀχληρός, οὐ δοκῶν με κοιράνους στυγεῖν.
οἴμοι κακοδαίμων, ὡς ἀπόλωλ᾽. ἐπελαθόμην
ἐν ᾧπέρ ἐστι πάντα μοι τὰ πράγματα.
475 Εὐριπίδιον ὦ γλυκύτατον καὶ φίλτατον,
κάκιστ᾽ ἀπολοίμην, εἴ τί σ᾽ αἰτήσαιμ᾽ ἔτι,
πλὴν ἓν μόνον, τουτὶ μόνον, τουτὶ μόνον,
σκάνδικά μοι δὸς μητρόθεν δεδεγμένος.

ΕΤΡΙΠΙΔΗΣ
ἁνὴρ ὑβρίζει· κλῇε πηκτὰ δωμάτων.

ΔΙΚΑΙΟΠΟΛΙΣ
480 ὦ θύμ᾽, ἄνευ σκάνδικος ἐμπορευτέα.

116

yourself! — But my sweetest Euripides, just give me that
little bottle plugged with a sponge.

EURIPIDES

Fellow, you'll make off with my whole tragedy! Take this
and begone.

DICAEOPOLIS

I'm off. Hold on, what am I doing? There's one thing miss-
ing, which if I don't have, I'm lost. Listen, my sweetest
Euripides, with this I'll go, and never come again. Give me
some withered greenery for my little basket.

EURIPIDES

You'll destroy me! Here you are. Gone are my plays!

DICAEOPOLIS

No more; I'll go. Indeed I am too troublesome, though
little thought I the chieftans hate me so![62] Good heavens
me, I'm ruined! I've forgotten the one thing on which all
my plans depend. My sweetest, dearest Euripidoodle, a
wretched death be mine if ever again I ask you for any-
thing—save just one thing, only this one, only this one: give
me some chervil from your mother's store. [63]

EURIPIDES

The man's outrageous! Batten the barriers of my domicile!

EURIPIDES is wheeled inside.

DICAEOPOLIS

My soul, without chervil must you venture forth. Don't you

---

[62] The line, in tragic style, is probably taken from *Telephus*.

[63] Aristophanes, for reasons unclear, often refers to Euripides'
mother as an impoverished hawker of wild herbs.

ARISTOPHANES

ἆρ' οἶσθ' ὅσον τὸν ἀγῶν' ἀγωνιεῖ τάχα,
μέλλων ὑπὲρ Λακεδαιμονίων ἀνδρῶν λέγειν;
πρόβαινέ νυν, ὦ θυμέ· γραμμὴ δ' αὑτηί.
ἔστηκας; οὐκ εἶ καταπιὼν Εὐριπίδην;
485 ἐπήνεσ'· ἄγε νυν, ὦ τάλαινα καρδία,
ἄπελθ' ἐκεῖσε, κᾆτα τὴν κεφαλὴν ἐκεῖ
παράσχες εἰποῦσ' ἅττ' ἂν αὐτῇ σοὶ δοκῇ.
τόλμησον, ἴθι, χώρησον· ἄγαμαι καρδίας.

XOΡΟΣ

(στρ) τί δράσεις; τί φήσεις; <εὖ> ἴσθι νυν
491 ἀναίσχυντος ὢν σιδηροῦς τ' ἀνήρ,
ὅστις παρασχὼν τῇ πόλει τὸν αὐχένα
ἅπασι μέλλεις εἷς λέγειν τἀναντία.
495 ἀνὴρ οὐ τρέμει τὸ πρᾶγμ'. εἶά νυν,
ἐπειδήπερ αὐτὸς αἱρεῖ, λέγε.

ΔΙΚΑΙΟΠΟΛΙΣ

μή μοι φθονήσητ', ἄνδρες οἱ θεώμενοι,
εἰ πτωχὸς ὢν ἔπειτ' ἐν Ἀθηναίοις λέγειν
μέλλω περὶ τῆς πόλεως, τρυγῳδίαν ποιῶν.
500 τὸ γὰρ δίκαιον οἶδε καὶ τρυγῳδία.
ἐγὼ δὲ λέξω δεινὰ μέν, δίκαια δέ.
οὐ γάρ με νῦν γε διαβαλεῖ Κλέων ὅτι
ξένων παρόντων τὴν πόλιν κακῶς λέγω.
αὐτοὶ γάρ ἐσμεν οὑπὶ Ληναίῳ τ' ἀγών,
505 κοὔπω ξένοι πάρεισιν· οὔτε γὰρ φόροι
ἥκουσιν οὔτ' ἐκ τῶν πόλεων οἱ ξύμμαχοι·
ἀλλ' ἐσμὲν αὐτοὶ νῦν γε περιεπτισμένοι·

118

realize what a great contest you will soon contest, when you speak in defence of Spartan foemen? Forward now, my soul; there's your mark. You hesitate? Won't you get going, now that you've downed a draught of Euripides? Bravo! Come on now, my foolish heart, get on over there, and then offer up your head on the spot, after you've told them what you yourself believe. Be bold, go on, move out. Well done, heart!

CHORUS

What will you do? What will you say? You must realize
that you are a shameless and a steely man,
you who have offered your neck to the city
and mean to speak alone against everyone.
The man does not tremble at his task. Very well:
since you've made the choice yourself, speak!

DICAEOPOLIS

Do not be aggrieved with me, gentleman spectators, if, though a beggar, I am ready to address the Athenians about the city while making comedy. For even comedy knows about what's right; and what I say will be shocking, but right. This time Cleon will not accuse me of defaming the city in the presence of foreigners; for we are by ourselves; it's the Lenaean competition, and no foreigners are here yet; neither tribute nor troops have arrived from the allied cities.[64] This time we are by ourselves, clean-hulled—for I

---

[64] Tribute payments from Athens' subject allies were presented at the Greater Dionysia in the spring, when allied troops would be mustered for the campaign season.

ARISTOPHANES

τοὺς γὰρ μετοίκους ἄχυρα τῶν ἀστῶν λέγω.
ἐγὼ δὲ μισῶ μὲν Λακεδαιμονίους σφόδρα,
510 καὐτοῖς ὁ Ποσειδῶν, οὑπὶ Ταινάρῳ θεός,
σείσας ἅπασιν ἐμβάλοι τὰς οἰκίας·
κἀμοὶ γάρ ἐστι τἀμπέλια κεκομμένα.
ἀτάρ, φίλοι γὰρ οἱ παρόντες ἐν λόγῳ,
τί ταῦτα τοὺς Λάκωνας αἰτιώμεθα;
515 ἡμῶν γὰρ ἄνδρες, — οὐχὶ τὴν πόλιν λέγω·
μέμνησθε τοῦθ᾽, ὅτι οὐχὶ τὴν πόλιν λέγω, —
ἀλλ᾽ ἀνδράρια μοχθηρά, παρακεκομμένα,
ἄτιμα καὶ παράσημα καὶ παράξενα,
ἐσυκοφάντει Μεγαρέων τὰ χλανίσκια.
520 κεἴ που σίκυον ἴδοιεν ἢ λαγῴδιον
ἢ χοιρίδιον ἢ σκόροδον ἢ χόνδρους ἅλας,
ταῦτ᾽ ἦν Μεγαρικὰ κἀπέπρατ᾽ αὐθημερόν.
καὶ ταῦτα μὲν δὴ σμικρὰ κἀπιχώρια·
πόρνην δὲ Σιμαίθαν ἰόντες Μεγαράδε
525 νεανίαι ᾽κκλέπτουσι μεθυσοκότταβοι·
κᾆθ᾽ οἱ Μεγαρῆς ὀδύναις πεφυσιγγωμένοι
ἀντεξέκλεψαν Ἀσπασίας πόρνα δύο·
κἀντεῦθεν ἀρχὴ τοῦ πολέμου κατερράγη
Ἕλλησι πᾶσιν ἐκ τριῶν λαικαστριῶν.
530 ἐντεῦθεν ὀργῇ Περικλέης οὐλύμπιος
ἤστραπτ᾽, ἐβρόντα, ξυνεκύκα τὴν Ἑλλάδα,

---

65 A cape at the southwestern tip of the Peloponnese.
66 An allusion to the great earthquake that devastated Laconia
c. 464 and that many attributed to the anger of Poseidon following

120

count the resident foreigners as the bran of our populace.
Myself, I hate the Spartans vehemently; and may Poseidon,
the god at Tainarum,[65] send them an earthquake and shake
all their houses down on them;[66] for I too have had vines
cut down. And yet I ask—for only friends are present for
this speech—why do we blame the Spartans for this? For
it was men of ours—I do not say the city, remember that,
I do not say the city—but some trouble-making excuses
for men, misminted, worthless, brummagem, and foreign-
made, who began denouncing the Megarians' little
cloaks.[67] If anywhere they spotted a cucumber or a bunny,
or a piglet or some garlic or rock salt, these were
"Megarian" and sold off the very same day. Now granted,
this was trivial and strictly local. But then some tipsy, cot-
tabus-playing[68] youths went to Megara and kidnapped the
whore Simaetha.[69] And then the Megarians, garlic-stung
by their distress, in retaliation stole a couple of Aspasia's
whores,[70] and from that the onset of war broke forth upon
all the Greeks: from three sluts! And then in wrath Peri-
cles, that Olympian, did lighten and thunder and stir up

the Spartans' execution of some of their subjects, who had taken
refuge in his temple at Cape Taenarum.

[67] On the suspicion that they had been imported without pay-
ment of duties.

[68] The game of cottabus, in which drinkers tossed wine lees at
a target, was associated with dissolute behavior.

[69] A lover of Alcibiades, according to the scholia.

[70] Popular gossip held that Aspasia, an immigrant citizen of
Miletus who lived with Pericles as his unmarried wife, procured
free-born women for him, or even trained prostitutes. In *Peace*
603-15 a different personal motive for starting the war is attrib-
uted to Pericles.

ἐτίθει νόμους ὥσπερ σκόλια γεγραμμένους,
ὡς χρὴ Μεγαρέας μήτε γῇ μήτ' ἐν ἀγορᾷ
μήτ' ἐν θαλάττῃ μήτ' ἐν ἠπείρῳ μένειν.
535 ἐντεῦθεν οἱ Μεγαρῆς, ὅτε δὴ 'πείνων βάδην,
Λακεδαιμονίων ἐδέοντο τὸ ψήφισμ' ὅπως
μεταστραφείη τὸ διὰ τὰς λαικαστρίας·
οὐκ ἠθέλομεν δ' ἡμεῖς δεομένων πολλάκις.
κἀντεῦθεν ἤδη πάταγος ἦν τῶν ἀσπίδων.
540 ἐρεῖ τις· "οὐ χρῆν" ἀλλὰ τί ἐχρῆν εἴπατε.
φέρ', εἰ Λακεδαιμονίων τις εἰσπλεύσαν σκάφει
ἀπέδοτο φήνας κυνίδιον Σεριφίων,
καθῆσθ' ἂν ἐν δόμοισιν; ἦ πολλοῦ γε δεῖ·
καὶ κάρτα μεντἂν εὐθέως καθείλκετε
545 τριακοσίας ναῦς, ἦν δ' ἂν ἡ πόλις πλέα
θορύβου στρατιωτῶν, περὶ τριηράρχου βοῆς,
μισθοῦ διδομένου, παλλαδίων χρυσουμένων,
στοᾶς στεναχούσης, σιτίων μετρουμένων,
ἀσκῶν, τροπωτήρων, κάδους ὠνουμένων,
550 σκορόδων, ἐλαῶν, κρομμύων ἐν δικτύοις,
στεφάνων, τριχίδων, αὐλητρίδων, ὑπωπίων·
τὸ νεώριον δ' αὖ κωπέων πλατουμένων,
τύλων ψοφούντων, θαλαμιῶν τρυπουμένων,
αὐλῶν, κελευστῶν, νιγλάρων, συριγμάτων.
555 ταῦτ' οἶδ' ὅτι ἂν ἐδρᾶτε· τὸν δὲ Τήλεφον
οὐκ οἰόμεσθα; νοῦς ἄρ' ἡμῖν οὐκ ἔνι.

ΗΜΙΧΟΡΙΟΝ Α'
ἄληθες, ὦπίτριπτε καὶ μιαρώτατε;

122

ACHARNIANS

Greece, and started making laws worded like drinking
songs, that Megarians should abide neither on land nor in
market nor on sea nor on shore.[71] Whereupon the Megari-
ans, starving by degrees, asked the Spartans to bring about
a reversal of the decree in response to the sluts; but we
refused, though they asked us many times. And then there
was a clashing of the shields. Someone will say, "they
shouldn't have!" But tell me, what should they have? Look,
if some Spartan had denounced and sold a Seriphian
puppy[72] imported in a rowboat, would you have sat quietly
by in your abodes? Far from it! No indeed: you'd have
instantaneously dispatched three hundred ships; the city
would fill with the hubbub of soldiers, clamor around the
skipper, pay disbursed, emblems of Pallas being gilded, the
Colonnade reverberating, rations being measured out,
wallets, oarloops, buyers of jars, garlic, olives, onions in
nets, garlands, anchovies, piper girls, black eyes. And the
dockyards would be full of oarspars being planed, thudding
dowelpins, oarports being bored, pipes, bosuns, whistling
and tooting. I know that's what you'd have done: and do we
reckon that Telephus wouldn't? Then we've got no brains!

LEADER OF THE FIRST SEMICHORUS
Is that so, you damned scum of the earth? Do you, a beggar,

71 For this decree of 432 see Thucydides 1.39, 67, 144; Aristo-
phanes models his parody of the decree on a "drinking song" by
Timocreon of Rhodes (*PMG* 731).   72 Seriphus, a small cy-
cladic island, was one of the least important Athenian allies.

---

541 εἰσπλεῦσαν van Leeuwen: ἐκπλεύσας z
553 τρυπ- Morrison: τροπ- z
556 ἡμῖν R Vp3 a: ὑμῖν t

123

ταυτὶ σὺ τολμᾷς πτωχὸς ὢν ἡμᾶς λέγειν,
καὶ συκοφάντης εἴ τις ἦν ὠνείδισας;

HMIXOPION B'

560 νὴ τὸν Ποσειδῶ, καὶ λέγει γ' ἅπερ λέγει
δίκαια πάντα κοὐδὲν αὐτῶν ψεύδεται.

HMIXOPION A'

εἶτ' εἰ δίκαια, τοῦτον εἰπεῖν αὔτ' ἐχρῆν;
ἀλλ' οὔτι χαίρων ταῦτα τολμήσει λέγειν.

HMIXOPION B'

οὗτος σύ, ποῖ θεῖς; οὐ μενεῖς; ὡς εἰ θενεῖς
565 τὸν ἄνδρα τοῦτον, αὐτὸς ἀρθήσει τάχα.

HMIXOPION A'

ἰὼ Λάμαχ', ὦ βλέπων ἀστραπάς,
βοήθησον, ὦ γοργολόφα, φανείς,
ἰὼ Λάμαχ', ὦ φίλ', ὦ φυλέτα·
εἴτ' ἔστι ταξίαρχος ἢ στρατηγὸς ἢ
570 τειχομάχας ἀνήρ, βοηθησάτω
τις ἀνύσας· ἐγὼ γὰρ ἔχομαι μέσος.

ΛΑΜΑΧΟΣ

πόθεν βοῆς ἤκουσα πολεμιστηρίας;
ποῖ χρὴ βοηθεῖν; ποῖ κυδοιμὸν ἐμβαλεῖν;
τίς Γοργόν' ἐξήγειρεν ἐκ τοῦ σάγματος;

---

[73] Aristophanes probably chose Lamachus (parodying the
Achilleus of *Telephus*) to represent war not only because of his

124

dare say this of us, and scold us, if we had the odd informer?

LEADER OF THE SECOND SEMICHORUS
He does, by Poseidon, and what he says is right, entirely,
and at no point does he lie.

LEADER OF THE FIRST SEMICHORUS
Even so, was he the one to say it? He'll be sorry that he
dared make this speech.

LEADER OF THE SECOND SEMICHORUS
Hey you, where are you running? Stop, I say! Because if
you hit this man, you'll be upended yourself, and quickly!

FIRST SEMICHORUS
O Lamachus[73] who looks lightning,
appear and help us, you of the fearsome crest!
O Lamachus, friend and fellow tribesman!
Or if there is a taxiarch, or general,
or wall-storming champion, let him come to our aid,
anyone, and quickly! I'm caught in a waistlock.

LAMACHUS enters in full panoply, with Soldiers.

LAMACHUS
Whence have I heard a martial shout? Whither must I
charge? Where hurl the hullabaloo? Who's roused my Gorgon from her shield case?

appropriately warlike name (cf. 270 n.) and his reputation as an
energetic soldier, but also because he was the least wealthy of
contemporary commanders and thus vulnerable to the charge of
promoting the war for personal gain (cf. 597-617).

125

ARISTOPHANES

ΔΙΚΑΙΟΠΟΛΙΣ
575 ὦ Λάμαχ᾽, ἥρως τῶν λόφων καὶ τῶν λόχων.

ΚΟΡΥΦΑΙΟΣ Α΄
ὦ Λάμαχ᾽, οὐ γὰρ οὗτος ἄνθρωπος πάλαι
ἅπασαν ἡμῶν τὴν πόλιν κακορροθεῖ;

ΛΑΜΑΧΟΣ
οὗτος, σὺ τολμᾷς πτωχὸς ὢν λέγειν τάδε;

ΔΙΚΑΙΟΠΟΛΙΣ
ὦ Λάμαχ᾽ ἥρως, ἀλλὰ συγγνώμην ἔχε,
εἰ πτωχὸς ὢν εἶπόν τι κἀστωμυλάμην.

ΛΑΜΑΧΟΣ
τί δ᾽ εἶπας ἡμᾶς; οὐκ ἐρεῖς;

ΔΙΚΑΙΟΠΟΛΙΣ
580   οὐκ οἶδά πω·
ὑπὸ τοῦ δέους γὰρ τῶν ὅπλων εἰλιγγιῶ.
ἀλλ᾽, ἀντιβολῶ σ᾽, ἀπένεγκέ μου τὴν μορμόνα.

ΛΑΜΑΧΟΣ
ἰδού.

ΔΙΚΑΙΟΠΟΛΙΣ
παράθες νυν ὑπτίαν αὐτὴν ἐμοί.

ΛΑΜΑΧΟΣ
κεῖται.

ΔΙΚΑΙΟΠΟΛΙΣ
φέρε νυν ἀπὸ τοῦ κράνους μοι τὸ πτερόν.

DICAEOPOLIS

Lamachus, hero! What crests and ambuscades!

LEADER OF THE FIRST SEMICHORUS

Lamachus, don't you realize that this man has long been
spewing slander at our whole city?

LAMACHUS

You there! Do you dare, beggar as you are, to say such
things?

DICAEOPOLIS

Lamachus, hero, please be merciful if, beggar that I am, I
spoke and prattled some.

LAMACHUS

What did you say about me? Speak up!

DICAEOPOLIS

I'm not certain yet; the terror of your armor makes me
dizzy. (*pointing at the Gorgon on Lamachus' shield*)
Please, take that scare-face away from me!

LAMACHUS

(*reversing his shield*) There.

DICAEOPOLIS

Now lay it upside down in front of me.

LAMACHUS

There it lies.

DICAEOPOLIS

Now hand me that plume from your helmet.

ΛΑΜΑΧΟΣ

τουτὶ πτίλον σοι.

ΔΙΚΑΙΟΠΟΛΙΣ

585   τῆς κεφαλῆς νύν μου λαβοῦ,
ἵν᾽ ἐξεμέσω· βδελύττομαι γὰρ τοὺς λόφους.

ΛΑΜΑΧΟΣ

οὗτος, τί δράσεις; τῷ πτίλῳ μέλλεις ἐμεῖν;

ΔΙΚΑΙΟΠΟΛΙΣ

πτίλον γάρ ἐστιν; εἰπέ μοι, τίνος ποτὲ
ὄρνιθός ἐστιν; ἆρα κομπολακύθου;

ΛΑΜΑΧΟΣ

οἴμ᾽ ὡς τεθνήξεις.

ΔΙΚΑΙΟΠΟΛΙΣ

590   μηδαμῶς, ὦ Λάμαχε·
οὐ γὰρ κατ᾽ ἰσχύν ἐστιν· εἰ δ᾽ ἰσχυρὸς εἶ,
τί μ᾽ οὐκ ἀπεψώλησας; εὔοπλος γὰρ εἶ.

ΛΑΜΑΧΟΣ

ταυτὶ λέγεις σὺ τὸν στρατηγὸν πτωχὸς ὤν;

ΔΙΚΑΙΟΠΟΛΙΣ

ἐγὼ γάρ εἰμι πτωχός;

ΛΑΜΑΧΟΣ

          ἀλλὰ τίς γὰρ εἶ;

ΔΙΚΑΙΟΠΟΛΙΣ

595 ὅστις; πολίτης χρηστός, οὐ σπουδαρχίδης,
ἀλλ᾽ ἐξ ὅτουπερ ὁ πόλεμος, στρατωνίδης,
σὺ δ᾽ ἐξ ὅτουπερ ὁ πόλεμος, μισθαρχίδης.

ACHARNIANS

LAMACHUS
Here's a tuft for you.

DICAEOPOLIS
Now take hold of my head, so I can puke. I'm sickened by your crests!

LAMACHUS
Hey there, what are you up to? You'd use my tuft to puke with?

DICAEOPOLIS
This tuft here? Tell me, what sort of bird is if from? Perhaps the roaring boastard?

LAMACHUS
Oh! Now you're doomed!

DICAEOPOLIS
Not at all, Lamachus! It's not a matter of strength—though if you're really strong, why not peel back my foreskin? You're well enough equipped!

LAMACHUS
Do you, a beggar, say this to a general?

DICAEOPOLIS
Me, a beggar?

LAMACHUS
Well, what are you then?

DICAEOPOLIS
What am I? A solid citizen, not a Mr. Placehunter, but ever since the war began, a Mr. Trooper; while you, ever since the war began, have been a Mr. Highpay!

ΛΑΜΑΧΟΣ

ἐχειροτόνησαν γάρ με.

ΔΙΚΑΙΟΠΟΛΙΣ

κόκκυγές γε τρεῖς.

ταῦτ᾽ οὖν ἐγὼ βδελυττόμενος ἐσπεισάμην,
600 ὁρῶν πολιοὺς μὲν ἄνδρας ἐν ταῖς τάξεσιν,
νεανίας δ᾽ οἵους σὺ διαδεδρακότας,
τοὺς μὲν ἐπὶ Θρᾴκης μισθοφοροῦντας τρεῖς
δραχμάς,
Τεισαμενοφαινίππους Πανουργιππαρχίδας,
ἑτέρους δὲ παρὰ Χάρητι, τοὺς δ᾽ ἐν Χάοσιν,
605 Γερητοθεοδώρους Διομειαλαζόνας,
τοὺς δ᾽ ἐν Καμαρίνῃ κἀν Γέλᾳ κἀν Καταγέλᾳ.

ΛΑΜΑΧΟΣ

ἐχειροτονήθησαν γάρ.

ΔΙΚΑΙΟΠΟΛΙΣ

αἴτιον δὲ τί
ὑμᾶς μὲν ἀεὶ μισθοφορεῖν ἀμηγέπῃ,
τωνδὶ δὲ μηδέν; ἐτεόν, ὦ Μαριλάδη,
610 ἤδη πεπρέσβευκας σὺ πολιὸς ὢν ἔνῃ;
ἀνένευσε· καίτοι γ᾽ ἐστὶ σώφρων κἀργάτης.
τί δ᾽ Ἀνθράκυλλος ἢ Εὐφορίδης ἢ Πρινίδης;

612 δ᾽ Ἀνθράκυλλος Reiske: δαὶ Δράκυλλος z

---

[74] That is, the Assembly was poorly attended.
[75] None of the men mentioned here is certainly identifiable,
though the only political figure from Diomeia known in this pe-

LAMACHUS

They did elect me.

DICAEOPOLIS

Three cuckoos did![74] That's why I was sickened and poured
a truce, when I saw grey-haired men in the ranks, and lads
like you arrantly malingering, some drawing three drach-
mas' pay on the Thracian coast—Teisamenus-Phaenippus,
Scoundrel-Hipparchides—others with Chares, others
among the Chaonians—Geres-Theodorus, Humbug from
Diomeia—still others in Camarina and Gela and
Catagela.[75]

LAMACHUS

They did get elected.

DICAEOPOLIS

But how come you're all drawing pay somewhere or other,
while none of these people ever does? (*to members of the
chorus*) Say, Marilades,[76] have you ever served on an em-
bassy, though you're a greybeard of long standing? He
shakes his head; and yet he's solid and hard-working. And
what about Anthracyllus and Euphorides and Prinides?[77]

riod is the Philoxenus ridiculed in *Clouds* 686 and *Wasps* 84.
The name of the Chaonians, a warlike people of Epirus, is used
here and elsewhere in comedy to pun on *chaos* "void" or *chaskein*
"gape." Camerina and Gela (suggesting *gelos* "laughter") were
Sicilian towns; Catagela is a comic coinage suggesting *katagelos*
"derision."

[76] "Coalson": the Acharnians are given invented names appro-
priate to charcoal burning, their chief local industry.

[77] "Ember" (with Reiske: Dracyllus MSS), "Totewell," and
"Oakson."

εἶδέν τις ὑμῶν τἀκβάταν᾽ ἢ τοὺς Χάονας;
οὔ φασιν. ἀλλ᾽ ὁ Κοισύρας καὶ Λάμαχος,
615 οἷς ὑπ᾽ ἐράνων τε καὶ χρεῶν πρώην ποτέ,
ὥσπερ ἀπόνιπτρον ἐκχέοντες ἑσπέρας,
ἅπαντες "ἐξίστω" παρήνουν οἱ φίλοι.

ΛΑΜΑΧΟΣ

ὦ δημοκρατία, ταῦτα δῆτ᾽ ἀνασχετά;

ΔΙΚΑΙΟΠΟΛΙΣ

οὐ δῆτ᾽, ἐὰν μὴ μισθοφορῇ γε Λάμαχος.

ΛΑΜΑΧΟΣ

620 ἀλλ᾽ οὖν ἐγὼ μὲν πᾶσι Πελοποννησίοις
ἀεὶ πολεμήσω καὶ ταράξω πανταχῇ,
καὶ ναυσὶ καὶ πεζοῖσι, κατὰ τὸ καρτερόν.

ΔΙΚΑΙΟΠΟΛΙΣ

ἐγὼ δὲ κηρύττω γε Πελοποννησίοις
ἅπασι καὶ Μεγαρεῦσι καὶ Βοιωτίοις
625 πωλεῖν ἀγοράζειν πρὸς ἐμέ, Λαμάχῳ δὲ μή.

ΚΟΡΥΦΑΙΟΣ

ἁνὴρ νικᾷ τοῖσι λόγοισιν, καὶ τὸν δῆμον μεταπείθει
περὶ τῶν σπονδῶν. ἀλλ᾽ ἀποδύντες τοῖς ἀνα-
παίστοις ἐπίωμεν.
ἐξ οὗ γε χοροῖσιν ἐφέστηκεν τρυγικοῖς ὁ διδάσκα-
λος ἡμῶν,

---

[78] Evidently referring to Megacles, an Alcmaeonid and thus typifying the bluest blood; so identified in order to emphasize his non-Athenian ancestry on his mother's side (she was Eretrian); cf. *Clouds* 46-48.

Has any of you ever seen Ecbatana or the Chaonians? They say they haven't. But the son of Coisyra[78] and Lamachus have, though just the other day, on account of dues and debts, all their friends were advising them to stand back, like people dumping the evening washwater.

LAMACHUS
Oh, Democracy! Will such talk be tolerated?

DICAEOPOLIS
No indeed, unless Lamachus draws his pay!

LAMACHUS
Be that as it may, I for one will ever make war on all the Peloponnesians, and everywhere harass them, with ships and footsoldiers, with all my might.

DICAEOPOLIS
And I announce to all Peloponnesians, Megarians, and Boeotians that they may trade in my marketplace, but not Lamachus.

DICAEOPOLIS, LAMACHUS, and his Soldiers exit on their separate ways.

CHORUS LEADER
That man has won the debate, and he's changed the people's mind about the truce. Now let's doff our cloaks and essay the anapests.[79]

Never yet, since our producer first directed comic

---

[79] The verse form in which the speeches of a *parabasis* were most often written, and the usual way to refer to its speech on behalf of the poet.

οὔπω παρέβη πρὸς τὸ θέατρον λέξων ὡς δεξιός ἐστιν
630 διαβαλλόμενος δ' ὑπὸ τῶν ἐχθρῶν ἐν Ἀθηναίοις
 ταχυβούλοις,
ὡς κωμῳδεῖ τὴν πόλιν ἡμῶν καὶ τὸν δῆμον καθυ-
 βρίζει,
ἀποκρίνασθαι δεῖται νυνὶ πρὸς Ἀθηναίους μετα-
 βούλους.
φησὶν δ' εἶναι πολλῶν ἀγαθῶν ἄξιος ὑμῖν ὁ ποιητής,
παύσας ὑμᾶς ξενικοῖσι λόγοις μὴ λίαν ἐξαπατᾶσθαι,
635 μήθ' ἥδεσθαι θωπευομένους, μήτ' εἶναι χαυνοπολίτας.
πρότερον δ' ὑμᾶς ἀπὸ τῶν πόλεων οἱ πρέσβεις ἐξα-
 πατῶντες
πρῶτον μὲν ἰοστεφάνους ἐκάλουν· κἀπειδὴ τοῦτό
 τις εἴποι,
εὐθὺς διὰ τοὺς στεφάνους ἐπ' ἄκρων τῶν πυγιδίων
 ἐκάθησθε.
εἰ δέ τις ὑμᾶς ὑποθωπεύσας "λιπαρὰς" καλέσειεν
 Ἀθήνας,
640 ηὕρετο πᾶν ἂν διὰ τὰς λιπαράς, ἀφύων τιμὴν
 περιάψας.
ταῦτα ποιήσας πολλῶν ἀγαθῶν αἴτιος ὑμῖν
 γεγένηται,
καὶ τοὺς δήμους ἐν ταῖς πόλεσιν δείξας ὡς δημο-
 κρατοῦνται.
τοιγάρτοι νῦν οὐκ τῶν πόλεων τὸν φόρον ὑμῖν
 ἀπάγοντες

choruses, has he come forward to tell the audience he is intelligent.[80] But since he has been accused by his enemies before Athenians quick to make up their minds, as one who makes comedy of our city and outrages the people, he now asks to defend himself before Athenians just as quick to change their minds. Our poet says that he deserves rich rewards from you, since he has stopped you from being deceived overmuch by foreigners' speeches, from being cajoled by flattery, from being citizens of Simpletonia. Before he did that, the ambassadors from the allied states who meant to deceive you would start by calling you "violet-crowned";[81] and when anyone said that, those "crowns" would promptly have you sitting on the tips of your little buttocks. And if anyone fawned on you by calling Athens "gleaming," that "gleaming" would get him everything, just for tagging you with an honor fit only for sardines. For this he's the source of rich benefits for you,[82] and also for showing how the peoples of the allied states were "democratically" governed.[83] That's why the allied emissaries who bring you their tribute will henceforth come: they'll be

[80] Since in this *parabasis* "producer" and "poet" evidently refer to the same person, the chorus leader's statements may refer either to Aristophanes or (less likely) to Callistratus.

[81] The epithets "violet-crowned" and "gleaming" are first attested for Athens in Pindar (*I.* 2.20, fr. 76).

[82] Or, with Blaydes' emendation, "for doing that, he deserves rich benefits from you."

[83] Referring to misadministration by the Athenians or by the democratic regimes in the allied states, or both.

ἥξουσιν ἰδεῖν ἐπιθυμοῦντες τὸν ποιητὴν τὸν ἄριστον,
645 ὅστις παρεκινδύνευσ᾽ εἰπεῖν ἐν Ἀθηναίοις τὰ δίκαια.
οὕτω δ᾽ αὐτοῦ περὶ τῆς τόλμης ἤδη πόρρω κλέος ἥκει,
ὅτε καὶ βασιλεὺς Λακεδαιμονίων τὴν πρεσβείαν
   βασανίζων
ἠρώτησεν πρῶτα μὲν αὐτοὺς πότεροι ταῖς ναυσὶ
   κρατοῦσιν,
εἶτα δὲ τοῦτον τὸν ποιητὴν ποτέρους εἴποι κακὰ
   πολλά·
650 τούτους γὰρ ἔφη τοὺς ἀνθρώπους πολὺ βελτίους
   γεγενῆσθαι
καὶ τῷ πολέμῳ πολὺ νικήσειν τοῦτον ξύμβουλον
   ἔχοντας.
διὰ ταῦθ᾽ ὑμᾶς Λακεδαιμόνιοι τὴν εἰρήνην προ-
   καλοῦνται
καὶ τὴν Αἴγιναν ἀπαιτοῦσιν· καὶ τῆς νήσου μὲν
   ἐκείνης
οὐ φροντίζουσ᾽, ἀλλ᾽ ἵνα τοῦτον τὸν ποιητὴν
   ἀφέλωνται.
655 ἀλλ᾽ ὑμεῖς τοι μή ποτ᾽ ἀφῆσθ᾽· ὡς κωμῳδήσει τὰ
   δίκαια.
φησὶν δ᾽ ὑμᾶς πολλὰ διδάξειν ἀγάθ᾽, ὥστ᾽ εὐδαί-
   μονας εἶναι,
οὐ θωπεύων οὐδ᾽ ὑποτείνων μισθοὺς οὐδ᾽ ἐξαπα-
   τύλλων,
οὐδὲ πανουργῶν οὐδὲ κατάρδων, ἀλλὰ τὰ βέλτιστα
   διδάσκων.
πρὸς ταῦτα Κλέων καὶ παλαμάσθω

ACHARNIANS

eager to lay eyes on this outstanding poet who has ventured
to tell the Athenians what's right. So far has the renown of
his boldness already spread that even the King, in ques-
tioning the envoys from Sparta,[84] asked them first which
side was stronger in ships, and then which side this poet
profusely abused; because those folks, he said, have be-
come far better and far likelier to win the war, with him as
an adviser. And therefore the Spartans offer you peace and
ask for the return of Aegina;[85] not that they care about that
island, but so that they can take away this poet. But listen,
don't you ever let him go, for he'll keep on making comedy
of what's right. He promises to give you plenty of fine
direction, so that you'll enjoy good fortune, and not to
flatter or dangle bribes or bamboozle you, nor play the
villain or butter you up, but to give you only the best di-
rection.

That said, let Cleon hatch his plots and build his traps

[84] See Thucydides 4.50.
[85] By the terms of the treaty of 445 Aegina, hitherto an ally of
Athens, was guaranteed autonomy (Thucydides 1.67), which on
the eve of the war the Spartans accused the Athenians of violating
(ibid. 1.139). In 431 the Athenians settled the island with their
own shareholders, expelling the Aeginetans (ibid. 2.27), who were
finally restored by the Spartans in 405 (Xenophon, *HG* 2.2.9). This
passage suggests that Aristophanes had a residence on Aegina.

137

660   καὶ πᾶν ἐπ' ἐμοὶ τεκταινέσθω.
τὸ γὰρ εὖ μετ' ἐμοῦ καὶ τὸ δίκαιον
ξύμμαχον ἔσται, κοὐ μή ποθ' ἁλῶ
περὶ τὴν πόλιν ὢν ὥσπερ ἐκεῖνος
δειλὸς καὶ λακαταπύγων.

ΧΟΡΟΣ

(στρ) δεῦρο Μοῦσ' ἐλθὲ φλεγυ-
666   ρὰ πυρὸς ἔχουσα μένος
ἔντονος Ἀχαρνική.
οἷον ἐξ ἀνθράκων πρινίνων
φέψαλος ἀνήλατ' ἐρεθιζόμενος
οὐρίᾳ ῥιπίδι,
670   ἡνίκ' ἂν ἐπανθρακίδες
ὦσι παρακείμεναι,
οἱ δὲ Θασίαν ἀνακυ-
κῶσι λιπαράμπυκα,
οἱ δὲ μάττωσιν, οὕ-
τω σοβαρὸν ἐλθὲ μέλος
εὔτονον, ἀγροικότερον,
675   ὡς ἐμὲ λαβοῦσα τὸν δημότην.

ΚΟΡΥΦΑΙΟΣ

οἱ γέροντες οἱ παλαιοὶ μεμφόμεσθα τῇ πόλει·
οὐ γὰρ ἀξίως ἐκείνων ὧν ἐναυμαχήσαμεν
γηροβοσκούμεσθ' ὑφ' ὑμῶν, ἀλλὰ δεινὰ πάσχομεν,
οἵτινες γέροντας ἄνδρας ἐμβαλόντες εἰς γραφὰς
680   ὑπὸ νεανίσκων ἐᾶτε καταγελᾶσθαι ῥητόρων,
οὐδὲν ὄντας, ἀλλὰ κωφοὺς καὶ παρεξηυλημένους,

against me to his utmost, for Good and Right will be my
allies, and never will I be caught behaving toward the city
as he does, a coward and a punk-arse.

CHORUS

Come this way, refulgent Muse,
wearing the force of fire,
ardent, Acharnian!
Even as a spark that from oaken embers
leaps aloft, excited
by a fan's fair wind,
when the herring
are lying there ready,
and some are mixing
the Thasian sauce with its gleaming fillet,
and others are kneading the dough: so
come, bringing with you a tempestuous,
a well-tuned, a countrified song,
to me, your fellow demesman.

CHORUS LEADER

We old men, the elderly, have a complaint against the city.
The care we receive from you in our old age is unworthy
of the sea battles we've fought; in fact you treat us terribly.
You throw aged men into lawsuits and let them be the
sport of stripling speechmakers, old men who are finished,
soundless and played out, men whose Poseidon Unfalter-

οἷς Ποσειδῶν ἀσφάλειός ἐστιν ἡ βακτηρία·
τονθορύζοντες δὲ γήρᾳ τῷ λίθῳ προσέσταμεν,
οὐχ ὁρῶντες οὐδὲν εἰ μὴ τῆς δίκης τὴν ἠλύγην.
685 ὁ δὲ νεανίας, ἐπ᾽ αὐτῷ σπουδάσας ξυνηγορεῖν,
εἰς τάχος παίει ξυνάπτων στρογγύλοις τοῖς
    ῥήμασιν·
κᾆτ᾽ ἀνελκύσας ἐρωτᾷ σκανδάληθρ᾽ ἱστὰς ἐπῶν
ἄνδρα Τιθωνὸν σπαράττων καὶ ταράττων καὶ κυκῶν.
ὁ δ᾽ ὑπὸ γήρως μασταρύζει, κᾆτ᾽ ὀφλὼν ἀπέρχεται·
690 εἶτα λύζει καὶ δακρύει καὶ λέγει πρὸς τοὺς φίλους·
"οὗ μ᾽ ἐχρῆν σορὸν πρίασθαι τοῦτ᾽ ὀφλὼν
    ἀπέρχομαι."

ΧΟΡΟΣ

(ἀντ) ταῦτα πῶς εἰκότα, γέ-
    ροντ᾽ ἀπολέσαι πολιὸν
    ἄνδρα περὶ κλεψύδραν,
πολλὰ δὴ ξυμπονήσαντα καὶ
695   θερμὸν ἀπομορξάμενον ἀνδρικὸν ἱ-
    δρῶτα δὴ καὶ πολύν,
ἄνδρ᾽ ἀγαθὸν ὄντα Μαρα-
    θῶνι περὶ τὴν πόλιν;
εἶτα Μαραθῶνι μὲν ὅτ᾽
    ἦμεν, ἐδιώκομεν,
νῦν δ᾽ ὑπ᾽ ἀνδρῶν πονη-
700   ρῶν σφόδρα διωκόμεθα,
    κᾆτα πρὸς ἁλισκόμεθα.

ing is but their walking stick. We stand by the stone[86] mumbling in our dotage, seeing nothing of our case but a blur. And the young man, who's cut a deal to plead against the old man, quickly throws a hold on him and hits him with hard-ball phrases; then he drags him up for questioning, sets verbal pitfalls, harries and flusters and confounds a Tithonus of a man.[87] And in his decrepitude he gums his reply, and leaves the court convicted. Then he wails and weeps and says to his loved ones, "The money meant to buy my coffin I end up owing in fines!"

CHORUS

How can that be fair?
To ruin a man old and grey,
hard by the water clock,[88]
a man who's toiled at your side
and wiped off warm manly sweat,
and lots of it,
when he was a brave fighter
at Marathon, in the city's cause?
What's more, when we were at Marathon
we chased the enemy;
but now we're being chased hard
by bad people,
and getting bagged as well.

[86] I.e., the table on which the jurymen's votes were counted.

[87] Tithonus, mortal husband of the goddess Dawn, asked Zeus for immortality but forgot to include agelessness, so that he eventually withered away to a mere squeaking voice.

[88] The device used in lawcourts to time each litigant's speech.

ARISTOPHANES

πρὸς τάδε τίς ἀντερεῖ Μαρψίας;

ΚΟΡΥΦΑΙΟΣ

τῷ γὰρ εἰκὸς ἄνδρα κυφόν, ἡλίκον Θουκυδίδην,
ἐξολέσθαι συμπλακέντα τῇ Σκυθῶν ἐρημίᾳ,
705   τῷδε τῷ Κηφισοδήμου, τῷ λάλῳ ξυνηγόρῳ;
ὥστ᾽ ἐγὼ μὲν ἠλέησα κἀπεμορξάμην ἰδὼν
ἄνδρα πρεσβύτην ὑπ᾽ ἀνδρὸς τοξότου κυκώμενον
ὃς μὰ τὴν Δήμητρ᾽, ἐκεῖνος ἡνίκ᾽ ἦν Θουκυδίδης,
οὐδ᾽ ἂν αὐτὸν Ἀρταχαίην ῥᾳδίως ἠνέσχετο,
710   ἀλλὰ κατεπάλαισε μέν ‹γ᾽› ἂν πρῶτον Εὐάθλους
δέκα,
κατεβόησε δ᾽ ἂν κεκραγὼς τοξότας τρισχιλίους,
περιετόξευσεν δ᾽ ἂν αὐτοῦ τοῦ πατρὸς τοὺς ξυγ-
γενεῖς.
ἀλλ᾽ ἐπειδὴ τοὺς γέροντας οὐκ ἐᾷθ᾽ ὕπνου τυχεῖν,
ψηφίσασθε χωρὶς εἶναι τὰς γραφάς, ὅπως ἂν ᾖ
715   τῷ γέροντι μὲν γέρων καὶ νωδὸς ὁ ξυνήγορος,
τοῖς νέοισι δ᾽ εὐρύπρωκτος καὶ λάλος χὠ Κλεινίου.

705 -δήμου Hamaker: -δήμῳ z
709 αὐτὸν Ἀρταχαίην Borthwick: αὐτὴν τὴν Ἀχαίαν z

89 The name, meaning "grappler," appears also in Eupolis fr.
179 as a flatterer of Callias, but is unattested outside comedy; it
may be a nickname, or generic for litigators.
90 Thucydides, son of Milesias, now nearly eighty years old,
had been Pericles' principal rival until he was exiled for ten years
in 443. Upon his return he tried to make a comeback by prosecut-
ing Pericles' friend, the philosopher Anaxagoras. But his career
came to an end in the trial mentioned here, when he became

142

What Marpsias will try to disprove it?[89]

CHORUS LEADER

Yes, how can it be fair that a stooped man of Thucydides' age should be destroyed in the grip of that Scythian wilderness, this man here, Cephisodemus' son, the prattling advocate?[90] I for one felt pity and wiped away a tear at the sight of an old gentleman being confounded by a bowman. By Demeter, when Thucydides was himself, he wouldn't lightly have brooked Artachaees himself,[91] but would have first outwrestled ten Euathluses, outshouted with a roar three thousand bowmen, and shot circles round the kinsmen of the advocate's father. But since you won't allow the old men to get a moment's sleep, at least decree that their cases be separate; then an old man's prosecutor would be old and toothless, and the young men's would be the wide-arsed, prattling son of Cleinias.[92] From now on you

tongue-tied during his defence speech. Cephisodemus' son, Euathlus, is mentioned elsewhere in comedy as a zealous prosecutor; apparently there was an Asiatic on his mother's side of the family, non-Athenian women having been eligible for marriage until 451. Scythians were familiar barbarians at Athens, where because of their skill as archers many were owned by the city and used as policemen.

[91] A huge and stentorian Persian nobleman who had accompanied Xerxes on his invasion of Greece and was worshiped as a hero at Acanthus, where he died (Herodotus 7.117); it is hard to make sense of the MSS' "Achaea herself" (a cult name of Demeter: Herodotus 5.61.2).

[92] Alcibiades, nephew of Pericles, was in 425 only twenty-five years old; he would later become one of the leading generals and politicians of the Peloponnesian War period, and one of its most notorious personalities.

ARISTOPHANES

κἀξελαύνειν χρὴ τὸ λοιπόν—κἂν φύγῃ τις
    ζημιοῦν—
τὸν γέροντα τῷ γέροντι, τὸν νέον δὲ τῷ νέῳ.

ΔΙΚΑΙΟΠΟΛΙΣ

ὅροι μὲν ἀγορᾶς εἰσιν οἵδε τῆς ἐμῆς.
720 ἐνταῦθ᾽ ἀγοράζειν πᾶσι Πελοποννησίοις
ἔξεστι καὶ Μεγαρεῦσι καὶ Βοιωτίοις,
ἐφ᾽ ᾧτε πωλεῖν πρὸς ἐμέ, Λαμάχῳ δὲ μή.
ἀγορανόμους δὲ τῆς ἀγορᾶς καθίσταμαι
τρεῖς τοὺς λαχόντας τούσδ᾽ ἱμάντας ἐκ Λεπρῶν.
725 ἐνταῦθα μήτε συκοφάντης εἰσίτω
μήτ᾽ ἄλλος ὅστις Φασιανός ἐστ᾽ ἀνήρ.
ἐγὼ δὲ τὴν στήλην καθ᾽ ἣν ἐσπεισάμην
μέτειμ᾽, ἵνα στήσω φανερὰν ἐν τἀγορᾷ.

ΜΕΓΑΡΕΥΣ

ἀγορὰ 'ν Ἀθάναις, χαῖρε, Μεγαρεῦσιν φίλα.
730 ἐπόθουν τυ ναὶ τὸν Φίλιον ᾇπερ ματέρα.
ἀλλ᾽, ὦ πόνηρα κουρίχι᾽ ἀθλίου πατρός,
ἄμβατε ποττὰν μᾶδδαν, αἴ χ᾽ εὕρητέ πᾳ.
ἀκούετε δή, ποτέχετ᾽ ἐμὶν τὰν γαστέρα·
πότερα πεπρᾶσθαι χρῇδδετ᾽ ἢ πεινῆν κακῶς;

ΚΟΡΑ

735 πεπρᾶσθαι πεπρᾶσθαι.

731 κουρίχι᾽ Robertson: κόριχ᾽ R: κόρι᾽ c
733 ἀκούετε Vp3: ἀκούετον cett.

144

should banish elderly defendants by using elderly prosecutors, and youths by using youths.

DICAEOPOLIS comes out of his house with boundary markers, leather straps, and a table.

DICAEOPOLIS

These are the boundaries of my market. Here all Peloponnesians, Megarians and Boeotians are free to trade, provided they sell to me and not to Lamachus. As trade commissioners I hereby appoint these three duly allotted straps from Flogwell. Let no informer enter here nor any other canary man. I'll go fetch the pillar with my treaty inscribed, and set it up in the market for all to see. (*goes inside.*)

A MEGARIAN with two young GIRLS, his daughters, enters and stops before Dicaeopolis' house.

MEGARIAN[93]

Hail, Athenian market, dear to Megarians! By the God of Friendship, I've missed you as a son misses a mother! But you, you miserable father's rotten little kids, go up the steps there for bread, if you can find some anywhere. (*pointing to the steps leading to Dicaeopolis' door*) Now listen, give me your undivided bellies: do you want to be sold or miserably starve?

GIRLS

Sold! Sold!

---

[93] The Megarian speaks his local dialect.

ARISTOPHANES

ΜΕΓΑΡΕΤΣ

ἐγώνγα καὐτός φαμι. τίς δ᾽ οὕτως ἄνους
ὃς ὑμέ κα πρίαιτο, φανερὰν ζαμίαν;
ἀλλ᾽ ἔστι γάρ μοι Μεγαρικά τις μαχανά·
χοίρους γὰρ ὑμὲ σκευάσας φασῶ φέρειν.
740 περίθεσθε τάσδε τὰς ὁπλὰς τῶν χοιρίων·
ὅπως δὲ δοξεῖτ᾽ εἶμεν ἐξ ἀγαθᾶς ὑός·
ὡς ναὶ τὸν Ἑρμᾶν, αἴπερ εἰξεῖτ᾽ οἴκαδις
ἄπρατα, πειρασεῖσθε τᾶς λιμοῦ κακῶς.
ἀλλ᾽ ἀμφίθεσθε καὶ ταδὶ τὰ ῥυγχία,
745 κἤπειτεν εἰς τὸν σάκκον ὧδ᾽ εἰσβαίνετε.
ὅπως δὲ γρυλλιξεῖτε καὶ κοΐξετε
χἠσεῖτε φωνὰν χοιρίων μυστηρικῶν.
ἐγὼν δὲ καρυξῶ Δικαιόπολιν ὅπᾳ.
Δικαιόπολι, ἦ λῇς πρίασθαι χοιρία;

ΔΙΚΑΙΟΠΟΛΙΣ

τί; ἀνὴρ Μεγαρικός;

ΜΕΓΑΡΕΤΣ

750   ἀγορασοῦντες ἴκομες.

ΔΙΚΑΙΟΠΟΛΙΣ

πῶς ἔχετε;

ΜΕΓΑΡΕΤΣ

διαπεινᾶμες ἀεὶ ποττὸ πῦρ.

ΔΙΚΑΙΟΠΟΛΙΣ

ἀλλ᾽ ἡδύ τοι νὴ τὸν Δί᾽, ἢν αὐλὸς παρῇ.
τί δ᾽ ἄλλο πράττεθ᾽ οἱ Μεγαρῆς νῦν;

MEGARIAN

So say I myself. But who'd be brainless enough to buy you,
an obvious waste of money? No matter, I've got a real
Megarian trick: I'll dress you up and say I've got piggies.[94]
Put on these piggy-hoofs, and see that you look like a fine
sow's farrow. Because if you get home unsold, by Hermes
you'll find out what famine is! Put on these snouts too, and
then get into the sack here, and be sure you grunt and oink
and sound like pigs at the Mysteries.[95] And I'll call around
for Dicaeopolis. Dicaeopolis! Want to buy some piggies?

DICAEOPOLIS

(*coming out*) What's this? A Megarian?

MEGARIAN

We've come to trade.

DICAEOPOLIS

How are you all doing?

MEGARIAN

We're always in front of the fire, fasting.

DICAEOPOLIS

Feasting, yes, that's certainly nice, if there's music. Other-
wise, how are you Megarians doing these days?

[94] The following exchange plays on the double sense of Greek
choiros = "pig(let)" (a staple meat and sacrificial animal) and
"hairless vulva"; compare English "pussy."

[95] At Eleusis, where initiands sacrificed suckling pigs.

ΜΕΓΑΡΕΥΣ

οἷα δή.

ὅκα μὲν ἐγὼν τηνῶθεν ἐμπορευόμαν,
755   τὤνδρες πρόβουλοι τοῦτ᾽ ἔπρασσον τᾷ πόλι,
ὅπως τάχιστα καὶ κάκιστ᾽ ἀπολοίμεθα.

ΔΙΚΑΙΟΠΟΛΙΣ

αὐτίκ᾽ ἄρ᾽ ἀπαλλάξεσθε πραγμάτων.

ΜΕΓΑΡΕΥΣ

σά μάν;

ΔΙΚΑΙΟΠΟΛΙΣ

τί δ᾽ ἄλλο Μεγαροῖ; πῶς ὁ σῖτος ὤνιος;

ΜΕΓΑΡΕΥΣ

πὰρ ἁμὲ πολυτίματος ᾇπερ τοὶ θεοί.

ΔΙΚΑΙΟΠΟΛΙΣ

ἅλας οὖν φέρεις;

ΜΕΓΑΡΕΥΣ

760   οὐχ ὑμὲς αὐτῶν ἄρχετε;

ΔΙΚΑΙΟΠΟΛΙΣ

οὐδὲ σκόροδα;

ΜΕΓΑΡΕΥΣ

ποῖα σκόροδ᾽; ὑμὲς τῶν ἀεί,
ὅκκ᾽ εἰσβάλητε, τὼς ἀρωραῖοι μύες,
πάσσακι τὰς ἄγλιθας ἐξορύσσετε.

ΔΙΚΑΙΟΠΟΛΙΣ

τί δαὶ φέρεις;

148

MEGARIAN

Same as ever. As I was starting on this trip our councilmen were hard at work for the city, providing for our quickest and direst destruction.

DICAEOPOLIS

Then you'll soon be rid of your troubles.

MEGARIAN

That's right.

DICAEOPOLIS

What else at Megara? How's the price of grain?

MEGARIAN

Where we are it's mighty high, like the gods.

DICAEOPOLIS

What have you got there? Must be salt.

MEGARIAN

Don't you all control it?

DICAEOPOLIS

Garlic, then?

MEGARIAN

Garlic! Every time you invade, you dig up the bulbs with a hoe, like field mice.

DICAEOPOLIS

What *have* you got, then?

ΜΕΓΑΡΕΤΣ

χοίρους ἐγῶνγα μυστικάς.

ΔΙΚΑΙΟΠΟΛΙΣ

καλῶς λέγεις· ἐπίδειξον.

ΜΕΓΑΡΕΤΣ

765   ἀλλὰ μὰν καλαί.

ἄντεινον, αἰ λῇς· ὡς παχεῖα καὶ καλά.

ΔΙΚΑΙΟΠΟΛΙΣ

τουτὶ τί ἦν τὸ πρᾶγμα;

ΜΕΓΑΡΕΤΣ

χοῖρος ναὶ Δία.

ΔΙΚΑΙΟΠΟΛΙΣ

τί λέγεις σύ; ποδαπὴ χοῖρος ἥδε;

ΜΕΓΑΡΕΤΣ

                    Μεγαρικά.

ἢ οὐ χοῖρός ἐσθ᾽ ἅδ᾽;

ΔΙΚΑΙΟΠΟΛΙΣ

              οὐκ ἔμοιγε φαίνεται.

ΜΕΓΑΡΕΤΣ

770   οὐ δεινά; θᾶσθε, τῶδε τᾶς ἀπιστίας·

οὔ φατι τάνδε χοῖρον εἶμεν. ἀλλὰ μάν,

αἰ λῇς, περίδου μοι περὶ θυμιτιδᾶν ἁλῶν,

αἰ μή ᾽στιν οὗτος χοῖρος Ἑλλάνων νόμῳ.

ΔΙΚΑΙΟΠΟΛΙΣ

ἀλλ᾽ ἔστιν ἀνθρώπου γε.

ACHARNIANS

MEGARIAN

I've got piggies for the Mysteries.

DICAEOPOLIS

That's fine! Let's see them.

MEGARIAN

Aren't they fine, though? Have a feel, if you like. How plump and pretty she is!

DICAEOPOLIS

What's this supposed to be?

MEGARIAN

A piggy, by Zeus!

DICAEOPOLIS

What are you talking about? What sort of piggy is this?

MEGARIAN

Megarian. Isn't this a piggy?

DICAEOPOLIS

It doesn't look like one to me.

MEGARIAN

(*to the spectators*) Isn't this awful? Look! The skepticism of the man! He says this isn't a piggy. (*to Dicaeopolis*) I tell you what: if you like, bet me some thyme-seasoned salt that this isn't a piggy, in the Greek sense.

DICAEOPOLIS

All right, but it belongs to a human being.

ARISTOPHANES

ΜΕΓΑΡΕΥΣ
ναὶ τὸν Διοκλέα,
775 ἐμά γα. τὺ δέ νιν εἴμεναι τίνος δοκεῖς;
ἢ λῇς ἀκοῦσαι φθεγγομένας;

ΔΙΚΑΙΟΠΟΛΙΣ
νὴ τοὺς θεοὺς
ἔγωγε.

ΜΕΓΑΡΕΥΣ
φώνει δὴ τὺ ταχέως, χοιρίον.
οὐ χρῆσθα; σιγῇς, ὦ κάκιστ᾽ ἀπολουμένα;
πάλιν τυ ἀποισῶ ναὶ τὸν Ἑρμᾶν οἴκαδις.

ΚΟΡΗ
780 κοΐ κοΐ.

ΜΕΓΑΡΕΥΣ
αὕτα ᾽στὶ χοῖρος;

ΔΙΚΑΙΟΠΟΛΙΣ
νῦν γε χοῖρος φαίνεται.
ἀτὰρ ἐκτραφείς γε κύσθος ἔσται.

ΜΕΓΑΡΕΥΣ
πέντ᾽ ἐτῶν,
σάφ᾽ ἴσθι, ποττὰν ματέρ᾽ εἰκασθήσεται.

ΔΙΚΑΙΟΠΟΛΙΣ
ἀλλ᾽ οὐχὶ θύσιμός ἐστιν αὑτηγί.

ΜΕΓΑΡΕΥΣ
σά μάν;
πᾷ δ᾽ οὐκὶ θύσιμός ἐστι;

152

MEGARIAN

Yes, by Diocles:[96] it belongs to me! Whose do you think it is? Would you like to hear it squeal?

DICAEOPOLIS

I certainly would.

MEGARIAN

Sound off, then, little piggy. Right now. You won't? Damn you to perdition, you're keeping mum? By Hermes, I'll take you home again!

FIRST GIRL

Oink! Oink!

MEGARIAN

Is that a piggy?

DICAEOPOLIS

It looks like a piggy now, but all grown up it'll be a pussy!

MEGARIAN

Rest assured, in five years she'll be just like her mother.

DICAEOPOLIS

But this one isn't even suitable for sacrifice.

MEGARIAN

Indeed? In what way unsuitable for sacrifice?

[96] A Megarian hero who had an annual festival there.

ΔΙΚΑΙΟΠΟΛΙΣ

785 κέρκον οὐκ ἔχει.

ΜΕΓΑΡΕΥΣ

νεαρὰ γάρ ἐστιν· ἀλλὰ δελφακουμένα
ἑξεῖ μεγάλαν τε καὶ παχεῖαν κἠρυθράν.
ἀλλ᾿ αἰ τράφειν λῇς, ἅδε τοι χοῖρος καλά.

ΔΙΚΑΙΟΠΟΛΙΣ

ὡς ξυγγενὴς ὁ κύσθος αὐτῆς θἀτέρᾳ.

ΜΕΓΑΡΕΥΣ

790 ὁμοματρία γάρ ἐστι κἠκ τωὐτῶ πατρός.
αἰ δ᾿ ἀμπαχυνθῇ κἀναχνοιανθῇ τριχί,
κάλλιστος ἔσται χοῖρος Ἀφροδίτᾳ θύειν.

ΔΙΚΑΙΟΠΟΛΙΣ

ἀλλ᾿ οὐχὶ χοῖρος τἀφροδίτῃ θύεται.

ΜΕΓΑΡΕΥΣ

οὐ χοῖρος Ἀφροδίτᾳ; μόνᾳ γα δαιμόνων.
795 καὶ γίνεταί γα τᾶνδε τᾶν χοίρων τὸ κρῆς
ἅδιστον ἂν τὸν ὀδελὸν ἀμπεπαρμένον.

ΔΙΚΑΙΟΠΟΛΙΣ

ἤδη δ᾿ ἄνευ τῆς μητρὸς ἐσθίοιεν ἄν;

ΜΕΓΑΡΕΥΣ

ναὶ τὸν Ποτειδᾶ, καί κ᾿ ἄνις γα τοῦ πατρός.

ΔΙΚΑΙΟΠΟΛΙΣ

τί δ᾿ ἐσθίει μάλιστα;

DICAEOPOLIS

It's got no tail![97]

MEGARIAN

She's still young, but when she's grown to sowhood she'll get a big, fat pink one. (*taking the other girl from the sack*) But if you want to rear one, here's a fine piggy for you.

DICAEOPOLIS

Why, this one's pussy is the twin of the other one's!

MEGARIAN

Sure, she's got the same mother and father. If she fills out and gets downy with hair, she'll be a very fine piggy to sacrifice to Aphrodite.[98]

DICAEOPOLIS

But a pig isn't sacrificed to Aphrodite.

MEGARIAN

A piggy not sacrificed to Aphrodite? Why, to her alone of deities! What's more, the meat of these piggies is absolutely delicious when it's skewered on a spit.

DICAEOPOLIS

Are they ready to eat without their mother?

MEGARIAN

Yes, and without their father, too, by Poseidon.

DICAEOPOLIS

What's their favorite food?

[97] Also a slang term for penis.
[98] Goddess of sexual enjoyment.

ARISTOPHANES

ΜΕΓΑΡΕΥΣ
πάνθ᾽ ἅ κα διδῷς.

αὐτὸς δ᾽ ἐρώτη.

ΔΙΚΑΙΟΠΟΛΙΣ
χοῖρε, χοῖρε.

ΚΟΡΗ
800   κοῒ κοΐ.

ΔΙΚΑΙΟΠΟΛΙΣ
τρώγοιτ᾽ ἂν ἐρεβίνθους;

ΚΟΡΗ
κοῒ κοῒ κοΐ.

ΔΙΚΑΙΟΠΟΛΙΣ
τί δαί; Φιβάλεως ἰσχάδας;

ΚΟΡΑ
κοῒ κοΐ.

ΔΙΚΑΙΟΠΟΛΙΣ
τί δαὶ σύ; τρώγοις ἄν;

ΚΟΡΗ
κοῒ κοῒ κοΐ.

ΔΙΚΑΙΟΠΟΛΙΣ
ὡς ὀξὺ πρὸς τὰς ἰσχάδας κεκράγατον.
805 ἐνεγκάτω τις ἔνδοθεν τῶν ἰσχάδων
τοῖς χοιριδίοισιν. ἆρα τρώξονται; βαβαί,
οἷον ῥοθιάζουσ᾽, ὦ πολυτίμηθ᾽ Ἡράκλεις.
ποδαπὰ τὰ χοιρί᾽; ὡς Τραγασαῖα φαίνεται.

156

MEGARIAN

Anything you give them. Ask them yourself.

DICAEOPOLIS

Piggy, piggy!

FIRST GIRL

Oink! Oink!

DICAEOPOLIS

Will you eat chickpeas?[99]

FIRST GIRL

Oink. Oink.

DICAEOPOLIS

Then how about Phibalean figs?[100]

FIRST GIRL

Oink! Oink!

DICAEOPOLIS

How about you? Will you eat them?

SECOND GIRL

Oink! Oink! Oink!

DICAEOPOLIS

How keenly you both squeal at the word "figs"! Someone fetch some figs from inside for the little piggies. (*tossing figs to the girls*) Will they eat them? Good heavens, how they slurp them down. Holy Heracles! Where are these piggies from? Evidently from Hungary!

[99] The following items of food have phallic double meanings.
[100] The name derives from an otherwise unknown place name, Phibalis.

ΜΕΓΑΡΕΤΣ

ἀλλ᾽ οὔτι πάσας κατέτραγον τὰς ἰσχάδας.
810 ἐγὼν γὰρ αὐτᾶν τάνδε μίαν ἀνειλόμαν.

ΔΙΚΑΙΟΠΟΛΙΣ

νὴ τὸν Δί᾽, ἀστείω γε τὼ βοσκήματε.
πόσου πρίωμαί σοι τὰ χοιρίδια; λέγε.

ΜΕΓΑΡΕΤΣ

τὸ μὲν ἄτερον τοῦτο σκορόδων τροπαλίδος,
τὸ δ᾽ ἄτερον, αἱ λῇς, χοίνικος μόνας ἁλῶν.

ΔΙΚΑΙΟΠΟΛΙΣ

ὠνήσομαί σοι· περίμεν᾽ αὐτοῦ.

ΜΕΓΑΡΕΤΣ

815   ταῦτα δή.
Ἑρμᾶ ᾽μπολαῖε, τὰν γυναῖκα τὰν ἐμὰν
οὕτω μ᾽ ἀποδόσθαι τάν τ᾽ ἐμαυτῶ ματέρα.

ΣΤΚΟΦΑΝΤΗΣ

ὤνθρωπε, ποδαπός;

ΜΕΓΑΡΕΤΣ

                    χοιροπώλας Μεγαρικός.

ΣΤΚΟΦΑΝΤΗΣ

τὰ χοιρίδια τοίνυν ἐγὼ φανῶ ταδὶ
πολέμια καὶ σέ.

ΜΕΓΑΡΕΤΣ

820   τοῦτ᾽ ἐκεῖν᾽· ἴκει πάλιν
ὅθενπερ ἀρχὰ τῶν κακῶν ἁμῖν ἔφυ.

MEGARIAN

Well, they didn't bolt down all the figs; I managed to pick up this one for myself.

DICAEOPOLIS

By god, they're a delightful pair of creatures. How much will the piggies cost me? Name your price.

MEGARIAN

This one here for a bunch of garlic; the other one, if you like, for only a peck of salt.

DICAEOPOLIS

I'll take them. Wait here.

MEGARIAN

All right. (*Dicaeopolis goes inside*) Hermes of Traders, may I sell that wife of mine on such terms, and my own mother too!

Enter INFORMER.

INFORMER

Your nationality, sir?

MEGARIAN

Megarian, a piggy dealer.

INFORMER

In that case, I'll expose these piggies as contraband, and you as well!

MEGARIAN

Here we go again, back to where our troubles first began!

ARISTOPHANES

ΣΥΚΟΦΑΝΤΗΣ

κλάων μεγαριεῖς. οὐκ ἀφήσεις τὸν σάκον;

ΜΕΓΑΡΕΥΣ

Δικαιόπολι Δικαιόπολι, φαντάδδομαι.

ΔΙΚΑΙΟΠΟΛΙΣ

ὑπὸ τοῦ; τίς ὁ φαίνων σ' ἐστίν; ἀγορανόμοι,
825   τοὺς συκοφάντας οὐ θύραζ' ἐξείρξετε;
τί δαὶ μαθὼν φαίνεις ἄνευ θρυαλλίδος;

ΣΥΚΟΦΑΝΤΗΣ

οὐ γὰρ φανῶ τοὺς πολεμίους;

ΔΙΚΑΙΟΠΟΛΙΣ

            κλάων γε σύ,
εἰ μὴ 'τέρωσε συκοφαντήσεις τρέχων.

ΜΕΓΑΡΕΥΣ

οἷον τὸ κακὸν ἐν ταῖς Ἀθάναις τοῦτ' ἔνι.

ΔΙΚΑΙΟΠΟΛΙΣ

830   θάρρει, Μεγαρίκ'· ἀλλ' ἧς ἀπέδου τὰ χοιρία
τιμῆς, λαβὲ ταυτὶ τὰ σκόροδα καὶ τοὺς ἅλας,
καὶ χαῖρε πόλλ'.

ΜΕΓΑΡΕΥΣ

        ἀλλ' ἁμὶν οὐκ ἐπιχώριον.

ΔΙΚΑΙΟΠΟΛΙΣ

πολυπραγμοσύνη νυν ἐς κεφαλὴν τράποιτ' ἐμοί.

830 ἀπέδου τὰ χοιρία Elmsley: τὰ χοιρίδι' ἀπέδου z

160

INFORMER

You'll regret that Megarian talk. Surrender that sack!

MEGARIAN

Dicaeopolis! Dicaeopolis! I'm being exposed!

DICAEOPOLIS

(*running out*) By whom? Who's exposing you? (*flicking his straps*) Market Commissioners, aren't you going to keep these informers out? (*to the Informer*) Who taught you to expose without a wick?[101]

INFORMER

I'm not to expose our enemies, then?

DICAEOPOLIS

You'll regret it, if you don't run off and do your informing elsewhere.

INFORMER runs away.

MEGARIAN

What a curse this is in Athens!

DICAEOPOLIS

Never mind, Megarian. Take this garlic and salt, the price you asked for the little piggies, and best of luck to you.

MEGARIAN

Luck's not native to us.

DICAEOPOLIS

If I was being meddlesome, let it be on my head.[102]

---

[101] Perhaps referring to the Informer's lack of a comic phallus.

[102] Interference in other states' internal affairs was a common criticism of Athens.

ARISTOPHANES

ΜΕΓΑΡΕΥΣ

ὦ χοιρίδια, πειρῆσθε κἄνις τοῦ πατρὸς
835 παίειν ἐφ᾽ ἁλὶ τὰν μάδδαν, αἴ κά τις διδῷ.

ΧΟΡΟΣ

εὐδαιμονεῖ γ᾽ ἄνθρωπος. οὐκ
ἤκουσας οἷ προβαίνει
τὸ πρᾶγμα τοῦ βουλεύματος;
καρπώσεται γὰρ ἀνὴρ
ἐν τἀγορᾷ καθήμενος·
κἂν εἰσίῃ τις Κτησίας
840 ἢ συκοφάντης ἄλλος, οἰ-
μώζων καθεδεῖται.

οὐδ᾽ ἄλλος ἀνθρώπων ὑπο—
ψωνῶν σε πημανεῖ τι,
οὐδ᾽ ἐναπομόρξεται Πρέπις
τὴν εὐρυπρωκτίαν σοι,
οὐδ᾽ ὠστιεῖ Κλεωνύμῳ·
845 χλαῖναν δ᾽ ἔχων φανὴν δίει
κοὐ ξυντυχών σ᾽ Ὑπέρβολος
δικῶν ἀναπλήσει·

οὐδ᾽ ἐντυχὼν ἐν τἀγορᾷ

---

103 "Grasper," an actual name here chosen for its comic significance, like "Marpsias" at 702.

MEGARIAN

Little piggies, even without your father, try to get salt with
the loaf you gobble, if anyone gives you one.

Exit MEGARIAN; DICAEOPOLIS *takes the* GIRLS *into his
house.*

CHORUS

The man is truly blessed. Didn't
you hear how his enterprising plan
is progressing?
The man will reap a bumper crop
by sitting in his market.
And if some Ctesias[103] intrudes
or any other informer,
he'll groan when he sits down.

Nor will anyone else vex you
by cutting into the queue,
nor will Prepis[104] smear off
his wide-arsedness on you,
nor will you bump into Cleonymus;
you'll saunter through your market wearing a bright
    cloak,
and Hyperbolus[105] won't run into you
and infect you with his lawsuits.

Nor in your market will you meet

[104] Son of Eupherus; served as Council Secretary in 422/1.
[105] After Cleon's death in 422 Hyperbolus, owner of a lamp-
making business, would replace him as the leading popular poli-
tician.

ARISTOPHANES

πρόσεισί σοι βαδίζων
Κρατῖνος ἀποκεκαρμένος
μοιχὸν μιᾷ μαχαίρᾳ,
850   ὁ περιπόνηρος Ἀρτέμων,
ὁ ταχὺς ἄγαν τὴν μουσικήν,
ὄζων κακὸν τῶν μασχαλῶν
πατρὸς Τραγασαίου·

οὐδ᾽ αὖθις αὖ σε σκώψεται
Παύσων ὁ παμπόνηρος
Λυσίστρατός τ᾽ ἐν τἀγορᾷ,
855   Χολαργέων ὄνειδος,
ὁ περιαλουργὸς τοῖς κακοῖς,
ῥιγῶν τε καὶ πεινῶν ἀεὶ
πλεῖν ἢ τριάκονθ᾽ ἡμέρας
τοῦ μηνὸς ἑκάστου.

ΘΗΒΑΙΟΣ
860   ἴττω Ἡρακλῆς, ἔκαμόν γα τὰν τύλαν κακῶς.
κατάθου τὺ τὰν γλάχων᾽ ἀτρέμας, Ἰσμηνία·

---

[106] The leading comic poet of the generation before Aristophanes, now elderly but still active: he was competing in this very festival with his play *Stormtossed,* which won second prize behind *Acharnians.*   [107] Referring either to a style fashionable among young roués or to one of the degrading forms of depilation meted out to adulterers.

[108] Artemon was a contemporary of the sixth-century poet Anacreon, who satirized his morals and assigned him the epithet

Cratinus[106] strolling about
with an adulterer's cut[107]
done with a straight razor,
an Artemon "the miscarried,"[108]
too hasty with his poetry,
his armpits smelling nasty,
son of a father from the Goat d'Azur.

Nor again in your market
will the thoroughly depraved Pauson[109] ridicule you,
nor will Lysistratus,[110]
the disgrace of Cholargus,
soaked in the slough of despond,
ever freezing and starving
more than thirty days
in every month.

Enter a THEBAN *with his slave Ismenias, both carrying wares and accompanied by Pipers.*

THEBAN[111]

Heracles bear witness, my shoulder's damned weary. Put the pennyroyal down easy, Ismenias. And all you pipers

periphoretos "borne in a litter" (frr. 372, 388), which Aristophanes transforms into *periponeros* "very wicked."

[109] An impoverished painter known for caricatures, jokes and riddles.

[110] Of several known contemporaries by this name the likeliest candidate is the Lysistratus mentioned in *Knights* 1266 and *Wasps* 787-95, 1308-13 as a poor man (or affecting the plain Spartan style of dress) and a practical joker.

[111] Like the Megarian, the Theban speaks in his native dialect and comes from an enemy state.

165

ARISTOPHANES

ὑμὲς δ᾽, ὅσοι Θείβαθεν αὐλειταὶ πάρα,
τοῖς ὀστίνοις φυσεῖτε τὸν πρωκτὸν κυνός.

ΔΙΚΑΙΟΠΟΛΙΣ

παῦ᾽· ἐς κόρακας. οἱ σφῆκες, οὐκ ἀπὸ τῶν θυρῶν;
865 πόθεν προσέπτανθ᾽ οἱ κακῶς ἀπολούμενοι
ἐπὶ τὴν θύραν μοι Χαιριδῆς βομβαύλιοι;

ΘΗΒΑΙΟΣ

νεὶ τὸν Ἰόλαον ἐπεχαρίττω γ᾽, ὦ ξένε·
Θείβαθε γὰρ φυσᾶντες ἐξόπισθέ μου
τἄνθεια τᾶς γλάχωνος ἀπέκιξαν χαμαί.
870 ἀλλ᾽ εἴ τι βούλει, πρίασο τῶν ἐγὼ φέρω,
τῶν ὀρταλίχων ἢ τῶν τετραπτερυλλίδων.

ΔΙΚΑΙΟΠΟΛΙΣ

ὦ χαῖρε, κολλικοφάγε Βοιωτίδιον.
τί φέρεις;

ΘΗΒΑΙΟΣ

        ὅσ᾽ ἐστὶν ἀγαθὰ Βοιωτοῖς· ἁπλῶς
ὀρίγανον, γλαχώ, ψιάθως, θρυαλλίδας,
875 νάσσας, κολοιώς, ἀτταγᾶς, φαλαρίδας,
τροχίλως, κολύμβως.

ΔΙΚΑΙΟΠΟΛΙΣ

        ὡσπερεὶ χειμὼν ἄρα
ὀρνιθίας εἰς τὴν ἀγορὰν ἐλήλυθας.

ΘΗΒΑΙΟΣ

καὶ μὰν φέρω χᾶνας, λαγώς, ἀλώπεκας,
σκάλοπας, ἐχίνως, αἰελώρως, πικτίδας,

166

ACHARNIANS

who are here with me from Thebes, puff on those bones
to the tune of "The Dog's Arsehole."

DICAEOPOLIS

(*coming out of his house*) Stop, damn you! Away from my
doorway, you hornets! Where did these dadblasted buzz-
pipers fly to my door from, these sons of Chaeris?

THEBAN

By Iolaus,[112] you've done me a favor there, friend. All the
way from Thebes they've been puffing behind me and
blowing my pennyroyal blossoms to the ground. But if you
like, buy some of the goods I've got, some fowl or some
four-wingers.

DICAEOPOLIS

Welcome, my baguette-eating Boeotian! What have you
got?

THEBAN

Just everything good that the Boeotians have: marjoram,
pennyroyal, rush mats, lamp wicks, ducks, jackdaws, fran-
colins, coots, wrens, grebes.

DICAEOPOLIS

Then you've hit my market like a fowl nor'easter!

THEBAN

I've also got geese, hares, foxes, moles, hedgehogs, cats,

112 Heracles' nephew and fellow hero.

880 ἰκτίδας, ἐνύδριας, ἐγχέλιας Κωπαΐδας.

ΔΙΚΑΙΟΠΟΛΙΣ

ὦ τερπνότατον σὺ τέμαχος ἀνθρώποις φέρων,
δός μοι προσειπεῖν, εἰ φέρεις, τὰς ἐγχέλεις.

ΘΗΒΑΙΟΣ

πρέσβειρα πεντήκοντα Κωπάδων κορᾶν,
ἔκβαθι τῶδε κἠπιχάριτται τῷ ξένῳ.

ΔΙΚΑΙΟΠΟΛΙΣ

885 ὦ φιλτάτη σὺ καὶ πάλαι ποθουμένη,
ἦλθες ποθεινὴ μὲν τρυγῳδικοῖς χοροῖς,
φίλη δὲ Μορύχῳ. δμῶες, ἐξενέγκατε
τὴν ἐσχάραν μοι δεῦρο καὶ τὴν ῥιπίδα.
σκέψασθε, παῖδες, τὴν ἀρίστην ἔγχελυν,
890 ἥκουσαν ἕκτῳ μόλις ἔτει ποθουμένην.
προσείπατ᾽ αὐτήν, ὦ τέκν᾽· ἄνθρακας δ᾽ ἐγὼ
ὑμῖν παρέξω τῆσδε τῆς ξένης χάριν.
ἀλλ᾽ ἔκφερ᾽ αὐτήν· μηδὲ γὰρ θανών ποτε
σοῦ χωρὶς εἴην ἐντετευτλιωμένης.

ΘΗΒΑΙΟΣ

895 ἐμοὶ δὲ τιμὰ τᾶσδε πᾶ γενήσεται;

ΔΙΚΑΙΟΠΟΛΙΣ

ἀγορᾶς τέλος ταύτην γέ που δώσεις ἐμοί.
ἀλλ᾽ εἴ τι πωλεῖς τῶνδε τῶν ἄλλων, λέγε.

badgers, martens, otters, Copaic eels.[113]

DICAEOPOLIS

O you who bring mankind's most delectable cutlet, permit me to greet the eels, if you've got them!

THEBAN

(*producing an eel*) Most venerable mistress of fifty Copaic maidens,[114] step forth here and grant your favors to our host!

DICAEOPOLIS

O dearest and long desired, you have come, the heart's desire of comic choruses and dear to Morychus![115] Servants, fetch me forth the brazier and the fan. (*these are brought out, followed by Dicaeopolis' children*) Children, look at the excellent eel we've been pining for, just arrived after six years. Say hello to her, kids, and in honor of this lady guest I'll provide you with coals. Now place her on her bier, "for even in death may I never be parted from you," enshrouded in beet![116]

THEBAN

And how am I going to be paid for her?

DICAEOPOLIS

I guess you'll give her to me as market tax. But if you're selling any of these other things, speak up.

---

[113] From Lake Copais in northeast Boeotia, and a delicacy.

[114] Adapted from an address to Thetis in Aeschylus' *Award of the Arms* (fr. 174).

[115] A wealthy gourmand.

[116] "for even ..." is quoted from Euripides, *Alcestis* 367-8 (Admetus to his dying wife), with "enshrouded in beet" substituted for "the woman who alone has been faithful to me."

ΘΗΒΑΙΟΣ
ἰώγα ταῦτα πάντα.

ΔΙΚΑΙΟΠΟΛΙΣ
φέρε, πόσου λέγεις;
ἢ φορτί᾽ ἕτερ᾽ ἐνθένδ᾽ ἐκεῖσ᾽ ἄξεις;

ΘΗΒΑΙΟΣ
ἰών;
900 ὅ τι γ᾽ ἔστ᾽ ἐν Ἀθάναις, ἐν Βοιωτοῖσιν δὲ μή.

ΔΙΚΑΙΟΠΟΛΙΣ
ἀφύας ἄρ᾽ ἄξεις πριάμενος Φαληρικὰς
ἢ κέραμον.

ΘΗΒΑΙΟΣ
ἀφύας ἢ κέραμον; ἀλλ᾽ ἔντ᾽ ἐκεῖ·
ἀλλ᾽ ὅ τι πὰρ ἁμὶν μή ᾽στι, τάδε δ᾽ αὖ πολύ.

ΔΙΚΑΙΟΠΟΛΙΣ
ἐγᾦδα τοίνυν· συκοφάντην ἔξαγε,
ὥσπερ κέραμον ἐνδησάμενος.

ΘΗΒΑΙΟΣ
905   νεὶ τὼ θεώ,
λάβοιμι μέντἂν κέρδος ἀγαγὼν καὶ πολύ,
ἅπερ πίθακον ἀλιτρίας πολλᾶς πλέων.

ΔΙΚΑΙΟΠΟΛΙΣ
καὶ μὴν ὁδὶ Νίκαρχος ἔρχεται φανῶν.

ΘΗΒΑΙΟΣ
μικκός γα μᾶκος οὗτος.

170

THEBAN

I'm selling everything here.

DICAEOPOLIS

All right, name your price. Or will you take an equivalent
load from here back home with you?

THEBAN

I will! Something that's found in Athens but not among the
Boeotians.

DICAEOPOLIS

You'll probably want to buy some sprats from Phalerum to
take with you, or pottery.

THEBAN

Sprats or pottery? We have them back home. No, some-
thing that's absent among us, but plentiful here.

DICAEOPOLIS

I've got it! An informer: pack him up like crockery and
export him.

THEBAN

Twin Gods, I'd surely make a sizeable profit by importing
one—one filled with lots of deviltry, like a monkey.

DICAEOPOLIS

Hey, look here: Nicarchus[117] is coming to expose us.

Enter NICARCHUS.

THEBAN

He's not very big.

---

[117] Otherwise unknown.

ARISTOPHANES

ΔΙΚΑΙΟΠΟΛΙΣ
    ἀλλὰ πᾶν κακόν.

ΝΙΚΑΡΧΟΣ
ταυτὶ τίνος τὰ φορτί᾽ ἐστί;

ΘΗΒΑΙΟΣ
910   τῶδ᾽ ἐμὰ
Θείβαθε, ἴττω Δεύς.

ΝΙΚΑΡΧΟΣ
        ἐγὼ τοίνυν ὁδὶ
φαίνω πολέμια ταῦτα.

ΘΗΒΑΙΟΣ
        τί δὲ κακὸν παθὼν
ὀρναπετίοισι πόλεμον ἦρα καὶ μάχαν;

ΝΙΚΑΡΧΟΣ
καὶ σέ γε φανῶ πρὸς τοῖσδε.

ΘΗΒΑΙΟΣ
            τί ἀδικείμενος;

ΝΙΚΑΡΧΟΣ
915 ἐγὼ φράσω σοι τῶν περιεστώτων χάριν.
ἐκ τῶν πολεμίων εἰσάγεις θρυαλλίδας.

ΔΙΚΑΙΟΠΟΛΙΣ
ἔπειτα φαίνεις δῆτα διὰ θρυαλλίδα;

ΝΙΚΑΡΧΟΣ
αὕτη γὰρ ἐμπρήσειεν ἂν τὸ νεώριον.

172

DICAEOPOLIS

But every inch of him's bad!

NICARCHUS

These wares, whose are they?

THEBAN

They're mine, from Thebes, as Zeus is my witness.

NICARCHUS

In that case, I hereby expose them as contraband.

THEBAN

What's the matter with you, declaring war and battle on my birdies?

NICARCHUS

And in addition to these, I shall expose you.

THEBAN

What have I done to you?

NICARCHUS

I'll explain it to you for the bystanders' benefit. You're importing lamp wicks from hostile territory.

DICAEOPOLIS

So you're actually exposing him because of a lamp wick?

NICARCHUS

This could burn up the shipyard!

ARISTOPHANES

ΔΙΚΑΙΟΠΟΛΙΣ
νεώριον θρυαλλίς;

ΝΙΚΑΡΧΟΣ
οἶμαι.

ΔΙΚΑΙΟΠΟΛΙΣ
τίνι τρόπῳ;

ΝΙΚΑΡΧΟΣ
920 ἐνθεὶς ἂν εἰς τίφην ἀνὴρ Βοιώτιος
ἅψας ἂν εἰσπέμψειεν εἰς τὸ νεώριον
δι' ὑδρορρόας, βορέαν ἐπιτηρήσας μέγαν.
κεἴπερ λάβοιτο τῶν νεῶν τὸ πῦρ ἅπαξ,
σελαγοῖντ' ἂν εὐθύς.

ΔΙΚΑΙΟΠΟΛΙΣ
ὦ κάκιστ' ἀπολούμενε,
925 σελαγοῖντ' ἂν ὑπὸ τίφης τε καὶ θρυαλλίδος;

ΝΙΚΑΡΧΟΣ
μαρτύρομαι.

ΔΙΚΑΙΟΠΟΛΙΣ
ξυλλάμβαν' αὐτοῦ τὸ στόμα.
δός μοι φορυτόν, ἵν' αὐτὸν ἐνδήσας φέρω
ὥσπερ κέραμον, ἵνα μὴ καταγῇ φερόμενος.

ΚΟΡΥΦΑΙΟΣ
(στρ) ἔνδησον, ὦ βέλτιστε, τῷ
930 ξένῳ καλῶς τὴν ἐμπολὴν
οὕτως ὅπως
ἂν μὴ φέρων κατάξῃ.

174

DICAEOPOLIS

A wick burn up a shipyard?

NICARCHUS

I reckon.

DICAEOPOLIS

In what way?

NICARCHUS

A man from Boeotia could put it on a beetle's back, light it, and send it into the shipyard through a water main, waiting for a stiff north wind. And if the fire once caught the ships, they'd be ablaze in no time.[118]

DICAEOPOLIS

(*hitting him with the straps*) Damn and blast you, they'd be ablaze from a beetle and a wick?

NICARCHUS

I call witnesses!

DICAEOPOLIS

Arrest his mouth. Give me some sawdust so I can pack him like pottery before I hand him over, so he won't get broken in transit.

CHORUS LEADER

Dear fellow, pack the merchandise
nicely for our foreign friend,
so that he can carry it
without breaking it.

[118] For a Boeotian incendiary device actually deployed in the following year see Thucydides 4.100.

ΔΙΚΑΙΟΠΟΛΙΣ

ἐμοὶ μελήσει ταῦτ᾽, ἐπεί
τοι καὶ ψοφεῖ λάλον τι καὶ
πυρορραγὲς
κἄλλως θεοῖσιν ἐχθρόν.

ΚΟΡΥΦΑΙΟΣ

935 τί χρήσεταί ποτ᾽ αὐτῷ;

ΔΙΚΑΙΟΠΟΛΙΣ

πάγχρηστον ἄγγος ἔσται,
κρατὴρ κακῶν, τριπτὴρ δικῶν,
φαίνειν ὑπευθύνους λυχνοῦ–
χος καὶ κύλιξ
τὰ πράγματ᾽ ἐγκυκᾶσθαι.

ΚΟΡΥΦΑΙΟΣ

(ἀντ) πῶς δ᾽ ἂν πεποιθοίη τις ἀγ–
941 γείῳ τοιούτῳ χρώμενος
κατ᾽ οἰκίαν
τοσόνδ᾽ ἀεὶ ψοφοῦντι;

ΔΙΚΑΙΟΠΟΛΙΣ

ἰσχυρόν ἐστιν, ὦγάθ᾽, ὥστ᾽
οὐκ ἂν καταγείη ποτ᾽, εἴ–
περ ἐκ ποδῶν
945 κατωκάρα κρέμαιτο.

ΚΟΡΥΦΑΙΟΣ

ἤδη καλῶς ἔχει σοι.

DICAEOPOLIS

I'll take care of that, because
—listen—it makes a chattering
and fire-cracked noise,
altogether godforsaken.

CHORUS LEADER

Whatever will he use it for?

DICAEOPOLIS

It will be a pot for every purpose:
a bowl for mixing evils, a mortar for pounding
    lawsuits,
a lampstand to expose outgoing officials,
and a cup
for blending trouble.

CHORUS LEADER

But how could anyone feel safe
using a pot like this
in the house,
when it's always making so much noise?

DICAEOPOLIS

It's sturdy, sir, so
it will never get broken,
even if it's hung head-downwards
by its feet.

CHORUS LEADER

(*to the Theban*)
You're all set now!

ΘΗΒΑΙΟΣ

μέλλω γά τοι θερίδδειν.

ΚΟΡΥΦΑΙΟΣ

ἀλλ᾽, ὦ ξένων βέλτιστε, συν–
θέριζε καὶ πρόσβαλλ᾽ ὅποι
950 βούλει φέρων
πρὸς πάντα συκοφάντην.

ΔΙΚΑΙΟΠΟΛΙΣ

μόλις γ᾽ ἐνέδησα τὸν κακῶς ἀπολούμενον.
αἶρου λαβὼν τὸν κέραμον; ὦ Βοιώτιε.

ΘΗΒΑΙΟΣ

ὑπόκυπτε τὰν τύλαν ἰών, Ἰσμείνιχε.

ΔΙΚΑΙΟΠΟΛΙΣ

955 χὤπως κατοίσεις αὐτὸν εὐλαβουμένως.
πάντως μὲν οἴσεις οὐδὲν ὑγιές, ἀλλ᾽ ὅμως·
κἂν τοῦτο κερδάνῃς ἄγων τὸ φορτίον,
εὐδαιμονήσεις συκοφαντῶν γ᾽ οὕνεκα.

ΟΙΚΕΤΗΣ

Δικαιόπολι.

ΔΙΚΑΙΟΠΟΛΙΣ

τί ἐστι; τί με βωστρεῖς;

ΟΙΚΕΤΗΣ

ὅ τι;

960 ἐκέλευε Λάμαχός σε ταυτησὶ δραχμῆς

THEBAN

I'll surely rake in a profit!

CHORUS LEADER

Rake away, most excellent guest;
toss him onto your load
and take him wherever you want,
an informer for every occasion.

DICAEOPOLIS

I had my hands full packing up the blasted wretch. Now take your pottery and load it up, Boeotian.

THEBAN

Come here and get your shoulder under it, Ismenichus.

DICAEOPOLIS

Make sure you carry him back carefully. You certainly won't be carrying anything wholesome, but no matter. And if you make a profit importing this shipment, you'll make a fortune in the informer trade!

THEBANS depart; enter SLAVE.

SLAVE

Dicaeopolis!

DICAEOPOLIS

Who's that? Why are you yelling for me?

SLAVE

Why? Lamachus orders you, for this drachma here, to give

ARISTOPHANES

εἰς τοὺς Χοᾶς αὑτῷ μεταδοῦναι τῶν κιχλῶν,
τριῶν δραχμῶν δ' ἐκέλευε Κωπᾷδ' ἔγχελυν.

ΔΙΚΑΙΟΠΟΛΙΣ

ὁ ποῖος οὗτος Λάμαχος τὴν ἔγχελυν;

ΟΙΚΕΤΗΣ

ὁ δεινός, ὁ ταλαύρινος, ὃς τὴν Γοργόνα
965 πάλλει κραδαίνων τρεῖς κατασκίους λόφους.

ΔΙΚΑΙΟΠΟΛΙΣ

οὐκ ἂν μὰ Δί', εἰ δοίη γέ μοι τὴν ἀσπίδα·
ἀλλ' ἐπὶ ταρίχει τοὺς λόφους κραδαινέτω·
ἢν δ' ἀπολιγαίνῃ, τοὺς ἀγορανόμους καλῶ.
ἐγὼ δ' ἐμαυτῷ τόδε λαβὼν τὸ φορτίον
970 εἴσειμ' ὑπαὶ πτερύγων κιχλᾶν καὶ κοψίχων.

ΧΟΡΟΣ

(στρ) εἶδες, ὦ πᾶσα πόλι, τὸν φρόνιμον
    ἄνδρα, τὸν ὑπέρσοφον,
οἷ' ἔχει σπεισάμενος ἐμπορικὰ
    χρήματα διεμπολᾶν,
ὧν τὰ μὲν ἐν οἰκίᾳ

---

119 The Pitcher Feast (*Choes*) was celebrated on the second day (of three) of the Anthesteria, a great mid-winter festival honoring Dionysus. The pitcher in question (the *chous*) held about three quarts. Among the many festivities were drinking contests and a state banquet to which guests were invited by the priest of Dionysus. Also relevant to our play, with its quasi-hymeneal ending, was the sacred marriage between the wife of the King Archon (the official in charge of the state religion) and Dionysus.

180

him some of your thrushes for the Pitcher Feast,[119] and he orders a Copaic eel for three drachmas.

DICAEOPOLIS
Which Lamachus is it who orders the eel?

SLAVE
Lamachus the awesome, the tough as leather, who brandishes the Gorgon as he shakes "three overshadowing crests"![120]

DICAEOPOLIS
No deal, by Zeus, not even if he gave me his shield. Let him shake his crests for salt fish.[121] And if he squawks about it, I'll summon the commissioners.

SLAVE runs away.

I'll take this load for myself and go inside, lofted on wings of thrushes and blackbirds.

DICAEOPOLIS goes inside.

CHORUS
Have you seen him, all you people, the smart
and exceedingly sagacious man,
seen what fine merchandise, thanks to his truce,
he's got for sale?
Some of his things are useful

---

[120] The phrase is taken from Aeschylus, *Seven Against Thebes* 384, where it refers to Tydeus, after whom Lamachus apparently named his own son.

[121] Among the cheapest and least respectable foods.

975   χρήσιμα, τὰ δ᾽ αὖ πρέπει
χλιαρὰ κατεσθίειν.

ΚΟΡΥΦΑΙΟΣ

αὐτόματα πάντ᾽ ἀγαθὰ τῷδέ γε πορίζεται.
οὐδέποτ᾽ ἐγὼ Πόλεμον οἴκαδ᾽ ὑποδέξομαι,
980   οὐδὲ παρ᾽ ἐμοί ποτε τὸν Ἁρμόδιον ᾄσεται
ξυγκατακλινείς, ὅτι παροινικὸς ἀνὴρ ἔφυ,
ὅστις ἐπὶ πάντ᾽ ἀγάθ᾽ ἔχοντας ἐπικωμάσας
ἠργάσατο πάντα κακά, κἀνέτρεπε κἀξέχει
κἀμάχετο καὶ προσέτι πολλὰ προκαλουμένου·
985   "πῖνε, κατάκεισο, λαβὲ τήνδε φιλοτησίαν,"
τὰς χάρακας ἧπτε πολὺ μᾶλλον ἔτι τῷ πυρί,
ἐξέχει θ᾽ ἡμῶν βίᾳ τὸν οἶνον ἐκ τῶν ἀμπέλων.

ΧΟΡΟΣ

(ἀντ) ἐπτέρωταί τ᾽ ἐπὶ τὸ δεῖπνον ἅμα
καὶ μεγάλα δὴ φρονεῖ,
τοῦ βίου δ᾽ ἐξέβαλε δεῖγμα τάδε
τὰ πτερὰ πρὸ τῶν θυρῶν.
ὦ Κύπριδι τῇ καλῇ
καὶ Χάρισι ταῖς φίλαις
ξύντροφε Διαλλαγή,

ΚΟΡΥΦΑΙΟΣ

990   ὡς καλὸν ἔχουσα τὸ πρόσωπον ἄρ᾽ ἐλάνθανες.
πῶς ἂν ἐμὲ καὶ σέ τις Ἔρως ξυναγάγοι λαβών

---

122 A traditional patriotic drinking song celebrating Harmodius and his friend Aristogeiton, who in 514 assassinated Hip-

around the house, while others
should be eaten hot.

CHORUS LEADER

To this man all bounties are supplied spontaneously. I will
never welcome the War God into my house, nor will he
ever recline at my side and sing the Harmodius Song,[122]
for he is an unruly fellow when he drinks. When we en-
joyed every bounty, he crashed our party and inflicted all
kinds of damage, upending, spilling, and fighting; and the
more I kept inviting him "to drink, recline, take this cup of
fellowship," the more he kept setting our vine props afire
and violently spilling the wine from our vines.

CHORUS

He's in flight to his dinner
and grand indeed are his thoughts;
as a token of his life style
he's tossed out these feathers before his door.
O Reconciliation, companion
of Cypris[123] the fair
and the beloved Graces,

CHORUS LEADER[124]

I didn't realize what a lovely face you have. How I wish that
some Eros, like the one in the painting who wears a garland

parchus, the brother of the last Athenian tyrant, Hippias; four
versions are preserved (*PMG* 893-96).

[123] Aphrodite.

[124] In this passage the Chorus Leader reacts as if Reconcili-
ation, answering the Chorus' invocation, has physically appeared
in the guise of a blooming girl; she is actually so staged in *Lysis-
trata*.

ὥσπερ ὁ γεγραμμένος ἔχων στέφανον ἀνθέμων;
ἢ πάνυ γερόντιον ἴσως νενόμικάς με σύ;
ἀλλά σε λαβὼν τρία δοκῶ γ᾽ ἂν ἔτι προσβαλεῖν·
995   πρῶτα μὲν ἂν ἀμπελίδος ὄρχον ἐλάσαι μακρόν,
εἶτα παρὰ τόνδε νέα μοσχίδια συκίδων,
καὶ τὸ τρίτον ἡμερίδος ὠσχόν, ὁ γέρων ὁδί,
καὶ περὶ τὸ χωρίον ἐλᾴδας ἅπαν ἐν κύκλῳ,
ὥστ᾽ ἀλείφεσθαι σ᾽ ἀπ᾽ αὐτῶν κἀμὲ ταῖς νουμηνίαις.

ΚΗΡΥΞ

1000   ἀκούετε λεῴ· κατὰ τὰ πάτρια τοὺς Χοᾶς
πίνειν ὑπὸ τῆς σάλπιγγος· ὃς δ᾽ ἂν ἐκπίῃ
πρώτιστος, ἀσκὸν Κτησιφῶντος λήψεται.

ΔΙΚΑΙΟΠΟΛΙΣ

ὦ παῖδες, ὦ γυναῖκες, οὐκ ἠκούσατε;
τί δρᾶτε; τοῦ κήρυκος οὐκ ἀκούετε;
1005   ἀναβράττετ᾽, ἐξοπτᾶτε, τρέπετ᾽, ἀφέλκετε
τὰ λαγῷα ταχέως, τοὺς στεφάνους ἀνείρετε.
φέρε τοὺς ὀβελίσκους, ἵν᾽ ἀναπείρω τὰς κίχλας.

ΧΟΡΟΣ

(στρ)   ζηλῶ σε τῆς εὐβουλίας,
μᾶλλον δὲ τῆς εὐωχίας,
1010   ἄνθρωπε, τῆς παρούσης.

997 ὠσχόν Brunck: ὄρχον t: κλάδον cett.

---

125 A painting by Zeuxis "in the temple of Aphrodite at Athens," according to the scholia.

126 The first day of the month was an occasion for religious and

of rosettes,[125] could bring you and me together! Or perhaps
you think I'm an absolute geezer? Ah but if I got hold of
you, I think I could still strike home three times. First, I'd
shove in a long rank of tender vines, and beside that some
fresh fig shoots, and thirdly a well hung vine branch—this
oldster would!—and, around the whole plot, a stand of
olive trees, so that you and I could anoint ourselves for the
New Moon feasts.[126]

Enter HERALD.

HERALD

Hear this, people! According to ancestral custom, drink
your pitchers when the trumpet sounds; and whoever is the
very first to drink up will win a Ctesiphon-size wineskin![127]

*The eccyclema is rolled out, revealing Dicaeopolis' Slaves
and Womenfolk as they prepare the feast.* DICAEOPOLIS
runs from the house.

DICAEOPOLIS

You slaves, you women, didn't you hear? What are you
doing? Don't you hear the herald? Braise the hare fillets,
roast them, turn them, pull them off the skewers quickly,
string the garlands. Hand me the skewers, so I can spit the
thrushes!

CHORUS

I envy you your well laid plan,
and more so your well laid table,
sir, here before us.

social festivities; cf. also *Wasps* 96.   [127] Evidently this man
(otherwise unknown) had a belly of impressive size.

ΔΙΚΑΙΟΠΟΛΙΣ

τί δῆτ᾽, ἐπειδὰν τὰς κίχλας
ὀπτωμένας ἴδητε;

ΧΟΡΟΣ

οἶμαί σε καὶ τοῦτ᾽ εὖ λέγειν.

ΔΙΚΑΙΟΠΟΛΙΣ

τὸ πῦρ ὑποσκάλευε.

ΧΟΡΟΣ

1015 ἤκουσας ὡς μαγειρικῶς
κομψῶς τε καὶ δειπνητικῶς
αὑτῷ διακονεῖται;

ΔΕΡΚΕΤΗΣ

οἴμοι τάλας.

ΔΙΚΑΙΟΠΟΛΙΣ

ὦ Ἡράκλεις, τίς οὑτοσί;

ΔΕΡΚΕΤΗΣ

ἀνὴρ κακοδαίμων.

ΔΙΚΑΙΟΠΟΛΙΣ

κατὰ σεαυτόν νυν τρέπου.

ΔΕΡΚΕΤΗΣ

1020 ὦ φίλτατε, σπονδαὶ γάρ εἰσι σοὶ μόνῳ,
μέτρησον εἰρήνης τί μοι, κἂν πέντ᾽ ἔτη.

ΔΙΚΑΙΟΠΟΛΙΣ

τί δ᾽ ἔπαθες;

DICAEOPOLIS
What will you say when you see
the thrushes being roasted!

CHORUS
You're right about that too, I think.

DICAEOPOLIS
Start poking up the fire!

CHORUS
Did you hear how master-chef-ily,
how subtly and how gourmettily
he caters for himself?

Enter DERCETES.

DERCETES
O woe is me!

DICAEOPOLIS
Heracles! Who's this?

DERCETES
A man ill-fated!

DICAEOPOLIS
Then keep it to yourself.

DERCETES
Dear friend, since you've got a truce all to yourself, measure out some peace for me, even if it's only five years' worth.

DICAEOPOLIS
What's the matter?

ARISTOPHANES

ΔΕΡΚΕΤΗΣ

ἐπετρίβην ἀπολέσας τὼ βόε.

ΔΙΚΑΙΟΠΟΛΙΣ

πόθεν;

ΔΕΡΚΕΤΗΣ

ἀπὸ Φυλῆς ἔλαβον οἱ Βοιώτιοι.

ΔΙΚΑΙΟΠΟΛΙΣ

ὦ τρισκακόδαιμον, εἶτα λευκὸν ἀμπέχει;

ΔΕΡΚΕΤΗΣ

1025 καὶ ταῦτα μέντοι νὴ Δί᾽ ὥπερ μ᾽ ἐτρεφέτην
ἐν πᾶσι βολίτοις.

ΔΙΚΑΙΟΠΟΛΙΣ

εἶτα νυνὶ τοῦ δέει;

ΔΕΡΚΕΤΗΣ

ἀπόλωλα τὠφθαλμὼ δακρύων τὼ βόε.
ἀλλ᾽ εἴ τι κήδει Δερκέτου Φυλασίου,
ὑπάλειψον εἰρήνῃ με τὠφθαλμὼ ταχύ.

ΔΙΚΑΙΟΠΟΛΙΣ

1030 ἀλλ᾽, ὦ πόνηρ᾽, οὐ δημοσιεύων τυγχάνω.

ΔΕΡΚΕΤΗΣ

ἴθ᾽ ἀντιβολῶ σ᾽, ἤν πως κομίσωμαι τὼ βόε.

DERCETES

I'm shattered; I've lost my pair of oxen!

DICAEOPOLIS

Where?

DERCETES

At Phyle; the Boeotians rustled them.

DICAEOPOLIS

Thrice ill-fated man! And you're still wearing white clothes?

DERCETES

And by god, those two supported me with all the manure I could want!

DICAEOPOLIS

So what do you want now?

DERCETES

I've ruined my eyes, sobbing for my oxen. But if you care at all for Dercetes of Phyle,[128] anoint my eyes with some peace, right away!

DICAEOPOLIS

You rascal, I'm not a public doctor![129]

DERCETES

Come on, I'm begging you; then maybe I can recover my oxen!

[128] The name means "bright-eyes" and so has comic point, but there was a contemporary Dercetes of Phyle (a supporter of the war?).

[129] A certain number of doctors were salaried by the city to give free treatment to the indigent.

ARISTOPHANES

ΔΙΚΑΙΟΠΟΛΙΣ

οὐκ ἔστιν, ἀλλὰ κλᾶε πρὸς τοὺς Πιττάλου.

ΔΕΡΚΕΤΗΣ

σὺ δ' ἀλλά μοι σταλαγμὸν εἰρήνης ἕνα
εἰς τὸν καλαμίσκον ἐνστάλαξον τουτονί.

ΔΙΚΑΙΟΠΟΛΙΣ

1035 οὐδ' ἂν στριβιλικίγξ· ἀλλ' ἀπιὼν οἴμωζέ ποι.

ΔΕΡΚΕΤΗΣ

οἴμοι κακοδαίμων τοῖν γεωργοῖν βοιδίοιν.

ΧΟΡΟΣ

(αντ) ἀνὴρ ἐνηύρηκέν τι ταῖς
σπονδαῖσιν ἡδύ, κοὐκ ἔοι–
κεν οὐδενὶ μεταδώσειν.

ΔΙΚΑΙΟΠΟΛΙΣ

1040 κατάχει σὺ τῆς χορδῆς τὸ μέλι·
τὰς σηπίας στάθενε.

ΧΟΡΟΣ

ἤκουσας ὀρθιασμάτων;

ΔΙΚΑΙΟΠΟΛΙΣ

ὀπτᾶτε τἀγχέλεια.

ΧΟΡΟΣ

ἀποκτενεῖς λιμῷ 'μὲ καὶ
1045 τοὺς γείτονας κνίσῃ τε καὶ
φωνῇ τοιαῦτα λάσκων.

DICAEOPOLIS
Impossible. Go squawk to Pittalus' people.[130]

DERCETES
No, please drip me just one drop of peace into this fennel stalk!

DICAEOPOLIS
Not even a teensy peep! Go and grieve somewhere else.

DERCETES
Ah, poor me! My little beasts of burden!

DERCETES trudges off.

CHORUS
The man's discovered in his treaty
something delightful, and evidently
won't share it with anyone.

DICAEOPOLIS
You, pour the honey on the sausage;
grill the squid.

CHORUS
Did you hear his ringing tones?

DICAEOPOLIS
Broil the eels.

CHORUS
You'll starve us to death,
me and my neighbors, with the smell
and with your voice too, shouting such orders.

---

[130] Pittalus, mentioned also in *Wasps* 1432, evidently held an appointment as a public doctor (1030 n.).

ΔΙΚΑΙΟΠΟΛΙΣ

ὀπτᾶτε ταυτὶ καὶ καλῶς ξανθίζετε.

ΠΑΡΑΝΥΜΦΟΣ

Δικαιόπολι.

ΔΙΚΑΙΟΠΟΛΙΣ

τίς οὑτοσί; τίς οὑτοσί;

ΠΑΡΑΝΥΜΦΟΣ

ἔπεμψέ τίς σοι νυμφίος ταυτὶ κρέα
ἐκ τῶν γάμων.

ΔΙΚΑΙΟΠΟΛΙΣ

1050   καλῶς γε ποιῶν ὅστις ἦν.

ΠΑΡΑΝΥΜΦΟΣ

ἐκέλευε δ᾽ ἐγχέαι σε τῶν κρεῶν χάριν,
ἵνα μὴ στρατεύοιτ᾽, ἀλλὰ κινοίη μένων,
εἰς τὸν ἀλάβαστον κύαθον εἰρήνης ἕνα.

ΔΙΚΑΙΟΠΟΛΙΣ

ἀπόφερ᾽, ἀπόφερε τὰ κρέα καὶ μή μοι δίδου,
1055   ὡς οὐκ ἂν ἐγχέαιμι χιλίων δραχμῶν.
ἀλλ᾽ αὑτηὶ τίς ἐστιν;

ΠΑΡΑΝΥΜΦΟΣ

ἡ νυμφεύτρια

δεῖται παρὰ τῆς νύμφης τι σοὶ λέξαι μόνῳ.

ΔΙΚΑΙΟΠΟΛΙΣ

φέρε δή, τί σὺ λέγεις; ὡς γελοῖον, ὦ θεοί,
τὸ δέημα τῆς νύμφης, ὃ δεῖταί μου σφόδρα,
1060   ὅπως ἂν οἰκουρῇ τὸ πέος τοῦ νυμφίου.

192

DICAEOPOLIS

Broil these here, and grill these nicely.

Enter a BEST MAN *with a Bridesmaid.*

BEST MAN

Dicaeopolis!

DICAEOPOLIS

Who's that? Who's that?

BEST MAN

A bridegroom has sent you this meat from the wedding feast.

DICAEOPOLIS

A fine gesture, whoever he is.

BEST MAN

And he asks you, in return for the meat—so he won't have to go on campaign but can stay home and screw—to pour just one spoonful of peace into this tube.

DICAEOPOLIS

Take the meat back, take it back and don't offer it to me! I wouldn't pour a drop for a thousand drachmas. But who's this girl here?

BEST MAN

The bridesmaid, who wants to give you a private message from the bride.

DICAEOPOLIS

Well, now, what's your message? (*she whispers in his ear*) Dear gods, how droll the bride's request is! Her very earnest request to me is, that her husband's cock be allowed

φέρε δεῦρο τὰς σπονδάς, ἵν᾽ αὐτῇ δῶ μόνῃ,
ὁτιὴ γυνή ᾽στι τοῦ πολέμου τ᾽ οὐκ ἀξία.
ὕπεχ᾽ ὧδε δεῦρο τοὐξάλειπτρον, ὦ γύναι.
οἶσθ᾽ ὡς ποιεῖται; τοῦτο τῇ νύμφῃ φράσον·
1065 ὅταν στρατιώτας καταλέγωσι, τουτῳὶ
νύκτωρ ἀλειφέτω τὸ πέος τοῦ νυμφίου.
ἀπόφερε τὰς σπονδάς. φέρε τὴν οἰνήρυσιν,
ἵν᾽ οἶνον ἐγχέω λαβὼν εἰς τοὺς χοᾶς.

KOΡΥΦΑΙΟΣ

καὶ μὴν ὁδί τις τὰς ὀφρῦς ἀνεσπακὼς
1070 ὥσπερ τι δεινὸν ἀγγελῶν ἐπείγεται.

ΑΓΓΕΛΟΣ Α΄

ἰὼ πόνοι τε καὶ μάχαι καὶ Λάμαχοι.

ΛΑΜΑΧΟΣ

τίς ἀμφὶ χαλκοφάλαρα δώματα κτυπεῖ;

ΑΓΓΕΛΟΣ Α΄

ἰέναι σ᾽ ἐκέλευον οἱ στρατηγοὶ τήμερον
ταχέως λαβόντα τοὺς λόχους καὶ τοὺς λόφους·
1075 κἄπειτα τηρεῖν νειφόμενον τὰς εἰσβολάς.
ὑπὸ τοὺς Χοᾶς γὰρ καὶ Χύτρους αὐτοῖσί τις
ἤγγειλε λῃστὰς ἐμβαλεῖν Βοιωτίους.

to stay at home! Bring the treaty here; I'll give some to her and her alone, since she's a woman and doesn't deserve to suffer from the war. Hold the tube over here, this way, ma'am. Do you know how it's done? Tell the bride this: whenever they call up troops, she should rub her husband's cock at night with this.

BEST MAN and Bridesmaid depart.

Take the treaty away. Bring me the wine ladle, so I can draw wine and pour it into the pitchers.

CHORUS LEADER
But look, a man speeds toward us with furrowed brows, as if he has some dire news to report.

Enter FIRST MESSENGER

FIRST MESSENGER
Ah, hardships and battles and Lamachuses!

LAMACHUS
(*emerging from his door*) Who makes a racket round my bronze-bossed halls?

FIRST MESSENGER
The generals order you this very day, with your crests and your ambuscades, to march out in the snow on the double, to guard the passes. They've received a report that Boeotian bandits will make a raid around the time of the Pitcher and Pot Feasts.

Exit FIRST MESSENGER.

ΛΑΜΑΧΟΣ

ἰὼ στρατηγοὶ πλείονες ἢ βελτίονες.
οὐ δεινὰ μὴ 'ξεῖναί με μηδ' ἑορτάσαι;

ΔΙΚΑΙΟΠΟΛΙΣ

1080 ἰὼ στράτευμα πολεμολαμαχαϊκόν.

ΛΑΜΑΧΟΣ

οἴμοι κακοδαίμων, καταγελᾷς ἤδη σύ μου.

ΔΙΚΑΙΟΠΟΛΙΣ

βούλει μάχεσθαι, Γηρυόνη τετραπτίλε;

ΛΑΜΑΧΟΣ

αἰαῖ,
οἴαν ὁ κῆρυξ ἀγγελίαν ἤγγειλέ μοι.

ΔΙΚΑΙΟΠΟΛΙΣ

αἰαῖ, τίνα δ' αὖ 'μοὶ προστρέχει τις ἀγγελῶν;

ΑΓΓΕΛΟΣ Β'

Δικαιόπολι.

ΔΙΚΑΙΟΠΟΛΙΣ

τί ἐστιν;

ΑΓΓΕΛΟΣ Β'

1085   ἐπὶ δεῖπνον ταχὺ
βάδιζε τὴν κίστην λαβὼν καὶ τὸν χοᾶ.
ὁ τοῦ Διονύσου γάρ σ' ἱερεὺς μεταπέμπεται.
ἀλλ' ἐγκόνει· δειπνεῖν κατακωλύεις πάλαι.
τὰ δ' ἄλλα πάντ' ἐστὶ παρεσκευασμένα,
1090 κλῖναι, τράπεζαι, προσκεφάλαια, στρώματα,
στέφανοι, μύρον, τραγήμαθ', αἱ πόρναι πάρα,

196

ACHARNIANS

LAMACHUS

Oh generals more numerous than capable! Isn't it terrible
that I'm not even allowed to join the feasting?

DICAEOPOLIS

Hooray for the po*lam*ical expedition!

LAMACHUS

Alas and damn the luck, are you now mocking me?

DICAEOPOLIS

(*picking up a locust from the table*) Would you like to fight,
you four-feathered Geryon?[131]

LAMACHUS

Alas, what an order the messenger messaged me!

DICAEOPOLIS

Alas, what is this second messenger running up to tell *me?*

Enter SECOND MESSENGER.

SECOND MESSENGER

Dicaeopolis!

DICAEOPOLIS

What is it?

SECOND MESSENGER

Go along to dinner right away, and take your hamper and
your pitcher; the Priest of Dionysus invites you! But hurry;
you've held up dinner a long time. Everything else stands
ready: couches, tables, pillows, coverlets, garlands, per-
fume, tasty tidbits; the whores are there; cakes, pastries,

[131] The winged monster Geryon, slain by Heracles, was tradi-
tionally triple-bodied.

197

ARISTOPHANES

ἄμυλοι, πλακοῦντες, σησαμοῦντες, ἴτρια,
ὀρχηστρίδες, τὰ φίλταθ᾽ Ἁρμοδίου, καλαί.
ἀλλ᾽ ὡς τάχιστα σπεῦδε.

ΛΑΜΑΧΟΣ
                    κακοδαίμων ἐγώ.

ΔΙΚΑΙΟΠΟΛΙΣ
1095 καὶ γὰρ σὺ μεγάλην ἐπεγράφου τὴν Γοργόνα.
σύγκλῃε, καὶ δεῖπνόν τις ἐνσκευαζέτω.

ΛΑΜΑΧΟΣ
παῖ παῖ, φέρ᾽ ἔξω δεῦρο τὸν γυλιὸν ἐμοί.

ΔΙΚΑΙΟΠΟΛΙΣ
παῖ παῖ, φέρ᾽ ἔξω δεῦρο τὴν κίστην ἐμοί.

ΛΑΜΑΧΟΣ
ἅλας θυμίτας οἶσε, παῖ, καὶ κρόμμυα.

ΔΙΚΑΙΟΠΟΛΙΣ
1100 ἐμοὶ δὲ τεμάχη· κρομμύοις γὰρ ἄχθομαι.

ΛΑΜΑΧΟΣ
θρῖον ταρίχους οἶσε δεῦρο, παῖ, σαπροῦ.

ΔΙΚΑΙΟΠΟΛΙΣ
κἀμοὶ σὺ δή, παῖ, θρῖον· ὀπτήσω δ᾽ ἐκεῖ.

ΛΑΜΑΧΟΣ
ἔνεγκε δεῦρο τὼ πτερὼ τὠκ τοῦ κράνους.

ΔΙΚΑΙΟΠΟΛΙΣ
ἐμοὶ δὲ τὰς φάττας γε φέρε καὶ τὰς κίχλας.

ACHARNIANS

sesame crackers, rolls, dancing girls, Harmodius' beloveds,[132] pretty ones! But hurry up, as fast as you can!

Exit SECOND MESSENGER.

LAMACHUS

I'm under a bad sign!

DICAEOPOLIS

It serves you right, for signing up with a big Gorgon! (*to a slave*) Close up, and someone pack my dinner!

LAMACHUS

Boy, boy, bring my mess kit out here to me.

DICAEOPOLIS

Boy, boy, bring my picnic basket out here to me.

LAMACHUS

Get the seasoned salt, boy, and the onions.

DICAEOPOLIS

For me the fish fillets; I'm sick of onions.

LAMACHUS

Bring me a fig leaf, boy, full of stale salt fish.

DICAEOPOLIS

And you can bring me a stuffed fig leaf; I'll cook it when I get there.

LAMACHUS

Bring here the twin plumes from my helmet.

DICAEOPOLIS

Bring me the pigeons and the thrushes.

[132] Punning on the opening words of the Harmodius song (see 980 n.).

199

ARISTOPHANES

ΛΑΜΑΧΟΣ

1105 καλόν γε καὶ λευκὸν τὸ τῆς στρούθου πτερόν.

ΔΙΚΑΙΟΠΟΛΙΣ

καλόν γε καὶ ξανθὸν τὸ τῆς φάττης κρέας.

ΛΑΜΑΧΟΣ

ὦνθρωπε, παῦσαι καταγελῶν μου τῶν ὅπλων.

ΔΙΚΑΙΟΠΟΛΙΣ

ὦνθρωπε, βούλει μὴ βλέπειν εἰς τὰς κίχλας;

ΛΑΜΑΧΟΣ

1113 ὦνθρωπε, βούλει μὴ προσαγορεύειν ἐμέ;

ΔΙΚΑΙΟΠΟΛΙΣ

1114 οὔκ, ἀλλ᾽ ἐγὼ χὠ παῖς ἐρίζομεν πάλαι.

1115 βούλει περιδόσθαι κἀπιτρέψαι Λαμάχῳ,

1116 πότερον ἀκρίδες ἥδιόν ἐστιν ἢ κίχλαι;

ΛΑΜΑΧΟΣ

οἴμ᾽ ὡς ὑβρίζεις.

ΔΙΚΑΙΟΠΟΛΙΣ

1117   τὰς ἀκρίδας κρίνει πολύ.

ΛΑΜΑΧΟΣ

1109 τὸ λοφεῖον ἐξένεγκε τῶν τριῶν λόφων.

ΔΙΚΑΙΟΠΟΛΙΣ

1110 κἀμοὶ λεκάνιον τῶν λαγῴων δὸς κρεῶν.

ΛΑΜΑΧΟΣ

1111 ἀλλ᾽ ἦ τριχοβρῶτες τοὺς λόφους μοι κατέφαγον;

LAMACHUS

So fair and white the ostrich plume!

DICAEOPOLIS

So fair and brown the pigeon meat!

LAMACHUS

Mister, stop laughing at my armor.

DICAEOPOLIS

Mister, please stop looking at my thrushes.

LAMACHUS

Mister, please stop addressing me.

DICAEOPOLIS

I'm not; my boy and I have been having an argument for
a while now. (*to his slave*) Do you want to bet, and have La-
machus decide it, whether locusts are tastier, or thrushes?

LAMACHUS

Oh! What impudence!

DICAEOPOLIS

He's strongly for the locusts.

LAMACHUS

Bring out the crest case with the triple crests.

DICAEOPOLIS

And give me a casserole with the hares' meat.

LAMACHUS

What, have moths consumed my crests?

1109-12 post 1117 transposuit Sommerstein

ARISTOPHANES

ΔΙΚΑΙΟΠΟΛΙΣ
1112   ἀλλ᾽ ἦ πρὸ δείπνου τὴν μίμαρκυν κατέδομαι;

ΛΑΜΑΧΟΣ
1118   παῖ παῖ, καθελών μοι τὸ δόρυ δεῦρ᾽ ἔξω φέρε.

ΔΙΚΑΙΟΠΟΛΙΣ
       παῖ παῖ, σὺ δ᾽ ἀφελὼν δεῦρο τὴν χορδὴν φέρε.

ΛΑΜΑΧΟΣ
1120   φέρε, τοῦ δόρατος ἀφελκύσωμαι τοὔλυτρον.
       ἔχ᾽, ἀντέχου, παῖ.

ΔΙΚΑΙΟΠΟΛΙΣ
                      καὶ σύ, παῖ, τοῦδ᾽ ἀντέχου.

ΛΑΜΑΧΟΣ
       τοὺς κιλλίβαντας οἶσε, παῖ, τῆς ἀσπίδος.

ΔΙΚΑΙΟΠΟΛΙΣ
       καὶ τῆς ἐμῆς τοὺς κριβανίτας ἔκφερε.

ΛΑΜΑΧΟΣ
       φέρε δεῦρο γοργόνωτον ἀσπίδος κύκλον.

ΔΙΚΑΙΟΠΟΛΙΣ
1125   κἀμοὶ πλακοῦντος τυρόνωτον δὸς κύκλον.

ΛΑΜΑΧΟΣ
       ταῦτ᾽ οὐ κατάγελώς ἐστιν ἀνθρώποις πλατύς;

ΔΙΚΑΙΟΠΟΛΙΣ
       ταῦτ᾽ οὐ πλακοῦς δῆτ᾽ ἐστὶν ἀνθρώποις γλυκύς;

ΛΑΜΑΧΟΣ
       κατάχει σύ, παῖ, τοὔλαιον. ἐν τῷ χαλκίῳ

202

DICAEOPOLIS

What, am I to eat the hare stew before dinner?

LAMACHUS

Boy, boy, take down my spear and bring it out here.

DICAEOPOLIS

Boy, boy, you take the sausage off and bring it here.

LAMACHUS

Come, let me draw the case off my spear. Ready, hold on, boy.

DICAEOPOLIS

And you, boy, hold on to this. (*the slave holds the skewer while Dicaeopolis removes the sausage*)

LAMACHUS

Bring me the staves, boy, to support my shield.

DICAEOPOLIS

Bring out the baguettes to support mine (*rubbing his belly*).

LAMACHUS

Bring hither my buckler round and Gorgon-bossed.

DICAEOPOLIS

And give me a pizza round and cheese-bossed.

LAMACHUS

Isn't this what men call flat insolence?

DICAEOPOLIS

Isn't this what men call delicious pizza?

LAMACHUS

Boy, you pour on the oil. (*buffing his shield*) In this bronze

ἐνορῶ γέροντα δειλίας φευξούμενον.

ΔΙΚΑΙΟΠΟΛΙΣ

1130 κατάχει σὺ τὸ μέλι. κἀνθάδ᾽ εὔδηλος γέρων
κλάειν κελεύων Λάμαχον τὸν Γοργάσου.

ΛΑΜΑΧΟΣ

φέρε δεῦρο, παῖ, θώρακα πολεμιστήριον.

ΔΙΚΑΙΟΠΟΛΙΣ

ἔξαιρε, παῖ, θώρακα κἀμοὶ τὸν χοᾶ.

ΛΑΜΑΧΟΣ

ἐν τῷδε πρὸς τοὺς πολεμίους θωρήξομαι.

ΔΙΚΑΙΟΠΟΛΙΣ

1135 ἐν τῷδε πρὸς τοὺς συμπότας θωρήξομαι.

ΛΑΜΑΧΟΣ

τὰ στρώματ᾽, ὦ παῖ, δῆσον ἐκ τῆς ἀσπίδος.

ΔΙΚΑΙΟΠΟΛΙΣ

τὸ δεῖπνον, ὦ παῖ, δῆσον ἔκ τῆς κιστίδος.

ΛΑΜΑΧΟΣ

ἐγὼ δ᾽ ἐμαυτῷ τὸν γυλιὸν οἴσω λαβών.

ΔΙΚΑΙΟΠΟΛΙΣ

ἐγὼ δὲ θοἰμάτιον λαβὼν ἐξέρχομαι.

ΛΑΜΑΧΟΣ

1140 τὴν ἀσπίδ᾽ αἴρου καὶ βάδιζ᾽, ὦ παῖ, λαβών.
νείφει. βαβαιάξ· χειμέρια τὰ πράγματα.

I see an old man about to be prosecuted for cowardice.

DICAEOPOLIS

And you pour on the honey. (*gazing into the pizza*) Here too an old man is visible, telling Lamachus, son of Gorgasus,[133] to go to hell!

LAMACHUS

Hand hither, boy, my warlike corslet.

DICAEOPOLIS

Boy, fetch me forth a corslet too—my pitcher.

LAMACHUS

In this I bolster me to meet the foe.

DICAEOPOLIS

In this I bolster me to meet my fellow drinkers.

LAMACHUS

Boy, bind my bedding to the shield.

DICAEOPOLIS

Boy, bind my dinner to the picnic basket.

LAMACHUS

And I shall carry the mess kit by myself.

DICAEOPOLIS

And I'll grab my cloak and be leaving.

LAMACHUS

Enclasp and raise the shield, boy, and be off. It's snowing! Brrr, I've wintry business!

Exit LAMACHUS *in one direction.*

[133] The name of Lamachus' father was actually Xenophanes.

ΔΙΚΑΙΟΠΟΛΙΣ

αἴρου τὸ δεῖπνον· συμποτικὰ τὰ πράγματα.

ΚΟΡΥΦΑΙΟΣ

ἴτε δὴ χαίροντες ἐπὶ στρατιάν.
ὡς ἀνομοίαν ἔρχεσθον ὁδόν·
1145 τῷ μὲν πίνειν στεφανωσαμένῳ,
σοὶ δὲ ῥιγῶν καὶ προφυλάττειν,
τῷ δὲ καθεύδειν
μετὰ παιδίσκης ὡραιοτάτης,
ἀνατριβομένῳ γε τὸ δεῖνα.

ΧΟΡΟΣ

(στρ) Ἀντίμαχον τὸν Ψακάδος, τὸν ξυγγραφῆ,
1151 τὸν μελέων ποιητήν,
ὡς μὲν ἁπλῷ λόγῳ κακῶς
ἐξολέσειεν ὁ Ζεύς·
ὅς γ' ἐμὲ τὸν τλήμονα Λήναια χορη-
1155 γῶν ἀπέλυσ' ἄδειπνον.
ὃν ἔτ' ἐπίδοιμι τευθίδος
δεόμενον, ἡ δ' ὠπτημένη
σίζουσα πάραλος ἐπὶ τραπέζῃ κειμένη
ὀκέλλοι· κᾆτα μέλ-
1160 λοντος λαβεῖν αὐτοῦ κύων
ἁρπάσασα φεύγοι.

DICAEOPOLIS
Pick up the dinner, I've festive business!

Exit DICAEOPOLIS in the other direction.

CHORUS LEADER
Good luck on your expeditions!
How dissimilar the paths you travel:
he'll wear a garland and drink;
you'll stand watch and freeze.
He'll be sleeping
with a very fresh young girl,
getting his thingum squeezed.

CHORUS
Antimachus son of Drizzler,[134] the drafter of bills,
the composer of bad songs:
to put it bluntly,
may Zeus terribly eradicate him!
He's the one who, as producer[135] at the Lenaea,
unkindly dismissed me[136] without dinner.
May I yet see him hungry for squid,
and may it lie grilled and sizzling by the shore
and make port safely at his table;
and then, when he's about
to grab it, may a dog snap it up
and run away with it!

---

[134] Otherwise unknown; the scholia say that "son of Drizzler" refers to Antimachus' habit of spraying saliva when he talked.

[135] Producers were expected to hold a banquet for the troupe after the competition.

[136] They speak as the generic comic chorus.

(ἀντ) τοῦτο μὲν αὐτῷ κακὸν ἔν, κᾆθ' ἕτερον
νυκτερινὸν γένοιτο.
ἠπιαλῶν γὰρ οἴκαδ' ἐξ
1165 ἱππασίας βαδίζων,
εἶτα πατάξειέ τις αὐτοῦ μεθύων
τῆς κεφαλῆς Ὀρέστης
μαινόμενος· ὁ δὲ λίθον λαβεῖν
βουλόμενος ἐν σκότῳ λάβοι
1170 τῇ χειρὶ πέλεθον ἀρτίως κεχεσμένον·
ἐπάξειεν δ' ἔχων
τὸν μάρμαρον, κἄπειθ' ἁμαρ-
τὼν βάλοι Κρατῖνον.

ΑΓΓΕΛΟΣ Γ΄

ὦ δμῶες οἳ κατ' οἶκόν ἐστε Λαμάχου,
1175 ὕδωρ, ὕδωρ ἐν χυτριδίῳ θερμαίνετε·
ὀθόνια, κηρωτὴν παρασκευάζετε,
ἔρι' οἰσυπηρά, λαμπάδιον περὶ τὸ σφυρόν.
ἀνὴρ τέτρωται χάρακι διαπηδῶν τάφρον,
καὶ τὸ σφυρὸν παλίνορρον ἐξεκόκκισεν,
1180 καὶ τῆς κεφαλῆς κατέαγε περὶ λίθῳ πεσών,
καὶ Γοργόν' ἐξήγειρεν ἐκ τῆς ἀσπίδος·
πτίλον δὲ τὸ μέγ' ⟨ὡς εἶδεν ἐκ κράνους⟩ πεσὸν
πρὸς ταῖς πέτραισι δεινὸν ἐξηύδα μέλος·
"ὦ κλεινὸν ὄμμα νῦν πανύστατόν σ' ἰδὼν

1182 μέγ' ⟨ὡς εἶδεν ἐκ κράνους⟩ πεσὸν exempli gratia Sommerstein: μέγα κομπολακύθου z: πεσὸν R^{pc} j: πεσὼν R^{ac} a

208

That's one curse for him; and here's another,
to happen to him in the night.
As he walks home shivering
after galloping his horse,
I hope some drunkard—
mad Orestes![137]—knocks him on the head;
and when he wants to grab a stone
I hope in the darkness
he grabs in his hand a fresh-shat turd,
and holding that glittering missile
let him charge at his foe, then miss him
and hit Cratinus!

A THIRD MESSENGER *rushes in and bangs on Lamachus'
door.*

THIRD MESSENGER

Ye vassals of the house of Lamachus, water, heat water in
a basin, prepare linen strips, wax salve, oily wool, a bandage
for his ankle! The man's been wounded by a stake, from
jumping over a trench, and twisted his ankle backwards
and dislocated it, and fractured his head by falling on a
stone, and waked the sleeping Gorgon from his shield! And
‹when he saw› the great plume had fallen ‹from his hel-
met› against the rocks, he voiced a direful cry: "O brilliant

---

[137] The nickname of the son of one Timocrates (schol. *Birds*
1487), after the mythical hero who wandered insane to Athens
after killing his own mother.

1185 λείπω, φάος γε τοὐμόν. οὐκέτ᾽ εἰμ᾽ ἐγώ."
τοσαῦτα λέξας εἰς ὑδρορρόαν πεσὼν
ἀνίσταταί τε καὶ ξυναντᾷ δραπέταις
ληστὰς ἐλαύνων καὶ κατασπέρχων δορί.
ὁδὶ δὲ καὐτός. ἀλλ᾽ ἄνοιγε τὴν θύραν.

ΛΑΜΑΧΟΣ

1190 ἀτταταῖ ἀτταταῖ,
στυγερὰ τάδε γε κρυερὰ πάθεα· τάλας ἐγώ.
διόλλυμαι δορὸς ὑπὸ πολεμίου τυπείς.
1195 ἐκεῖνο δ᾽ οὖν αἰακτὸν ἂν γένοιτο,
Δικαιόπολις εἴ μ᾽ ἴδοι τετρωμένον
κᾆτ᾽ ἐγχάνοι ταῖς ἐμαῖς τύχαισιν.

ΔΙΚΑΙΟΠΟΛΙΣ

Ἀτταταῖ ἀτταταῖ,
τῶν τιτθίων, ὡς σκληρὰ καὶ κυδώνια.
1200 φιλήσατόν με μαλθακῶς, ὦ χρυσίω,
τὸ περιπεταστὸν κἀπιμανδαλωτόν.
τὸν γὰρ χοᾶ πρῶτος ἐκπέπωκα.

ΛΑΜΑΧΟΣ

ὦ συμφορὰ τάλαινα τῶν ἐμῶν κακῶν.
1205 ἰὼ ἰὼ τραυμάτων ἐπωδύνων.

ΔΙΚΑΙΟΠΟΛΙΣ

ἰὴ ἰή, χαῖρε, Λαμαχίππιον.

visage, now for the last time do I behold you, light of mine;
I am no more!" This he said when he fell into a drainage
ditch; then he stood up and faced his fleeing men, as he
pressed and routed the brigands with his spear.

Enter LAMACHUS, *wounded and bedraggled, supported by
two Soldiers.*

And here he is himself! Come, open the door!

LAMACHUS

Oh oh! Ah ah!
Hateful as hell these icy pains; wretched am I!
I am undone, by foeman's spear struck down.
But it would be true agony
if Dicaeopolis should see me wounded
and jeer at my misfortunes.

Enter DICAEOPOLIS, *intoxicated, supported by two danc-
ing girls.*

DICAEOPOLIS

Oh oh! Ah ah!
What tits! How firm, like quinces!
Kiss me softly, my two bangles,
one with open mouth, one with plunging tongue.
Because I'm the first to drain my pitcher!

LAMACHUS

O lamentable conjunction of my woes!
Ah, ah, my afflictive wounds!

DICAEOPOLIS

Hey, hey! Hello there, little Lamachippus!

211

ΛΑΜΑΧΟΣ

στυγερὸς ἐγώ.

ΔΙΚΑΙΟΠΟΛΙΣ

τί με σὺ κυνεῖς;

ΛΑΜΑΧΟΣ

μογερὸς ἐγώ.

ΔΙΚΑΙΟΠΟΛΙΣ

τί με σὺ δάκνεις;

ΛΑΜΑΧΟΣ

1210 τάλας ἐγὼ ξυμβολῆς βαρείας.

ΔΙΚΑΙΟΠΟΛΙΣ

τοῖς Χουσὶ γάρ τις ξυμβολὰς ἐπράττετο;

ΛΑΜΑΧΟΣ

ἰὼ ἰώ, Παιὰν Παιάν.

ΔΙΚΑΙΟΠΟΛΙΣ

ἀλλ᾽ οὐχὶ νυνὶ τήμερον Παιώνια.

ΛΑΜΑΧΟΣ

λάβεσθέ μου, λάβεσθε τοῦ σκέλους· παπαῖ,
1215 προσλάβεσθ᾽, ὦ φίλοι.

ΔΙΚΑΙΟΠΟΛΙΣ

ἐμοῦ δέ γε σφὼ τοῦ πέους ἄμφω μέσου
προσλάβεσθ᾽, ὦ φίλαι.

ΛΑΜΑΧΟΣ

εἰλιγγιῶ κάρα λίθῳ πεπληγμένος
καὶ σκοτοδινιῶ.

212

ACHARNIANS

LAMACHUS

Accursed am I!

DICAEOPOLIS

(*to one girl*)
Smooching me, eh?

LAMACHUS

Beleaguered am I!

DICAEOPOLIS

(*to the other girl*)
Nibbling me, eh?

LAMACHUS

Woe is me, what a costly fray!

DICAEOPOLIS

What, somebody made you defray their expenses at the
Pitcher Feast?

LAMACHUS

Oh, oh, Healer, Healer!

DICAEOPOLIS

But it's not the Healer's Festival today.

LAMACHUS

Hold, o hold this leg of mine! Ouch!
Take hold, my friends!

DICAEOPOLIS

And you two hold the thick of my cock;
take hold, my girls!

LAMACHUS

I reel, my pate smitten by a stone,
and swoon in darkness.

ΔΙΚΑΙΟΠΟΛΙΣ

1220 κἀγὼ καθεύδειν βούλομαι καὶ στύομαι
καὶ σκοτοβινιῶ.

ΛΑΜΑΧΟΣ

θύραζέ μ' ἐξενέγκατ' εἰς τοῦ Πιττάλου
παιωνίαισι χερσίν.

ΔΙΚΑΙΟΠΟΛΙΣ

ὡς τοὺς κριτάς με φέρετε. ποῦ 'στιν ὁ βασιλεύς;
1225 ἀπόδοτέ μοι τὸν ἀσκόν.

ΛΑΜΑΧΟΣ

λόγχη τις ἐμπέπηγέ μοι
δι' ὀστέων ὀδυρτά.

ΔΙΚΑΙΟΠΟΛΙΣ

ὁρᾶτε τουτονὶ κενόν.
τήνελλα καλλίνικος.

ΚΟΡΥΦΑΙΟΣ

τήνελλα δῆτ', εἴπερ καλεῖς γ',
ὦ πρέσβυ, καλλίνικος.

ΔΙΚΑΙΟΠΟΛΙΣ

καὶ πρός γ' ἄκρατον ἐγχέας
ἄμυστιν ἐξέλαψα.

ΚΟΡΥΦΑΙΟΣ

τήνελλά νυν, ὦ γεννάδα· χώρει

---

138 I.e., the judges of the drinking contest, perhaps with an

DICAEOPOLIS
I too want to go to bed; I have a hard-on,
and want to fuck in darkness.

LAMACHUS
Bear me off to Pittalus' clinic,
with healing hands.

DICAEOPOLIS
Take me to the judges. Where's the King?[138]
Give me the wine skin!

LAMACHUS
A lance has pierced me through,
most woefully, to the bone!

LAMACHUS is borne away.

DICAEOPOLIS
(*holding up his pitcher*)
Look, this pitcher's empty!
Hail the Champion!

CHORUS LEADER
Hail then—since you bid me,
old sir—the Champion!

DICAEOPOLIS
And what's more, I poured the wine neat
and chugged it straight down!

CHORUS LEADER
Then Hail, old chap!

allusion to the dramatic judges as well. For the King (Archon) see
961 n.

1230   λαβὼν τὸν ἀσκόν.

ΔΙΚΑΙΟΠΟΛΙΣ

ἕπεσθέ νυν ᾄδοντες· ὦ
τήνελλα καλλίνικος.

ΧΟΡΟΣ

ἀλλ᾽ ἐψόμεσθα σὴν χάριν
τήνελλα καλλίνικον ᾄ–
δοντες σὲ καὶ τὸν ἀσκόν.

Take the wineskin and go.

DICAEOPOLIS
Then follow me, singing
"Hail the Champion"!

CHORUS
Yes, we'll follow, in your honor,
singing "Hail the Champion"
for you and your wineskin.

DICAEOPOLIS leads the Chorus off in song.

KNIGHTS

INTRODUCTORY NOTE

Knights was produced at the Lenaea of 424, placing first; Cratinus placed second with *Satyrs* and Aristomenes third with *Porters*. *Knights*, the first play that Aristophanes produced in his own name (cf. 512-45), made good his promise at the previous year's Lenaea to "cut Cleon up into shoeleather for the Knights" (*Acharnians* 299-302), even though Cleon in the meantime had become more powerful than ever.

In the preceding summer, Athenian troops under the command of the general Demosthenes had stranded a force of Spartan infantrymen on an island off Pylos in the western Peloponnese. Cleon broke the subsequent strategic and diplomatic impasse by rising in the Assembly and challenging the generals to attack the Spartans; when Nicias, spokesman for the generals, demurred, the Assembly invited Cleon to assume Nicias' authority over the Pylos campaign. Cleon accepted, vowing to kill or capture the Spartans within three weeks, and then fulfilled his vow, returning to Athens with 292 Spartan hostages (Thucydides 4.1-41). This was a key victory for Athens: it diminished the legend of Spartan invincibility on land, and the hostages could be used to force an end to the annual invasions of Attica. It also made a hero of Cleon, who was honored with a civic crown, lifetime meals in the Prytaneum, and front-row seating at festivals and in the theater. And it seemed to vindicate Cleon's warlike policies, so that the Athenians now rejected out of hand all proposals to negotiate a peace treaty and instead embarked on an ambitious and aggressive series of campaigns. One of these, which involved Nicias and the Knights, is even invoked in the play as a counterbalance to Cleon's victory at Pylos (595-610).

Knights is a remarkably savage indictment, both personal and political, of Cleon, of the other popular politicians who had succeeded Pericles upon his death in 429, and of the complacency of the demos (sovereign people) in following their advice. In Aristophanes' eyes, Cleon and his ilk were crude but cunning tradesmen of questionable ancestry who had made their way into politics as blackmailers and malicious prosecutors; who deceived the people into authorizing the sort of reckless military and imperialistic adventures that would enable them to enrich themselves by embezzlement, extortion, and bribe-taking; who impoverished both rich and poor by their rapacity; who corrupted the morals of the young; and who tarnished the glory, and were threatening the future, of Athens. The play resounds with the noise, the vulgarity, the violence, and the selfish cynicism that for Aristophanes typified the new style of Athenian leadership. As for the victory at Pylos, Cleon had simply stolen the credit from the real generals. No doubt there were other Athenians, though apparently not a majority, who shared these opinions.[1]

---

[1] Thucydides' assessment of Pericles' successors (2.65) is essentially the same, and his treatment of Cleon in general is unmistakably hostile.

To dramatize these spacious themes Aristophanes devised, with brilliant economy of means, an allegorical plot as simple as a folk tale. The house (Athens) of Mr. Demos, a decrepit old man, has been taken over by a newly bought slave, a barbaric tanner from Paphlagonia (Cleon, in real life a tanner). This Paphlagon has entranced Mr. Demos with lies, petty gifts, and flattery, while hoarding Mr. Demos' wealth to himself and violently alienating the home-bred slaves (political competitors) from Mr. Demos, whom they would serve. Two of these Slaves[2] hit on the idea of stealing Paphlagon's oracles, where they discover that he is but the latest in a succession of demagogues, each worse than the last. The oracles predict that Paphlagon is to be overthrown by someone even worse, a sausage seller. Such a Sausage Seller appears, is recruited by the Slaves and backed by a Chorus representing the aristocratic Knights, who, like Aristophanes, were (for reasons now obscure) enemies of Cleon. There follows a series of contests in which the Sausage Seller outdoes Paphlagon at his own demagogic techniques and, as predicted, succeeds him as Mr. Demos's steward. At the end of the play, the Sausage Seller magically restores Mr. Demos to his youthful prime, revealing him as he was in the days of Marathon and Sala-

---

[2] The two were interpreted in antiquity, as by many scholars today, as representing the generals Demosthenes and Nicias. But their characterization suggests rather that they represent the political "outs" more generally: only line 55 has a particular referent, Demosthenes, but other details in the passage do not suit him, and nowhere do the slaves' words and actions depend for intelligibility on personal caricature. In this edition the slaves are simply called (as in the text) First Slave and Second Slave.

mis when he, and the Athenians, were at the pinnacle of their greatness. Guided by the now-honest Sausage Seller, Mr. Demos promises never to repeat his recent mistakes, and in traditional comic fashion is sent back to his farm with a "well hung boy" and two girls, who represent peace treaties.

In subsequent years Aristophanes expressed greater pride in *Knights* than in any other of his plays, claiming that it inaugurated a new genre of "demagogue comedy" and boasting of his own personal courage, and success, in attacking the most dangerous of the demagogues (see esp. *Clouds* 549-62). Despite Eupolis' counterclaim that he had shared in the composition of *Knights* (fr. 89), Aristophanes' pride seems justified on both counts. Although the play's allegorical mode of attack has its own artistic advantages, the fact that no character is explicitly identified with an actual person—Cleon is named only once in the play (976) in a choral song not explicitly associated with the character Paphlagon—suggests fear of retaliation. In the event, Cleon did retaliate, indicting Aristophanes a second time (see *Acharnians,* Introductory Note), this time settling out of court (*Wasps* 1284-91). That Cleon was elected general in his own right shortly after the success of *Knights* is not incompatible with Aristophanes' claim that the play indeed damaged Cleon: after Pylos Cleon could hardly be denied a command, and in any case *Knights* concentrates its fire not on Cleon's military ability but on his persuasiveness in the Assembly, and in that respect the poet's attack may well have struck home.

Text

Five papyri preserve fragments of *Knights*.[3] There are 31 medieval MSS, which divide into two main families: R and the sources of S on the one side, and the MSS designated by the siglum *y* on the other. In addition, M and one of the correcting hands in Γ derive from lost early MSS related to but independent of R S and *y*. The recensions made by Triclinius (at least three) and by later Byzantine scholars were based on *recentiores* of the *y* family. In this edition the *y* family is represented by VEΓAΘVp3C. Accompanying the text of *Knights* is a substantial corpus of scholia both metrical and exegetic.

Sigla

R	Ravennas 429 (*c.* 950)
S	readings found in the Suda
M	Ambrosianus L 39 sup. (*c.* 1320)
V	Venetus Marcianus 474 (XI/XII)
E	Estensis a.U.5.10 (XIV/XVin)
Γ	Laurentianus 31.15 (*c.* 1325)
A	Parisinus gr. 2712 (XIVin)
Θ	Laurentianus conv. soppr. 140 (XIVin)
Vp3	Vaticanus Palatinus gr. 128 (XV)
C	Parisinus gr. 2717 (XV/XVI)
z	the archetype of RM*y*
y	the consensus of VEΓAΘCVp3

---

[3] *Pap. Oxyr.* 11.1373 (V), lines 6-15, 1013-17, 1057-62; *Pap. Bodl. gr. class.* f 72(P) (IV/V), lines 37-46, 86-95; *Pap. Berol.* 13929 et 21105 (IV), lines 546-54, 574-83; *Pap. Oxyr.* 13.2545 (I a.C./II p.C.), lines 1057-76; *Pap. Mich. inv.* 6035 (II/III), lines 1127-41.

Annotated Editions

F. H. M. Blaydes (Halle 1892)
W. W. Merry (Oxford 1895)
F. A. von Velsen, rev. by K. Zacher (Leipzig 1898)
J. van Leeuwen (Leiden 1900)
R. A. Neil (Cambridge 1901)
B. B. Rogers (London 1910), with English translation.
A. H. Sommerstein (Warminster 1981), with English trans-
    lation.
G. Mastromarco (Turin 1983), with Italian translation.

ΤΑ ΤΟΥ ΔΡΑΜΑΤΟΣ ΠΡΟΣΩΠΑ

ΟΙΚΕΤΗΣ Α *Δήμου*
ΟΙΚΕΤΗΣ Β *Δήμου*
ΑΛΛΑΝΤΟΠΩΛΗΣ
ΠΑΦΛΑΓΩΝ *ταμίας*
   Δήμου
ΔΗΜΟΣ Πυκνίτης

ΧΟΡΟΣ *ἱππέων*

ΚΩΦΑ ΠΡΟΣΩΠΑ
ΠΑΙΣ
ΑΙ ΣΠΟΝΔΑΙ
ΟΙΚΕΤΑΙ *Δήμου*

DRAMATIS PERSONAE

FIRST SLAVE of Demos
SECOND SLAVE of Demos
SAUSAGE SELLER
PAPHLAGON, steward of
   Demos
DEMOS of Pnyx Hill

CHORUS of Athenian
   Knights

SILENT CHARACTERS
SLAVE BOY
PEACE TREATIES, two girls
SLAVES of Demos

ΙΠΠΗΣ

ΟΙΚΕΤΗΣ Α΄

Ἰατταταιὰξ τῶν κακῶν, ἰατταταῖ.
κακῶς Παφλαγόνα τὸν νεώνητον κακὸν
αὐταῖσι βουλαῖς ἀπολέσειαν οἱ θεοί.
ἐξ οὗ γὰρ εἰσήρρησεν εἰς τὴν οἰκίαν
5 πληγὰς ἀεὶ προστρίβεται τοῖς οἰκέταις.

ΟΙΚΕΤΗΣ Β΄

κάκιστα δῆθ᾽ οὑτός γε πρῶτος Παφλαγόνων
αὐταῖς διαβολαῖς.

ΟΙΚΕΤΗΣ Α΄

ὦ κακόδαιμον, πῶς ἔχεις;

ΟΙΚΕΤΗΣ Β΄

κακῶς καθάπερ σύ.

ΟΙΚΕΤΗΣ Α΄

δεῦρό νυν πρόσελθ᾽, ἵνα

1–497 Οἰκέτης Α΄ Dindorf: Δημοσθένης z
6–154 Οἰκέτης Β΄ Dindorf: Νικίας z

---

[1] The reputed founder of Greek *aulos* music, of music without

KNIGHTS

The scene building represents the house of Demos.

FIRST SLAVE rushes from the house.

FIRST SLAVE

Yow, ow ow ow! Damn it all! Yow ow ow! That damn new-bought Paphlagon, may the gods damnably destroy him, him and all his schemes! Ever since he turned up at our house, he's been getting the homebred servants beaten nonstop.

SECOND SLAVE comes out of the house.

SECOND SLAVE

Yes, of all Paphlagons I hope he's the first to perish most damnably, him and his slanders too!

FIRST SLAVE

Poor fellow, how goes it?

SECOND SLAVE

Damn badly, just like you.

FIRST SLAVE

Then join me over here, and let's wail a tune by Olympus[1]

words, and of the Phrygian and Lydian modes, which conservative Athenians considered slavish and barbaric.

ξυναυλίαν κλαύσωμεν Οὐλύμπου νόμον.

ΟΙΚΕΤΗΣ Α΄ καὶ Β΄

10 μυμῦ μυμῦ μυμῦ μυμῦ μυμῦ μυμῦ.

ΟΙΚΕΤΗΣ Α΄

τί κινυρόμεθ᾽ ἄλλως; οὐκ ἐχρῆν ζητεῖν τινα
σωτηρίαν νῷν, ἀλλὰ μὴ κλάειν ἔτι;

ΟΙΚΕΤΗΣ Β΄

τίς οὖν γένοιτ᾽ ἄν; λέγε σύ.

ΟΙΚΕΤΗΣ Α΄

σὺ μὲν οὖν μοι λέγε,

ἵνα μὴ μάχωμαι.

ΟΙΚΕΤΗΣ Β΄

μὰ τὸν Ἀπόλλω ᾽γὼ μὲν οὔ.

ΟΙΚΕΤΗΣ Α΄

15 ἀλλ᾽ εἰπὲ θαρρῶν, εἶτα κἀγὼ σοὶ φράσω.

ΟΙΚΕΤΗΣ Β΄

πῶς ἂν σύ μοι λέξειας ἁμὲ χρὴ λέγειν;

ΟΙΚΕΤΗΣ Α΄

ἀλλ᾽ οὐκ ἔνι μοι τὸ θρέττε.

ΟΙΚΕΤΗΣ Β΄

πῶς ἂν οὖν ποτε

εἴποιμ᾽ ἂν αὐτὸ δῆτα κομψευριπικῶς;

ΟΙΚΕΤΗΣ Α΄

μή μοί γε, μή μοι, μὴ διασκανδικίσῃς·
20 ἀλλ᾽ εὑρέ τιν᾽ ἀπόκινον ἀπὸ τοῦ δεσπότου.

as a wind duet.

FIRST AND SECOND SLAVES
Hoo hoo hoo hoo hoo hoo.

FIRST SLAVE
Why are we standing here wailing? Shouldn't we be looking for some way out of this, instead of just sobbing on?

SECOND SLAVE
All right, what way? Do tell.

FIRST SLAVE
No, you tell me; I don't want to squabble about it.

SECOND SLAVE
Not me, by Apollo, no!

FIRST SLAVE
Come on, out with it; then I'll tell you.

SECOND SLAVE
"Could you but say for me what I must say!"[2]

FIRST SLAVE
But I haven't got an inkling.

SECOND SLAVE
All right, how can I possibly express it in smart Euripidean fashion?

FIRST SLAVE
Please don't, please don't, don't chervil me over![3] Just think of some kind of skidoo away from the master!

---

[2] = Euripides' *Hippolytus* 345 (Phaedra to the Nurse).

[3] For the reference to Euripides' mother see *Acharnians* 475-78.

ΟΙΚΕΤΗΣ Β΄
λέγε δὴ μο λω μεν ξυνεχὲς ὡδὶ ξυλλαβών.

ΟΙΚΕΤΗΣ Α΄
καὶ δὴ λέγω· μολωμεν.

ΟΙΚΕΤΗΣ Β΄
                                    ἐξόπισθέ νυν
αὖ το φάθι τοῦ μολωμεν.

ΟΙΚΕΤΗΣ Α΄
                    αὐτο.

ΟΙΚΕΤΗΣ Β΄
                                    πάνυ καλῶς.
ὥσπερ δεφόμενός νυν ἀτρέμα πρῶτον λέγε
25 τὸ μολωμεν, εἶτα δ᾽ αὐτο, κᾆτ᾽ ἐπάγων πυκνόν.

ΟΙΚΕΤΗΣ Α΄
μολωμεν αὐτομολωμεν αὐτομολῶμεν.

ΟΙΚΕΤΗΣ Β΄
                                            ἦν,
οὐχ ἡδύ;

ΟΙΚΕΤΗΣ Α΄
            νὴ Δία· πλήν γε περὶ τῷ δέρματι
δέδοικα τουτονὶ τὸν οἰωνόν.

ΟΙΚΕΤΗΣ Β΄
                            τί δαί;

ΟΙΚΕΤΗΣ Α΄
ὁτιὴ τὸ δέρμα δεφομένων ἀπέρχεται.

KNIGHTS

SECOND SLAVE

Very well, say "wall lets," and put it together like this.

FIRST SLAVE

All right, "wallets."

SECOND SLAVE

Now, next after "wallets" say "go way."

FIRST SLAVE

"Go way."

SECOND SLAVE

Very good! Now, as if you were masturbating, slowly say "wallets" first, then "go way," and then start speeding it up fast.

FIRST SLAVE

Wallets, go way, wallets go way, lets go AWOL!

SECOND SLAVE

There, wasn't that nice?

FIRST SLAVE

Zeus yes, except I'm afraid this doesn't bode well for my skin.

SECOND SLAVE

How so?

FIRST SLAVE

Because masturbators get their skins peeled off.

ΟΙΚΕΤΗΣ Β΄

30 κράτιστα τοίνυν τῶν παρόντων ἐστὶ νῷν,
θεῶν ἰόντε προσπεσεῖν του πρὸς βρέτας.

ΟΙΚΕΤΗΣ Α΄

ποῖον βρετέτετας; ἐτεὸν ἡγεῖ γὰρ θεούς;

ΟΙΚΕΤΗΣ Β΄

ἔγωγε.

ΟΙΚΕΤΗΣ Α΄

ποίῳ χρώμενος τεκμηρίῳ;

ΟΙΚΕΤΗΣ Β΄

ὁτιὴ θεοῖσιν ἐχθρός εἰμ᾽. οὐκ εἰκότως;

ΟΙΚΕΤΗΣ Α΄

35 εὖ προσβιβάζεις μ᾽. ἀλλ᾽ ἕτερά πη σκεπτέον.
βούλει τὸ πρᾶγμα τοῖς θεαταῖσιν φράσω;

ΟΙΚΕΤΗΣ Β΄

οὐ χεῖρον· ἓν δ᾽ αὐτοὺς παραιτησώμεθα,
ἐπίδηλον ἡμῖν τοῖς προσώποισιν ποιεῖν,
ἢν τοῖς ἔπεσι χαίρωσι καὶ τοῖς πράγμασιν.

ΟΙΚΕΤΗΣ Α΄

40 λέγοιμ᾽ ἂν ἤδη. νῷν γάρ ἐστι δεσπότης
ἄγροικος ὀργήν, κυαμοτρώξ, ἀκράχολος,
Δῆμος Πυκνίτης, δύσκολον γερόντιον
ὑπόκωφον. οὗτος τῇ προτέρᾳ νουμηνίᾳ
ἐπρίατο δοῦλον βυρσοδέψην Παφλαγόνα
45 πανουργότατον καὶ διαβολώτατόν τινα.
οὗτος καταγνοὺς τοῦ γέροντος τοὺς τρόπους,

234

SECOND SLAVE

Well then, our best option is to make for some god's image and kowtow.

FIRST SLAVE

What do you mean, "immmage?" Say, do you really believe in the gods?

SECOND SLAVE

Sure.

FIRST SLAVE

What's your evidence?

SECOND SLAVE

Because I'm godforsaken. Isn't that enough?

FIRST SLAVE

You've certainly convinced me. But we've got to consider something else. Would you like me to explain the situation to the spectators?

SECOND SLAVE

Not a bad idea. But let's ask them one favor: to make it obvious to us by their expressions whether they're enjoying our dialogue and action.

FIRST SLAVE

Now I'll tell them. We two have a master with a farmer's temperament, a bean chewer, prickly in the extreme, known as Mr. Demos of Pnyx Hill,[4] a cranky, half-deaf little codger. Last market day he bought a slave, Paphlagon, a tanner, an arch criminal, and a slanderer. He sized up the old man's character, this rawhide Paphlagon did, so

---

[4] Where the Athenian Assembly met.

ὁ βυρσοπαφλαγών, ὑποπεσὼν τὸν δεσπότην
ἤκαλλ᾽, ἐθώπευ᾽, ἐκολάκευ᾽, ἐξηπάτα
κοσκυλματίοις ἄκροισι, τοιαυτὶ λέγων·
50 "ὦ Δῆμε, λοῦσαι πρῶτον ἐκδικάσας μίαν,
ἐνθοῦ, ῥόφησον, ἔντραγ᾽, ἔχε τριώβολον.
βούλει παραθῶ σοι δόρπον;" εἶτ᾽ ἀναρπάσας
ὅ τι ἄν τις ἡμῶν σκευάσῃ τῷ δεσπότῃ
Παφλαγὼν κεχάρισται τοῦτο. καὶ πρώην γ᾽ ἐμοῦ
55 μᾶζαν μεμαχότος ἐν Πύλῳ Λακωνικήν,
πανουργότατά πως παραδραμὼν ὑφαρπάσας
αὐτὸς παρέθηκε τὴν ὑπ᾽ ἐμοῦ μεμαγμένην.
ἡμᾶς δ᾽ ἀπελαύνει κοὐκ ἐᾷ τὸν δεσπότην
ἄλλον θεραπεύειν, ἀλλὰ βυρσίνην ἔχων
60 δειπνοῦντος ἑστὼς ἀποσοβεῖ τοὺς ῥήτορας.
ᾄδει δὲ χρησμούς· ὁ δὲ γέρων σιβυλλιᾷ.
ὁ δ᾽ αὐτὸν ὡς ὁρᾷ μεμακκοακότα,
τέχνην πεποίηται· τοὺς γὰρ ἔνδον ἄντικρυς
ψευδῆ διαβάλλει· κᾆτα μαστιγούμεθα
65 ἡμεῖς· Παφλαγὼν δὲ περιθέων τοὺς οἰκέτας
αἰτεῖ, ταράττει, δωροδοκεῖ λέγων τάδε·
"ὁρᾶτε τὸν Ὕλαν δι᾽ ἐμὲ μαστιγούμενον;
εἰ μή μ᾽ ἀναπείσετ᾽, ἀποθανεῖσθε τήμερον."
ἡμεῖς δὲ δίδομεν· εἰ δὲ μή, πατούμενοι
70 ὑπὸ τοῦ γέροντος ὀκταπλάσιον χέζομεν.
νῦν οὖν ἀνύσαντε φροντίσωμεν, ὦγαθέ,
ποίαν ὁδὸν νὼ τρεπτέον καὶ πρὸς τίνα.

he crouched before the master and started flattering and
fawning and toadying and swindling him with odd tidbits
of waste leather, saying things like, "Mr. Demos, do have
your bath as soon as you've tried only one case."—"Here's
something to nibble, wolf down, savor: a 3-obol piece."[5]—
"Shall I serve you a snack?" And then Paphlagon swipes
whatever any of the rest of us has prepared and presents it
to the master. Why, just the other day I whipped up a
Spartan cake at Pylos,[6] and by some very dirty trick he
outmaneuvered me, snatched the cake, and served it up
himself—the one I'd whipped up! He shuts us out and
won't allow anyone else to court the master; no, when
master's having supper he stands by with a leather swatter
and bats away the politicians. And he chants oracles; the
old man's crazy about sibyls. And since he sees that the
master's a mooncalf, he's devised an artful technique: he
tells outright lies about the household staff; then we get
whippings, and Paphlagon chases after the servants, shak-
ing us down, shaking us up, demanding bribes, making
threats like, "See how I got Hylas that whipping? You'd
better be reasonable or you've lived your last day!" And we
pay the price, because if we don't, the master will pound
on us till we shit out eight times as much. (to Second Slave)
So now, my friend, let's figure out quickly what path to take,
and to whom.

[5] The juryman's daily payment, recently raised from 2 to 3
obols on Cleon's motion.
[6] See Introductory Note.

ΟΙΚΕΤΗΣ Β΄

κράτιστ᾽ ἐκείνην τὴν μολωμεν, ὦγαθέ.

ΟΙΚΕΤΗΣ Α΄

ἀλλ᾽ οὐχ οἷόν τε τὸν Παφλαγόν᾽ οὐδὲν λαθεῖν·
75 ἐφορᾷ γὰρ οὗτος πάντ᾽. ἔχει γὰρ τὸ σκέλος
τὸ μὲν ἐν Πύλῳ, τὸ δ᾽ ἕτερον ἐν τἠκκλησίᾳ.
τοσόνδε δ᾽ αὐτοῦ βῆμα διαβεβηκότος
ὁ πρωκτός ἐστιν αὐτόχρημ᾽ ἐν Χάοσιν,
τὼ χεῖρ᾽ ἐν Αἰτωλοῖς, ὁ νοῦς δ᾽ ἐν Κλωπιδῶν.

ΟΙΚΕΤΗΣ Β΄

κράτιστον οὖν νῷν ἀποθανεῖν.

ΟΙΚΕΤΗΣ Α΄

80   ἀλλὰ σκόπει,
ὅπως ἂν ἀποθάνωμεν ἀνδρικώτατα.

ΟΙΚΕΤΗΣ Β΄

πῶς δῆτα, πῶς γένοιτ᾽ ἂν ἀνδρικώτατα;
βέλτιστον ἡμῖν αἷμα ταύρειον πιεῖν·
ὁ Θεμιστοκλέους γὰρ θάνατος αἱρετώτερος.

ΟΙΚΕΤΗΣ Α΄

85 μὰ Δί᾽ ἀλλ᾽ ἄκρατον οἶνον ἀγαθοῦ δαίμονος.
ἴσως γὰρ ἂν χρηστόν τι βουλευσαίμεθα.

ΟΙΚΕΤΗΣ Β΄

ἰδού γ᾽ ἄκρατον. περὶ ποτοῦ γοῦν ἐστί σοι.
πῶς δ᾽ ἂν μεθύων χρηστόν τι βουλεύσαιτ᾽ ἀνήρ;

ΟΙΚΕΤΗΣ Α΄

ἄληθες, οὗτος; κρουνοχυτρολήραιον εἶ.

KNIGHTS

SECOND SLAVE
Our best option, my friend, is that "go way."

FIRST SLAVE
But nothing can get past Paphlagon; he keeps an eye on everything. He's got one foot in Pylos, and the other in the Assembly. He's got his legs spread so far apart that his arsehole's smack dab over Buggerland, his hand's in Shake Downs, and his mind's on Crimea.

SECOND SLAVE
Then our best option is death.

FIRST SLAVE
Well, figure out what would be the most manly death for us.

SECOND SLAVE
Let's see then, what would be the most manly? Our best course is to drink bull's blood: we should choose the death Themistocles chose.[7]

FIRST SLAVE
God no, we should toast the Good Genie with neat wine instead! Maybe that way we might think up a good plan.

SECOND SLAVE
Listen to him, neat wine! You're always looking for an excuse to drink. But how could a tipsy person think up a good plan?

FIRST SLAVE
Oh, is that right? You babbling bucket of birchwater! How

[7] For this legend about Themistocles—the Athenian hero of the Persian Wars and architect of Athens' naval supremacy—see Sophocles fr. 178, Plutarch *Themistocles* 31, Diodorus 11.58.

90 οἶνον σὺ τολμᾷς εἰς ἐπίνοιαν λοιδορεῖν;
οἴνου γὰρ εὕροις ἄν τι πρακτικώτερον;
ὁρᾷς, ὅταν πίνωσιν ἄνθρωποι, τότε
πλουτοῦσι, διαπράττουσι, νικῶσιν δίκας,
εὐδαιμονοῦσιν, ὠφελοῦσι τοὺς φίλους.
95 ἀλλ᾽ ἐξένεγκέ μοι ταχέως οἴνου χοᾶ,
τὸν νοῦν ἵν᾽ ἄρδω καὶ λέγω τι δεξιόν.

ΟΙΚΕΤΗΣ Β΄
οἴμοι, τί ποθ᾽ ἡμᾶς ἐργάσει τῷ σῷ ποτῷ;

ΟΙΚΕΤΗΣ Α΄
ἀγάθ᾽· ἀλλ᾽ ἔνεγκ᾽· ἐγὼ δὲ κατακλινήσομαι.
ἢν γὰρ μεθυσθῶ, πάντα ταυτὶ καταπάσω
100 βουλευματίων καὶ γνωμιδίων καὶ νοιδίων.

ΟΙΚΕΤΗΣ Β΄
ὡς εὐτυχῶς ὅτι οὐκ ἐλήφθην ἔνδοθεν
κλέπτων τὸν οἶνον.

ΟΙΚΕΤΗΣ Α΄
εἰπέ μοι, Παφλαγών τί δρᾷ;

ΟΙΚΕΤΗΣ Β΄
ἐπίπαστα λείξας δημιόπραθ᾽ ὁ βάσκανος
ῥέγκει μεθύων ἐν ταῖσι βύρσαις ὕπτιος.

ΟΙΚΕΤΗΣ Α΄
105 ἴθι νυν, ἄκρατον ἐγκάναξόν μοι πολὺν
σπονδήν.

ΟΙΚΕΤΗΣ Β΄
λαβὲ δὴ καὶ σπεῖσον ἀγαθοῦ δαίμονος.

dare you cast aspersions on the creative power of wine?
Can you come up with anything more effective? Don't you
see, it's when people drink that they get rich, they're suc-
cessful, they win lawsuits, they're happy, they can help
their friends. So quick, go in and fetch me a jug of wine; I
want to water my wit and come up with something smart.

SECOND SLAVE

Oh dear, what are you and your drink going to get us into?

FIRST SLAVE

A good spot! Now go in and get it. (*first Slave goes inside*)
I'm going to stretch out on the ground, because if I get
drunk I'm going to sprinkle everything with bits of plans,
thoughts, and ideas.

SECOND SLAVE

(*returning with a jug, a cup, and a garland*) It's a lucky
thing I wasn't caught swiping the wine from in there!

FIRST SLAVE

Say, what's Paphlagon doing?

SECOND SLAVE

That devil's been licking the sauce off confiscated goodies,
and now he's belly-up drunk on his hides, snoring away.

FIRST SLAVE

Come on then, slosh me the wine neat, a double libation.

SECOND SLAVE

Here you are; now pour one for the Good Genie.

ARISTOPHANES

ΟΙΚΕΤΗΣ Α'
ἕλχ', ἕλκε τὴν τοῦ δαίμονος τοῦ Πραμνίου.
ὦ δαῖμον ἀγαθέ, σὸν τὸ βούλευμ', οὐκ ἐμόν.

ΟΙΚΕΤΗΣ Β'
εἴπ', ἀντιβολῶ, τί ἐστι;

ΟΙΚΕΤΗΣ Α'
τοὺς χρησμοὺς ταχὺ
110 κλέψας ἔνεγκε τοῦ Παφλαγόνος ἔνδοθεν,
ἕως καθεύδει.

ΟΙΚΕΤΗΣ Β'
ταῦτ'. ἀτὰρ τοῦ δαίμονος
δέδοιχ' ὅπως μὴ τεύξομαι κακοδαίμονος.

ΟΙΚΕΤΗΣ Α'
φέρε νυν, ἐγὼ 'μαυτῷ προσαγάγω τὸν χοᾶ,
τὸν νοῦν ἵν' ἄρδω καὶ λέγω τι δεξιόν.

ΟΙΚΕΤΗΣ Β'
115 ὡς μεγάλ' ὁ Παφλαγὼν πέρδεται καὶ ῥέγκεται,
ὥστ' ἔλαθον αὐτὸν τὸν ἱερὸν χρησμὸν λαβών,
ὅνπερ μάλιστ' ἐφύλαττεν.

ΟΙΚΕΤΗΣ Α'
ὦ σοφώτατε.
φέρ' αὐτόν, ἵν' ἀναγνῶ· σὺ δ' ἔγχεον πιεῖν
ἀνύσας τι. φέρ' ἴδω, τί ἄρ' ἔνεστιν αὐτόθι;
120 ὦ λόγια. δός μοι, δὸς τὸ ποτήριον ταχύ.

ΟΙΚΕΤΗΣ Β'
ἰδού. τί φησ' ὁ χρησμός;

242

FIRST SLAVE

Down the hatch, down goes the libation for the Pramnian Genie![8] Ah, Good Genie, that idea's yours, not mine!

SECOND SLAVE

Tell me, please, what idea?

FIRST SLAVE

Quick, go steal Paphlagon's oracles and bring them out here while he's still asleep.

SECOND SLAVE

(*going inside*) OK, but I'm afraid I may transform our Genie from Good to Bad.

FIRST SLAVE

Well then, I'll just pass myself the jug, to water my wit and come up with something smart.

SECOND SLAVE

(*returning with a scroll*) Paphlagon's snoring and farting so loud, he didn't notice when I grabbed his holy oracle, the one he most closely guarded.

FIRST SLAVE

You're a genius! Give it here, so I can read it. And you hurry up and pour me a drink. Let's see, what's in here? What prophecies! Give me the cup, give it here quickly!

SECOND SLAVE

Here. What's the oracle say?

[8] Pramnian wine was a fine, strong red.

ΟΙΚΕΤΗΣ Α´
ἑτέραν ἔγχεον.

ΟΙΚΕΤΗΣ Β´
ἐν τοῖς λογίοις ἔνεστιν "ἑτέραν ἔγχεον;"

ΟΙΚΕΤΗΣ Α´
ὦ Βάκι.

ΟΙΚΕΤΗΣ Β´
τί ἐστι;

ΟΙΚΕΤΗΣ Α´
δὸς τὸ ποτήριον ταχύ.

ΟΙΚΕΤΗΣ Β´
πολλῷ γ᾽ ὁ Βάκις ἐχρῆτο τῷ ποτηρίῳ.

ΟΙΚΕΤΗΣ Α´
125   ὦ μιαρὲ Παφλαγών, ταῦτ᾽ ἄρ᾽ ἐφυλάττου πάλαι,
τὸν περὶ σεαυτοῦ χρησμὸν ὀρρωδῶν.

ΟΙΚΕΤΗΣ Β´
τιή;

ΟΙΚΕΤΗΣ Α´
ἐνταῦθ᾽ ἔνεστιν, αὐτὸς ὡς ἀπόλλυται.

ΟΙΚΕΤΗΣ Β´
καὶ πῶς;

ΟΙΚΕΤΗΣ Α´
ὅπως; ὁ χρησμὸς ἄντικρυς λέγει

FIRST SLAVE

Pour me a refill!

SECOND SLAVE

The prophecies say "pour me a refill"?

FIRST SLAVE

Oh Bacis![9]

SECOND SLAVE

What is it?

FIRST SLAVE

Quick, give me the cup!

SECOND SLAVE

Bacis certainly made use of that cup!

FIRST SLAVE

Paphlagon, you scum! So that's why you were so watchful all that time: you were shitting in your pants about the oracle concerning yourself!

SECOND SLAVE

Why?

FIRST SLAVE

Herein lies the secret of his own destruction!

SECOND SLAVE

Well? How?

FIRST SLAVE

How? The oracle explicitly says that first there arises a

---

[9] The legendary author of oracles that were compiled into books and enjoyed great popular esteem.

ὡς πρῶτα μὲν στυππειοπώλης γίγνεται,
130 ὃς πρῶτος ἕξει τῆς πόλεως τὰ πράγματα.

ΟΙΚΕΤΗΣ Βʹ
εἷς οὑτοσὶ πώλης. τί τοὐντεῦθεν; λέγε.

ΟΙΚΕΤΗΣ Αʹ
μετὰ τοῦτον αὖθις προβατοπώλης δεύτερος.

ΟΙΚΕΤΗΣ Βʹ
δύο τώδε πώλα. καὶ τί τόνδε χρὴ παθεῖν;

ΟΙΚΕΤΗΣ Αʹ
κρατεῖν, ἕως ἕτερος ἀνὴρ βδελυρώτερος
135 αὐτοῦ γένοιτο· μετὰ δὲ ταῦτ᾽ ἀπόλλυται.
ἐπιγίγνεται γὰρ βυρσοπώλης ὁ Παφλαγών,
ἅρπαξ, κεκράκτης, Κυκλοβόρου φωνὴν ἔχων.

ΟΙΚΕΤΗΣ Βʹ
τὸν προβατοπώλην ἦν ἄρ᾽ ἀπολέσθαι χρεὼν
ὑπὸ βυρσοπώλου;

ΟΙΚΕΤΗΣ Αʹ
νὴ Δί᾽.

ΟΙΚΕΤΗΣ Βʹ
οἴμοι δείλαιος.
140 πόθεν οὖν ἂν ἔτι γένοιτο πώλης εἷς μόνος;

ΟΙΚΕΤΗΣ Αʹ
ἔτ᾽ ἔστιν εἷς ὑπερφυᾶ τέχνην ἔχων.

ΟΙΚΕΤΗΣ Βʹ
εἴπ᾽, ἀντιβολῶ, τίς ἐστιν;

hemp seller,[10] who will be the first to manage the city's affairs.

SECOND SLAVE

That's one seller. What's next? Tell me!

FIRST SLAVE

After him there's another one again, a sheep seller.[11]

SECOND SLAVE

That makes a pair of sellers. And what's in store for him?

FIRST SLAVE

To hold power, until another champion arises who's more disgusting than he, whereupon he perishes. For his successor is a hide seller, our Paphlagon, a robber, a screamer with a voice like the Cycloborus in spate.

SECOND SLAVE

So the sheep seller was fated to perish at the hands of a hide seller?

FIRST SLAVE

That's right.

SECOND SLAVE

Heaven save us! I wish that just one more seller would appear from somewhere!

FIRST SLAVE

There *is* one still to come, with an extraordinary trade.

SECOND SLAVE

Tell me, please, who is it?

10 I.e. Eucrates of Melite, who had been a general in 432/1 and went on to have a long political career.

11 I.e. Lysicles, who lived with Aspasia after Pericles' death and fell in battle in 428.

ARISTOPHANES

ΟΙΚΕΤΗΣ Α΄

εἴπω;

ΟΙΚΕΤΗΣ Β΄

νὴ Δία.

ΟΙΚΕΤΗΣ Α΄

ἀλλαντοπώλης ἔσθ᾽ ὁ τοῦτον ἐξολῶν.

ΟΙΚΕΤΗΣ Β΄

ἀλλαντοπώλης; ὦ Πόσειδον, τῆς τέχνης.

145 φέρε, ποῦ τὸν ἄνδρα τοῦτον ἐξευρήσομεν;

ΟΙΚΕΤΗΣ Α΄

ζητῶμεν αὐτόν.

ΟΙΚΕΤΗΣ Β΄

ἀλλ᾽ ὁδὶ προσέρχεται

ὥσπερ κατὰ θεῖον εἰς ἀγοράν.

ΟΙΚΕΤΗΣ Α΄

ὦ μακάριε

ἀλλαντοπῶλα, δεῦρο δεῦρ᾽, ὦ φίλτατε,

ἀνάβαινε σωτὴρ τῇ πόλει καὶ νῷν φανείς.

ΑΛΛΑΝΤΟΠΩΛΗΣ

τί ἐστι; τί με καλεῖτε;

ΟΙΚΕΤΗΣ Α΄

150 δεῦρ᾽ ἔλθ᾽, ἵνα πύθῃ

ὡς εὐτυχὴς εἶ καὶ μεγάλως εὐδαιμονεῖς.

---

143 ἐξολῶν M y v.l. S^λΣΘ: ἐξελῶν R² λΣR

248

FIRST SLAVE

You want me to tell you?

SECOND SLAVE

Certainly!

FIRST SLAVE

The man who shall destroy Paphlagon is a sausage seller.

SECOND SLAVE

A sausage seller! Holy Poseidon, what a trade! Come on, where do we find this man?

FIRST SLAVE

Let's look for him!

SECOND SLAVE

Wait, here he is going to market, as if by providence!

Enter SAUSAGE SELLER carrying his table and paraphernalia.

FIRST SLAVE

Oh blessed sausage seller, step this way, this way, dear fellow, the city's revealed savior, and ours!

SAUSAGE SELLER

What is it? Why are you hailing me?

FIRST SLAVE

Come over here and find out how fortunate you are, how greatly blessed.

ARISTOPHANES

OIKETHΣ B′

ἴθι δή, κάθελ᾽ αὑτοῦ τοὐλεὸν καὶ τοῦ θεοῦ
τὸν χρησμὸν ἀναδίδαξον αὐτὸν ὡς ἔχει·
ἐγὼ δ᾽ ἰὼν προσκέψομαι τὸν Παφλαγόνα.

OIKETHΣ A′

155 ἄγε δὴ σὺ κατάθου πρῶτα τὰ σκεύη χαμαί·
ἔπειτα τὴν γῆν πρόσκυσον καὶ τοὺς θεούς.

ΑΛΛΑΝΤΟΠΩΛΗΣ

ἰδού· τί ἐστιν;

OIKETHΣ A′

ὦ μακάρι᾽, ὦ πλούσιε,
ὦ νῦν μὲν οὐδείς, αὔριον δ᾽ ὑπέρμεγας,
ὦ τῶν Ἀθηνῶν ταγὲ τῶν εὐδαιμόνων.

ΑΛΛΑΝΤΟΠΩΛΗΣ

160 τί μ᾽, ὦγάθ᾽, οὐ πλύνειν ἐᾷς τὰς κοιλίας
πωλεῖν τε τοὺς ἀλλᾶντας, ἀλλὰ καταγελᾷς;

OIKETHΣ A′

ὦ μῶρε, ποίας κοιλίας; δευρὶ βλέπε.
τὰς στίχας ὁρᾷς τὰς τῶνδε τῶν λαῶν;

ΑΛΛΑΝΤΟΠΩΛΗΣ

ὁρῶ.

OIKETHΣ A′

τούτων ἁπάντων αὐτὸς ἀρχέλας ἔσει,
165 καὶ τῆς ἀγορᾶς καὶ τῶν λιμένων καὶ τῆς πυκνός·
βουλὴν πατήσεις καὶ στρατηγοὺς κλαστάσεις,

KNIGHTS

SECOND SLAVE

All right then, take his table off him and brief him on the gist of the god's oracle; I'll go in and keep Paphlagon under surveillance.

SECOND SLAVE goes inside.

FIRST SLAVE

Now then, first put down that gear of yours, then kowtow to the earth and the gods.

SAUSAGE SELLER

Very well; what's it all about?

FIRST SLAVE

You're lucky! You're rich! You're nothing now, but tomorrow supremely great! You're the captain of flourishing Athens!

SAUSAGE SELLER

Look, mister, why don't you let me soak my tripe and hawk my sausages, instead of making fun of me?

FIRST SLAVE

Tripe, you idiot? Look out there: do you see the ranks of this assembled host?

SAUSAGE SELLER

Sure I do.

FIRST SLAVE

You're going to be top dog of them all, of the market, the harbors, and the Pnyx! You'll trample the Council, dock the generals, put people in chains and lock them up, suck cocks

δήσεις, φυλάξεις, ἐν πρυτανείῳ λαικάσεις.

ΑΛΛΑΝΤΟΠΩΛΗΣ

ἐγώ;

ΟΙΚΕΤΗΣ Α'

σὺ μέντοι· κοὐδέπω γε πάνθ' ὁρᾷς.
ἀλλ' ἐπανάβηθι κἀπὶ τοὐλεὸν τοδὶ
170 καὶ κάτιδε τὰς νήσους ἁπάσας ἐν κύκλῳ.

ΑΛΛΑΝΤΟΠΩΛΗΣ

καθορῶ.

ΟΙΚΕΤΗΣ Α'

τί δαί; τἀμπόρια καὶ τὰς ὁλκάδας;

ΑΛΛΑΝΤΟΠΩΛΗΣ

ἔγωγε.

ΟΙΚΕΤΗΣ Α'

πῶς οὖν οὐ μεγάλως εὐδαιμονεῖς;
ἔτι νυν τὸν ὀφθαλμὸν παράβαλλ' εἰς Καρίαν
τὸν δεξιόν, τὸν δ' ἕτερον εἰς Καρχηδόνα.

ΑΛΛΑΝΤΟΠΩΛΗΣ

175 εὐδαιμονήσω γ', εἰ διαστραφήσομαι.

ΟΙΚΕΤΗΣ Α'

οὔκ, ἀλλὰ διὰ σοῦ ταῦτα πάντα πέρναται·
γίγνει γάρ, ὡς ὁ χρησμὸς οὑτοσὶ λέγει,
ἀνὴρ μέγιστος.

ΑΛΛΑΝΤΟΠΩΛΗΣ

εἰπέ μοι, καὶ πῶς ἐγὼ
ἀλλαντοπώλης ὢν ἀνὴρ γενήσομαι;

in the Prytaneum![12]

SAUSAGE SELLER

Me?

FIRST SLAVE

Yes, you! And that's not all. Here, climb higher up, on this table, and survey the islands all around.

SAUSAGE SELLER

I see them.

FIRST SLAVE

What else? Ports and cargo ships?

SAUSAGE SELLER

Sure.

FIRST SLAVE

Then how can you deny that you're flourishing? Here then, swivel your right eye toward Caria and the other one toward Carthage.

SAUSAGE SELLER

I'll really flourish if I swivel myself wall-eyed!

FIRST SLAVE

No, the point is that all this is yours to buy and sell! You're going to be a tremendous big shot; this oracle here says so.

SAUSAGE SELLER

Tell me, just how does a sausage seller like me become a big shot?

---

[12] See *Acharnians* 125 n. For his success at Pylos the people had awarded Cleon privileges there for life.

---

174 Καλχηδόνα Σ^Θ cf. 1303

ARISTOPHANES

ΟΙΚΕΤΗΣ Α΄

180 δι' αὐτὸ γάρ τοι τοῦτο καὶ γίγνει μέγας,
ὁτιὴ πονηρὸς κἀξ ἀγορᾶς εἶ καὶ θρασύς.

ΑΛΛΑΝΤΟΠΩΛΗΣ

οὐκ ἀξιῶ 'γὼ 'μαυτὸν ἰσχύειν μέγα.

ΟΙΚΕΤΗΣ Α΄

οἴμοι, τί ποτ' ἔσθ' ὅτι σαυτὸν οὐ φὴς ἄξιον;
ξυνειδέναι τί μοι δοκεῖς σαυτῷ καλόν.
μῶν ἐκ καλῶν εἶ κἀγαθῶν;

ΑΛΛΑΝΤΟΠΩΛΗΣ

185   μὰ τοὺς θεούς,
εἰ μὴ 'κ πονηρῶν γ'.

ΟΙΚΕΤΗΣ Α΄

                    ὦ μακάριε τῆς τύχης,
ὅσον πέπονθας ἀγαθὸν εἰς τὰ πράγματα.

ΑΛΛΑΝΤΟΠΩΛΗΣ

ἀλλ', ὦγάθ', οὐδὲ μουσικὴν ἐπίσταμαι
πλὴν γραμμάτων, καὶ ταῦτα μέντοι κακὰ κακῶς.

ΟΙΚΕΤΗΣ Α΄

190 τουτὶ μόνον σ' ἔβλαψεν, ὅτι καὶ κακὰ κακῶς.
ἡ δημαγωγία γὰρ οὐ πρὸς μουσικοῦ
ἔτ' ἐστὶν ἀνδρὸς οὐδὲ χρηστοῦ τοὺς τρόπους,
ἀλλ' εἰς ἀμαθῆ καὶ βδελυρόν. ἀλλὰ μὴ παρῇς
ἅ σοι διδόασ' ἐν τοῖς λογίοισιν οἱ θεοί.

ΑΛΛΑΝΤΟΠΩΛΗΣ

πῶς δῆτά φησ' ὁ χρησμός;

FIRST SLAVE

That's precisely why you are going to be great, because you're loudmouthed, low class and down market.

SAUSAGE SELLER

Even I don't think I deserve great power.

FIRST SLAVE

Uh oh, what makes you say you don't deserve it? You sound as though you've got something good on your conscience. Don't tell me you come from a distinguished family!

SAUSAGE SELLER

Heavens no, they're nothing if not low class.

FIRST SLAVE

Congratulations, what blessed luck! Right there you've got a fine start in politics.

SAUSAGE SELLER

Look, mister, I'm uneducated except for reading and writing, and I'm damn poor even at those.

FIRST SLAVE

The only thing that hurts you there is that you're only damn poor. No, political leadership's no longer a job for a man of education and good character, but for the ignorant and disgusting. Please don't throw away what the gods are offering you in their prophecies!

SAUSAGE SELLER

What does the oracle say, then?

ΟΙΚΕΤΗΣ Α'

195   εὖ νὴ τοὺς θεοὺς
καὶ ποικίλως πως καὶ σοφῶς ᾐνιγμένος·
ἀλλ᾽ ὁπόταν μάρψῃ βυρσαίετος ἀγκυλοχήλης
γαμφηλῇσι δράκοντα κοάλεμον αἱματοπώτην,
δὴ τότε Παφλαγόνων μὲν ἀπόλλυται ἡ σκοροδάλμη,
200 κοιλιοπώλῃσιν δὲ θεὸς μέγα κῦδος ὀπάζει,
αἴ κεν μὴ πωλεῖν ἀλλᾶντας μᾶλλον ἕλωνται.

ΑΛΛΑΝΤΟΠΩΛΗΣ

πῶς οὖν πρὸς ἐμὲ ταῦτ᾽ ἐστίν; ἀναδίδασκέ με.

ΟΙΚΕΤΗΣ Α'

βυρσαίετος μὲν ὁ Παφλαγών ἐσθ᾽ οὑτοσί.

ΑΛΛΑΝΤΟΠΩΛΗΣ

τί δ᾽ ἀγκυλοχήλης ἐστίν;

ΟΙΚΕΤΗΣ Α'

                αὐτό που λέγει,
205 ὅτι ἀγκύλαις ταῖς χερσὶν ἁρπάζων φέρει.

ΑΛΛΑΝΤΟΠΩΛΗΣ

ὁ δράκων δὲ πρὸς τί;

ΟΙΚΕΤΗΣ Α'

                τοῦτο περιφανέστατον.
ὁ δράκων γάρ ἐστι μακρὸν ὅ τ᾽ ἀλλᾶς αὖ μακρόν·
εἶθ᾽ αἱματοπώτης ἐσθ᾽ ὅ τ᾽ ἀλλᾶς χὠ δράκων.
τὸν οὖν δράκοντά φησι τὸν βυρσαίετον
210 ἤδη κρατήσειν, αἴ κε μὴ θαλφθῇ λόγοις.

FIRST SLAVE

By heaven it's a good one, rather intricate and subtly enigmatic:

> "Yea, when the crook-taloned rawhide eagle shall
>   snatch
> in its beak the dimwitted blood-guzzling serpent,
> even then shall perish the garlic breath of the
>   Paphlagons,
> while to tripe sellers the god grants great glory,
> unless they choose rather to sell sausages."

SAUSAGE SELLER

Well, how does this apply to me? Clue me in.

FIRST SLAVE

(*pointing to Cleon among the spectators*) This Paphlagon here is the rawhide eagle.

SAUSAGE SELLER

And what's crook-taloned?

FIRST SLAVE

That's pretty self-explanatory: with crooked hands he snatches and takes.

SAUSAGE SELLER

And what about the serpent?

FIRST SLAVE

That's quite obvious: the serpent's long, and so is a sausage; and both sausage and serpent are blood guzzlers. So the oracle says that the serpent will soon overpower the rawhide eagle, if he isn't melted by verbiage.

ARISTOPHANES

ΑΛΛΑΝΤΟΠΩΛΗΣ

τὰ μὲν λόγι᾽ αἰκάλλει με· θαυμάζω δ᾽ ὅπως
τὸν δῆμον οἷός τ᾽ ἐπιτροπεύειν εἴμ᾽ ἐγώ.

ΟΙΚΕΤΗΣ Α´

φαυλότατον ἔργον· ταῦθ᾽ ἅπερ ποιεῖς ποίει·
τάραττε καὶ χόρδευ᾽ ὁμοῦ τὰ πράγματα
215 ἅπαντα, καὶ τὸν δῆμον ἀεὶ προσποιοῦ
ὑπογλυκαίνων ῥηματίοις μαγειρικοῖς.
τὰ δ᾽ ἄλλα σοι πρόσεστι δημαγωγικά,
φωνὴ μιαρά, γέγονας κακῶς, ἀγοραῖος εἶ·
ἔχεις ἅπαντα πρὸς πολιτείαν ἃ δεῖ·
220 χρησμοί τε συμβαίνουσι καὶ τὸ Πυθικόν.
ἀλλὰ στεφανοῦ καὶ σπένδε τῷ Κοαλέμῳ·
χὤπως ἀμυνεῖ τὸν ἄνδρα.

ΑΛΛΑΝΤΟΠΩΛΗΣ

καὶ τίς ξύμμαχος
γενήσεταί μοι; καὶ γὰρ οἵ τε πλούσιοι
δεδίασιν αὐτὸν ὅ τε πένης βδύλλει λεώς.

ΟΙΚΕΤΗΣ Α´

225 ἀλλ᾽ εἰσὶν ἱππῆς ἄνδρες ἀγαθοὶ χίλιοι
μισοῦντες αὐτόν, οἳ βοηθήσουσί σοι,
καὶ τῶν πολιτῶν οἱ καλοί τε κἀγαθοί.
καὶ τῶν θεατῶν ὅστις ἐστὶ δεξιός,
κἀγὼ μετ᾽ αὐτῶν χὠ θεὸς ξυλλήψεται.
230 καὶ μὴ δέδιθ᾽· οὐ γάρ ἐστιν ἐξῃκασμένος·
ὑπὸ τοῦ δέους γὰρ αὐτὸν οὐδεὶς ἤθελεν
τῶν σκευοποιῶν εἰκάσαι. πάντως γε μὴν

SAUSAGE SELLER

The prophecies are flattering, but it's an amazing idea, me being fit to supervise the people.

FIRST SLAVE

Nothing's easier. Just keep doing what you're doing: make a hash of all their affairs and turn it into baloney, and always keep the people on your side by sweetening them with gourmet bons mots. You've got everything else a demagogue needs: a repulsive voice, low birth, marketplace morals—you've got all the ingredients for a political career. Plus, the oracles and Delphic Apollo agree. (*extending the cup and garland*) So put on this garland, pour a libation to the god Dimwit, and see that you settle our enemy's hash.

SAUSAGE SELLER

And just who will be my ally? He makes the rich tremble and the poor folk shit in their pants.

FIRST SLAVE

But there are the Knights, fine gentlemen a thousand strong, who detest him and will rally to your side, and all fine and upstanding citizens, and every smart spectator, and myself along with them, and the god will lend a hand too. And never fear, he's not portrayed to the life: none of the mask makers had the guts to make a portrait mask.

ARISTOPHANES

γνωσθήσεται· τὸ γὰρ θέατρον δεξιόν.

ΟΙΚΕΤΗΣ Β′

οἴμοι κακοδαίμων, ὁ Παφλαγὼν ἐξέρχεται.

ΠΑΦΛΑΓΩΝ

235 οὔτοι μὰ τοὺς δώδεκα θεοὺς χαιρήσετον,
ὁτιὴ ’πὶ τῷ δήμῳ ξυνόμνυτον πάλαι.
τουτὶ τί δρᾷ τὸ Χαλκιδικὸν ποτήριον;
οὐκ ἔσθ’ ὅπως οὐ Χαλκιδέας ἀφίστατον.
ἀπολεῖσθον, ἀποθανεῖσθον, ὦ μιαρωτάτω.

ΟΙΚΕΤΗΣ Α′

240 οὗτος, τί φεύγεις; οὐ μενεῖς; ὦ γεννάδα
ἀλλαντοπῶλα μὴ προδῷς τὰ πράγματα.

ἄνδρες ἱππῆς, παραγένεσθε· νῦν ὁ καιρός. ὦ Σίμων,
ὦ Παναίτι’, οὐκ ἐλᾶτε πρὸς τὸ δεξιὸν κέρας;
ἄνδρες ἐγγύς. ἀλλ’ ἀμύνου κἀπαναστρέφου πάλιν.
245 ὁ κονιορτὸς δῆλος αὐτῶν ὡς ὁμοῦ προσκειμένων.
ἀλλ’ ἀμύνου καὶ δίωκε καὶ τροπὴν αὐτοῦ ποιοῦ.

ΚΟΡΥΦΑΙΟΣ

παῖε παῖε τὸν πανοῦργον καὶ ταραξιππόστρατον

235–1252 Παφλαγών Dindorf: Κλέων z

13 Probably the Simon who wrote a treatise on horsemanship
(cf. Xenophon *On Horsemanship* 1.1) and/or the Simon of *In-
scriptiones Graecae* ii² 2343 (see the General Introduction), but
the name was not unusual.

He'll be recognized all the same, because the audience is smart.

SECOND SLAVE

(*within*) Heaven help me, Paphlagon's coming out!

Enter PAPHLAGON

PAPHLAGON

By the Twelve Gods, you two won't get away with your unending plots against the people! What's that Chalcidian cup doing here? It can only mean you're inciting the Chalcidians to revolt! You two are goners, done for, you utter scum!

SECOND SLAVE

Hey, why are you running away? Please stay! Worthy Sausage Seller, don't betray the cause!

Gentlemen of the cavalry, ride to our aid; now's the time!

Enter the CHORUS.

Simon,[13] Panaetius,[14] drive for the right wing! (*to the Sausage Seller*) Our troops are nearby. Now turn back around and put up a fight! The dust cloud's plain to see as they get closer, galloping to the fray. Come on, put up a fight! Chase him! Repulse him!

FIRST SLAVE and SAUSAGE SELLER join the attack.

CHORUS LEADER

Hit him, hit the scoundrel, the harrrier of the horse troops,

[14] Probably the Panaetius (or one of two men by that name) denounced in the scandals of 415; see Andocides 1.13.

καὶ τελώνην καὶ φάραγγα καὶ Χάρυβδιν ἁρπαγῆς,
καὶ πανοῦργον καὶ πανοῦργον· πολλάκις γὰρ αὖτ᾽
   ἐρῶ.
250 καὶ γὰρ οὗτος ἦν πανοῦργος πολλάκις τῆς ἡμέρας.
   ἀλλὰ παῖε καὶ δίωκε καὶ τάραττε καὶ κύκα
   καὶ βδελύττου, καὶ γὰρ ἡμεῖς, κἀπικείμενος βόα·
   εὐλαβοῦ δὲ μὴ ᾽κφύγῃ σε· καὶ γὰρ οἶδε τὰς ὁδούς,
   ἅσπερ Εὐκράτης ἔφευγεν εὐθὺ τῶν κυρηβίων.

ΠΑΦΛΑΓΩΝ

255 ὦ γέροντες ἡλιασταί, φράτερες τριωβόλου,
   οὓς ἐγὼ βόσκω κεκραγὼς καὶ δίκαια κἄδικα,
   παραβοηθεῖθ᾽, ὡς ὑπ᾽ ἀνδρῶν τύπτομαι ξυνωμοτῶν.

ΚΟΡΥΦΑΙΟΣ

ἐν δίκῃ γ᾽, ἐπεὶ τὰ κοινὰ πρὶν λαχεῖν κατεσθίεις,
   κἀποσυκάζεις πιέζων τοὺς ὑπευθύνους σκοπῶν
260 ὅστις αὐτῶν ὠμός ἐστιν ἢ πέπων ἢ μὴ πέπων.
264 καὶ σκοπεῖς γε τῶν πολιτῶν ὅστις ἐστὶν ἀμνοκῶν,
265 πλούσιος καὶ μὴ πονηρὸς καὶ τρέμων τὰ πράγματα.
261 κἄν τιν᾽ αὐτῶν γνῷς ἀπράγμον᾽ ὄντα καὶ κεχηνότα,
262 καταγαγὼν ἐκ Χερρονήσου, διαβαλὼν ἀγκυρίσας,
263 εἶτ᾽ ἀποστρέψας τὸν ὦμον αὐτὸν ἐνεκολήβασας.

ΠΑΦΛΑΓΩΝ

266 ξυνεπίκεισθ᾽ ὑμεῖς; ἐγὼ δ᾽, ἄνδρες, δι᾽ ὑμᾶς τύπ-
   τομαι,
   ὅτι λέγειν γνώμην ἔμελλον ὡς δίκαιον ἐν πόλει
   ἱστάναι μνημεῖον ὑμῶν ἐστιν ἀνδρείας χάριν.

264–5 post 260 transp. Brunck

262

the tax farmer, the chasm and Charybdis of rapacity, the scoundrel, the scoundrel! I'll keep calling him that, because he acts the scoundrel many times each day. Come on, hit him, pursue him, shake him up, mix him up, loathe him as we do, give out with a war cry as you attack him! Take care he doesn't get away; he knows the routes Eucrates took to decamp straight to the hemp market.

PAPHLAGON

Elders of the jury courts, brethren of the three obols,[15] whom I cater to by loud denunciations fair and foul, reinforce me: I'm being roughed up by enemy conspirators!

CHORUS LEADER

And rightly so, since you gobble public funds before you're allotted an office; and like a fig picker you squeeze magistrates under review, looking to see which of them is raw, which ripe and unripe; yes, and what's more, you scan the citizenry for anyone who's an innocent lamb, rich and innocuous and afraid of litigation. And if you hear of anyone who's apolitical and naive, you drag him back from the Chersonnese,[16] trip him up with your slanders, then twist his shoulder back and stomp him.

PAPHLAGON

Are you Knights joining the attack on me? But gentlemen, it's on your behalf that I'm being beaten: I was just about to move a decree declaring it right and proper to erect a monument in honor of your courage!

[15] See 51 n.
[16] The Gallipoli Peninsula, where many Athenian settlers and grain merchants resided.

ARISTOPHANES

ΚΟΡΥΦΑΙΟΣ

ὡς δ᾽ ἀλαζών, ὡς δὲ μάσθλης. εἶδες οἷ᾽ ὑπέρχεται
270 ὡσπερεὶ γέροντας ἡμᾶς κἀκκοβαλικεύεται;
ἀλλ᾽ ἐὰν ταύτῃ ⟨τρέπηται⟩, ταυτηὶ πεπλήξεται·
ἢν δ᾽ ὑπεκκλίνῃ γε, δευρὶ πρὸς σκέλος κυρηβάσει.

ΠΑΦΛΑΓΩΝ

ὦ πόλις καὶ δῆμ᾽, ὑφ᾽ οἵων θηρίων γαστρίζομαι.

ΑΛΛΑΝΤΟΠΩΛΗΣ

καὶ κέκραγας, ὥσπερ ἀεὶ τὴν πόλιν καταστρέφει.

ΠΑΦΛΑΓΩΝ

275 ἀλλ᾽ ἐγώ σε τῇ βοῇ ταύτῃ γε πρῶτα τρέψομαι.

ΚΟΡΥΦΑΙΟΣ

ἀλλ᾽ ἐὰν μέντοι γε νικᾷς τῇ βοῇ, τήνελλά σοι·
ἢν δ᾽ ἀναιδείᾳ παρέλθῃ σ᾽, ἡμέτερος ὁ πυραμοῦς.

ΠΑΦΛΑΓΩΝ

τουτονὶ τὸν ἄνδρ᾽ ἐγὼ ᾽νδείκνυμι, καὶ φήμ᾽ ἐξάγειν
ταῖσι Πελοποννησίων τριήρεσι ζωμεύματα.

ΑΛΛΑΝΤΟΠΩΛΗΣ

280 ναὶ μὰ Δία κἄγωγε τοῦτον, ὅτι κενῇ τῇ κοιλίᾳ
εἰσδραμὼν εἰς τὸ πρυτανεῖον, εἶτα πάλιν ἐκθεῖ πλέᾳ.

ΟΙΚΕΤΗΣ Α᾽

νὴ Δί᾽, ἐξάγων γε τἀπόρρηθ᾽, ἅμ᾽ ἄρτον καὶ κρέας

271 ⟨τρέπηται⟩ Zacher: γε νικᾷ z

264

CHORUS LEADER

What a phony! Smooth as calfskin! Do you see how far he'll go to get round us and bamboozle us as if we were codgers? Well, if he tries to ‹escape› this way, he'll get hit with this; and if he tries to duck out that way, he'll butt against a leg!

PAPHLAGON

Ah, city! Ah, people! What sort of beasts are punching me in the guts?

SAUSAGE SELLER

There you go shouting, the same way you're always subjugating the city!

PAPHLAGON

Well, you're the first one I'm going to rout with that very shout!

CHORUS LEADER

Well, if you manage to beat him with your shouting, you're the man of the hour; but if he outdoes you in brazenness, we take the cake.

PAPHLAGON

I denounce this man here and accuse him of smuggling plank steaks[17] for Spartan triremes!

SAUSAGE SELLER

And I denounce this man, by Zeus, for running into the Prytaneum with an empty gut and running out again with a full one!

FIRST SLAVE

Damn right, and for smuggling out what he shouldn't—

[17] Punning on *zomeumata* (stew) and *hypozomata* (ship's ropes).

265

καὶ τέμαχος, οὗ Περικλέης οὐκ ἠξιώθη πώποτε.

ΠΑΦΛΑΓΩΝ
ἀποθανεῖσθον αὐτίκα μάλα.

ΑΛΛΑΝΤΟΠΩΛΗΣ
285 τριπλάσιον κεκράξομαί σου.

ΠΑΦΛΑΓΩΝ
καταβοήσομαι βοῶν σε.

ΑΛΛΑΝΤΟΠΩΛΗΣ
κατακεκράξομαί σε κράζων.

ΠΑΦΛΑΓΩΝ
διαβαλῶ σ᾽, ἐὰν στρατηγῇς.

ΑΛΛΑΝΤΟΠΩΛΗΣ
κυνοκοπήσω σου τὸ νῶτον.

ΠΑΦΛΑΓΩΝ
290 περιελῶ σ᾽ ἀλαζονείαις.

ΑΛΛΑΝΤΟΠΩΛΗΣ
ὑποτεμοῦμαι τὰς ὁδούς σου.

ΠΑΦΛΑΓΩΝ
βλέψον εἴς μ᾽ ἀσκαρδάμυκτον.

ΑΛΛΑΝΤΟΠΩΛΗΣ
ἐν ἀγορᾷ κἀγὼ τέθραμμαι.

ΠΑΦΛΑΓΩΝ
διαφορήσω σ᾽, εἴ τι γρύξει.

ΑΛΛΑΝΤΟΠΩΛΗΣ
295 κοπροφορήσω σ᾽, εἰ λαλήσεις.

bread, meat, a fish fillet—goodies that Pericles himself was never awarded.

PAPHLAGON
You two are dead meat now!

SAUSAGE SELLER
I'll shout three times as loud as you!

PAPHLAGON
I'll outbellow you with my bellowing!

SAUSAGE SELLER
I'll shout you down with my shouting!

PAPHLAGON
I'll slander you if become a general!

SAUSAGE SELLER
I'll beat your back like a dog's!

PAPHLAGON
I'll harass you with quackeries!

SAUSAGE SELLER
I'll cut off your escape routes!

PAPHLAGON
Look at me without blinking.

SAUSAGE SELLER
I was raised in the markets too!

PAPHLAGON
One peep from you and I'll rip you apart!

SAUSAGE SELLER
Any blather from you and I'll cart you off like a load of dung!

ΠΑΦΛΑΓΩΝ

ὁμολογῶ κλέπτειν· σὺ δ' οὐχί.

ΑΛΛΑΝΤΟΠΩΛΗΣ

νὴ τὸν Ἑρμῆν τὸν Ἀγοραῖον,
κἀπιορκῶ γε βλεπόντων.

ΠΑΦΛΑΓΩΝ

ἀλλότρια τοίνυν σοφίζει·
300 καὶ φανῶ σε τοῖς πρυτάνεσιν
ἀδεκατεύτους τῶν θεῶν ἱε–
ρὰς ἔχοντα κοιλίας.

ΧΟΡΟΣ

(στρ) ὦ μιαρὲ καὶ βδελυρὲ καὶ κατακεκρᾶκτα, τοῦ σοῦ
θράσους
305 πᾶσα μὲν γῆ πλέα, πᾶσα δ' ἐκκλησία,
καὶ τέλη καὶ γραφαὶ καὶ δικαστήρι', ὦ
βορβοροτάραξι καὶ τὴν πόλιν ἅπασαν ἡ–
310 μῶν ἀνατετυρβακώς,
ὅστις ἡμῶν τὰς Ἀθήνας ἐκκεκώφωκας βοῶν
κἀπὸ τῶν πετρῶν ἄνωθεν τοὺς φόρους θυννοσκοπῶν.

ΠΑΦΛΑΓΩΝ

οἶδ' ἐγὼ τὸ πρᾶγμα τοῦθ' ὅθεν πάλαι καττύεται.

ΑΛΛΑΝΤΟΠΩΛΗΣ

315 εἰ δὲ μὴ σύ γ' οἶσθα κάττυμ', οὐδ' ἐγὼ χορδεύματα,
ὅστις ὑποτέμνων ἐπώλεις δέρμα μοχθηροῦ βοὸς
τοῖς ἀγροίκοισιν πανούργως, ὥστε φαίνεσθαι παχύ,
καὶ πρὶν ἡμέραν φορῆσαι μεῖζον ἦν δυοῖν δοχμαῖν.

KNIGHTS

PAPHLAGON

I admit I'm a thief; you don't.

SAUSAGE SELLER

I do so, by Hermes of the Markets! And even when people
see me do it, I swear I didn't!

PAPHLAGON

Then you're stealing someone else's tricks! And I expose
you to the police for possession of sacred tripe belonging
to the gods, and with failure to pay the tithe on it.

CHORUS

You filthy disgusting shout-downer, your brazenness
fills the whole land, the whole Assembly,
the taxes, the indictments and lawcourts,
you muckraker, you who have thrown our whole city
into a sea of troubles,
who have deafened our Athens with your bellowing,
watching from the rocks like a tuna fisher for shoals
    of tribute!

PAPHLAGON

I know where this longterm conspiracy was cobbled up!

SAUSAGE SELLER

If you don't know cobbling, I don't know sausage making.
You're the one who used to slant-cut the hide of a low-
grade ox so it looked thick and sell it to the farmers at a
dishonest price; before they'd worn it a day, it was two
handbreadths wider!

---

[304] κατακεκρᾶκτα Hermann, cf. 287: κεκράκτα z: κράκτα
ΑΓΘ

ΟΙΚΕΤΗΣ Α΄

νὴ Δία κἀμὲ τοῦτ᾽ ἔδρασε ταὐτόν, ὥστε κατάγελων
320   πάμπολυν τοῖς δημόταισι καὶ φίλοις παρασχεθεῖν.
πρὶν γὰρ εἶναι Περγασῆσιν ἔνεον ἐν ταῖς ἐμβάσιν.

ΧΟΡΟΣ

ἆρα δῆτ᾽ οὐκ ἀπ᾽ ἀρχῆς ἐδήλους ἀναί-
325   δειαν, ἥπερ μόνη προστατεῖ ῥητόρων;
ἦ σὺ πιστεύων ἀμέργεις τῶν ξένων τοὺς καρπίμους,
πρῶτος ὤν· ὁ δ᾽ Ἱπποδάμου λείβεται θεώμενος.
ἀλλ᾽ ἐφάνη γὰρ ἀνὴρ ἕτερος πολὺ
σοῦ μιαρώτερος, ὥστε με χαίρειν,
330   ὅς σε παύσει καὶ πάρεισι, δῆλός ἐστιν αὐτόθεν,
πανουργίᾳ τε καὶ θράσει
καὶ κοβαλικεύμασιν.

ΚΟΡΥΦΑΙΟΣ

ἀλλ᾽ ὦ τραφεὶς ὅθενπέρ εἰσιν ἄνδρες οἵπερ εἰσίν,
νῦν δεῖξον ὡς οὐδὲν λέγει τὸ σωφρόνως τραφῆναι.

ΑΛΛΑΝΤΟΠΩΛΗΣ

335   καὶ μὴν ἀκούσαθ᾽ οἷός ἐστιν οὑτοσὶ πολίτης.

ΠΑΦΛΑΓΩΝ

οὔκουν μ᾽ ἐάσεις;

326 ἀμέργεις Bothe, cl. Σ: ἀμέλγει(ς) z

---

[18] Upper and Lower Pergase were two small demes about 8 miles north of Athens.

FIRST SLAVE

By Zeus, he pulled that one on me too! My friends and fellow demesmen got a big laugh at my expense when I started swimming in my shoes before we got as far as Pergase![18]

CHORUS

So then, didn't you from the very start display
Shamelessness, that sole bulwark of politicians?
Trusting in her, you pluck the most fruitful foreigners,
second to none, while Hippodamus' son can only
    look on and shed tears.[19]
Ah, but another man has shown up,
much slimier than you, I'm delighted to say,
one who from the word go is obviously going to
    stymie and outdo you
in villainy and brazennesss
and flimflammery!

CHORUS LEADER

(*to Sausage Seller*) Very well, since you were bred where men are what they are, show us now what nonsense a decent breeding is.

SAUSAGE SELLER

Sure! I'll tell you what sort of citizen this one is.

PAPHLAGON

So you won't let me speak first?

[19] The son of Hippodamus, the renowned city planner from Miletus, was Archeptolemus, who was granted Athenian citizenship and in 425 worked for a negotiated settlement of the war (see 794-96); in 411 he joined the oligarchic regime and was executed after it fell.

ΑΛΛΑΝΤΟΠΩΛΗΣ
μὰ Δί', ἐπεὶ κἀγὼ πονηρός εἰμι.

ΟΙΚΕΤΗΣ Α'
ἐὰν δὲ μὴ ταύτῃ γ' ὑπείκῃ, λέγ' ὅτι κὰκ πονηρῶν.

ΠΑΦΛΑΓΩΝ
οὐκ αὖ μ' ἐάσεις;

ΑΛΛΑΝΤΟΠΩΛΗΣ
μὰ Δία.

ΠΑΦΛΑΓΩΝ
ναὶ μὰ Δία.

ΑΛΛΑΝΤΟΠΩΛΗΣ
μὰ τὸν
Ποσειδῶ,
ἀλλ' αὐτὸ περὶ τοῦ πρότερος εἰπεῖν πρῶτα
διαμαχοῦμαι.

ΠΑΦΛΑΓΩΝ
οἴμοι, διαρραγήσομαι.

ΑΛΛΑΝΤΟΠΩΛΗΣ
340   καὶ μὴν ἐγὼ οὐ παρήσω.

ΟΙΚΕΤΗΣ Α'
πάρες πάρες πρὸς τῶν θεῶν αὐτῷ διαρραγῆναι.

ΠΑΦΛΑΓΩΝ
τῷ καὶ πεποιθὼς ἀξιοῖς ἐμοῦ λέγειν ἔναντα;

ΑΛΛΑΝΤΟΠΩΛΗΣ
ὁτιὴ λέγειν οἷός τε κἀγὼ καὶ καρυκοποιεῖν.

SAUSAGE SELLER

Certainly not, because I'm sleazy too.

FIRST SLAVE

And if that doesn't make him yield the floor, tell him your
ancestors were sleazy too.

PAPHLAGON

You still won't let me speak first?

SAUSAGE SELLER

Certainly not!

PAPHLAGON

Certainly yes!

SAUSAGE SELLER

By Poseidon, no! First to speak? I'll fight you for that here
and now!

PAPHLAGON

I'm going to burst my seams!

SAUSAGE SELLER

I said, I won't let you.

FIRST SLAVE

Good heavens, let him! Let him burst his seams!

PAPHLAGON

Just what makes you so sure you're fit to speak against me?

SAUSAGE SELLER

Because I can speak too, and make a stew of everything.

ARISTOPHANES

ΠΑΦΛΑΓΩΝ

ἰδοὺ λέγειν. καλῶς γ᾽ ἂν οὖν σὺ πρᾶγμα
προσπεσόν σοι
345 ὠμοσπάρακτον παραλαβὼν μεταχειρίσαιο χρηστῶς.
ἀλλ᾽ οἶσθ᾽ ὅ μοι πεπονθέναι δοκεῖς; ὅπερ τὸ πλῆθος.
εἴ που δικίδιον εἶπας εὖ κατὰ ξένου μετοίκου,
τὴν νύκτα θρυλῶν καὶ λαλῶν ἐν ταῖς ὁδοῖς σεαυτῷ,
ὕδωρ τε πίνων κἀπιδεικνὺς τοὺς φίλους τ᾽ ἀνιῶν,
350 ᾤου δυνατὸς εἶναι λέγειν. ὦ μῶρε, τῆς ἀνοίας.

ΑΛΛΑΝΤΟΠΩΛΗΣ

τί δαὶ σὺ πίνων τὴν πόλιν πεποίηκας, ὥστε νυνὶ
ὑπὸ σοῦ μονωτάτου κατεγλωττισμένην σιωπᾶν;

ΠΑΦΛΑΓΩΝ

ἐμοὶ γὰρ ἀντέθηκας ἀνθρώπων τίν᾽; ὅστις εὐθὺς
θύννεια θερμὰ καταφαγὼν, κᾆτ᾽ ἐπιπιὼν ἀκράτου
355 οἴνου χοᾶ κασαλβάσω τοὺς ἐν Πύλῳ στρατηγούς.

ΑΛΛΑΝΤΟΠΩΛΗΣ

ἐγὼ δέ γ᾽ ἤνυστρον βοὸς καὶ κοιλίαν ὑείαν
καταβροχθίσας κᾆτ᾽ ἐπιπιὼν τὸν ζωμὸν ἀναπόνιπτος
λαρυγγιῶ τοὺς ῥήτορας καὶ Νικίαν ταράξω.

ΟΙΚΕΤΗΣ Α΄

τὰ μὲν ἄλλα μ᾽ ἤρεσας λέγων· ἓν δ᾽ οὐ προσίεταί με,
360 τῶν πραγμάτων ὁτιὴ μόνος τὸν ζωμὸν ἐκροφήσει.

PAPHLAGON

Speak, ha! A pretty speech you'd make if you stumbled into
a case you received fresh slaughtered; you'd take it in hand
like a pro! Want to know my opinion? That the same thing
as happens to most people has happened to you. You prob-
ably spoke well in a bitty lawsuit against an immigrant
foreigner, after droning your speech all night long, bab-
bling it to yourself in the streets, swearing off wine, and
rehearsing with your friends till you got on their nerves,
and then you started thinking you're a powerful speaker.
You fool, what a delusion![20]

SAUSAGE SELLER

And what do you drink, to have fixed it so the city's now
gagged speechless by the thrust of your tongue, and yours
alone?

PAPHLAGON

I'd like to know who in the world you compare me with!
Me, I'll polish off a plateful of hot tuna right now, wash it
down with a pitcher of neat wine, and then screw the gen-
erals at Pylos!

SAUSAGE SELLER

Yes, and it's cow belly and hog tripe I'll gobble down, and
drink up the gravy, and then without washing my hands I'll
throttle the politicians and harass Nicias!

FIRST SLAVE

I like most of what you said, but one thing doesn't sit well
with me, that you mean to slurp up the political gravy all
by yourself.

[20] Compare Cleon's remarks as reported by Thucydides
3.38.2.

ΠΑΦΛΑΓΩΝ

ἀλλ᾽ οὐ λάβρακας καταφαγὼν Μιλησίους
κλονήσεις.

ΑΛΛΑΝΤΟΠΩΛΗΣ

ἀλλὰ σχελίδας ἐδηδοκὼς ὠνήσομαι μέταλλα.

ΠΑΦΛΑΓΩΝ

ἐγὼ δ᾽ ἐπεισπηδῶν γε τὴν βουλὴν βίᾳ κυκήσω.

ΑΛΛΑΝΤΟΠΩΛΗΣ

ἐγὼ δὲ βυνήσω γέ σου τὸν πρωκτὸν ἀντὶ φύσκης.

ΠΑΦΛΑΓΩΝ

365   ἐγὼ δέ γ᾽ ἐξέλξω σε τῆς πυγῆς θύραζε κύβδα.

ΟΙΚΕΤΗΣ Α΄

νὴ τὸν Ποσειδῶ κἀμέ γ᾽ ἄρ᾽, ἤνπερ γε τοῦτον
ἕλκῃς.

ΠΑΦΛΑΓΩΝ

οἷόν σε δήσω ‹᾽ν› τῷ ξύλῳ.

ΑΛΛΑΝΤΟΠΩΛΗΣ

διώξομαί σε δειλίας.

ΠΑΦΛΑΓΩΝ

ἡ βύρσα σου θρανεύσεται.

ΑΛΛΑΝΤΟΠΩΛΗΣ

373   τὰς βλεφαρίδας σου παρατιλῶ.

ΠΑΦΛΑΓΩΝ

370   δερῶ σε θύλακον κλοπῆς.

364 βυνήσω Jackson: βινήσω R: κινήσω M y

276

PAPHLAGON

But you won't eat up the Milesians' big fish and then run
roughshod over them. [21]

SAUSAGE SELLER

But I will eat sides of beef and buy mining leases.

PAPHLAGON

I'll jump into the Council and stir it up with brute force.

SAUSAGE SELLER

And I'll stuff your arsehole like a sausage skin.

PAPHLAGON

And I'll drag you outside by the butt, upside down.

FIRST SLAVE

By Poseidon, if you drag him you'll have to drag me too!

PAPHLAGON

How I'll enjoy clamping you in the stocks!

SAUSAGE SELLER

I'll prosecute you for cowardice!

PAPHLAGON

Your hide will end up on my tanning bench!

SAUSAGE SELLER

I'll tweeze off your eyebrows!

PAPHLAGON

I'll use your skin for a loot bag!

[21] Perhaps Cleon had reneged on a bribe from a political faction on Miletus, a rich and loyal ally of Athens (cf. 927-40); or "big fish" may allude to oligarchs.

370-73 transp. Henderson

ΑΛΛΑΝΤΟΠΩΛΗΣ

372   περικόμματ᾽ ἔκ σου σκευάσω.

ΠΑΦΛΑΓΩΝ

371   διαπατταλευθήσει χαμαί.

ΑΛΛΑΝΤΟΠΩΛΗΣ

τὸν πρηγορεῶνά σου ᾽κτεμῶ.

ΟΙΚΕΤΗΣ Α᾽

375   καὶ νὴ Δί᾽ ἐμβαλόντες αὐ–
        τῷ πάτταλον μαγειρικῶς
        εἰς τὸ στόμ᾽, εἶτα δ᾽ ἔνδοθεν
        τὴν γλῶτταν ἐξείραντες αὐ–
        τοῦ σκεψόμεσθ᾽ εὖ κἀνδρικῶς
380   κεχηνότος
        τὸν πρωκτόν, εἰ χαλαζᾷ.

ΧΟΡΟΣ

(ἀντ)   ἦν ἄρα πυρός θ᾽ ἕτερα θερμότερα καὶ ⟨λόγοι τῶν⟩
        λόγων
385   ἐν πόλει τῶν ἀναιδῶν ἀναιδέστεροι·
        καὶ τὸ πρᾶγμ᾽ ἦν ἄρ᾽ οὐ φαῦλον ὧδ᾽ ⟨οὐδαμῶς.⟩
        ἀλλ᾽ ἔπιθι καὶ στρόβει, μηδὲν ὀλίγον ποίει·
        νῦν γὰρ ἔχεται μέσος.

ΚΟΡΥΦΑΙΟΣ

ὡς ἐὰν νυνὶ μαλάξῃς αὐτὸν ἐν τῇ προσβολῇ,
390   δειλὸν εὑρήσεις· ἐγὼ γὰρ τοὺς τρόπους ἐπίσταμαι.

ΑΛΛΑΝΤΟΠΩΛΗΣ

ἀλλ᾽ ὅμως οὗτος τοιοῦτος ὢν ἅπαντα τὸν βίον,

278

SAUSAGE SELLER

I'll make mincemeat of you!

PAPHLAGON

You'll be stretched out on the ground and pegged!

SAUSAGE SELLER

I'll crop out your gizzard!

FIRST SLAVE

And by god, we'll jam a peg in his mouth like butchers, and
yank out his tongue and take a good brave look down to his
gaping arsehole, to see if he's measly![22]

CHORUS

So there really are temperatures hotter than fire, and
  speeches
more brazen than the brazen speeches heard in the
  city.
And our job turns out to be nothing so trifling, ‹no
  indeed›!
Attack him and make his head spin; don't set your
  sights low,
for now you've got him around the middle.

CHORUS LEADER

That's right, if you soften him up now in the first onslaught,
you'll find he's a coward; I know his character.

SAUSAGE SELLER

He's been that sort of character his whole life, and then he

---

[22] As an animal before slaughter is inspected for signs of tape-
worm.

---

386 ‹οὐδαμῶς› Rogers

ARISTOPHANES

κᾆτ᾽ ἀνὴρ ἔδοξεν εἶναι, τἀλλότριον ἀμῶν θέρος.
νῦν δὲ τοὺς στάχυς ἐκείνους, οὓς ἐκεῖθεν ἤγαγεν,
ἐν ξύλῳ δήσας ἀφαύει κἀποδόσθαι βούλεται.

ΠΑΦΛΑΓΩΝ

395 οὐ δέδοιχ᾽ ὑμᾶς, ἕως ἂν ζῇ τὸ βουλευτήριον
καὶ τὸ τοῦ δήμου πρόσωπον μακκοᾷ καθήμενον.

ΧΟΡΟΣ

ὡς δὲ πρὸς πᾶν ἀναιδεύεται κοὐ μεθί-
στησι τοῦ χρώματος τοῦ παρεστηκότος.
400 εἴ σε μὴ μισῶ, γενοίμην ἐν Κρατίνου κῴδιον
καὶ διδασκοίμην προσᾴδειν Μορσίμου τραγῳδίᾳ.
ὦ περὶ πάντ᾽ ἐπὶ πᾶσί τε πράγμασι
δωροδόκοισιν ἐπ᾽ ἄνθεσιν ἵζων,
εἴθε φαύλως, ὥσπερ ηὗρες, ἐκβάλοις τὴν ἔνθεσιν.
405 ᾄσαιμι γὰρ τότ᾽ ἂν μόνον
"πῖνε πῖν᾽ ἐπὶ συμφοραῖς".

ΚΟΡΥΦΑΙΟΣ

τὸν Οὔλιόν τ᾽ ἂν οἴομαι, γέροντα πυροπίπην,
ἡσθέντ᾽ ἰηπαιωνίσαι καὶ βακχέβακχον ᾆσαι.

---

407 Οὔλιόν Raubitschek: Οὐλίου Bothe: Ἰουλίου z

---

[23] I.e. by getting credit for the victory at Pylos.
[24] I.e. using the Spartan prisoners to bargain for favorable terms; cf. Thucydides 4.41.

passes for a real man by reaping somebody else's harvest.[23]
And now those ears of corn he brought back with him, he's
clamped them in the stocks for parching, in hopes of selling
them back.[24]

PAPHLAGON

I'm not afraid of you people, as long as the Council lives
and Demos' booby face gapes from his seat!

CHORUS

See how he keeps up his boundless brazenness
without even changing his usual color!
If I don't hate you, may I turn into a blanket in
    Cratinus' house[25]
and be coached by Morsimus[26] to sing in a tragedy!
Oh, you're everywhere, in everyone's business,
lighting on bribery's blossoms;
I hope you throw up your mouthful as easily as you
    found it.
For only then will I sing,
"Drink, Drink on a Happy Occasion!"[27]

CHORUS LEADER

And I imagine Ulius,[28] the old grain ogler,[29] would whoop
a paean of joy and sing the Bacchebacchus.

---

[25] Referring to Cratinus' alleged incontinence, cf. 526 ff.

[26] Son of the tragic poet Philocles and great-nephew of Aeschylus.

[27] The title of a victory ode by Simonides (*PMG* 512).

[28] One of the sons of the statesman Cimon.

[29] Slang for one of the official cereal inspectors, who might be blamed for price increases.

ARISTOPHANES

ΠΑΦΛΑΓΩΝ

οὗτοί μ' ὑπερβαλεῖσθ' ἀναιδείᾳ μὰ τὸν Ποσειδῶ,
410 ἢ μήποτ' Ἀγοραίου Διὸς σπλάγχνοισι παρα-
γενοίμην.

ΑΛΛΑΝΤΟΠΩΛΗΣ

ἔγωγε, νὴ τοὺς κονδύλους, οὓς πολλὰ δὴ 'πὶ πολ-
λοῖς
ἠνεσχόμην ἐκ παιδίου, μαχαιρίδων τε πληγάς,
ὑπερβαλεῖσθαί σ' οἴομαι τούτοισιν, ἢ μάτην γ' ἂν
ἀπομαγδαλιὰς σιτούμενος τοσοῦτος ἐκτραφείην.

ΠΑΦΛΑΓΩΝ

415 ἀπομαγδαλιὰς ὥσπερ κύων; ὦ παμπόνηρε, πῶς οὖν
κυνὸς βορὰν σιτούμενος μαχεῖ σὺ κυνοκεφάλῳ;

ΑΛΛΑΝΤΟΠΩΛΗΣ

καὶ νὴ Δί' ἄλλα γ' ἐστί μου κόβαλα παιδὸς ὄντος·
ἐξηπάτων γὰρ τοὺς μαγείρους ἂν λέγων τοιαυτί·
"σκέψασθε, παῖδες· οὐχ ὁρᾶθ'; ὥρα νέα, χελιδών."
420 οἱ δ' ἔβλεπον, κἀγὼ 'ν τοσούτῳ τῶν κρεῶν ἔκλεπ-
τον.

ΟΙΚΕΤΗΣ Α'

ὦ δεξιώτατον κρέας, σοφῶς γε προὐνοήσω·
ὥσπερ ἀκαλήφας ἐσθίων πρὸ χελιδόνων ἔκλεπτες.

ΑΛΛΑΝΤΟΠΩΛΗΣ

καὶ ταῦτα δρῶν ἐλάνθανόν ⟨γ'.⟩ εἰ δ' οὖν ἴδοι τις
αὐτῶν,
ἀποκρυπτόμενος εἰς τὼ κοχώνα τοὺς θεοὺς ἀπώμνυν·

KNIGHTS

PAPHLAGON

By Poseidon, you aren't going to outshoot me in brazenness, or I hope never again to share in the feast of Marketplace Zeus!

SAUSAGE SELLER

So help me the punches and knife slashes I've taken many times over since childhood, I'm sure I will overshoot you in all this, or else I've grown this big on a diet of sops for nothing.

PAPHLAGON

Sops, like a dog? How can a cheap joker like you eat dog-food and expect to fight a dog-faced baboon?

SAUSAGE SELLER

I swear, when I was I boy I had a lot more monkey tricks. I used to fool the butchers by saying things like, "Look, boys, don't you see? Spring is here, there's a swallow!" And just when they were looking up, I swiped some meat.

FIRST SLAVE

A most meaty machination; smart planning! You got your booty, like eating nettles before the swallows come.

SAUSAGE SELLER

And I never got caught in the act, because if any of them spotted me, I'd stash it up my crotch and swear to god I'm

---

[410] συγγενοίμην Casaubon

425 ὥστ᾽ εἶπ᾽ ἀνὴρ τῶν ῥητόρων ἰδών με τοῦτο δρῶντα·
"οὐκ ἔσθ᾽ ὅπως ὁ παῖς ὅδ᾽ οὐ τὸν δῆμον ἐπιτροπεύσει."

OIKETHΣ A´

εὖ γε ξυνέβαλεν αὔτ᾽· ἀτὰρ δῆλόν γ᾽ ἀφ᾽ οὗ ξυνέγνω·
ὁτιὴ 'πιώρκεις θ᾽ ἡρπακὼς καὶ κρέας ὁ πρωκτὸς
εἶχεν.

ΠΑΦΛΑΓΩΝ

ἐγώ σε παύσω τοῦ θράσους, οἶμαι δὲ μᾶλλον ἄμφω.
430 ἔξειμι γάρ σοι λαμπρὸς ἤδη καὶ μέγας καθιείς,
ὁμοῦ ταράττων τήν τε γῆν καὶ τὴν θάλατταν εἰκῇ.

ΑΛΛΑΝΤΟΠΩΛΗΣ

ἐγὼ δὲ συστείλας γε τοὺς ἀλλᾶντας εἶτ᾽ ἀφήσω
κατὰ κῦμ᾽ ἐμαυτὸν οὔριον, κλάειν σε μακρὰ
κελεύσας.

OIKETHΣ A´

κἄγωγ᾽, ἐάν τι παραχαλᾷ, τὴν ἀντλίαν φυλάξω.

ΠΑΦΛΑΓΩΝ

435 οὔτοι μὰ τὴν Δήμητρα καταπροίξει τάλαντα πολλὰ
κλέψας Ἀθηναίων.

OIKETHΣ A´

                        ἄθρει καὶ τοῦ ποδὸς παρίει·
ὡς οὗτος ἤδη καικίας ἢ συκοφαντίας πνεῖ.

ΑΛΛΑΝΤΟΠΩΛΗΣ

σὲ δ᾽ ἐκ Ποτειδαίας ἔχοντ᾽ εὖ οἶδα δέκα τάλαντα.

ΠΑΦΛΑΓΩΝ

τί δῆτα; βούλει τῶν ταλάντων ἓν λαβὼν σιωπᾶν;

innocent. So when one of the politicians saw me doing that he said, "There's no way this boy won't someday govern the people."

FIRST SLAVE

That was a good guess! But it's obvious how he figured it out: you perjured yourself about a robbery and took meat up your arse.

PAPHLAGON

I'll put a stop to your insolence, and I mean both of you. I'll hit you like a hurricane, awesome and strong, roiling land and sea every which way!

SAUSAGE SELLER

But I'll furl my sausages and let myself run fairly before the waves, after bidding you fare-ill.

FIRST SLAVE

And I'll man the bilges in case of a leak.

PAPHLAGON

By Demeter, you won't get away with the huge pile of money you've filched from the Athenians!

FIRST SLAVE

Ahoy there, slacken the sheets! He's ready to blow up a nor'easter, or a frame-upper.

SAUSAGE SELLER

I know all about the ten talents you got out of Potidaea.[30]

PAPHLAGON

What about it? Want to take one of those talents to keep quiet?

[30] Athens took this strategically important city in 429, but only after a long and costly siege (Thucydides 2.70).

ΟΙΚΕΤΗΣ Α΄

440 ἀνὴρ ἂν ἡδέως λάβοι. τοὺς τερθρίους παρίει·
τὸ πνεῦμ᾽ ἔλαττον γίγνεται.

ΠΑΦΛΑΓΩΝ

φεύξει γραφὰς ⟨δωροδοκίας⟩
ἑκατονταλάντους τέτταρας.

ΑΛΛΑΝΤΟΠΩΛΗΣ

σὺ δ᾽ ἀστρατείας γ᾽ εἴκοσιν,
κλοπῆς δὲ πλεῖν ἢ χιλίας.

ΠΑΦΛΑΓΩΝ

445 ἐκ τῶν ἀλιτηρίων σέ φη–
μι γεγονέναι τῶν τῆς θεοῦ.

ΑΛΛΑΝΤΟΠΩΛΗΣ

τὸν πάππον εἶναι φημί σου
τῶν δορυφόρων—

ΠΑΦΛΑΓΩΝ

ποίων; φράσον.

ΑΛΛΑΝΤΟΠΩΛΗΣ

—τῶν Βυρσίνης τῆς Ἱππίου.

ΠΑΦΛΑΓΩΝ

κόβαλος εἶ.

ΑΛΛΑΝΤΟΠΩΛΗΣ

450   πανοῦργος εἶ.

442 ⟨δωροδοκίας⟩ Göttling

286

FIRST SLAVE

The gentleman would be glad to! Slacken the ropes; the wind's dropping.

PAPHLAGON

You'll face charges ‹of bribe-taking,› four of them at a hundred talents each!

SAUSAGE SELLER

And you'll face twenty for draft-dodging, and more than a thousand for embezzlement!

PAPHLAGON

I say that you're descended from the polluters of our Goddess![31]

SAUSAGE SELLER

And I say your grandfather was among the bodyguards—

PAPHLAGON

What bodyguards? Go on.

SAUSAGE SELLER

—of Hippias' wife, Pursine![32]

PAPHLAGON

You scamp!

SAUSAGE SELLER

You crook!

[31] The seventh-century aristocratic faction who killed the followers of Cylon in Athena's sanctuary and whose descendants were accursed (Herodotus 5.71, Thucydides 1.126).

[32] Tyrant of Athens from 527 until his expulsion in 510; his wife's name was Myrsine, here Byrsine, punning on *byrsa* "hide."

287

ΟΙΚΕΤΗΣ Α΄

παῖ ἀνδρικῶς.

ΠΑΦΛΑΓΩΝ

ἰοὺ ἰού,
τύπτουσί μ᾽ οἱ ξυνωμόται.

ΟΙΚΕΤΗΣ Α΄

παῖ αὐτὸν ἀνδρικώτατα καὶ
γάστριζε καὶ τοῖς ἐντέροις
455   καὶ τοῖς κόλοις,
χὤπως κολᾷ τὸν ἄνδρα.

ΚΟΡΥΦΑΙΟΣ

ὦ γεννικώτατον κρέας ψυχήν τ᾽ ἄριστε πάντων,
καὶ τῇ πόλει σωτὴρ φανεὶς ἡμῖν τε τοῖς πολίταις,
ὡς εὖ τὸν ἄνδρα ποικίλως τ᾽ ἐπῆλθες ἐν λόγοισιν.
460   πῶς ἄν σ᾽ ἐπαινέσαιμεν οὕτως ὥσπερ ἡδόμεσθα;

ΠΑΦΛΑΓΩΝ

ταυτὶ μὰ τὴν Δήμητρά μ᾽ οὐκ ἐλάνθανεν
τεκταινόμενα τὰ πράγματ᾽, ἀλλ᾽ ἠπιστάμην
463   γομφούμεν᾽ αὐτὰ πάντα καὶ κολλώμενα.

ΑΛΛΑΝΤΟΠΩΛΗΣ

465   οὔκουν μ᾽ ἐν Ἄργει γ᾽ οἷα πράττεις λανθάνει.
466   πρόφασιν μὲν Ἀργείους φίλους ἡμῖν ποιεῖ,
467   ἰδίᾳ δ᾽ ἐκεῖ Λακεδαιμονίοις ξυγγίγνεται.

ΟΙΚΕΤΗΣ Α΄

464   οἴμοι, σὺ δ᾽ οὐδὲν ἐξ ἁμαξουργοῦ λέγεις;

FIRST SLAVE

Hit him a good one!

PAPHLAGON

Ow! Help! The conspirators are beating me!

FIRST SLAVE

Hit him a really good one! Belly-punch him with your guts and tripe, and see that you mete out the man's comeuppance.

CHORUS LEADER

You're a prime cut of meat and surpass all men in guts, appearing as savior to our city and us her citizens! How well and adroitly you've mounted your verbal attack! How can we find the praise to match our delight?

PAPHLAGON

By Demeter, I caught on to the fabrication of this business; I knew how everything was being bolted and glued!

SAUSAGE SELLER

And I'm on to what you're up to in Argos. He pretends he's making the Argives our friends, but he's down there cutting his own deal with the Spartans![33]

FIRST SLAVE

Uh oh, hadn't you better use some jargon from the blacksmith's?

[33] In 424 Argos was neutral, but her treaty with Sparta was due to expire in 421.

---

464 post 467 Hermann, cf. Σ

ΑΛΛΑΝΤΟΠΩΛΗΣ

468 καὶ ταῦτ᾽ ἐφ᾽ οἷσίν ἐστι συμφυσώμενα
ἐγῷδ᾽· ἐπὶ γὰρ τοῖς δεδεμένοις χαλκεύεται.

ΟΙΚΕΤΗΣ Α΄

470 εὖ γ᾽, εὖ γε· χάλκευ᾽ ἀντὶ τῶν κολλωμένων.

ΑΛΛΑΝΤΟΠΩΛΗΣ

καὶ ξυγκροτοῦσιν ἄνδρες αὔτ᾽ ἐκεῖθεν αὖ.
καὶ ταῦτά μ᾽ οὔτ᾽ ἀργύριον οὔτε χρυσίον
διδοὺς ἀναπείσεις οὔτε προσπέμπων φίλους,
ὅπως ἐγὼ ταῦτ᾽ οὐκ Ἀθηναίοις φράσω.

ΠΑΦΛΑΓΩΝ

475 ἐγὼ μὲν οὖν αὐτίκα μάλ᾽ εἰς βουλὴν ἰὼν
ὑμῶν ἁπάντων τὰς ξυνωμοσίας ἐρῶ,
καὶ τὰς ξυνόδους τὰς νυκτερινὰς ἐν τῇ πόλει,
καὶ πάνθ᾽ ἃ Μήδοις καὶ βασιλεῖ ξυνόμνυτε,
καὶ τἀκ Βοιωτῶν ταῦτα συντυρούμενα.

ΑΛΛΑΝΤΟΠΩΛΗΣ

480 πῶς οὖν ὁ τυρὸς ἐν Βοιωτοῖς ὤνιος;

ΠΑΦΛΑΓΩΝ

ἐγώ σε νὴ τὸν Ἡρακλέα παραστορῶ.

ΟΙΚΕΤΗΣ Α΄

ἄγε δὴ σὺ τίνα νοῦν ἢ τίνα γνώμην ἔχεις,
νυνὶ διδάξεις, εἴπερ ἀπεκρύψω τότε

482 γνώμην R: ψυχὴν Μ y

SAUSAGE SELLER

And I know the design for this welding of his: he's forging it on the men in irons.[34]

FIRST SLAVE

That's good, that's good: meet his gluing with forging!

SAUSAGE SELLER

And men on the other side are helping him hammer it out. (*to Paphlagon*) And you may offer me bribes of silver or gold, or send your colleagues round to visit, but you won't talk me out of revealing all this to the Athenians.

PAPHLAGON

Quite the reverse: I'm off to the Council this very minute to inform on all of you for your conspiracies, your nocturnal meetings within the city, all your plots with the Medes and their King,[35] and that cheesy business with the Boeotians.[36]

SAUSAGE SELLER

So, what's the price of cheese in Boeotia?

PAPHLAGON

By Heracles, I'll spread your hide!

EXIT PAPHLAGON.

FIRST SLAVE

Come on now, what's your idea? What's your plan? You'll

[34] Cf. 394-95. [35] Athens was still negotiating with the Persians (Thucydides 4.50.3); the term "Medes," recalling the Persian invasions, was used to evoke popular prejudice.
[36] For secret contacts with democratic factions in Boeotia see Thucydides 4.76.

εἰς τὼ κοχώνα τὸ κρέας, ὡς αὐτὸς λέγεις.
485 θεύσει γὰρ ᾄξας εἰς τὸ βουλευτήριον,
ὡς οὗτος εἰσπεσὼν ἐκεῖσε διαβαλεῖ
ἡμᾶς ἅπαντας καὶ κράγον κεκράξεται.

ΑΛΛΑΝΤΟΠΩΛΗΣ
ἀλλ᾽ εἶμι· πρῶτον δ᾽, ὡς ἔχω, τὰς κοιλίας
καὶ τὰς μαχαίρας ἐνθαδὶ καταθήσομαι.

ΟΙΚΕΤΗΣ Α´
490 ἔχε νυν, ἄλειψον τὸν τράχηλον τουτῳί,
ἵν᾽ ἐξολισθάνειν δύνῃ τὰς διαβολάς.

ΑΛΛΑΝΤΟΠΩΛΗΣ
ἀλλ᾽ εὖ λέγεις καὶ παιδοτριβικῶς ταυταγί.

ΟΙΚΕΤΗΣ Α´
ἔχε νυν, ἐπέγκαψον λαβὼν ταδί.

ΑΛΛΑΝΤΟΠΩΛΗΣ
                              τί δαί;

ΟΙΚΕΤΗΣ Α´
ἵν᾽ ἄμεινον, ὦ τᾶν, ἐσκοροδισμένος μάχῃ.
καὶ σπεῦδε ταχέως.

ΑΛΛΑΝΤΟΠΩΛΗΣ
                    ταῦτα δρῶ.

ΟΙΚΕΤΗΣ Α´
495   μέμνησό νυν
δάκνειν, διαβάλλειν, τοὺς λόφους κατεσθίειν,
χὤπως τὰ κάλλαι᾽ ἀποφαγὼν ἥξεις πάλιν.

show it to us now, if you really did hide that meat up your crotch that time, as you claim you did, because you've got to run in a flash to the Council; he's going to charge in there slandering all of us and screaming his scream.

SAUSAGE SELLER

I'm off. But first I'll leave my tripe and knives right here.

FIRST SLAVE

Here, smear this on your neck, so you can slip out of his slanders.[37]

SAUSAGE SELLER

That's good, spoken like a coach!

FIRST SLAVE

Here now, take this and bolt it down.

SAUSAGE SELLER

How come?

FIRST SLAVE

You'll fight better, my boy, if you're primed with garlic.[38] Now off with you!

SAUSAGE SELLER

I'm gone!

SAUSAGE SELLER runs off.

FIRST SLAVE

Now remember: bite him, slander him, gobble up his comb, and make sure you chew off his wattles before you return!

[37] As a wrestler is oiled before a match.
[38] Like a fighting cock.

ΚΟΡΥΦΑΙΟΣ

ἀλλ᾽ ἴθι χαίρων, καὶ πράξειας
κατὰ νοῦν τὸν ἐμόν, καί σε φυλάττοι
500   Ζεὺς Ἀγοραῖος· καὶ νικήσας
αὖθις ἐκεῖθεν πάλιν ὡς ἡμᾶς
ἔλθοις στεφάνοις κατάπαστος.
ὑμεῖς δ᾽ ἡμῖν προσέχετε τὸν νοῦν
τοῖς ἀναπαίστοις, ὦ παντοίας
505   ἤδη μούσης
πειραθέντες καθ᾽ ἑαυτούς.

εἰ μέν τις ἀνὴρ τῶν ἀρχαίων κωμῳδοδιδάσκαλος ἡμᾶς
ἠνάγκαζεν λέξοντας ἔπη πρὸς τὸ θέατρον παραβῆναι,
οὐκ ἂν φαύλως ἔτυχεν τούτου· νῦν δ᾽ ἄξιός ἐσθ᾽ ὁ
   ποιητής,
510   ὅτι τοὺς αὐτοὺς ἡμῖν μισεῖ τολμᾷ τε λέγειν τὰ δίκαια,
καὶ γενναίως πρὸς τὸν Τυφῶ χωρεῖ καὶ τὴν ἐριώλην.
ἃ δὲ θαυμάζειν ὑμῶν φησιν πολλοὺς αὐτῷ προσιόντας
καὶ βασανίζειν ὡς οὐχὶ πάλαι χορὸν αἰτοίη καθ᾽
   ἑαυτόν,
ἡμᾶς ὑμῖν ἐκέλευε φράσαι περὶ τούτου. φησὶ γὰρ
   ἀνὴρ
515   οὐχ ὑπ᾽ ἀνοίας τοῦτο πεπονθὼς διατρίβειν, ἀλλὰ
   νομίζων
κωμῳδοδιδασκαλίαν εἶναι χαλεπώτατον ἔργον
   ἁπάντων·
πολλῶν γὰρ δὴ πειρασάντων αὐτὴν ὀλίγοις
   χαρίσασθαι·

KNIGHTS

CHORUS LEADER

Go, and good luck, and may you accomplish
our aims, and may Zeus of the Marketplace
watch over you! I hope you're victorious there,
and come back to us
spangled with crowns!
But now we ask that you all listen
to our anapests, you who are in your own right
well versed
in every kind of art.

If any old-time comic producer had tried to force us to
face the theater and make a speech, he wouldn't easily
have succeeded. But today our poet deserves it, because he
hates the same people we do, and dares to say what's right,
and nobly strides forth against the typhoon and the whirl-
wind. As to a question that he says has many of you puzzled
and approaching him for an answer—why he's waited so
long to apply for a chorus in his own name—he's author-
ized us to explain that to you. The gentleman says that he
wasn't lingering in that position out of stupidity, but in the
belief that producing comedies is the hardest of all tasks,
for many have courted this muse, few have enjoyed her

ὑμᾶς τε πάλαι διαγιγνώσκων ἐπετείους τὴν φύσιν
   ὄντας
καὶ τοὺς προτέρους τῶν ποιητῶν ἅμα τῷ γήρᾳ προ-
   διδόντας·
520 τοῦτο μὲν εἰδὼς ἅπαθε Μάγνης ἅμα ταῖς πολιαῖς
   κατιούσαις,
ὃς πλεῖστα χορῶν τῶν ἀντιπάλων νίκης ἔστησε
   τροπαῖα·
πάσας δ' ὑμῖν φωνὰς ἱεὶς καὶ ψάλλων καὶ πτερυγίζων
καὶ λυδίζων καὶ ψηνίζων καὶ βαπτόμενος βατρα-
   χείοις
οὐκ ἐξήρκεσεν, ἀλλὰ τελευτῶν ἐπὶ γήρως, οὐ γὰρ
   ἐφ' ἥβης,
525 ἐξεβλήθη πρεσβύτης ὤν, ὅτι τοῦ σκώπτειν ἀπε-
   λείφθη·
εἶτα Κρατίνου μεμνημένος, ὃς πολλῷ ῥεύσας ποτ'
   ἐπαίνῳ
διὰ τῶν ἀφελῶν πεδίων ἔρρει, καὶ τῆς στάσεως
   παρασύρων
ἐφόρει τὰς δρῦς καὶ τὰς πλατάνους καὶ τοὺς
   ἐχθροὺς προθελύμνους·
ᾆσαι δ' οὐκ ἦν ἐν συμποσίῳ πλὴν Δωροῖ συκοπέδιλε,
530 καὶ Τέκτονες εὐπαλάμων ὕμνων· οὕτως ἤνθησεν
   ἐκεῖνος.
νυνὶ δ' ὑμεῖς αὐτὸν ὁρῶντες παραληροῦντ' οὐκ
   ἐλεεῖτε,
ἐκπιπτουσῶν τῶν ἠλέκτρων καὶ τοῦ τόνου οὐκέτ'
   ἐνόντος

favors; and he was long aware that your tastes change every year, and that you abandoned his predecessors as they grew older. He knew what happened to Magnes[39] as soon as the grey hairs appeared, the poet who'd posted so many victories over his rivals' choruses: though he vocalized all kinds of sounds, strumming, flapping, singing Lydian, buzzing, dying himself green as a frog, it wasn't enough; in his old age, though never in his prime, he ended up getting booed off the stage, veteran that he was, because his powers of mockery had deserted him. Then he recalled Cratinus,[40] who once rode the high wave of your applause and coursed through the open plains, sweeping oaks, plane trees, and enemies from their moorings and bearing them off uprooted. At a party there was no singing anything but "Goddess of Bribery with Shoes of Impeach Wood" and "Builders of Handy Hymns," so lush was his flowering! But now you see him driveling around town, his frets falling out,[41]

[39] Magnes won a record eleven victories, the only datable one in 472.

[40] In the present competition Cratinus' play *Satyrs* would win second prize; he won nine victories overall.

[41] Like a worn-out lyre.

τῶν θ᾽ ἁρμονιῶν διαχασκουσῶν· ἀλλὰ γέρων ὢν
περιέρρει,
ὥσπερ Κοννᾶς, στέφανον μὲν ἔχων αὖον, δίψῃ δ᾽
ἀπολωλώς,
535 ὃν χρῆν διὰ τὰς προτέρας νίκας πίνειν ἐν τῷ πρυ-
τανείῳ,
καὶ μὴ ληρεῖν, ἀλλὰ θεᾶσθαι λιπαρὸν παρὰ τῷ
Διονύσῳ.
οἵας δὲ Κράτης ὀργὰς ὑμῶν ἠνέσχετο καὶ στυφε-
λιγμούς,
ὃς ἀπὸ σμικρᾶς δαπάνης ὑμᾶς ἀριστίζων ἀπέπεμ-
πεν,
ἀπὸ κραμβοτάτου στόματος μάττων ἀστειοτάτας
ἐπινοίας·
540 χοὖτος μέντοι μόνον ἀντήρκει, τοτὲ μὲν πίπτων,
τοτὲ δ᾽ οὐχί.
ταῦτ᾽ ὀρρωδῶν διέτριβεν ἀεί, καὶ πρὸς τούτοισιν
ἔφασκεν
ἐρέτην χρῆναι πρῶτα γενέσθαι πρὶν πηδαλίοις
ἐπιχειρεῖν,
κᾆτ᾽ ἐντεῦθεν πρῳρατεῦσαι καὶ τοὺς ἀνέμους δια-
θρῆσαι,
κᾆτα κυβερνᾶν αὐτὸν ἑαυτῷ. τούτων οὖν οὕνεκα
πάντων,
545 ὅτι σωφρονικῶς κοὐκ ἀνοήτως εἰσπηδήσας ἐφλυάρει,
αἴρεσθ᾽ αὐτῷ πολὺ τὸ ῥόθιον, παραπέμψατ᾽ ἐφ᾽ ἕν-
δεκα κώπαις,
θόρυβον χρηστὸν ληναΐτην,

his tuning gone and his shapeliness all disjointed, but you feel no pity; no, he's just an old man doddering about, like Conn-ass[42] wearing a withered crown and perishing of thirst, who for his earlier victories should be getting free drinks in the Prytaneum,[43] and instead of driveling should be sitting pretty in the front row next to Dionysus. And what violent rebuffs Crates[44] had to endure at your hands, who used to send you home with a low-cost snack, baking up very witty ideas from his dainty palate. And he merely survived, sometimes losing, sometimes not. It was in dread of these precedents that our poet kept delaying. And in addition, he held that one should be an oarsman before handling the tiller, and from there take charge of the bow and watch the weather, and only then become a pilot in one's own right. So for all these reasons, that he acted discreetly, and didn't leap mindlessly in and spout rubbish, raise a big wave of applause for him, and give him an eleven-oar cheer worthy of the Lenaea, so that our poet

---

[42] A derogatory nickname for Connus, the renowned musician and teacher of Socrates, who had become a byword for washed-up celebrity; he was the title character in a comedy by Ameipsias.

[43] See 167 n.

[44] Crates flourished *c.* 450-430 and won three victories. On his homespun style cf. Aristotle, *Poetics* 1449b.

---

[540] μόνον Sommerstein: μόνος z
[546] παραπέμψατέ θ' Bentley

ἵν᾽ ὁ ποιητὴς ἀπίῃ χαίρων
κατὰ νοῦν πράξας,
550 φαιδρὸς λάμποντι μετώπῳ.

ΧΟΡΟΣ

(στρ) ἵππι᾽ ἄναξ Πόσειδον, ᾧ
χαλκοκρότων ἵππων κτύπος
καὶ χρεμετισμὸς ἁνδάνει
καὶ κυανέμβολοι θοαὶ
555 μισθοφόροι τριήρεις,
μειρακίων θ᾽ ἅμιλλα λαμ—
πρυνομένων ἐν ἅρμασιν
καὶ βαρυδαιμονούντων,
δεῦρ᾽ ἔλθ᾽ εἰς χορόν, ὦ χρυσοτρίαιν᾽, ὦ
560 δελφίνων μεδέων Σουνιάρατε,
ὦ Γεραίστιε παῖ Κρόνου,
Φορμίωνί τε φίλτατ᾽ ἐκ
τῶν ἄλλων τε θεῶν Ἀθη—
ναίοις πρὸς τὸ παρεστός.

ΚΟΡΥΦΑΙΟΣ

565 εὐλογῆσαι βουλόμεσθα τοὺς πατέρας ἡμῶν, ὅτι
ἄνδρες ἦσαν τῆσδε τῆς γῆς ἄξιοι καὶ τοῦ πέπλου,
οἵτινες πεζαῖς μάχαισιν ἔν τε ναυφάρκτῳ στρατῷ
πανταχοῦ νικῶντες ἀεὶ τήνδ᾽ ἐκόσμησαν πόλιν·
οὐ γὰρ οὐδεὶς πώποτ᾽ αὐτῶν τοὺς ἐναντίους ἰδὼν
570 ἠρίθμησεν, ἀλλ᾽ ὁ θυμὸς εὐθὺς ἦν ἀμυνίας·
εἰ δέ που πέσοιεν εἰς τὸν ὦμον ἐν μάχῃ τινί,
τοῦτ᾽ ἀπεψήσαντ᾽ ἄν, εἶτ᾽ ἠρνοῦντο μὴ πεπτωκέναι,

may go away happy and successful, gleaming to the top of
his shining head![45]

CHORUS

Poseidon, Lord of Horses,
thrilling to the ring of horses' hooves
clashing like bronze, and their neighing,
and to the swift triremes
with their blue rams and their payloads,
and to the contest of youths
in their chariots, heading for the heights of glory
or the depths of ill fortune,
come join our dance, god of the golden trident,
master of dolphins at Sunium,
son of Cronus at Geraestus,
dearest of gods to Phormio[46]
and the Athenians
in time of war!

CHORUS LEADER

We want to praise our forebears for being gentlemen wor-
thy of this land and the Robe,[47] who in infantry battles and
naval expeditions were always victorious everywhere and
adorned our city. For not one of them ever reckoned the
enemy's numbers, but as soon as he saw them his spirit was
defiant. If in any battle they happened to fall on their
shoulder, they would slap off the dirt, deny they'd fallen,

---

45 A reference to Aristophanes' early baldness.
46 This successful and respected admiral died *c.* 428.
47 The robe presented to Athena at the Panathenaea.

ARISTOPHANES

ἀλλὰ διεπάλαιον αὖθις. καὶ στρατηγὸς οὐδ᾽ ἂν εἷς
τῶν πρὸ τοῦ σίτησιν ἤτησ᾽ ἐρόμενος Κλεαίνετον·
575 νῦν δ᾽ ἐὰν μὴ προεδρίαν φέρωσι καὶ τὰ σιτία,
οὐ μαχεῖσθαί φασιν. ἡμεῖς δ᾽ ἀξιοῦμεν τῇ πόλει
προῖκα γενναίως ἀμύνειν καὶ θεοῖς ἐγχωρίοις.
καὶ πρὸς οὐκ αἰτοῦμεν οὐδὲν πλὴν τοσουτονὶ μόνον·
ἢν ποτ᾽ εἰρήνη γένηται καὶ πόνων παυσώμεθα,
580 μὴ φθονεῖθ᾽ ἡμῖν κομῶσι μηδ᾽ ἀπεστλεγγισμένοις.

ΧΟΡΟΣ

(ἀντ) ὦ πολιοῦχε Παλλάς, ὦ
τῆς ἱερωτάτης ἁπα–
σῶν πολέμῳ τε καὶ ποιη–
ταῖς δυνάμει θ᾽ ὑπερφερού–
585 σης μεδέουσα χώρας,
δεῦρ᾽ ἀφικοῦ λαβοῦσα τὴν
ἐν στρατιαῖς τε καὶ μάχαις
ἡμετέραν ξυνεργὸν
Νίκην, ἣ χορικῶν ἐστιν ἑταίρα
590 τοῖς τ᾽ ἐχθροῖσι μεθ᾽ ἡμῶν στασιάζει.
νῦν οὖν δεῦρο φάνηθι· δεῖ
γὰρ τοῖς ἀνδράσι τοῖσδε πά–
σῃ τέχνῃ πορίσαι σε νί–
κην εἴπερ ποτὲ καὶ νῦν.

ΚΟΡΥΦΑΙΟΣ

595 ἃ ξύνισμεν τοῖσιν ἵπποις, βουλόμεσθ᾽ ἐπαινέσαι.
ἄξιοι δ᾽ εἴσ᾽ εὐλογεῖσθαι· πολλὰ γὰρ δὴ πράγματα
ξυνδιήνεγκαν μεθ᾽ ἡμῶν, εἰσβολάς τε καὶ μάχας.

302

and get back into the match. And not a single general of the former generation would have applied to Cleainetus[48] for a state subsidy; whereas now if they don't get front-row seats and free meals, they refuse to fight! But we want only to fight nobly for the city and for its native gods. We ask nothing more, except for only this much: if peace ever comes and our toils are ended, don't begrudge us our long hair and our use of luxurious bathing utensils.

CHORUS

Pallas,[49] City Guardian,
mistress of the land
that is the holiest of all
and the most successful in war, poets,
and power,
come join us, and bring
our helper
in expeditions and battles,
Victory, our companion in choral dances,
who sides with us against our enemies.
Come then, appear to us, for you should
by all means bestow victory
on these gentlemen,
now if ever before!

CHORUS LEADER

We want to praise what we saw our horses accomplish.[50] They deserve our eulogy, for they've borne with us a great many hardships, invasions, and battles. But we aren't

---

[48] Cleon's father.
[49] Athena.
[50] In Nicias' recent victory at Solygeia, where the cavalry was transported on ships (Thucydides 4.42-4).

ἀλλὰ τἀν τῇ γῇ μὲν αὐτῶν οὐκ ἄγαν θαυμάζομεν,
ὡς ὅτ᾽ εἰς τὰς ἱππαγωγοὺς εἰσεπήδων ἀνδρικῶς,
600 πριάμενοι κώθωνας, οἱ δὲ καὶ σκόροδα καὶ κρόμμυα·
εἶτα τὰς κώπας λαβόντες ὥσπερ ἡμεῖς οἱ βροτοὶ
ἐμβαλόντες ἀνεφρυάξανθ᾽· "ἵππαπαῖ, τίς ἐμβαλεῖ;
ληπτέον μᾶλλον. τί δρῶμεν; οὐκ ἐλᾷς, ὦ σαμφόρα;"
ἐξεπήδων τ᾽ εἰς Κόρινθον· εἶτα δ᾽ οἱ νεώτατοι
605 ταῖς ὁπλαῖς ὤρυττον εὐνὰς καὶ μετῆσαν βρώματα·
ἤσθιον δὲ τοὺς παγούρους ἀντὶ ποίας Μηδικῆς,
εἴ τις ἐξέρποι θύραζε κἀκ βυθοῦ θηρώμενοι·
ὥστ᾽ ἔφη Θέωρος εἰπεῖν καρκίνον Κορίνθιον·
"δεινά γ᾽, ὦ Πόσειδον, εἰ μηδ᾽ ἐν βυθῷ δυνήσομαι
610 μήτε γῇ μήτ᾽ ἐν θαλάττῃ διαφυγεῖν τοὺς ἱππέας."

ὦ φίλτατ᾽ ἀνδρῶν καὶ νεανικώτατε,
ὅσην ἀπὼν παρέσχες ἡμῖν φροντίδα·
καὶ νῦν ἐπειδὴ σῶς ἐλήλυθας πάλιν,
ἄγγειλον ἡμῖν πῶς τὸ πρᾶγμ᾽ ἠγωνίσω.

ΑΛΛΑΝΤΟΠΩΛΗΣ
615 τί δ᾽ ἄλλο γ᾽ εἰ μὴ Νικόβουλος ἐγενόμην;

ΧΟΡΟΣ
(στρ) νῦν ἄρ᾽ ἄξιόν γε πᾶσίν
ἐστιν ἐπολολύξαι.
ὦ καλὰ λέγων, πολὺ δ᾽ ἀ-
μείνον᾽ ἔτι τῶν λόγων
ἐργασάμεν᾽ εἴθ᾽ ἐπέλ—

304

too amazed at their actions on land, considering how they
jumped manfully aboard the horse transports after buy-
ing canteens and rations of garlic and onions, then sat to
their oars like we humans, dipped their blades, and raised
a snort of "Heave Horse! Who'll dip his blade? Stroke
harder! What are we doing? Pull harder, S-Brand!" They
jumped ashore at Corinth, and the colts made dugouts with
their hooves and foraged for fodder. Instead of mede clo-
ver they ate crabs, whenever any crawled ashore and even
fishing them from the deep. So Theorus[51] claims a Corin-
thian crab said, "Lord Poseidon, it's awful if neither in the
deep nor on shore nor at sea will I succeed in escaping the
Knights!"

Enter SAUSAGE SELLER.

Dearest and bravest of men, you had us so worried while
you were gone! Now that you're safely back, tell us how
you fared in your contest.

SAUSAGE SELLER
How do you think? I'm a real Nicobulus![52]

CHORUS
Now *that* deserves from everyone
a shout of thanksgiving!
Ah, you've brought fine news
and done deeds far finer still,
so please tell me

[51] Identity unknown; the homonymous crony of Cleon men-
tioned e.g. in *Acharnians* 134 is out of place in this company.
[52] The name (a common one) can be rendered "Victor Fore-
council."

θοις ἅπαντά μοι σαφῶς·
620 ὡς ἐγώ μοι δοκῶ
κἂν μακρὰν ὁδὸν διελθεῖν
ὥστ᾽ ἀκοῦσαι. πρὸς τάδ᾽, ὦ βέλ–
τιστε, θαρρήσας λέγ᾽, ὡς ἅ–
παντες ἡδόμεσθά σοι.

ΑΛΛΑΝΤΟΠΩΛΗΣ
καὶ μὴν ἀκοῦσαί γ᾽ ἄξιον τῶν πραγμάτων.
625 εὐθὺς γὰρ αὐτοῦ κατόπιν ἐνθένδ᾽ ἱέμην·
ὁ δ᾽ ἄρ᾽ ἔνδον ἐλασίβροντ᾽ ἀναρρηγνὺς ἔπη
τερατευόμενος ἤρειδε κατὰ τῶν ἱππέων,
κρημνοὺς ἐρείδων καὶ ξυνωμότας λέγων
πιθανώταθ᾽· ἡ βουλὴ δ᾽ ἅπασ᾽ ἀκροωμένη
630 ἐγένεθ᾽ ὑπ᾽ αὐτοῦ ψευδατραφάξυος πλέα,
κἄβλεψε νᾶπυ καὶ τὰ μέτωπ᾽ ἀνέσπασεν.
κἄγωγ᾽ ὅτε δὴ ᾽γνων ἐνδεχομένην τοὺς λόγους
καὶ τοῖς φενακισμοῖσιν ἐξαπατωμένην·
"ἄγε δὴ Σκίταλοι καὶ Φένακες, ἦν δ᾽ ἐγώ,
635 Βερέσχεθοί τε καὶ Κόβαλοι καὶ Μόθων,
ἀγορά τ᾽, ἐν ᾗ παῖς ὢν ἐπαιδεύθην ἐγώ,
νῦν μοι θράσος καὶ γλῶτταν εὔπορον δότε
φωνήν τ᾽ ἀναιδῆ". ταῦτα φροντίζοντί μοι
ἐκ δεξιᾶς ἐπέπαρδε καταπύγων ἀνήρ.
640 κἀγὼ προσέκυσα· κᾆτα τῷ πρωκτῷ θενὼν
τὴν κιγκλίδ᾽ ἐξήραξα κἀναχανὼν μέγα
ἀνέκραγον· "ὦ βουλή, λόγους ἀγαθοὺς φέρων
εὐαγγελίσασθαι πρῶτος ὑμῖν βούλομαι·

306

the whole story plainly,
for I think
I'd travel a long way
to hear it. Very well, my
excellent fellow, speak boldly,
since we're all enjoying this!

SAUSAGE SELLER

Yes, the story is certainly worth hearing. I took off from
here right on his heels, and there he was in the Council
chamber, breaking out thunderous phrases and assault-
ing the Knights with his bombast, launching mountainous
tirades and calling them conspirators, most persuasively.
The ears of the whole Council were as quickly overgrown
by his lies as by weeds, their eyes looked mustard, and
their brows were knitted together. When I saw that they
were swallowing his story and being fooled by his flimflam,
I said, "Come on, you demons of Puffery, Quackery, Fool-
ery, Chicanery, and Debauchery, and you Marketplace
where I was reared as a boy, now give me boldness, a ready
tongue, and a shameless voice!" As I was pondering this
prayer, some bugger validated it by farting on my lucky
side. I kowtowed, then striking the turnstile with my arse
I knocked it from its hinges, and opening my mouth wide
I bellowed, "Councillors, I've got good news and want to

ἐξ οὗ γὰρ ἡμῖν ὁ πόλεμος κατερράγη,
645   οὐπώποτ᾽ ἀφύας εἶδον ἀξιωτέρας."
ἡ δ᾽ εὐθέως τὰ πρόσωπα διεγαλήνισεν·
εἶτ᾽ ἐστεφάνουν μ᾽ εὐαγγέλια· κἀγὼ ᾽φρασα
αὐτοῖς ἀπόρρητον ποιησάμενος, ταχύ,
ἵνα τὰς ἀφύας ὠνοῖντο πολλὰς τοὐβολοῦ,
650   τῶν δημιουργῶν ξυλλαβεῖν τὰ τρύβλια.
οἱ δ᾽ ἀνεκρότησαν καὶ πρὸς ἔμ᾽ ἐκεχήνεσαν.
ὁ δ᾽ ὑπονοήσας, ὁ Παφλαγών, εἰδὼς ἄρα
οἷς ἥδεθ᾽ ἡ βουλὴ μάλιστα ῥήμασιν,
γνώμην ἔλεξεν· "ἄνδρες, ἤδη μοι δοκεῖ
655   ἐπὶ συμφοραῖς ἀγαθαῖσιν εἰσηγγελμέναις
εὐαγγέλια θύειν ἑκατὸν βοῦς τῇ θεῷ.
ἐπένευσεν εἰς ἐκεῖνον ἡ βουλὴ πάλιν.
κἀγώγ᾽ ὅτε δὴ ᾽γνων τοῖς βολίτοις ἡττώμενος,
διηκοσίῃσι βουσὶν ὑπερηκόντισα,
660   τῇ δ᾽ Ἀγροτέρᾳ κατὰ χιλίων παρήνεσα
εὐχὴν ποιήσασθαι χιμάρων εἰς αὔριον,
αἱ τριχίδες εἰ γενοίαθ᾽ ἑκατὸν τοὐβολοῦ.
ἐκαραδόκησεν εἰς ἔμ᾽ ἡ βουλὴ πάλιν.
ὁ δὲ ταῦτ᾽ ἀκούσας ἐκπλαγεὶς ἐφληνάφα·
665   κᾆθ᾽ εἷλκον αὐτὸν οἱ πρυτάνεις χοἰ τοξόται,
οἱ δ᾽ ἐθορύβουν περὶ τῶν ἀφύων ἑστηκότες·
ὁ δ᾽ ἠντεβόλει γ᾽ αὐτοὺς ὀλίγον μεῖναι χρόνον·
"ἵν᾽ ἅττ᾽ ὁ κῆρυξ οὑκ Λακεδαίμονος λέγει
πύθησθ᾽· ἀφῖκται γὰρ περὶ σπονδῶν", λέγων.
670   οἱ δ᾽ ἐξ ἑνὸς στόματος ἅπαντες ἀνέκραγον·
"νυνὶ περὶ σπονδῶν; ἐπειδή γ᾽, ὦ μέλε,

be the first to announce it: never since the war broke out have I ever seen sprats cheaper!" Right away their expressions turned sunny, and they moved to crown me for my glad tidings. And I recommended to them, making it their state secret, that to be able to buy lots of sprats for a penny, they should immediately confiscate all the bowls in the potters' market. They applauded loudly and gaped at me in admiration. But he caught on, that Paphlagon, knowing of course the sort of line that especially pleases the Council, and made a proposal: "Gentlemen, in view of the happy event just reported, I think we should sacrifice, in honor of the glad tidings, one hundred cows to the Goddess!"[53] The Council switched its allegiance back to him. When I realized I was being outplayed by his cow dung, I raised the bid to two hundred cows and recommended that they vow a thousand goats to the Wild Maiden[54] tomorrow, if anchovies should sell for a hundred a penny. The Council swung their heads back to me. He was stunned to hear it and started babbling. Then the magistrates and the policemen started to drag him away, and the Councillors stood up hollering about the anchovies. He kept begging them to hold on a moment "until you find out what the Spartan herald has to say," says he, "because he's here to discuss a peace treaty!" But all of them yelled back as one, "A peace treaty now? How convenient, sir, when they've just heard

[53] Athena, as at the Panathenaea.
[54] Artemis Agrotera, to whom 500 goats were sacrificed each year in fulfillment of a vow made before the battle of Marathon in 490.

ARISTOPHANES

ᾔσθοντο τὰς ἀφύας παρ' ἡμῖν ἀξίας.
οὐ δεόμεθα σπονδῶν· ὁ πόλεμος ἑρπέτω."
ἐκεκράγεσάν τε τοὺς πρυτάνεις ἀφιέναι·
675 εἶθ' ὑπερεπήδων τοὺς δρυφάκτους πανταχῇ.
ἐγὼ δὲ τὰ κορίανν' ἐπριάμην ὑποδραμὼν
ἅπαντα τά τε γήτει' ὅσ' ἦν ἐν τἀγορᾷ·
ἔπειτα ταῖς ἀφύαις ἐδίδουν ἡδύσματα
ἀποροῦσιν αὐτοῖς προῖκα κἀχαριζόμην.
680 οἱ δ' ὑπερεπήνουν ὑπερεπύππαζόν τέ με
ἅπαντες οὕτως ὥστε τὴν βουλὴν ὅλην
ὀβολοῦ κοριάννοις ἀναλαβὼν ἐλήλυθα.

ΧΟΡΟΣ
(ἀντ) πάντα τοι πέπραγας οἷα
χρὴ τὸν εὐτυχοῦντα·
ηὗρε δ' ὁ πανοῦργος ἕτε-
ρον πολὺ πανουργίαις
685 μείζοσι κεκασμένον
καὶ δόλοισι ποικίλοις
ῥήμασίν θ' αἱμύλοις.
ἀλλ' ὅπως ἀγωνιεῖ φρόν-
τιζε τἀπίλοιπ' ἄριστα·
συμμάχους δ' ἡμᾶς ἔχων εὔ–
690 νους ἐπίστασαι πάλαι.

ΑΛΛΑΝΤΟΠΩΛΗΣ
καὶ μὴν ὁ Παφλαγὼν οὑτοσὶ προσέρχεται,
ὠθῶν κολόκυμα καὶ ταράττων καὶ κυκῶν,
ὡς δὴ καταπιόμενός με. Μορμὼ τοῦ θράσους.

that anchovies are a bargain here! We don't need a peace treaty; let the war drag on!" And they hollered for the magistrates to adjourn, then started jumping over the turnstiles every which way. I cut ahead of them and bought up all the coriander and leeks in the market, then handed them out as a free gift to the Councillors when they needed seasoning for the sprats. And they all praised and cheered me so extravagantly that I've returned with the whole Council in my pocket for a pennyworth of coriander.

CHORUS
Your fortune has been all
that defines the successful man,
and that rascal has met
another who far excels him
in greater rascality
and intricate schemes
and wheedling words.
But mind you plan how best to fight
the remaining rounds;
you've long known that in us
you have partisan allies.

Enter PAPHLAGON.

SAUSAGE SELLER
Here comes that Paphlagon now, driving a long ground swell and chopping and churning, no doubt intent on pulling me under. What a brassy devil!

ARISTOPHANES

ΠΑΦΛΑΓΩΝ

εἰ μή σ᾽ ἀπολέσαιμ᾽, εἴ τι τῶν αὐτῶν ἐμοὶ
695 ψευδῶν ἐνείη, διαπέσοιμι πανταχῇ.

ΑΛΛΑΝΤΟΠΩΛΗΣ

ἥσθην ἀπειλαῖς, ἐγέλασα ψολοκομπίαις,
ἀπεπυδάρισα μόθωνα, περιεκόκκασα.

ΠΑΦΛΑΓΩΝ

οὔτοι μὰ τὴν Δήμητρ᾽ ἔτ᾽ εἰ μή σ᾽ ἐκφάγω
ἐκ τῆσδε τῆς γῆς, οὐδέποτε βιώσομαι.

ΑΛΛΑΝΤΟΠΩΛΗΣ

700 εἰ μὴ 'κφάγῃς; ἐγὼ δέ γ᾽, εἰ μή σ᾽ ἐκπίω,
κἂν ἐκροφήσας αὐτὸς ἐπιδιαρραγῶ.

ΠΑΦΛΑΓΩΝ

ἀπολῶ σε νὴ τὴν προεδρίαν τὴν ἐκ Πύλου.

ΑΛΛΑΝΤΟΠΩΛΗΣ

ἰδοὺ προεδρίαν· οἷον ὄψομαί σ᾽ ἐγὼ
ἐκ τῆς προεδρίας ἔσχατον θεώμενον.

ΠΑΦΛΑΓΩΝ

705 ἐν τῷ ξύλῳ δήσω σε νὴ τὸν οὐρανόν.

ΑΛΛΑΝΤΟΠΩΛΗΣ

ὡς ὀξύθυμος. φέρε τί σοι δῶ καταφαγεῖν;
ἐπὶ τῷ φάγοις ἥδιστ᾽ ἄν; ἐπὶ βαλλαντίῳ;

ΠΑΦΛΑΓΩΝ

ἐξαρπάσομαί σου τοῖς ὄνυξι τἄντερα.

312

KNIGHTS

PAPHLAGON

If I'm the liar that I used to be, and still can't destroy you, let me be blown to bits!

SAUSAGE SELLER

Your threats are music to my ears! Your fuming boasts make me laugh, dance the shimmy, and crow!

PAPHLAGON

I won't go on living, by Demeter I won't, if I don't devour you right off this earth!

SAUSAGE SELLER

If you don't devour me? Same goes for me if I don't guzzle you down, even if swallowing you makes me burst!

PAPHLAGON

I'll destroy you, so help me the front-row seat I won at Pylos!

SAUSAGE SELLER

Oho, front-row seat! How I'll love seeing you exchange that seat for one in the last row!

PAPHLAGON

By heaven, I'll clamp you in the stocks!

SAUSAGE SELLER

What a cranky temper! Here, what'll I give you to eat? What's your favorite snack? Wallet?

PAPHLAGON

I'll rip out your guts with my fingernails!

ARISTOPHANES

ΑΛΛΑΝΤΟΠΩΛΗΣ
ἀπονυχιῶ σου τἀν πρυτανείῳ σιτία.

ΠΑΦΛΑΓΩΝ
710 ἕλξω σε πρὸς τὸν δῆμον, ἵνα δῷς μοι δίκην.

ΑΛΛΑΝΤΟΠΩΛΗΣ
κἀγὼ δὲ σ᾽ ἕλξω καὶ διαβαλῶ πλείονα.

ΠΑΦΛΑΓΩΝ
ἀλλ᾽, ὦ πόνηρε, σοὶ μὲν οὐδὲν πείθεται·
ἐγὼ δ᾽ ἐκείνου καταγελῶ γ᾽ ὅσον θέλω.

ΑΛΛΑΝΤΟΠΩΛΗΣ
ὡς σφόδρα σὺ τὸν δῆμον σεαυτοῦ νενόμικας.

ΠΑΦΛΑΓΩΝ
715 ἐπίσταμαι γὰρ αὐτὸν οἷς ψωμίζεται.

ΑΛΛΑΝΤΟΠΩΛΗΣ
κᾆθ᾽ ὥσπερ αἱ τίτθαι γε σιτίζεις κακῶς·
μασώμενος γὰρ τῷ μὲν ὀλίγον ἐντίθης,
αὐτὸς δ᾽ ἐκείνου τριπλάσιον κατέσπακας.

ΠΑΦΛΑΓΩΝ
καὶ νὴ Δί᾽ ὑπό γε δεξιότητος τῆς ἐμῆς
720 δύναμαι ποιεῖν τὸν δῆμον εὐρὺν καὶ στενόν.

ΑΛΛΑΝΤΟΠΩΛΗΣ
χὠ πρωκτὸς οὑμὸς τουτογὶ σοφίζεται.

ΠΑΦΛΑΓΩΝ
οὐκ, ὦγάθ᾽, ἐν βουλῇ με δόξεις καθυβρίσαι.
ἴωμεν εἰς τὸν δῆμον.

314

KNIGHTS

SAUSAGE SELLER
I'll scratch out your free dinners in the Prytaneum!

PAPHLAGON
I'll haul you before Demos and get justice from you!

SAUSAGE SELLER
And I'll haul you, and outslander you!

PAPHLAGON
But Demos doesn't listen to anything you say, you creep,
whereas I can make a fool of him as much as I want.

SAUSAGE SELLER
You're pretty sure you've got Demos in your pocket.

PAPHLAGON
Right; I know the sort of tidbits he likes.

SAUSAGE SELLER
Sure, you feed him, just like the nannies: badly! You chew
some food and feed him a morsel, after you've bolted down
three times as much yourself.

PAPHLAGON
And what's more, by god, I can make Demos expand and
contract, thanks to my dexterity.

SAUSAGE SELLER
Even my arsehole can do that trick!

PAPHLAGON
Mister, you won't be taking credit for putting me down in
Council. Let's go before Demos.

315

ARISTOPHANES

ΑΛΛΑΝΤΟΠΩΛΗΣ
οὐδὲν κωλύει,
ἰδού· βάδιζε, μηδὲν ἡμᾶς ἰσχέτω.

ΠΑΦΛΑΓΩΝ
ὦ Δῆμε, δεῦρ᾽ ἔξελθε.

ΑΛΛΑΝΤΟΠΩΛΗΣ
725   νὴ Δί, ὦ πάτερ,
ἔξελθε δῆτ᾽.

ΠΑΦΛΑΓΩΝ
ὦ Δημίδιον ὦ φίλτατον,
ἔξελθ᾽, ἵν᾽ εἰδῇς οἷα περιυβρίζομαι.

ΔΗΜΟΣ
τίνες οἱ βοῶντες; οὐκ ἄπιτ᾽ ἀπὸ τῆς θύρας;
τὴν εἰρεσιώνην μου κατεσπαράξατε.
τίς, ὦ Παφλαγών, ἀδικεῖ σε;

ΠΑΦΛΑΓΩΝ
730   διὰ σὲ τύπτομαι
ὑπὸ τουτουὶ καὶ τῶν νεανίσκων.

ΔΗΜΟΣ
τιή;

ΠΑΦΛΑΓΩΝ
ὁτιὴ φιλῶ σ᾽, ὦ Δῆμ᾽, ἐραστής τ᾽ εἰμὶ σός.

ΔΗΜΟΣ
σὺ δ᾽ εἶ τίς ἐτεόν;

SAUSAGE SELLER

Nothing's stopping us. All right, move along; don't let anything keep us.

PAPHLAGON

(*knocking at Demos' door*) Oh, Demos, come out here!

SAUSAGE SELLER

Yes, sir, do come out!

PAPHLAGON

My dearest darling Demos, come out and see what outrageous insults I'm taking!

DEMOS

(*within*) What's all the shouting? Get away from my door!
(*emerging*) You've battered my harvest wreath to bits!
Paphlagon, who's doing you wrong?

PAPHLAGON

On account of you, this guy here and these young bloods are beating me up.

DEMOS

Why?

PAPHLAGON

Because I adore you, Mr. Demos, and because I'm your lover![55]

DEMOS

(*to the Sausage Seller*) And tell me, who are you?

[55] See *Acharnians* 144 n.

---

[727] post 729 *y*

ARISTOPHANES

ΑΛΛΑΝΤΟΠΩΛΗΣ
                ἀντεραστὴς τουτουί,
ἐρῶν πάλαι σου βουλόμενός τέ σ' εὖ ποιεῖν,
735 ἄλλοι τε πολλοὶ καὶ καλοί τε κἀγαθοί.
ἀλλ' οὐχ οἷοί τ' ἐσμὲν διὰ τουτονί. σὺ γὰρ
ὅμοιος εἶ τοῖς παισὶ τοῖς ἐρωμένοις·
τοὺς μὲν καλούς τε κἀγαθοὺς οὐ προσδέχει,
σαυτὸν δὲ λυχνοπώλαισι καὶ νευρορράφοις
740 καὶ σκυτοτόμοις καὶ βυρσοπώλαισιν δίδως.

ΠΑΦΛΑΓΩΝ
εὖ γὰρ ποιῶ τὸν δῆμον.

ΑΛΛΑΝΤΟΠΩΛΗΣ
                εἰπέ μοι, τί δρῶν;

ΠΑΦΛΑΓΩΝ
ὅ τι; τὸν στρατηγὸν ὑποδραμὼν τὸν ἐκ Πύλου,
πλεύσας ἐκεῖσε, τοὺς Λάκωνας ἤγαγον.

ΑΛΛΑΝΤΟΠΩΛΗΣ
ἐγὼ δὲ περιπατῶν γ' ἀπ' ἐργαστηρίου
745 ἕψοντος ἑτέρου τὴν χύτραν ὑφειλόμην.

ΠΑΦΛΑΓΩΝ
καὶ μὴν ποιήσας αὐτίκα μάλ' ἐκκλησίαν,
ὦ Δῆμ', ἵν' εἰδῇς ὁπότερος νῷν ἐστί σοι
εὐνούστερος, διάκρινον, ἵνα τοῦτον φιλῇς.

ΑΛΛΑΝΤΟΠΩΛΗΣ
ναί, ναί, διάκρινον δῆτα, πλὴν μὴ 'ν τῇ πυκνί.

318

SAUSAGE SELLER

His rival for your love, one who has long lusted for you and
wanted to treat you right, like many other fine upstanding
people. But because of him, we can't. You see, you're like
the boys who attract lovers: you say no to the fine upstand-
ing ones, but give yourself to lamp sellers[56] and cobblers
and shoemakers and tanners.

PAPHLAGON

Because I treat Demos right!

SAUSAGE SELLER

How so? Let's hear it.

PAPHLAGON

How? I got the jump on the general from Pylos, sailed
down there and brought back the Spartans.

SAUSAGE SELLER

And when I was strolling around, I entered a shop and
filched a pot someone else had on the boil.

PAPHLAGON

I suggest that you hold an Assembly right away, Mr. De-
mos, to find out which of us is more devoted to you, and
decide, so you can cherish that one.

SAUSAGE SELLER

Yes, yes, do decide between us, but not on the Pnyx.

---

[56] A jibe at Hyperbolus (see *Acharnians* 846-47).

---

742 τὸν στρατηγὸν...τὸν Γ² Vp3 t b: τῶν στρατηγῶν...τῶν
cett.: τοὺς στρατηγοὺς...τοὺς v.l. Σ

ARISTOPHANES

ΔΗΜΟΣ

750 οὐκ ἂν καθιζοίμην ἐν ἄλλῳ χωρίῳ.
ἀλλ᾽ εἰς τὸ πρόσθε. χρὴ παρεῖν᾽ εἰς τὴν πύκνα.

ΑΛΛΑΝΤΟΠΩΛΗΣ

οἴμοι κακοδαίμων, ὡς ἀπόλωλ᾽. ὁ γὰρ γέρων
οἴκοι μὲν ἀνδρῶν ἐστι δεξιώτατος,
ὅταν δ᾽ ἐπὶ ταυτησὶ καθῆται τῆς πέτρας,
755 κέχηνεν ὥσπερ ἐμποδίζων ἰσχάδας.

ΧΟΡΟΣ

(στρ) νῦν δή σε πάντα δεῖ κάλων ἐξιέναι σεαυτοῦ,
καὶ λῆμα θούριον φορεῖν καὶ λόγους ἀφύκτους,
ὅτοισι τόνδ᾽ ὑπερβαλεῖ. ποικίλος γὰρ ἀνὴρ
κἀκ τῶν ἀμηχάνων πόρους εὐμήχανος πορίζειν.
760 πρὸς ταῦθ᾽ ὅπως ἕξει πολὺς καὶ λαμπρὸς εἰς τὸν
ἄνδρα.

ΚΟΡΥΦΑΙΟΣ

ἀλλὰ φυλάττου καὶ πρὶν ἐκεῖνον προσκεῖσθαί σοι
πρότερον σὺ
τοὺς δελφῖνας μετεωρίζου καὶ τὴν ἄκατον
παραβάλλου.

ΠΑΦΛΑΓΩΝ

τῇ μὲν δεσποίνῃ Ἀθηναίῃ, τῇ τῆς πόλεως μεδεούσῃ,
εὔχομαι, εἰ μὲν περὶ τὸν δῆμον τὸν Ἀθηναίων
γεγένημαι
765 βέλτιστος ἀνὴρ μετὰ Λυσικλέα καὶ Κύνναν καὶ
Σαλαβακχώ,
ὥσπερ νυνὶ μηδὲν δράσας δειπνεῖν ἐν τῷ πρυτανείῳ·

320

DEMOS

I wouldn't sit anywhere else. Forward, then! All be in attendance on the Pnyx!

All move into the orchestra, where DEMOS *takes a seat on a rock.*

SAUSAGE SELLER

(*aside*) Oh blast my luck, I'm finished! When he's at home the old fellow's the shrewdest of men, but when he's sitting on that rock, he gapes like a chewer of dried figs!

CHORUS

Now you must spread all the sail you have,
and convey a commanding spirit and irresistible
    arguments,
with which to overthrow him. For your foe is wily,
good at working out what works in unworkable
    situations.
So advance on your man with the full force of a
    storm!

CHORUS LEADER

Now keep your eyes open, and before he attacks, you hoist your dolphins[57] to the yardarms and lay your boat alongside.

PAPHLAGON

I pray to Lady Athena, Mistress of the City: if in service to the Athenian Demos I have been the leading man, after Lysicles, Cynna, and Salabaccho,[58] may I continue to dine

---

[57] Lumps of iron or lead that were dropped on the enemy's decks.   [58] Cynna and Salabaccho were notorious courtesans.

ARISTOPHANES

εἰ δέ σε μισῶ καὶ μὴ περί σου μάχομαι μόνος
ἀντιβεβηκώς,
ἀπολοίμην καὶ διαπρισθείην κατατμηθείην τε
λέπαδνα.

ΑΛΛΑΝΤΟΠΩΛΗΣ

κἄγωγ᾽, ὦ Δῆμ᾽, εἰ μή σε φιλῶ καὶ μὴ στέργω,
κατατμηθεὶς
770   ἑψοίμην ἐν περικομματίοις· κεἰ μὴ τούτοισι πέποιθας,
ἐπὶ ταυτησὶ κατακνησθείην ἐν μυττωτῷ μετὰ τυροῦ
καὶ τῇ κρεάγρᾳ τῶν ὀρχιπέδων ἑλκοίμην εἰς Κερα-
μεικόν.

ΠΑΦΛΑΓΩΝ

καὶ πῶς ἂν ἐμοῦ μᾶλλόν σε φιλῶν, ὦ Δῆμε,
γένοιτο πολίτης;
ὃς πρῶτα μέν, ἡνίκ᾽ ἐβούλευον, σοὶ χρήματα
πλεῖστ᾽ ἀπέδειξα
775   ἐν τῷ κοινῷ, τοὺς μὲν στρεβλῶν, τοὺς δ᾽ ἄγχων,
τοὺς δὲ μεταιτῶν,
οὐ φροντίζων τῶν ἰδιωτῶν οὐδενός, εἰ σοὶ
χαριοίμην.

ΑΛΛΑΝΤΟΠΩΛΗΣ

τοῦτο μέν, ὦ Δῆμ᾽, οὐδὲν σεμνόν· κἀγὼ γὰρ τοῦτό
σε δράσω·
ἁρπάζων γὰρ τοὺς ἄρτους σοι τοὺς ἀλλοτρίους
παραθήσω.
ὡς δ᾽ οὐχὶ φιλεῖ σ᾽ οὐδ᾽ ἔστ᾽ εὔνους, τοῦτ᾽ αὐτό σε
πρῶτα διδάξω,

322

in the Prytaneum for doing nothing; but if I'm your enemy and cease standing alone in the forefront to fight for you, may I perish, sawn in two and sliced up for harnesses!

SAUSAGE SELLER

As for me, Demos, if I don't love and cherish you, may I be sliced up and boiled with mincemeat; and if you don't believe it, may I be grated on this very table in pesto with cheese, and be dragged by the balls with a meathook to Potters' Field!

PAPHLAGON

Just how could there be a citizen who cherishes you more than I do, Demos? First of all, when I was a Councillor, I showed record profits in the public accounts by putting men on the rack, or throttling them or demanding a cut, without regard for anyone's personal situation, so long as I could gratify you.

SAUSAGE SELLER

Demos, that's nothing to brag about; I'll do the same thing for you. I'll snatch other people's loaves and serve them to you. The first thing I'll prove to you is that he isn't your

ARISTOPHANES

780 ἀλλ᾽ ἢ διὰ τοῦτ᾽ αὖθ᾽ ὁτιή σου τῆς ἀνθρακιᾶς ἀπο-
λαύει.
σὲ γάρ, ὃς Μήδοισι διεξιφίσω περὶ τῆς χώρας
Μαραθῶνι,
καὶ νικήσας ἡμῖν μεγάλως ἐγγλωττοτυπεῖν παρέδω-
κας,
ἐπὶ ταῖσι πέτραις οὐ φροντίζει σκληρῶς σε καθή-
μενον οὕτως,
οὐχ ὥσπερ ἐγὼ ῥαψάμενός σοι τουτὶ φέρω. ἀλλ᾽
ἐπαναίρου,
785 κᾆτα καθίζου μαλακῶς, ἵνα μὴ τρίβῃς τὴν ἐν
Σαλαμῖνι.

ΔΗΜΟΣ
ἄνθρωπε, τίς εἶ; μῶν ἔγγονος εἶ τῶν Ἁρμοδίου τις
ἐκείνων;
τοῦτό γέ τοί σου τοὔργον ἀληθῶς γενναῖον καὶ
φιλόδημον.

ΠΑΦΛΑΓΩΝ
ὡς ἀπὸ μικρῶν εὔνους αὐτῷ θωπευματίων
γεγένησαι.

ΑΛΛΑΝΤΟΠΩΛΗΣ
καὶ σὺ γὰρ αὐτὸν πολὺ μικροτέροις τούτων
δελεάσμασιν εἷλες.

ΠΑΦΛΑΓΩΝ
790 καὶ μὴν εἴ πού τις ἀνὴρ ἐφάνη τῷ δήμῳ μᾶλλον
ἀμύνων

friend or your partisan, save only that he enjoys sitting by
your fire. At Marathon you outduelled the Medes in de-
fense of our country, and your victory bequeathed to our
tongues matter for minting great phrases. But he doesn't
care if you have to sit like that on the hard rocks, unlike
me, who bring this cushion I've had made for you. Here,
get up a moment; now sit back down comfortably, so you
don't chafe what sat to the oar at Salamis.[59]

DEMOS

Who are you, my man? You're not a descendant of Har-
modius' famous family, are you?[60] All I can say is, this act
of yours is truly outstanding and Demos-spirited!

PAPHLAGON

With that paltry bit of fawning you're suddenly his parti-
san!

SAUSAGE SELLER

Well, you hooked him with much paltrier baits than that.

PAPHLAGON

I say the man has never appeared who stuck up for Demos

---

[59] The major victory over the Persian fleet in 480.

[60] Cleon seems to have been related by marriage to one of
Harmodius' descendants.

ἢ μᾶλλον ἐμοῦ σε φιλῶν, ἐθέλω περὶ τῆς κεφαλῆς
περιδόσθαι.

ΑΛΛΑΝΤΟΠΩΛΗΣ

καὶ πῶς σὺ φιλεῖς, ὃς τοῦτον ὁρῶν οἰκοῦντ᾽ ἐν ταῖς
πιθάκναισιν
καὶ γυπαρίοις καὶ πυργιδίοις ἔτος ὄγδοον οὐκ
ἐλεαίρεις,
ἀλλὰ καθείρξας αὐτὸν βλίττεις; Ἀρχεπτολέμου δὲ
φέροντος
795 τὴν εἰρήνην ἐξεσκέδασας, τὰς πρεσβείας τ᾽
ἀπελαύνεις
ἐκ τῆς πόλεως ῥαθαπυγίζων, αἳ τὰς σπονδὰς
προκαλοῦνται.

ΠΑΦΛΑΓΩΝ

ἵνα γ᾽ Ἑλλήνων ἄρξῃ πάντων. ἔστι γὰρ ἐν τοῖς
λογίοισιν
ὡς τοῦτον δεῖ ποτ᾽ ἐν Ἀρκαδίᾳ πεντωβόλου
ἡλιάσασθαι,
ἢν ἀναμείνῃ· πάντως δ᾽ αὐτὸν θρέψω ᾽γὼ καὶ
θεραπεύσω,
800 ἐξευρίσκων εὖ καὶ μιαρῶς ὁπόθεν τὸ τριώβολον ἕξει.

ΑΛΛΑΝΤΟΠΩΛΗΣ

οὐχ ἵνα γ᾽ ἄρξῃ μὰ Δί᾽ Ἀρκαδίας προνοούμενος,
ἀλλ᾽ ἵνα μᾶλλον
σὺ μὲν ἁρπάζῃς καὶ δωροδοκῇς παρὰ τῶν πόλεων,
ὁ δὲ δῆμος

better than me, or cherished you more, and I don't mind staking my head on it!

SAUSAGE SELLER

Just how can you claim to cherish him, when you've seen him living in barrels and shanties and garrets for eight years now[61] and feel no pity, indeed shut him in and rifle his hut? And when Archeptolemus brought a peace proposal you tore it in pieces; and the embassies that offered a treaty, you kicked their butts and drove them from the city.

PAPHLAGON

Yes, so he could rule over all Greeks! It's right in the oracles: one day this Demos shall draw five obols[62] to hear cases in Arcadia,[63] if he stays the course; in any event, I'll nourish and cater to him, finding him his three obols by any means, fair and foul.

SAUSAGE SELLER

You certainly aren't figuring how he can rule Arcadia, but how you can steal and take bribes from the allied cities,

[61] On these conditions see Thucydides 2.14-17, 52.

[62] See 51 n.

[63] For Athenian ambitions in the Peloponnese see Thucydides 5.29, 47.

ARISTOPHANES

ὑπὸ τοῦ πολέμου καὶ τῆς ὁμίχλης ἃ πανουργεῖς μὴ
  καθορᾷ σου,
ἀλλ' ὑπ' ἀνάγκης ἅμα καὶ χρείας καὶ μισθοῦ πρός
  σε κεχήνῃ.
805 εἰ δέ ποτ' εἰς ἀγρὸν οὗτος ἀπελθὼν εἰρηναῖος δια-
  τρίψῃ,
καὶ χίδρα φαγὼν ἀναθαρρήσῃ καὶ στεμφύλῳ εἰς
  λόγον ἔλθῃ,
γνώσεται οἵων ἀγαθῶν αὐτὸν τῇ μισθοφορᾷ
  παρεκόπτου·
εἶθ' ἥξει σοι δριμὺς ἄγροικος κατά σου τὴν ψῆφον
  ἰχνεύων.
ἃ σὺ γιγνώσκων τόνδ' ἐξαπατᾷς καὶ ὀνειροπολεῖς
  περὶ σαυτοῦ.

ΠΑΦΛΑΓΩΝ
810 οὔκουν δεινὸν ταυτί σε λέγειν δῆτ' ἔστ' ἐμὲ καὶ
  διαβάλλειν
πρὸς Ἀθηναίους καὶ τὸν δῆμον, πεποιηκότα
  πλείονα χρηστὰ
νὴ τὴν Δήμητρα Θεμιστοκλέους πολλῷ περὶ τὴν
  πόλιν ἤδη;

ΑΛΛΑΝΤΟΠΩΛΗΣ
ὦ πόλις Ἄργους, κλύεθ' οἷα λέγει. σὺ Θεμιστοκλεῖ
  ἀντιφερίζεις;
ὃς ἐποίησεν τὴν πόλιν ἡμῶν μεστὴν εὑρὼν ἐπιχειλῆ,
815 καὶ πρὸς τούτοις ἀριστώσῃ τὸν Πειραιᾶ προσ-
  έμαξεν,

and how Demos can be made blind to your crimes amid
the fog of war, while mooning at you from necessity, dep-
rivation, and jury pay. But if Demos ever returns to his
peaceful life on the farm, and regains his spirit by eating
porridge and chewing the fat with some pressed olives,
he'll realize the many benefits you beat him out of with
your state pay; then he'll come after you with a farmer's
vengeful temper, tracking down a ballot to use against you.
You're aware of this, so you keep fooling him and rigging
up dreams about yourself.[64]

PAPHLAGON

Isn't it really awful that you presume to say such things and
to slander me before the Athenians and Demos, after my
many fine services—many more, by Demeter, than Them-
istocles ever did for the city?

SAUSAGE SELLER

"City of Argos, hearken to his words!"[65] Are you matching
yourself with Themistocles? He found our city's cup half-
full and filled it the rest of the way, and he baked the
Piraeus as dessert for her lunch,[66] and added new seafood

[64] Thucydides 5.16.1 similarly explains Cleon's aggressive poli-
cies.

[65] Euripides' *Telephus,* fr. 713.

[66] See Thucydides 1.93.

---

[809] σ(ε)αυτοῦ z: αὐτοῦ van Herwerden

ἀφελών τ᾽ οὐδὲν τῶν ἀρχαίων ἰχθῦς καινοὺς
   παρέθηκεν·
σὺ δ᾽ Ἀθηναίους ἐζήτησας μικροπολίτας ἀποφῆναι
διατειχίζων καὶ χρησμῳδῶν, ὁ Θεμιστοκλεῖ ἀντι-
   φερίζων.
κἀκεῖνος μὲν φεύγει τὴν γῆν, σὺ δ᾽ Ἀχιλλείων
   ἀπομάττει.

ΠΑΦΛΑΓΩΝ

820   οὔκουν ταυτὶ δεινὸν ἀκούειν, ὦ Δῆμ᾽, ἐστίν μ᾽ ὑπὸ
   τούτου,
ὁτιή σε φιλῶ;

ΔΗΜΟΣ

   παῦ παῦ, οὗτος, καὶ μὴ σκέρβολλε πονηρά.
πολλοῦ δὲ πολύν με χρόνον καὶ νῦν ἐλελήθεις
   ἐγκρυφιάζων.

ΑΛΛΑΝΤΟΠΩΛΗΣ

μιαρώτατος, ὦ Δημακίδιον, καὶ πλεῖστα πανοῦργα
   δεδρακώς.
ὁπόταν χασμᾷ, καὶ τοὺς καυλοὺς
825   τῶν εὐθυνῶν ἐκκαυλίζων
καταβροχθίζει, κἀμφοῖν χειροῖν
μυστιλᾶται τῶν δημοσίων.

ΠΑΦΛΑΓΩΝ

οὐ χαιρήσεις, ἀλλά σε κλέπτονθ᾽
αἱρήσω ᾽γὼ τρεῖς μυριάδας.

dishes to her menu while taking away none of the old;
whereas you've tried to turn the Athenians into tiny-town-
ies by building partitions and chanting oracles. Themisto-
cles' match! And he's exiled from the country, while you
wipe your fingers on "peerless Achilles" baguettes! [67]

PAPHLAGON

Isn't it awful to hear him say these things about me, De-
mos, just because I cherish you?

DEMOS

(*to Paphlagon*) Shut up, shut up, you, and stop your sleazy
mud-slinging! You've been getting away with hoodwinking
me for far too long already.

SAUSAGE SELLER

He's utter scum, my precious Demos, and a champion evil-
doer. While you're gaping into space, he breaks the choic-
est stalks off the audits of outgoing officials and gulps them
down, and with both hands sops the gravy from the people's
treasury.

PAPHLAGON

You won't get the last laugh; I'll convict you of stealing
thirty thousand drachmas!

[67] These were served in the Prytaneum (167 n.).

ARISTOPHANES

ΑΛΛΑΝΤΟΠΩΛΗΣ

830　τί θαλαττοκοπεῖς καὶ πλατυγίζεις,
　　　μιαρώτατος ὢν περὶ τὸν δῆμον
　　　τὸν Ἀθηναίων; καί σ᾽ ἐπιδείξω
　　　νὴ τὴν Δήμητρ᾽, ἢ μὴ ζῴην,
　　　δωροδοκήσαντ᾽ ἐκ Μυτιλήνης
835　πλεῖν ἢ μνᾶς τετταράκοντα.

ΧΟΡΟΣ

(ἀντ)　ὦ πᾶσιν ἀνθρώποις φανεὶς μέγιστον ὠφέλημα,
　　　ζηλῶ σε τῆς εὐγλωττίας. εἰ γὰρ ὧδ᾽ ἐποίσει,
　　　μέγιστος Ἑλλήνων ἔσει, καὶ μόνος καθέξεις
　　　τἀν τῇ πόλει τῶν συμμάχων τ᾽ ἄρξεις ἔχων τρίαιναν,
840　ᾗ πολλὰ χρήματ᾽ ἐργάσει σείων τε καὶ ταράττων.

ΚΟΡΥΦΑΙΟΣ

　　　καὶ μὴ μεθῇς τὸν ἄνδρ᾽, ἐπειδή σοι λαβὴν δέδωκεν·
　　　κατεργάσει γὰρ ῥᾳδίως πλευρὰς ἔχων τοιαύτας.

ΠΑΦΛΑΓΩΝ

　　　οὐκ, ὦγαθοί, ταῦτ᾽ ἐστί πω ταύτῃ μὰ τὸν Ποσειδῶ.
　　　ἐμοὶ γάρ ἐστ᾽ εἰργασμένον τοιοῦτον ἔργον ὥστε
845　ἁπαξάπαντας τοὺς ἐμοὺς ἐχθροὺς ἐπιστομίζειν,
　　　ἕως ἂν ᾖ τῶν ἀσπίδων τῶν ἐκ Πύλου τι λοιπόν.

ΑΛΛΑΝΤΟΠΩΛΗΣ

　　　ἐπίσχες· ἐν ταῖς ἀσπίσιν λαβὴν γὰρ ἐνδέδωκας.
　　　οὐ γάρ σ᾽ ἐχρῆν, εἴπερ φιλεῖς τὸν δῆμον, ἐκ προνοίας
　　　ταύτας ἐᾶν αὐτοῖσι τοῖς πόρπαξιν ἀνατεθῆναι.
850　ἀλλ᾽ ἔστι τοῦτ᾽, ὦ Δῆμε, μηχάνημ᾽, ἵν᾽, ἢν σὺ βούλῃ
　　　τὸν ἄνδρα κολάσαι τουτονί, σοὶ τοῦτο μὴ ᾿κγένηται.

KNIGHTS

SAUSAGE SELLER

Why slap the water with the flat of your oar, when you've
treated the Athenian people in the scurviest fashion? And
by Demeter and hope to die, I'll prove you took a bribe
from Mytilene of over forty minas![68]

CHORUS

O paramount benefactor of all mankind revealed,
I envy you your ready tongue! Keep thrusting
    forward this way,
and you'll be the greatest man in Greece, hold sole
    power in the city,
and rule over the allies, in your hand a trident
for shaking them and quaking them and making lots
    of money.

CHORUS LEADER

And don't let your man off the hook, now that he's let you
get a grip on him; you'll put him down easily, with a chest
like yours!

PAPHLAGON

No, gentlemen, we haven't reached that point quite yet, by
Poseidon. For I've accomplished a deed great enough to
put a gag bit in the mouths of all my enemies, as long as
there's anything left of those shields from Pylos!

SAUSAGE SELLER

Hold it: those shields have given me an opening. If you
really cherish the people, you shouldn't have deliberately
let those shields be displayed with their handles still on.
That, Demos, is a stratagem designed to frustrate any pun-
ishment you may want to mete out to this guy. You see what

---

[68] For Cleon and Mytilene see Thucydides 3.1-50.

ὁρᾷς γὰρ αὐτῷ στῖφος οἷόν ἐστι βυρσοπωλῶν
νεανιῶν· τούτους δὲ περιοικοῦσι μελιτοπῶλαι
καὶ τυροπῶλαι· τοῦτο δ᾽ εἰς ἕν ἐστι συγκεκυφός,
855 ὥστ᾽ εἰ σὺ βριμήσαιο καὶ βλέψειας ὀστρακίνδα,
νύκτωρ καθαρπάσαντες ἂν τὰς ἀσπίδας θέοντες
τὰς εἰσβολὰς τῶν ἀλφίτων ἂν καταλάβοιεν ἡμῶν.

ΔΗΜΟΣ

οἴμοι τάλας· ἔχουσι γὰρ πόρπακας; ὦ πόνηρε,
ὅσον με παρεκόπτου χρόνον τοιαῦτα κρουσιδημῶν.

ΠΑΦΛΑΓΩΝ

860 ὦ δαιμόνιε, μὴ τοῦ λέγοντος ἴσθι, μηδ᾽ οἰηθῇς
ἐμοῦ ποθ᾽ εὑρήσειν φίλον βελτίον᾽, ὅστις εἷς ὢν
ἔπαυσα τοὺς ξυνωμότας, καί μ᾽ οὐ λέληθεν οὐδὲν
ἐν τῇ πόλει ξυνιστάμενον, ἀλλ᾽ εὐθέως κέκραγα.

ΑΛΛΑΝΤΟΠΩΛΗΣ

ὅπερ γὰρ οἱ τὰς ἐγχέλεις θηρώμενοι πέπονθας.
865 ὅταν μὲν ἡ λίμνη καταστῇ, λαμβάνουσιν οὐδέν·
ἐὰν δ᾽ ἄνω τε καὶ κάτω τὸν βόρβορον κυκῶσιν,
αἱροῦσι· καὶ σὺ λαμβάνεις, ἢν τὴν πόλιν ταράττῃς.
ἐν δ᾽ εἰπέ μοι τοσουτονί· σκύτη τοσαῦτα πωλῶν
ἔδωκας ἤδη τουτῳὶ κάττυμα παρὰ σεαυτοῦ
ταῖς ἐμβάσιν φάσκων φιλεῖν;

ΔΗΜΟΣ

870   οὐ δῆτα μὰ τὸν Ἀπόλλω.

ΑΛΛΑΝΤΟΠΩΛΗΣ

ἔγνωκας οὖν δῆτ᾽ αὐτὸν οἷός ἐστιν; ἀλλ᾽ ἐγώ σοι

334

a pack of young leather sellers surround him, and around them live the honey sellers and cheese sellers. They're all in this together. So if you start growling and look to be toying with ostraca,[69] they'll take those shields down by night and in a flash seize the entrances to our grain market!

DEMOS

Dear me, their handles are on? You sneak, how long have you been gouging me like this by short-changing the people?

PAPHLAGON

My dear sir, don't believe the last thing you hear, and don't think you'll ever find a better friend than me, who single-handedly put a stop to the conspirators. And nothing gets plotted in the city that I'm not aware of and immediately screaming about.

SAUSAGE SELLER

Yes, you act just like the eel fishermen. When the lake is still, they catch nothing; but if they stir the mud up and down, they make a catch. You also make a catch if you stir up the city. Answer me just one question: though you sell so much leather, and profess to cherish Demos, have you ever given him a free patch for his shoes?

DEMOS

No, by Apollo, he never has!

SAUSAGE SELLER

So now do you recognize him for what he is? I, on the other

---

[69] Shards used both in children's games and in nominating candidates for ostracism (exile from Attica).

ARISTOPHANES

ζεῦγος πριάμενος ἐμβάδων τουτὶ φορεῖν δίδωμι.

ΔΗΜΟΣ

κρίνω σ' ὅσων ἐγῷδα περὶ τὸν δῆμον ἄνδρ' ἄριστον
εὐνούστατόν τε τῇ πόλει καὶ τοῖσι δακτύλοισιν.

ΠΑΦΛΑΓΩΝ

875   οὐ δεινὸν οὖν δῆτ' ἐμβάδας τοσουτονὶ δύνασθαι,
ἐμοῦ δὲ μὴ μνείαν ἔχειν ὅσων πέπονθας; ὅστις
ἔπαυσα τοὺς κινουμένους, τὸν Γρῦπον ἐξαλείψας.

ΑΛΛΑΝΤΟΠΩΛΗΣ

οὔκουν σε δῆτα ταῦτα δεινόν ἐστι πρωκτοτηρεῖν
παῦσαί τε τοὺς κινουμένους; κοὐκ ἔσθ' ὅπως
ἐκείνους

880   οὐχὶ φθονῶν ἔπαυσας, ἵνα μὴ ῥήτορες γένοιντο.
τονδὶ δ' ὁρῶν ἄνευ χιτῶνος ὄντα τηλικοῦτον
οὐπώποτ' ἀμφιμασχάλου τὸν Δῆμον ἠξίωσας
χειμῶνος ὄντος· ἀλλ' ἐγώ σοι τουτονὶ δίδωμι.

ΔΗΜΟΣ

τοιουτονὶ Θεμιστοκλῆς οὐπώποτ' ἐπενόησεν.

885   καίτοι σοφὸν κἀκεῖν' ὁ Πειραιεύς· ἔμοιγε μέντοι
οὐ μεῖζον εἶναι φαίνετ' ἐξεύρημα τοῦ χιτῶνος.

ΠΑΦΛΑΓΩΝ

οἴμοι τάλας, οἵοις πιθηκισμοῖς με περιελαύνεις.

ΑΛΛΑΝΤΟΠΩΛΗΣ

οὔκ, ἀλλ' ὅπερ πίνων ἀνὴρ πέπονθ' ὅταν χεσείῃ,

877 Γρῦπον S: Γρύππον v.l. Σᴹ: Γρύττον z

336

hand, have bought you this pair of shoes here to wear as my present.

DEMOS
I judge you, of all the men I know, the finest servant of Demos and the most devoted to the city and my toes!

PAPHLAGON
But isn't it shocking that a pair of shoes counts for so much, while you've quite forgotten all I've done for you? I put a stop to the buggers by striking Grypus[70] from the citizen rolls.

SAUSAGE SELLER
Well, isn't it shocking that you should pursue this arsehole sleuthing and try to stop the buggers? There's no question that you stopped them out of rivalry, for fear they'd become politicians! And though you see Demos here without a tunic—at his age!—you've never thought he deserves a tunic with two sleeves to wear in winter; *(to Demos)* whereas I'm giving you this one.

DEMOS
Themistocles never thought of this! I grant you the Piraeus was clever too,[71] but to my way of thinking it wasn't a greater piece of policy than this tunic.

PAPHLAGON
Damn it all, what monkey tricks you harass me with!

SAUSAGE SELLER
No, I'm just borrowing your methods, as a man at a drink-

---

[70] "Hook Nose," identity unknown.
[71] See 815 n.

ARISTOPHANES

τοῖσιν τρόποις τοῖς σοῖσιν ὥσπερ βλαυτίοισι χρῶμαι.

ΠΑΦΛΑΓΩΝ

890 ἀλλ᾽ οὐχ ὑπερβαλεῖ με θωπείαις· ἐγὼ γὰρ αὐτὸν
προσαμφιῶ τοδί· σὺ δ᾽ οἴμωζ᾽, ὦ πόνηρ᾽.

ΔΗΜΟΣ

ἰαιβοῖ.
οὐκ ἐς κόρακας ἀποφθερεῖ βύρσης κάκιστον ὄζων;

ΑΛΛΑΝΤΟΠΩΛΗΣ

καὶ τοῦτό γ᾽ ἐπίτηδές σε περιήμπεσχ᾽, ἵνα σ᾽ ἀπο-
πνίξῃ·
καὶ πρότερον ἐπεβούλευσέ σοι. τὸν καυλὸν οἶσθ᾽
ἐκεῖνον
τὸν σιλφίου τὸν ἄξιον γενόμενον;

ΔΗΜΟΣ

895   οἶδα μέντοι.

ΑΛΛΑΝΤΟΠΩΛΗΣ

ἐπίτηδες οὗτος αὐτὸν ἔσπευσ᾽ ἄξιον γενέσθαι,
ἵν᾽ ἐσθίοιτ᾽ ὠνούμενοι, κἄπειτ᾽ ἐν ἡλιαίᾳ
βδέοντες ἀλλήλους ἀποκτείνειαν οἱ δικασταί.

ΔΗΜΟΣ

νὴ τὸν Ποσειδῶ καὶ πρὸς ἐμὲ τοῦτ᾽ εἶπ᾽ ἀνὴρ
Κόπρειος.

ΑΛΛΑΝΤΟΠΩΛΗΣ

900 οὐ γὰρ τόθ᾽ ὑμεῖς βδεόμενοι δήπου ᾽γένεσθε πυρροί;

ΔΗΜΟΣ

καὶ νὴ Δί᾽ ἦν γε τοῦτο Πυρράνδρου τὸ μηχάνημα.

338

ing party borrows slippers when he needs to shit.

PAPHLAGON

Well, you can't outdo me when it comes to fawning. (*taking off his jacket*) I'm going to put this on him too, and you can eat your heart out, creep!

DEMOS

Ugh! Get the hell away from me with your terrible stink of rawhide!

SAUSAGE SELLER

And he tried to make you wear that thing deliberately, to suffocate you! He pulled the same trick on you before. Remember when asafetida stalks were such a bargain?

DEMOS

Sure I remember.

SAUSAGE SELLER

He deliberately fixed the price so that everybody would buy and eat them, and then in court the jurors would fart each other to death!

DEMOS

By Poseidon, that's exactly what I was told by a man from Dungstown!

SAUSAGE SELLER

And didn't you all fart each other brown?

DEMOS

God yes, and a real Brown Shirt tactic it was, too.[72]

---

[72] Literally "a contrivance of Pyrrhander," probably a proverbial phrase used here for the sake of the pun; but a contemporary of this name is attested (*IG* I^3 1190.8).

ARISTOPHANES

ΠΑΦΛΑΓΩΝ

οἵοισί μ᾽, ὦ πανοῦργε, βωμολοχεύμασιν ταράττεις.

ΑΛΛΑΝΤΟΠΩΛΗΣ

ἡ γὰρ θεός μ᾽ ἐκέλευε νικῆσαί σ᾽ ἀλαζονείαις.

ΠΑΦΛΑΓΩΝ

ἀλλ᾽ οὐχὶ νικήσεις. ἐγὼ γάρ φημί σοι παρέξειν,
905 ὦ Δῆμε, μηδὲν δρῶντι μισθοῦ τρύβλιον ῥοφῆσαι.

ΑΛΛΑΝΤΟΠΩΛΗΣ

ἐγὼ δὲ κυλίχνιόν γέ σοι καὶ φάρμακον δίδωμι
τὰν τοῖσιν ἀντικνημίοις ἑλκύδρια περιαλείφειν.

ΠΑΦΛΑΓΩΝ

ἐγὼ δὲ τὰς πολιάς γέ σου ᾽κλέγων νέον ποιήσω.

ΑΛΛΑΝΤΟΠΩΛΗΣ

ἰδοὺ δέχου κέρκον λαγῶ τὠφθαλμιδίω περιψῆν.

ΠΑΦΛΑΓΩΝ

910 ἀπομυξάμενος, ὦ Δῆμέ, μου πρὸς τὴν κεφαλὴν
ἀποψῶ.

ΑΛΛΑΝΤΟΠΩΛΗΣ

ἐμοῦ μὲν οὖν.

ΠΑΦΛΑΓΩΝ

ἐμοῦ μὲν οὖν.
ἐγώ σε ποιήσω τριη–
ραρχεῖν, ἀναλίσκοντα τῶν
σαυτοῦ, παλαιὰν ναῦν ἔχοντ᾽,
915 εἰς ἣν ἀναλῶν οὐκ ἐφέ–
ξεις οὐδὲ ναυπηγούμενος·

PAPHLAGON

You bastard, what clownish antics you use to fluster me!

SAUSAGE SELLER

Well, the Goddess told me to beat you with flimflammeries.

PAPHLAGON

But you won't beat me! I assure you, Demos, for doing absolutely nothing I'll provide you with a bowl of state pay to lap up.

SAUSAGE SELLER

And here's a little jar of ointment from me, to rub into the blisters on your shins.

PAPHLAGON

And I'll pluck out your white hairs and make you young.

SAUSAGE SELLER

Here, take this bunny tail and dab your darling eyes.

PAPHLAGON

Blow your nose, Demos, and wipe your hand on my head.

SAUSAGE SELLER

No, on mine.

PAPHLAGON

No, on mine! (*to Sausage Seller*) I'll put you in command of a trireme at your own expense, an ancient hulk that you'll never stop pouring money into and refitting, and I'll

διαμηχανήσομαί θ' ὅπως
ἂν ἱστίον σαπρὸν λάβῃς.

ΑΛΛΑΝΤΟΠΩΛΗΣ

ἀνὴρ παφλάζει, παῦε παῦ,
920 ὑπερζέων· ὑφελκτέον
τῶν δᾳδίων ἀπαρυστέον
τε τῶν ἀπειλῶν ταυτηί.

ΠΑΦΛΑΓΩΝ

δώσεις ἐμοὶ καλὴν δίκην
ἱπούμενος ταῖς εἰσφοραῖς.
925 ἐγὼ γὰρ εἰς τοὺς πλουσίους
σπεύσω σ' ὅπως ἂν ἐγγραφῇς.

ΑΛΛΑΝΤΟΠΩΛΗΣ

ἐγὼ δ' ἀπειλήσω μὲν οὐ—
δέν, εὔχομαι δέ σοι ταδί·
τὸ μὲν τάγηνον τευθίδων
930 ἐφεστάναι σῖζον, σὲ δὲ
γνώμην ἐρεῖν μέλλοντα περὶ
Μιλησίων καὶ κερδανεῖν
τάλαντον, ἢν κατεργάσῃ,
σπεύδειν ὅπως τῶν τευθίδων
935 ἐμπλήμενος φθαίης ἔτ' εἰς
ἐκκλησίαν ἐλθών· ἔπει-
τα πρὶν φαγεῖν ἀνὴρ μεθή-
κοι, καὶ σὺ τὸ τάλαντον λαβεῖν
βουλόμενος ἐ—
940 σθίων ἅμ' ἀποπνιγείης.

fix it so you get rotten sails!

SAUSAGE SELLER

The man's blowing his top—stop, stop!—he's boiling over! We've got to pull out some of that kindling and skim off some of those threats; use this!

PAPHLAGON

You'll pay me a fine penalty for this, when I crush you with tax bills; because I'll fix so you're registered among the rich!

SAUSAGE SELLER

I'll make no threats, but I wish you this: your squid is sizzling in the pan when you're scheduled to make a motion about the Milesians[73] that'll net you a talent if you get it passed, and you're hurrying to stuff yourself with the squid in time to get to the Assembly, and before you can eat it a man comes to fetch you, and you're so eager to get the talent that you choke to death on your meal!

---

[73] Perhaps a reference to the recent doubling of that state's annual tribute.

ARISTOPHANES

ΚΟΡΤΦΑΙΟΣ

εὖ γε νὴ τὸν Δία καὶ τὸν Ἀπόλλω καὶ τὴν Δήμητρα.

ΔΗΜΟΣ

κἀμοὶ δοκεῖ, καὶ τἆλλα γ᾽ εἶναι καταφανῶς
ἀγαθὸς πολίτης, οἷος οὐδείς πω χρόνου
945 ἀνὴρ γεγένηται τοῖσι πολλοῖς τοὐβολοῦ.
σὺ δ᾽, ὦ Παφλαγών, φάσκων φιλεῖν μ᾽ ἐσκορόδισας.
καὶ νῦν ἀπόδος τὸν δακτύλιον, ὡς οὐκέτι
ἐμοὶ ταμιεύσεις.

ΠΑΦΛΑΓΩΝ

ἔχε· τοσοῦτον δ᾽ ἴσθ᾽ ὅτι,
εἰ μή μ᾽ ἐάσεις ἐπιτροπεύειν, ἕτερος αὖ
950 ἐμοῦ πανουργότερός τις ἀναφανήσεται.

ΔΗΜΟΣ

οὐκ ἔσθ᾽ ὅπως ὁ δακτύλιός ἐσθ᾽ οὑτοσὶ
οὑμός· τὸ γοῦν σημεῖον ἕτερον φαίνεται.
ἀλλ᾽ ἦ οὐ καθορῶ;

ΑΛΛΑΝΤΟΠΩΛΗΣ

φέρ᾽ ἴδω, τί σοι σημεῖον ἦν;

ΔΗΜΟΣ

δημοῦ βοείου θρῖον ἐξωπτημένον.

ΑΛΛΑΝΤΟΠΩΛΗΣ

οὐ τοῦτ᾽ ἔνεστιν.

ΔΗΜΟΣ

955 οὐ τὸ θρῖον; ἀλλὰ τί;

CHORUS LEADER

That's a good one, by Zeus, Apollo, and Demeter!

DEMOS

I agree, and think that in general he's obviously a good citizen; it's been quite some time since the dime-a-dozens have had that sort of man on their side. But you, Paphlagon, have ruffled my feathers with your declarations of affection for me. Now return my ring; you're no longer my steward!

PAPHLAGON

Here, take it; but you can be sure of this much: if you won't let me be your steward, someone more villainous will appear in my place.

DEMOS

This can't possibly be my ring; it seems to have a different seal. It must be my eyesight.

SAUSAGE SELLER

Let's have a look. What was your seal?

DEMOS

A pea pulse sandwich, steaming hot.

SAUSAGE SELLER

Not on this ring.

DEMOS

No sandwich? Then what?

ARISTOPHANES

ΑΛΛΑΝΤΟΠΩΛΗΣ

λάρος κεχηνὼς ἐπὶ πέτρας δημηγορῶν.

ΔΗΜΟΣ

αἰβοῖ τάλας.

ΑΛΛΑΝΤΟΠΩΛΗΣ

τί ἐστιν;

ΔΗΜΟΣ

ἀπόφερ᾽ ἐκποδών.
οὐ τὸν ἐμὸν εἶχεν, ἀλλὰ τὸν Κλεωνύμου.
παρ᾽ ἐμοῦ δὲ τουτονὶ λαβὼν ταμίευέ μοι.

ΠΑΦΛΑΓΩΝ

960 μὴ δῆτά πώ γ᾽, ὦ δέσποτ᾽, ἀντιβολῶ σ᾽ ἐγώ,
πρὶν ἄν γε τῶν χρησμῶν ἀκούσῃς τῶν ἐμῶν.

ΑΛΛΑΝΤΟΠΩΛΗΣ

καὶ τῶν ἐμῶν νυν.

ΠΑΦΛΑΓΩΝ

ἀλλ᾽ ἐὰν τούτῳ πίθῃ,
μολγὸν γενέσθαι δεῖ σε.

ΑΛΛΑΝΤΟΠΩΛΗΣ

κἄν γε τουτῳί,
ψωλὸν γενέσθαι δεῖ σε μέχρι τοῦ μυρρίνου.

ΠΑΦΛΑΓΩΝ

965 ἀλλ᾽ οἵ γ᾽ ἐμοὶ λέγουσιν ὡς ἄρξαι σε δεῖ
χώρας ἁπάσης ἐστεφανωμένον ῥόδοις.

SAUSAGE SELLER

A large-mouthed seagull on a rock haranguing the people.

DEMOS

How revolting!

SAUSAGE SELLER

What's the matter?

DEMOS

Get it out of my sight! He wasn't wearing my ring, but Cleonymus'. But here's another; take it and be my steward.

PAPHLAGON

Not yet, master, I beg you, at least not until you've listened to my oracles!

SAUSAGE SELLER

And mine too, then.

PAPHLAGON

If you listen to him, you'll surely become a mere balloon.[74]

SAUSAGE SELLER

And if you listen to him, you'll surely get your cock skinned back to the short and curlies![75]

PAPHLAGON

But I've got oracles predicting that you shall wear a crown of roses and rule over every land.

[74] A slangy version of a famous oracle given to Theseus, predicting that Athens would be storm-tossed but like a wineskin would never be submerged.

[75] I.e. circumcised; see *Acharnians* 158 n.

ARISTOPHANES

ΑΛΛΑΝΤΟΠΩΛΗΣ

οὑμοὶ δέ γ᾽ αὖ λέγουσιν ὡς ἁλουργίδα
ἔχων κατάπαστον καὶ στεφάνην ἐφ᾽ ἅρματος
χρυσοῦ διώξεις Σμικύθην καὶ κύριον.

ΔΗΜΟΣ

970   καὶ μὴν ἔνεγκ᾽ αὐτοὺς ἰών, ἵν᾽ οὑτοσὶ
αὐτῶν ἀκούσῃ.

ΑΛΛΑΝΤΟΠΩΛΗΣ
        πάνυ γε.

ΔΗΜΟΣ
            καὶ σύ νυν φέρε.

ΠΑΦΛΑΓΩΝ
ἰδού.

ΑΛΛΑΝΤΟΠΩΛΗΣ
    ἰδοὺ νὴ τὸν Δί᾽· οὐδὲν κωλύει.

ΧΟΡΟΣ

(στρ) ἥδιστον φάος ἡμέρας
        ἔσται τοῖς τε παροῦσι καὶ
975   τοῖσιν εἰσαφικνουμένοις,
        ἢν Κλέων ἀπόληται.
        καίτοι πρεσβυτέρων τινῶν
        οἵων ἀργαλεωτάτων
        ἐν τῷ δείγματι τῶν δικῶν
980   ἤκουσ᾽ ἀντιλεγόντων,

348

KNIGHTS

SAUSAGE SELLER

And mine predict that you shall wear a diadem and a robe
spangled with crimson, and ride in a golden chariot, and
chase Smicythe and master[76] into court!

DEMOS

(*to Sausage Seller*) Very well, go and get them, so this guy
can hear them.

SAUSAGE SELLER

Sure thing!

DEMOS

And you get yours.

PAPHLAGON

OK!

SAUSAGE SELLER

OK it is! What are we waiting for?

SAUSAGE SELLER and PAPHLAGON *go inside.*

CHORUS

Bright and joyful that day
will be, for residents
and visitors alike,
if Cleon is destroyed!
And yet I heard some
litigious old fogeys
in the lawsuit market
arguing the case

---

[76] Probably a dig at a man named Smicythus (not an uncommon name) for effeminacy, but possibly the phrase is a legal tag, since Smicythe was also a common female name.

ὡς εἰ μὴ 'γένεθ' οὗτος ἐν
τῇ πόλει μέγας, οὐκ ἂν ἤ–
στην σκεύει δύο χρησίμω,
δοῖδυξ οὐδὲ τορύνη.

(ἀντ) ἀλλὰ καὶ τόδ' ἔγωγε θαυ–
986   μάζω τῆς ὑομουσίας
αὐτοῦ· φασὶ γὰρ αὐτὸν οἱ
παῖδες οἳ ξυνεφοίτων,
τὴν Δωριστὶ μόνην ἂν ἁρ–
990   μόττεσθαι θαμὰ τὴν λύραν,
ἄλλην δ' οὐκ ἐθέλειν μαθεῖν·
κᾆτα τὸν κιθαριστὴν
ὀργισθέντ' ἀπάγειν κελεύ–
ειν, ὡς ἁρμονίαν ὁ παῖς
995   οὗτος οὐ δύναται μαθεῖν
ἢν μὴ Δωροδοκιστί.

                    ΠΑΦΛΑΓΩΝ
ἰδοὺ θέασαι, κοὐχ ἅπαντας ἐκφέρω.

                    ΑΛΛΑΝΤΟΠΩΛΗΣ
οἴμ' ὡς χεσείω, κοὐχ ἅπαντας ἐκφέρω.

                    ΔΗΜΟΣ
ταυτὶ τί ἐστι;

that if he hadn't become
a big shot in the city, we wouldn't
have had two useful utensils:
a pestle and a ladle.

I also wonder at this
part of his education
as a swine: the boys
who were his classmates
say that often he would tune
his lyre only in the Dorian mode
and refuse to learn another;
and then the music teacher
angrily had him expelled
"because this boy
can't learn any mode
but the Quid Pro Quorian."[77]

Enter PAPHLAGON *with a load of scrolls.*

PAPHLAGON
Look at these, and that's not all of them!

Enter SAUSAGE SELLER *with a bigger load.*

SAUSAGE SELLER
Oh dear, I'm about to shit, and that's not all of them!

DEMOS
What's all this?

[77] *Dorodokisti* puns on "Dorian" and "bribe taking" (*doro-dokein*).

351

ΠΑΦΛΑΓΩΝ

λόγια.

ΔΗΜΟΣ

πάντ᾽;

ΠΑΦΛΑΓΩΝ

ἐθαύμασας;

1000   καὶ νὴ Δί᾽ ἔτι γέ μούστὶ κιβωτὸς πλέα.

ΑΛΛΑΝΤΟΠΩΛΗΣ

ἐμοὶ δ᾽ ὑπερῷον καὶ ξυνοικία δύο.

ΔΗΜΟΣ

φέρ᾽ ἴδω, τίνος γάρ εἰσιν οἱ χρησμοί ποτε;

ΠΑΦΛΑΓΩΝ

οὑμοὶ μέν εἰσι Βάκιδος.

ΔΗΜΟΣ

οἱ δὲ σοὶ τίνος;

ΑΛΛΑΝΤΟΠΩΛΗΣ

Γλάνιδος, ἀδελφοῦ τοῦ Βάκιδος γεραιτέρου.

ΔΗΜΟΣ

εἰσὶν δὲ περὶ τοῦ;

ΠΑΦΛΑΓΩΝ

1005   περὶ Ἀθηνῶν, περὶ Πύλου,

περὶ σοῦ, περὶ ἐμοῦ, περὶ ἁπάντων πραγμάτων.

ΔΗΜΟΣ

οἱ σοὶ δὲ περὶ τοῦ;

PAPHLAGON

Prophecies.

DEMOS

All of them?

PAPHLAGON

Surprised? By Zeus, I've still got a locker full of them!

SAUSAGE SELLER

And I've got an attic and two tenement buildings full of them!

DEMOS

Let's see. Who could be the source of these oracles?

PAPHLAGON

Mine are from Bacis.

DEMOS

And what about yours?

SAUSAGE SELLER

From Glanis,[78] Bacis' older brother.

DEMOS

And what are they about?

PAPHLAGON

About Athens, about Pylos, about you, about me, about everything.

DEMOS

And what about yours?

[78] Fictitious; *glanis* is a kind of shad.

ΑΛΛΑΝΤΟΠΩΛΗΣ

περὶ Ἀθηνῶν, περὶ φακῆς,
περὶ Λακεδαιμονίων, περὶ σκόμβρων νέων,
περὶ τῶν μετρούντων τἄλφιτ᾽ ἐν ἀγορᾷ κακῶς,
1010 περὶ σοῦ, περὶ ἐμοῦ. τὸ πέος οὑτοσὶ δάκοι.

ΔΗΜΟΣ

ἄγε νυν ὅπως αὐτοὺς ἀναγνώσεσθέ μοι,
καὶ τὸν περὶ ἐμοῦ ᾽κεῖνον ᾧπερ ἥδομαι,
ὡς ἐν νεφέλῃσιν αἰετὸς γενήσομαι.

ΠΑΦΛΑΓΩΝ

ἄκουε δή νυν καὶ πρόσεχε τὸν νοῦν ἐμοί·
1015 φράζευ, Ἐρεχθεΐδη, λογίων ὁδόν, ἥν σοι Ἀπόλλων
ἴαχεν ἐξ ἀδύτοιο διὰ τριπόδων ἐριτίμων.
σῴζεσθαί σ᾽ ἐκέλευ᾽ ἱερὸν κύνα καρχαρόδοντα,
ὃς πρὸ σέθεν χάσκων καὶ ὑπὲρ σοῦ δεινὰ κεκραγὼς
σοὶ μισθὸν ποριεῖ. κἂν μὴ δρᾷ ταῦτ᾽, ἀπολεῖται·
1020 πολλοὶ γὰρ μίσει σφε κατακρώζουσι κολοιοί.

ΔΗΜΟΣ

ταυτὶ μὰ τὴν Δήμητρ᾽ ἐγὼ οὐκ οἶδ᾽ ὅ τι λέγει.
τί γάρ ἐστ᾽ Ἐρεχθεῖ καὶ κολοιοῖς καὶ κυνί;

ΠΑΦΛΑΓΩΝ

ἐγὼ μέν εἰμ᾽ ὁ κύων· πρὸ σοῦ γὰρ ἀπύω·

---

79 Like Cecrops (1055) and Aegeus (1067), an early king of
Attica.
80 For Cleon's claim to be the people's watchdog cf. *Wasps*
894 ff.

SAUSAGE SELLER

About Athens, about lentil soup, about the Spartans, about fresh mackerel, about grain dealers in the market who give short measure, about you, about me. He can go suck himself!

DEMOS

Well then, both of you expound them to me, including the one about myself that I so enjoy, that I shall become an eagle in the clouds.

PAPHLAGON

Then listen, and give me your full attention.

"Mark well, son of Erechtheus,[79] the path of the prophecies, which Apollo

sent shrieking to you from his sanctum through the priceless tripods.

He bids you keep safe the holy sawtoothed watchdog,[80]

who yawns at your feet and by barking terribly on your behalf

provides you with pay, which if he cannot do, he'll die;

for many are the jackdaws that in their hatred croak against him."

DEMOS

By Demeter, I don't know what that one means. What's Erechtheus got to do with jackdaws and a dog?

PAPHLAGON

I'm the dog, because I howl on your behalf; and Phoebus[81]

---

[81] Phoebus, Loxias, and Son of Leto are epithets of Apollo.

ARISTOPHANES

σοὶ δ᾽ εἶπε σῴζεσθαι 'μ᾽ ὁ Φοῖβος τὸν κύνα.

ΑΛΛΑΝΤΟΠΩΛΗΣ

1025 οὐ τοῦτό φησ᾽ ὁ χρησμός, ἀλλ᾽ ὁ κύων ὁδὶ
ὥσπερ ἀθάρης σου τῶν λογίων παρεσθίει.
ἐμοὶ γάρ ἐστ᾽ ὀρθῶς περὶ τούτου τοῦ κυνός.

ΔΗΜΟΣ

λέγε νυν· ἐγὼ δὲ πρῶτα λήψομαι λίθον,
ἵνα μή μ᾽ ὁ χρησμὸς ὁ περὶ τοῦ κυνὸς δάκῃ.

ΑΛΛΑΝΤΟΠΩΛΗΣ

1030 φράζευ, Ἐρεχθεΐδη, κύνα Κέρβερον ἀνδραποδιστήν,
ὃς κέρκῳ σαίνων σ᾽, ὁπόταν δειπνῇς, ἐπιτηρῶν
ἐξέδεταί σου τοὖψον, ὅταν σύ ποι ἄλλοσε χάσκῃς·
εἰσφοιτῶν τ᾽ ἐς τοὐπτάνιον λήσει σε κυνηδὸν
νύκτωρ τὰς λοπάδας καὶ τὰς νήσους διαλείχων.

ΔΗΜΟΣ

1035 νὴ τὸν Ποσειδῶ πολύ γ᾽ ἄμεινον, ὦ Γλάνι.

ΠΑΦΛΑΓΩΝ

ὦ τᾶν, ἄκουσον, εἶτα διάκρινον, τόδε·
ἔστι γυνή, τέξει δὲ λέονθ᾽ ἱεραῖς ἐν Ἀθήναις,
ὃς περὶ τοῦ δήμου πολλοῖς κώνωψι μαχεῖται
ὥς τε περὶ σκύμνοισι βεβηκώς· τὸν σὺ φυλάξαι,
1040 τεῖχος ποιήσας ξύλινον πύργους τε σιδηροῦς.

1026 ἀθάρης Hermann: θύρας z

82 The mythical Hound of Hell; the epithet perhaps refers to the punishment of Mytilene (Thucydides 3.36).

356

is telling you to keep me, your dog, safe.

SAUSAGE SELLER

That's not what the oracle says. This dog here is treating your prophecies like gruel, sneaking bites. I've got the right reading about this dog.

DEMOS

Let's hear it then. But first I'll get a stone in case the oracle about the dog tries to bite me.

SAUSAGE SELLER

"Mark well, son of Erechtheus, the dog Cerberus,
    trafficker in bodies, [82]
who wags his tail at you when you're dining and
    watches,
and when you happen to gape in another direction,
    eats up your entree,
and at night steals into your kitchen all unseen, and
    doglike
licks clean the plates and the islands."

DEMOS

By Poseidon, that's much better, Glanis!

PAPHLAGON

Listen, sir, before you render your verdict:
    "There is a woman who shall bear a lion in holy
        Athens,
who will fight for Demos against a swarm of gnats
as stalwartly as for his cubs; keep him safe,
building a wooden wall and iron towers." [83]

[83] For the "wooden wall" oracle of 480 that justified Athenian confidence in their navy, see Herodotus 7.141.

357

ARISTOPHANES

ταῦτ᾽ οἶσθ᾽ ὅ τι λέγει;

ΔΗΜΟΣ

μὰ τὸν Ἀπόλλω ᾽γὼ μὲν οὔ.

ΠΑΦΛΑΓΩΝ

ἔφραζεν ὁ θεός σοι σαφῶς σῴζειν ἐμέ·
ἐγὼ γὰρ ἀντὶ τοῦ λέοντός εἰμί σοι.

ΔΗΜΟΣ

καὶ πῶς μ᾽ ἐλελήθεις Ἀντιλέων γεγενημένος;

ΑΛΛΑΝΤΟΠΩΛΗΣ

1045 ἐν οὐκ ἀναδιδάσκει σε τῶν λογίων ἑκών,
ὅ τι τὸ σιδήρου τεῖχός ἐστι καὶ ξύλων,
ἐν ᾧ σε σῴζειν τόνδ᾽ ἐκέλευ᾽ ὁ Λοξίας.

ΔΗΜΟΣ

πῶς δῆτα τοῦτ᾽ ἔφραζεν ὁ θεός;

ΑΛΛΑΝΤΟΠΩΛΗΣ
                                    τουτονὶ
δῆσαί σ᾽ ἐκέλευ᾽ ἐν πεντεσυρίγγῳ ξύλῳ.

ΔΗΜΟΣ

1050 ταυτὶ τελεῖσθαι τὰ λόγι᾽ ἤδη μοι δοκεῖ.

ΠΑΦΛΑΓΩΝ

μὴ πείθου· φθονεραὶ γὰρ ἐπικρώζουσι κορῶναι.
ἀλλ᾽ ἱέρακα φίλει μεμνημένος ἐν φρεσίν, ὅς σοι
ἤγαγε συνδήσας Λακεδαιμονίων κορακίνους.

---

[84] The Greek puns on Antileon, an early tyrant of Chalcis.

358

Do you know what that means?

DEMOS

By Apollo, not I.

PAPHLAGON

The god was clearly advising you to keep me safe, because
I stand for the lion you're to get.

DEMOS

And just how did you come to stand for lyin' behind my
back?[84]

SAUSAGE SELLER

One detail in the prophecy he purposely isn't explaining to
you: what the one wall is that's made of iron and wood,
where Loxias[85] ordered you to keep this guy safe.

DEMOS

Well then, what did the god mean by that?

SAUSAGE SELLER

He was ordering you to clamp this guy in the five-holed
wooden pillory.

DEMOS

I think that prophecy will very soon come true!

PAPHLAGON

Trust it not; for jealous are the ravens that squawk
    against me.
"Rather keep in your thoughts the hawk and cherish
    him,
who brought you in fetters the Spartan ravenfish."[86]

[85] See 1024 n.
[86] See 394-95.

ΑΛΛΑΝΤΟΠΩΛΗΣ

τοῦτό γέ τοι Παφλαγὼν παρεκινδύνευσε μεθυσθείς.

1055 Κεκροπίδη κακόβουλε, τί τοῦθ᾽ ἡγεῖ μέγα τοὔργον;

καί κε γυνὴ φέροι ἄχθος, ἐπεί κεν ἀνὴρ ἀναθείη·

ἀλλ᾽ οὐκ ἂν μαχέσαιτο· χέσαιτο γάρ, εἰ μαχέσαιτο.

ΠΑΦΛΑΓΩΝ

ἀλλὰ τόδε φράσσαι, πρὸ Πύλου Πύλον ἤν σοι

 ἔφραζεν·

ἔστι Πύλος πρὸ Πύλοιο—

ΔΗΜΟΣ

 τί τοῦτο λέγει, πρὸ Πύλοιο;

ΑΛΛΑΝΤΟΠΩΛΗΣ

1060 τὰς πυέλους φησὶν καταλήψεσθ᾽ ἐν βαλανείῳ.

ΔΗΜΟΣ

ἐγὼ δ᾽ ἄλουτος τήμερον γενήσομαι;

ΑΛΛΑΝΤΟΠΩΛΗΣ

οὗτος γὰρ ἡμῶν τὰς πυέλους ὑφήρπασεν.

ἀλλ᾽ οὑτοσὶ γάρ ἐστι περὶ τοῦ ναυτικοῦ

ὁ χρησμός, ᾧ σε δεῖ προσέχειν τὸν νοῦν πάνυ.

ΔΗΜΟΣ

1065 προσέχω· σὺ δ᾽ ἀναγίγνωσκε, τοῖς ναύταισί μου

ὅπως ὁ μισθὸς πρῶτον ἀποδοθήσεται.

SAUSAGE SELLER

The fact is, Paphlagon was drunk when he took that
bold gamble.[87]
"Ill-advised scion of Cecrops,[88] why do think this a
great deed?
Even a woman can bear a burden should a man put it
on her,
but fight she cannot, for if she should fight she would
shit."

PAPHLAGON

But ponder this, what the god's said about Pylos
before Pylos:
"there's a Pylos before Pylos…"

DEMOS

What does he mean, "before Pylos"?

SAUSAGE SELLER

He says he shall *pillage* a *pile* of tubs from the bath
house.

DEMOS

And I'm supposed to go bathless today?

SAUSAGE SELLER

That's because he's made off with the tubs. Now here's the
oracle about the fleet for you, so you should pay very close
attention to it.

DEMOS

I will; but mind you expound how my sailors are to get their
pay.

[88] See 1015 n.

ARISTOPHANES

ΑΛΛΑΝΤΟΠΩΛΗΣ

Αἰγεΐδη, φράσσαι κυναλώπεκα, μή σε δολώσῃ,
λαίθαργον, ταχύπουν, δολίαν κερδώ, πολύιδριν.
οἶσθ᾽ ὅ τι ἐστὶν τοῦτο;

ΔΗΜΟΣ

Φιλόστρατος ἡ κυναλώπηξ.

ΑΛΛΑΝΤΟΠΩΛΗΣ

1070 οὐ τοῦτό φησιν, ἀλλὰ ναῦς ἑκάστοτε
αἰτεῖ ταχείας ἀργυρολόγους οὑτοσί·
ταύτας ἀπαυδᾷ μὴ διδόναι σ᾽ ὁ Λοξίας.

ΔΗΜΟΣ

πῶς δὴ τριήρης ἐστὶ κυναλώπηξ;

ΑΛΛΑΝΤΟΠΩΛΗΣ

ὅπως;
ὅτι ἡ τριήρης ἐστὶ χὠ κύων ταχύ.

ΔΗΜΟΣ

1075 πῶς οὖν ἀλώπηξ προσετέθη πρὸς τῷ κυνί;

ΑΛΛΑΝΤΟΠΩΛΗΣ

ἀλωπεκίοισι τοὺς στρατιώτας ᾔκασεν,
ὁτιὴ βότρυς τρώγουσιν ἐν τοῖς χωρίοις.

ΔΗΜΟΣ

εἶέν.
τούτοις ὁ μισθὸς τοῖς ἀλωπεκίοισι ποῦ;

ΑΛΛΑΝΤΟΠΩΛΗΣ

ἐγὼ ποριῶ, καὶ τοῦτον ἡμερῶν τριῶν.

SAUSAGE SELLER

"Scion of Aegeus,[89] ponder the fox-dog lest he
  beguile you;
he's treacherous, swift of foot, a wily trickster, and
  very crafty."
Do you get that one?

DEMOS

The fox-dog is Philostratus.[90]

SAUSAGE SELLER

That's not it; no, this one keeps demanding swift ships for
collecting revenue; Loxias is warning you not to give them
to him.

DEMOS

How can a trireme be a fox-dog?

SAUSAGE SELLER

How? Because both triremes and dogs are fleet.

DEMOS

And how come "fox" is added to the dog?

SAUSAGE SELLER

Soldiers are like fox cubs because they eat grapes in the
farmlands.

THE DEMOS

Aha. And where's the pay for these fox cubs?

SAUSAGE SELLER

I'll provide it, and that within three days.[91]

---

[89] See 1015 n.
[90] A pimp who used that nickname, cf. *Lysistrata* 957.
[91] See 1054 n.

1080 ἀλλ᾽ ἔτι τόνδ᾽ ἐπάκουσον, ὃν εἶπέ σοι ἐξαλέασθαι
χρησμὸν Λητοΐδης Κυλλήνην, μή σε δολώσῃ.

ΔΗΜΟΣ

ποίαν Κυλλήνην;

ΑΛΛΑΝΤΟΠΩΛΗΣ
τὴν τούτου χεῖρ᾽ ἐποίησεν
Κυλλήνην ὀρθῶς, ὁτιή φησ᾽· "ἔμβαλε κυλλῇ."

ΠΑΦΛΑΓΩΝ
οὐκ ὀρθῶς φράζει· τὴν Κυλλήνην γὰρ ὁ Φοῖβος
1085 εἰς τὴν χεῖρ᾽ ὀρθῶς ᾐνίξατο τὴν Διοπείθους.
ἀλλὰ γάρ ἐστιν ἐμοὶ χρησμὸς περὶ σοῦ πτερυγωτός,
αἰετὸς ὡς γίγνει καὶ πάσης γῆς βασιλεύεις.

ΑΛΛΑΝΤΟΠΩΛΗΣ
καὶ γὰρ ἐμοί· καὶ γῆς καὶ τῆς ἐρυθρᾶς γε
θαλάσσης,
χὤτι γ᾽ ἐν Ἐκβατάνοις δικάσεις, λείχων ἐπίπαστα.

ΠΑΦΛΑΓΩΝ
1090 ἀλλ᾽ ἐγὼ εἶδον ὄναρ, καί μοὐδόκει ἡ θεὸς αὐτὴ
τοῦ δήμου καταχεῖν ἀρυταίνῃ πλουθυγίειαν.

ΑΛΛΑΝΤΟΠΩΛΗΣ
νὴ Δία καὶ γὰρ ἐγώ· καί μοὐδόκει ἡ θεὸς αὐτὴ
ἐκ πόλεως ἐλθεῖν καὶ γλαῦξ αὐτῇ ᾽πικαθῆσθαι·
εἶτα κατασπένδειν κατὰ τῆς κεφαλῆς ἀρυβάλλῳ

---

92 An expert on oracles and a prosecutor of atheists and intel-
lectuals; his hand seems to have been crippled.

"But listen also to this, the oracle wherein Leto's son
bids you shun the wiles of Crookhaven."

DEMOS

Crookhaven?

SAUSAGE SELLER

The verse properly refers to this guy's hand as
    Crookhaven,
because he says, "put something in my crooked hand."

PAPHLAGON

He's got it wrong: by "Crookhaven" Phoebus actually
meant to allude to the hand of Diopeithes.[92]
But here, I've got an oracle about you, a winged one,
that you are to become an eagle, and the king of
    every land.

SAUSAGE SELLER

Me too: over the earth and the Red Sea too,
and that you'll judge cases in Ecbatana,[93] nibbling
    canapés.

PAPHLAGON

Wait, I've had a dream: I saw the Goddess[94] herself
pouring healthy wealthiness over Demos with a big
    ladle.

SAUSAGE SELLER

By god I've had one too: I also saw the Goddess
    herself,
coming from the Acropolis with an owl sitting on her
    helmet;

[93] See *Acharnians* 64 n.
[94] Athena.

1095   ἀμβροσίαν κατὰ σοῦ, κατὰ τούτου δὲ σκοροδάλμην.

ΔΗΜΟΣ

ἰοὺ ἰού.
οὐκ ἦν ἄρ᾽ οὐδεὶς τοῦ Γλάνιδος σοφώτερος.
καὶ νῦν ἐμαυτὸν ἐπιτρέπω σοι τουτονὶ
γερονταγωγεῖν κἀναπαιδεύειν πάλιν.

ΠΑΦΛΑΓΩΝ

1100   μήπω γ᾽, ἱκετεύω σ᾽, ἀλλ᾽ ἀνάμεινον, ὡς ἐγὼ
κριθὰς ποριῶ σοι καὶ βίον καθ᾽ ἡμέραν.

ΔΗΜΟΣ

οὐκ ἀνέχομαι κριθῶν ἀκούων· πολλάκις
ἐξηπατήθην ὑπό τε σοῦ καὶ Θουφάνους.

ΠΑΦΛΑΓΩΝ

ἀλλ᾽ ἄλφιτ᾽ ἤδη σοι ποριῶ 'σκευασμένα.

ΑΛΛΑΝΤΟΠΩΛΗΣ

1105   ἐγὼ δὲ μαζίσκας γε διαμεμαγμένας
καὶ τοὔψον ὀπτόν· μηδὲν ἄλλ᾽ εἰ μὴ 'σθιε.

ΔΗΜΟΣ

ἀνύσατέ νυν, ὅ τι περ ποιήσεθ᾽· ὡς ἐγώ,
ὁπότερος ἂν σφῷν νῦν με μᾶλλον εὖ ποιῇ,
τούτῳ παραδώσω τῆς πυκνὸς τὰς ἡνίας.

ΠΑΦΛΑΓΩΝ

τρέχοιμ᾽ ἂν εἴσω πρότερος.

ΑΛΛΑΝΤΟΠΩΛΗΣ

1110   οὐ δῆτ᾽, ἀλλ᾽ ἐγώ.

then down she poured a pitcher of ambrosia over
    your head,
and over his a pitcher of garlic sauce.

DEMOS

Ha ha! There's really nobody more ingenious than that
Glanis! I hereby request that you be my own steward, "to
guide me in my old age and retrain me."[95]

PAPHLAGON

Not yet, I beg you! Please hold off, so I can provide you
with barley grain and a daily livelihood.

DEMOS

I can't stand hearing about barley grain! You and Thu-
phanes[96] have cheated me once too often.

PAPHLAGON

All right, I'll supply barley meal already processed.

SAUSAGE SELLER

And I'll supply barley cakes ready-made, and the hot meal
too; all you have to do is eat.

DEMOS

Then you two get on your marks and go to it, because to
the one who treats me best I intend to award the reins of
the Pnyx.[97]

PAPHLAGON

I'll run inside first!

SAUSAGE SELLER

Oh no, I'm first!

---

[95] A line from Sophocles' *Peleus* (fr. 487.2).
[96] Apparently a crony of Cleon's.   [97] See 42 n.

ΧΟΡΟΣ

ὦ Δῆμε, καλήν γ᾽ ἔχεις
ἀρχήν, ὅτε πάντες ἄν–
θρωποι δεδίασί σ᾽ ὥσ–
περ ἄνδρα τύραννον.
1115 ἀλλ᾽ εὐπαράγωγος εἶ,
θωπευόμενός τε χαί–
ρεις κἀξαπατώμενος,
πρὸς τόν τε λέγοντ᾽ ἀεὶ
κέχηνας· ὁ νοῦς δέ σου
1120 παρὼν ἀποδημεῖ.

ΔΗΜΟΣ

νοῦς οὐκ ἔνι ταῖς κόμαις
ὑμῶν, ὅτε μ᾽ οὐ φρονεῖν
νομίζετ᾽· ἐγὼ δ᾽ ἑκὼν
ταῦτ᾽ ἠλιθιάζω.
1125 αὐτός τε γὰρ ἥδομαι
βρύλλων τὸ καθ᾽ ἡμέραν,
κλέπτοντά τε βούλομαι
τρέφειν ἕνα προστάτην·
τοῦτον δ᾽, ὅταν ᾖ πλέως,
1130 ἄρας ἐπάταξα.

ΧΟΡΟΣ

οὕτω μὲν ἂν εὖ ποιοῖς,
καί σοι πυκνότης ἔνεστ᾽

1131 ἂν...ποιοῖς vel ποιῇς z: ἄρ᾽...ποιεῖς (C Vp3) Meineke

368

SAUSAGE SELLER precedes PAPHLAGON *into the house.*

CHORUS

Demos, you have a fine
sway, since all mankind
fears you like
a man with tyrannical power.[98]
But you're easily led astray:
you enjoy being flattered
and thoroughly deceived,
and every speechmaker
has you gaping. You've a mind,
but it's out to lunch.

DEMOS

There's no mind under your long hair,
since you consider me stupid;
but there's purpose
in this foolishness of mine.
I relish
my daily pap,
and I pick one thieving
political leader to fatten;
I raise him up, and when he's full,
I swat him down.

CHORUS

In that case you'll do well;
and your character really does

[98] For Athens as a "tyranny" cf. Pericles in Thucydides 2.63.2.

1132 καί Bergler: εἴ z

ἐν τῷ τρόπῳ, ὡς λέγεις,
τούτῳ πάνυ πολλή,
1135 εἰ τούσδ᾽ ἐπίτηδες ὥσ–
περ δημοσίους τρέφεις
ἐν τῇ πυκνί, κᾆθ᾽ ὅταν
μή σοι τύχῃ ὄψον ὄν,
τούτων ὃς ἂν ᾖ παχύς,
1140 θύσας ἐπιδειπνεῖς.

ΔΗΜΟΣ

σκέψασθε δέ μ᾽, εἰ σοφῶς
αὐτοὺς περιέρχομαι
τοὺς οἰομένους φρονεῖν
κἄμ᾽ ἐξαπατύλλειν.
1145 τηρῶ γὰρ ἑκάστοτ᾽ αὐ–
τοὺς οὐδὲ δοκῶν ὁρᾶν
κλέπτοντας· ἔπειτ᾽ ἀναγ–
κάζω πάλιν ἐξεμεῖν
ἅττ᾽ ἂν κεκλόφωσί μου,
1150 κημὸν καταμηλῶν.

ΠΑΦΛΑΓΩΝ

ἄπαγ᾽ ἐς μακαρίαν ἐκποδών.

ΑΛΛΑΝΤΟΠΩΛΗΣ
σύ γ᾽, ὦ φθόρε.

ΠΑΦΛΑΓΩΝ
ὦ Δῆμ᾽, ἐγὼ μέντοι παρεσκευασμένος

contain, as you claim,
very deep cunning,
if you deliberately fatten these men,
like public victims,
on the Pnyx, and then
when you chance to lack dinner,
you sacrifice one who's bloated
and have yourself a meal.

DEMOS

Just watch me and see if I don't
ingeniously trick them,
those who think they're smart
and that I'm their dupe.
I monitor them all the time,
pretending I don't even see them,
as they steal; and then I force
them to regurgitate
whatever they've stolen from me,
using a verdict tube[99] as a probe.

*Enter SAUSAGE SELLER and PAPHLAGON, each carrying a
large basket.*

PAPHLAGON

Get out of the blessed way!

SAUSAGE SELLER

You get out of the way, creep.

PAPHLAGON

Oh Mr. Demos, I've been sitting here for triennia, ready

[99] In Athenian courts a wicker funnel atop the voting urns
allowed jurors to cast their votes unseen.

ARISTOPHANES

τρίπαλαι κάθημαι βουλόμενός σ᾽ εὐεργετεῖν.

ΑΛΛΑΝΤΟΠΩΛΗΣ
ἐγὼ δὲ δεκάπαλαι γε καὶ δωδεκάπαλαι
1155 καὶ χιλιόπαλαι καὶ προπαλαιπαλαίπαλαι.

ΔΗΜΟΣ
ἐγὼ δὲ προσδοκῶν γε τρισμυριόπαλαι
βδελύττομαί σφω καὶ προπαλαιπαλαίπαλαι.

ΑΛΛΑΝΤΟΠΩΛΗΣ
οἶσθ᾽ οὖν ὃ δρᾶσον;

ΔΗΜΟΣ
εἰ δὲ μή, φράσῃς γε σύ.

ΑΛΛΑΝΤΟΠΩΛΗΣ
ἄφες ἀπὸ βαλβίδων ἐμέ τε καὶ τουτονί,
ἵνα σ᾽ εὖ ποιῶμεν ἐξ ἴσου.

ΔΗΜΟΣ
1160 δρᾶν ταῦτα χρή.
ἄπιτον.

ΑΛΛΑΝΤΟΠΩΛΗΣ καὶ ΠΑΦΛΑΓΩΝ
ἰδού.

ΔΗΜΟΣ
θέοιτ᾽ ἄν.

ΑΛΛΑΝΤΟΠΩΛΗΣ
ὑποθεῖν οὐκ ἐῶ.

ΔΗΜΟΣ
ἀλλ᾽ ἦ μεγάλως εὐδαιμονήσω τήμερον

and willing to serve you.

SAUSAGE SELLER

And I've been ready decennia, dodecennia, millenia, mil-
lenni-enni-ennia past.

DEMOS

And I've been waiting for billionennia, and getting sick of
you both for millenni-enni-ennia past.

SAUSAGE SELLER

Do you know what you should do?

DEMOS

If I don't, you'll tell me.

SAUSAGE SELLER

Start me and this guy from the same gate, so we have an
equal shot at serving you.

DEMOS

That's what we should do. Go to the gate!

SAUSAGE SELLER AND PAPHLAGON

Ready!

DEMOS

Go!

SAUSAGE SELLER and PAPHLAGON race into the house.

SAUSAGE SELLER

No cutting in!

DEMOS

By god, my lovers are certainly going to make me blissfully

ὑπὸ τῶν ἐραστῶν, νὴ Δί᾽, εἰ ᾽γὼ θρύψομαι.

ΠΑΦΛΑΓΩΝ

ὁρᾷς, ἐγώ σοι πρότερος ἐκφέρω δίφρον.

ΑΛΛΑΝΤΟΠΩΛΗΣ

1165 ἀλλ᾽ οὐ τράπεζαν· ἀλλ᾽ ἐγὼ προτεραίτερος.

ΠΑΦΛΑΓΩΝ

ἰδοὺ φέρω σοι τήνδε μαζίσκην ἐγὼ
ἐκ τῶν ὀλῶν τῶν ἐκ Πύλου μεμαγμένην.

ΑΛΛΑΝΤΟΠΩΛΗΣ

ἐγὼ δὲ μυστίλας μεμυστιλημένας
ὑπὸ τῆς θεοῦ τῇ χειρὶ τηλεφαντίνῃ.

ΔΗΜΟΣ

1170 ὡς μέγαν ἄρ᾽ εἶχες, ὦ πότνια, τὸν δάκτυλον.

ΠΑΦΛΑΓΩΝ

ἐγὼ δ᾽ ἔτνος γε πίσινον εὔχρων καὶ καλόν·
ἐτόρυνε δ᾽ αὐτὴ Παλλὰς ἡ Πυλαιμάχος.

ΑΛΛΑΝΤΟΠΩΛΗΣ

ὦ Δῆμ᾽, ἐναργῶς ἡ θεός σ᾽ ἐπισκοπεῖ.
καὶ νῦν ὑπερέχει σου χύτραν ζωμοῦ πλέαν.

ΔΗΜΟΣ

1175 οἴει γὰρ οἰκεῖσθ᾽ ἂν ἔτι τήνδε τὴν πόλιν,
εἰ μὴ φανερῶς ἡμῶν ὑπερεῖχε τὴν χύτραν;

1163 εἰ Bentley: ἢ z

100 *Pylaimachos* was an actual epithet of Athena, which Paphlagon uses to allude to Pylos.

happy today, if I play hard to get.

SAUSAGE SELLER and PAPHLAGON emerge.

PAPHLAGON
Look! I'm the first to fetch you something—a stool!

SAUSAGE SELLER
But not a table; I'm firster with that!

PAPHLAGON
Look, I've got this cookie for you, made from grain imported from Pylos.

SAUSAGE SELLER
And I've got this spoon bread, indented by the ivory hand of the Goddess.

DEMOS
Sovereign Goddess, you must have a very big finger!

PAPHLAGON
I've got pea soup, fragrant and fine. And it was stirred by Athena Battler at the Pylisades.[100]

SAUSAGE SELLER
Demos, I can see with my own eyes that the Goddess watches over you. Just now she's holding over your head a potful of beef broth.

DEMOS
Of course; do you think there'd still be a city here, if she didn't visibly hold her pot over us?[101]

[101] Misremembering a famous verse of Solon's (fr. 4.4 West), substituting "pot" for "hands."

375

ARISTOPHANES

ΠΑΦΛΑΓΩΝ

τουτὶ τέμαχός σοὔδωκεν ἡ Φοβεσιστράτη.

ΑΛΛΑΝΤΟΠΩΛΗΣ

ἡ δ' Ὀβριμοπάτρα γ' ἐφθὸν ἐκ ζωμοῦ κρέας
καὶ χόλικος ἠνύστρου τε καὶ γαστρὸς τόμον.

ΔΗΜΟΣ

1180 καλῶς γ' ἐποίησε τοῦ πέπλου μεμνημένη.

ΠΑΦΛΑΓΩΝ

ἡ Γοργολόφα σ' ἐκέλευε τουτουὶ φαγεῖν
ἐλατῆρος, ἵνα τὰς ναῦς ἐλαύνωμεν καλῶς.

ΑΛΛΑΝΤΟΠΩΛΗΣ

λαβὲ καὶ ταδί νυν.

ΔΗΜΟΣ

                    καὶ τί τούτοις χρήσομαι
τοῖς ἐντέροις;

ΑΛΛΑΝΤΟΠΩΛΗΣ

                    ἐπίτηδες αὔτ' ἔπεμψέ σοι

1185 εἰς τὰς τριήρεις ἐντερόνειαν ἡ θεός·
ἐπισκοπεῖ γὰρ περιφανῶς τὸ ναυτικόν.
ἔχε καὶ πιεῖν κεκραμένον τρία καὶ δύο.

ΔΗΜΟΣ

ὡς ἡδύς, ὦ Ζεῦ, καὶ τὰ τρία φέρων καλῶς.

ΑΛΛΑΝΤΟΠΩΛΗΣ

ἡ Τριτογενὴς γὰρ αὐτὸν ἐνετριτώνισεν.

PAPHLAGON

This fish fillet here is the gift of Athena Chiller of Armies.

SAUSAGE SELLER

And from Athena Strong Like Her Father, beef boiled in broth and a good cut of tripe and paunch.

DEMOS

Nice of her to remember the Robe we gave her![102]

PAPHLAGON

Athena of the Ghastly Plumes bids you taste this fine *roll*, so our oarsmen can *row well*.

SAUSAGE SELLER

Then take these, too.

DEMOS

Just what am I supposed to do with these belly tripes?

SAUSAGE SELLER

They're shipped to you from the Goddess to use in the bellies of our triremes; she obviously watches over the fleet. Have a drink, too, mixed two parts wine to three of water.

DEMOS

It's good, by god, and takes the three parts nicely!

SAUSAGE SELLER

Sure: Athena Tritogenes tritogenated it.[103]

---

[102] See 566 n.

[103] The epithet was explained in antiquity as deriving from Lake Tritonis in Libya; here the Sausage Seller puns on *Tri-* (three).

ΠΑΦΛΑΓΩΝ

1190 λαβέ νυν πλακοῦντος πίονος παρ᾽ ἐμοῦ τόμον.

ΑΛΛΑΝΤΟΠΩΛΗΣ

παρ᾽ ἐμοῦ δ᾽ ὅλον γε τὸν πλακοῦντα τουτονί.

ΠΑΦΛΑΓΩΝ

ἀλλ᾽ οὐ λαγῷ᾽ ἕξεις ὁπόθεν δῷς· ἀλλ᾽ ἐγώ.

ΑΛΛΑΝΤΟΠΩΛΗΣ

οἴμοι, πόθεν λαγῷά μοι γενήσεται;
ὦ θυμέ, νυνὶ βωμολόχον ἔξευρέ τι.

ΠΑΦΛΑΓΩΝ

ὁρᾷς τάδ᾽, ὦ κακόδαιμον;

ΑΛΛΑΝΤΟΠΩΛΗΣ

1195   ὀλίγον μοι μέλει·
ἐκεινοὶ γὰρ ὡς ἔμ᾽ ἔρχονταί τινες
πρέσβεις ἔχοντες ἀργυρίου βαλλάντια.

ΠΑΦΛΑΓΩΝ

ποῦ ποῦ;

ΑΛΛΑΝΤΟΠΩΛΗΣ

τί δέ σοι τοῦτ᾽; οὐκ ἐάσεις τοὺς ξένους;
ὦ Δημίδιον, ὁρᾷς τὰ λαγῷ᾽ ἅ σοι φέρω;

ΠΑΦΛΑΓΩΝ

1200 οἴμοι τάλας, ἀδίκως γε τἄμ᾽ ὑφήρπασας.

ΑΛΛΑΝΤΟΠΩΛΗΣ

νὴ τὸν Ποσειδῶ, καὶ σὺ γὰρ τοὺς ἐκ Πύλου.

PAPHLAGON

Now have a slice of luscious cheesecake, with my compliments.

SAUSAGE SELLER

And with my compliments, have this whole cheesecake.

PAPHLAGON

But you don't have a source for hare's meat to give him; I do.

SAUSAGE SELLER

(*aside*) Damn! Where will I come up with hare's meat? It's time, my soul, to think up some tomfoolery.

PAPHLAGON

(*producing a hare*) Take a look at this, you loser!

SAUSAGE SELLER

I don't care, because here come some ambassadors with bags of silver, to see me!

PAPHLAGON

(*dropping the hare*) Where? Where?

SAUSAGE SELLER

What's it to you? Why don't you leave the foreigners alone? (*picking up the hare*) My precious Demos, see the hare's meat I've got for you?

PAPHLAGON

Damn it all, you pinched my hare! That's unfair!

SAUSAGE SELLER

By Poseidon, it isn't: I'm just imitating you with the men from Pylos!

ARISTOPHANES

ΔΗΜΟΣ

εἴπ᾽, ἀντιβολῶ, πῶς ἐπενόησας ἁρπάσαι;

ΑΛΛΑΝΤΟΠΩΛΗΣ

τὸ μὲν νόημα τῆς θεοῦ, τὸ δὲ κλέμμ᾽ ἐμόν.

ΠΑΦΛΑΓΩΝ

ἐγὼ δ᾽ ἐκινδύνευσ᾽, ἐγὼ δ᾽ ὤπτησά γε.

ΔΗΜΟΣ

1205 ἄπιθ᾽· οὐ γὰρ ἀλλὰ τοῦ παραθέντος ἡ χάρις.

ΠΑΦΛΑΓΩΝ

οἴμοι κακοδαίμων, ὑπεραναιδευθήσομαι.

ΑΛΛΑΝΤΟΠΩΛΗΣ

τί οὐ διακρίνεις, Δῆμ᾽, ὁπότερός ἐστι νῷν
ἀνὴρ ἀμείνων περὶ σὲ καὶ τὴν γαστέρα;

ΔΗΜΟΣ

τῷ δῆτ᾽ ἂν ὑμᾶς χρησάμενος τεκμηρίῳ
1210 δόξαιμι κρίνειν τοῖς θεαταῖσιν σοφῶς;

ΑΛΛΑΝΤΟΠΩΛΗΣ

ἐγὼ φράσω σοι. τὴν ἐμὴν κίστην ἰὼν
ξύλλαβε σιωπῇ καὶ βασάνισον ἅττ᾽ ἔνι,
καὶ τὴν Παφλαγόνος· κἀμέλει κρινεῖς καλῶς.

ΔΗΜΟΣ

φέρ᾽ ἴδω, τί οὖν ἔνεστιν;

ΑΛΛΑΝΤΟΠΩΛΗΣ

                                           οὐχ ὁρᾷς κενήν,
1215 ὦ παππίδιον; ἅπαντα γάρ σοι παρεφόρουν.

380

DEMOS

Tell me, please, where you got the idea of pinching that?

SAUSAGE SELLER

The Goddess thought it up, I pulled the job.

PAPHLAGON

But it was I took the risk, and I that roasted the meat!

DEMOS

Go on! Nobody but the server gets thanked.

PAPHLAGON

Great heavens me, I'm going to be out-brazened!

SAUSAGE SELLER

Why not decide once and for all, Demos, which of us is the better man for you and your stomach?

DEMOS

Well, what do you think the audience would accept as evidence of a smart decision?

SAUSAGE SELLER

I'll tell you. Don't say a word, just go pick up my basket and examine what's in it; Paphlagon's too. Don't worry, you'll make a good decision.

DEMOS

(*opening the Sausage Seller's basket*) Let's see now, what's in it?

SAUSAGE SELLER

Daddy, don't you see it's empty? I brought everything to your table.

ΔΗΜΟΣ

αὕτη μὲν ἡ κίστη τὰ τοῦ δήμου φρονεῖ.

ΑΛΛΑΝΤΟΠΩΛΗΣ

βάδιζέ νυν καὶ δεῦρο πρὸς τὴν Παφλαγόνος.
ὁρᾷς τάδ';

ΔΗΜΟΣ

οἴμοι, τῶν ἀγαθῶν ὅσων πλέα.
ὅσον τὸ χρῆμα τοῦ πλακοῦντος ἀπέθετο·
1220 ἐμοὶ δ' ἔδωκεν ἀποτεμὼν τυννουτονί.

ΑΛΛΑΝΤΟΠΩΛΗΣ

τοιαῦτα μέντοι καὶ πρότερόν σ' ἠργάζετο·
σοὶ μὲν προσεδίδου μικρὸν ὧν ἐλάμβανεν,
αὐτὸς δ' ἑαυτῷ παρετίθει τὰ μείζονα.

ΔΗΜΟΣ

ὦ μιαρέ, κλέπτων δή με ταῦτ' ἐξηπάτας;
1225 ἐγὼ δέ τυ ἐστεφάνιξα κἠδωρησάμαν.

ΠΑΦΛΑΓΩΝ

ἐγὼ δ' ἔκλεπτον ἐπ' ἀγαθῷ γε τῇ πόλει.

ΔΗΜΟΣ

κατάθου ταχέως τὸν στέφανον, ἵν' ἐγὼ τουτῳὶ
αὐτὸν περιθῶ.

ΑΛΛΑΝΤΟΠΩΛΗΣ

κατάθου ταχέως, μαστιγία.

ΠΑΦΛΑΓΩΝ

οὐ δῆτ', ἐπεί μοι χρησμός ἐστι Πυθικὸς
1230 φράζων, ὑφ' οὗ 'δέησέ μ' ἡττᾶσθαι μόνον.

KNIGHTS

DEMOS
Say, this is a basket with Demos' interests at heart!

SAUSAGE SELLER
Now come over here to Paphlagon's. (*opening it*) See this?

DEMOS
My goodness, it's crammed; look at all the goodies! Have a look at the cheesecake he's put aside for himself! And he cut me off a slice no bigger than *this!*

SAUSAGE SELLER
That's what he did to you all along, tossing you a petty piece of his profits and putting away the lion's share for himself.

DEMOS
You scum, is that how you robbed me blind, and me that crowned and endowed you?

PAPHLAGON
But I stole for the good of the city!

DEMOS
Lay down that crown this instant; I'm going to put it on his head.

SAUSAGE SELLER
This instant, you scamp!

PAPHLAGON
No! I've got a Pythian oracle specifying the only one destined to defeat me.

ARISTOPHANES

ΑΛΛΑΝΤΟΠΩΛΗΣ

τοὐμόν γε φράζων ὄνομα καὶ λίαν σαφῶς.

ΠΑΦΛΑΓΩΝ

καὶ μήν σ' ἐλέγξαι βούλομαι τεκμηρίῳ,
εἴ τι ξυνοίσεις τοῦ θεοῦ τοῖς θεσφάτοις.
καί σου τοσοῦτο πρῶτον ἐκπειράσομαι·
1235 παῖς ὢν ἐφοίτας εἰς τίνος διδασκάλου;

ΑΛΛΑΝΤΟΠΩΛΗΣ

ἐν ταῖσιν εὔστραις κονδύλοις ἡρμοττόμην.

ΠΑΦΛΑΓΩΝ

πῶς εἶπας; ὥς μοῦ χρησμὸς ἅπτεται φρενῶν.
εἶέν.
ἐν παιδοτρίβου δὲ τίνα πάλην ἐμάνθανες;

ΑΛΛΑΝΤΟΠΩΛΗΣ

κλέπτων ἐπιορκεῖν καὶ βλέπειν ἐναντίον.

ΠΑΦΛΑΓΩΝ

1240 ὦ Φοῖβ' Ἄπολλον Λύκιε, τί ποτέ μ' ἐργάσει;
τέχνην δὲ τίνα ποτ' εἶχες ἐξανδρούμενος;

ΑΛΛΑΝΤΟΠΩΛΗΣ

ἠλλαντοπώλουν καί τι καὶ βινεσκόμην.

ΠΑΦΛΑΓΩΝ

οἴμοι κακοδαίμων· οὐκέτ' οὐδέν εἰμ' ἐγώ.
λεπτή τις ἐλπίς ἐστ' ἐφ' ἧς ὀχούμεθα.
1245 καί μοι τοσοῦτον εἰπέ· πότερον ἐν ἀγορᾷ
ἠλλαντοπώλεις ἐτεὸν ἢ 'πὶ ταῖς πύλαις;

SAUSAGE SELLER

Specifying my name, and with perfect clarity.

PAPHLAGON

Well then, I'd like to question you to see whether you match up with the god's prophetic utterances. First, let me ask you this: when you were a boy, whose school did you attend?

SAUSAGE SELLER

The school of hard knocks, in the slaughterhouse district.

PAPHLAGON

What's that you say? How the oracle bites me to the quick! Now then: at the wrestling school, what technique did you learn?

SAUSAGE SELLER

When stealing, to look them in the eye and swear I didn't do it.

PAPHLAGON

"Phoebus Apollo of Lycia, what do you mean to do to me?"[104] And when you were becoming a man, what sort of trade did you follow?

SAUSAGE SELLER

I sold sausages, and now and then I also sold my arse.

PAPHLAGON

Oh, I'm damned! This is the absolute end of me! There's but a splinter of hope keeping me afloat. And it's this: tell me, did you sell sausages in the marketplace or at the city gates?

[104] From Euripides' *Telephus,* fr 700.

ARISTOPHANES

ΑΛΛΑΝΤΟΠΩΛΗΣ

ἐπὶ ταῖς πύλαισιν, οὗ τὸ τάριχος ὤνιον.

ΠΑΦΛΑΓΩΝ

οἴμοι, πέπρακται τοῦ θεοῦ τὸ θέσφατον.
κυλίνδετ᾽ εἴσω τόνδε τὸν δυσδαίμονα.
1250 ὦ στέφανε, χαίρων ἄπιθι, καί σ᾽ ἄκων ἐγὼ
λείπω· σὲ δ᾽ ἄλλος τις λαβὼν κεκτήσεται,
κλέπτης μὲν οὐκ ἂν μᾶλλον, εὐτυχὴς δ᾽ ἴσως.

ΑΛΛΑΝΤΟΠΩΛΗΣ

Ἑλλάνιε Ζεῦ, σὸν τὸ νικητήριον.

ΟΙΚΕΤΗΣ Α΄

ὦ χαῖρε καλλίνικε· καὶ μέμνησ᾽ ὅτι
1255 ἀνὴρ γεγένησαι δι᾽ ἐμέ· καί σ᾽ αἰτῶ βραχύ,
ὅπως ἔσομαί σοι Φᾶνος ὑπογραφεὺς δικῶν.

ΔΗΜΟΣ

ἐμοὶ δέ γ᾽ ὅ τι σοι τοὔνομ᾽ εἴπ᾽.

ΑΛΛΑΝΤΟΠΩΛΗΣ

                              Ἀγοράκριτος·
ἐν τἀγορᾷ γὰρ κρινόμενος ἐβοσκόμην.

ΔΗΜΟΣ

Ἀγορακρίτῳ τοίνυν ἐμαυτὸν ἐπιτρέπω

---

105 From Euripides' *Bellerophon*, fr. 310, substituting "roll" for "take."   106 Parodies the heroine's farewell in Euripides' *Alcestis* 177-82.

107 Mentioned as a crony of Cleon's in *Wasps* 1220.

SAUSAGE SELLER
At the gates, where they sell cheap fish.

PAPHLAGON
Ah me, the god's own fateful prophecy has come to pass!
"Roll me inside, utterly ill-starred!"[105] Begone and fare-
well, my crown; against my will do I abandon you.

"Some other man will take you as his own,
no greater thief, but luckier perhaps."[106]

*Paphlagon tosses the Sausage Seller his crown and swoons
upon the eccyclema.*

SAUSAGE SELLER
Zeus of the Hellenes, yours the prize of victory!

FIRST SLAVE
(*appearing at the doorway*) Hail, fair victor, and bear in
mind that you became a big shot thanks to me. And I'll ask
only a small favor, that you make me your Phanus,[107] your
notary for indictments.

DEMOS
And now tell me what your name is.

SAUSAGE SELLER
Agoracritus, because I made my way by haggling in the
marketplace.[108]

DEMOS
Then to Agoracritus' stewardship I commit myself, and to

[108] Sausage Seller comically etymologizes the name, which
properly means "chosen by the assembly." Aristophanes probably
intends no allusion to the famous Parian sculptor who worked
with Phidias.

ARISTOPHANES

1260 καὶ τὸν Παφλαγόνα παραδίδωμι τουτονί.

ΑΛΛΑΝΤΟΠΩΛΗΣ

καὶ μὴν ἐγώ σ᾽, ὦ Δῆμε, θεραπεύσω καλῶς,
ὥσθ᾽ ὁμολογεῖν σε μηδέν᾽ ἀνθρώπων ἐμοῦ
ἰδεῖν ἀμείνω τῇ Κεχηναίων πόλει.

ΧΟΡΟΣ

(στρ) τί κάλλιον ἀρχομένοι–
1265   σιν ἢ καταπαυομένοισιν
ἢ θοᾶν ἵππων ἐλατῆρας ἀείδειν
   μηδὲν εἰς Λυσίστρατον,
μηδὲ Θούμαντιν τὸν ἀνέστιον αὖ λυ–
   πεῖν ἑκούσῃ καρδίᾳ;
1270 καὶ γὰρ οὗτος, ὦ φίλ᾽ Ἄπολλον, ἀεὶ πει–
   νῇ, θαλεροῖς δακρύοις
σᾶς ἁπτόμενος φαρέτρας
   Πυθῶνι δίᾳ μὴ κακῶς πένεσθαι.

ΚΟΡΥΦΑΙΟΣ

λοιδορῆσαι τοὺς πονηροὺς οὐδέν ἐστ᾽ ἐπίφθονον,
1275 ἀλλὰ τιμὴ τοῖσι χρηστοῖς, ὅστις εὖ λογίζεται.
εἰ μὲν οὖν ἄνθρωπος, ὃν δεῖ πόλλ᾽ ἀκοῦσαι καὶ κακά,
αὐτὸς ἦν ἔνδηλος, οὐκ ἂν ἀνδρὸς ἐμνήσθην φίλου.
νῦν δ᾽ Ἀρίγνωτον γὰρ οὐδεὶς ὅστις οὐκ ἐπίσταται,
ὅστις ἢ τὸ λευκὸν οἶδεν ἢ τὸν ὄρθιον νόμον.
1280 ἔστιν οὖν ἀδελφὸς αὐτῷ τοὺς τρόπους οὐ συγγενής,

109 Ridiculed for emaciation in Hermippus fr. 36.

388

his custody I commit this Paphlagon here.

SAUSAGE SELLER

And you can count on me, Demos, for fine service, so you'll agree you've never seen anyone better than me for the city of Suckerthenians!

The eccyclema is withdrawn as DEMOS *and* SAUSAGE SELLER *go inside.*

CHORUS

What finer way
for drivers of swift horses
to begin or end a song than by singing
nothing against Lysistratus,
nor bringing the homeless Thumantis[109] further grief
light-heartedly?
Because he's always hungry, dear Apollo,
and weeping hot tears
he clutches your quiver in holy Pytho,
begging relief from his cursed poverty.

CHORUS LEADER

There's nothing invidious about calling bad people names; it's a way to honor good people, if you stop to think about it. Thus, if the man who's about to be called lots of bad names were well known in his own right, I wouldn't mention a gentleman who's a friend of mine. But it's a fact that everyone who can tell good music from bad knows who Arignotus is.[110] Now Arignotus has a brother of dis-

---

[110] Son of Automenes, a very popular lyre player; cf. *Wasps* 1277-78.

Ἀριφράδης πονηρός. ἀλλὰ τοῦτο μὲν καὶ βούλεται·
ἐστὶ δ' οὐ μόνον πονηρός, οὐ γὰρ οὐδ' ἂν ᾐσθόμην,
οὐδὲ παμπόνηρος, ἀλλὰ καὶ προσεξηύρηκέ τι.
τὴν γὰρ αὑτοῦ γλῶτταν αἰσχραῖς ἡδοναῖς λυμαίνεται,
1285 ἐν κασαυρείοισι λείχων τὴν ἀπόπτυστον δρόσον,
καὶ μολύνων τὴν ὑπήνην καὶ κυκῶν τὰς ἐσχάρας,
καὶ Πολυμνήστεια ποιῶν καὶ ξυνῶν Οἰωνίχῳ.
ὅστις οὖν τοιοῦτον ἄνδρα μὴ σφόδρα βδελύττεται,
οὔποτ' ἐκ ταὐτοῦ μεθ' ἡμῶν πίεται ποτηρίου.

ΧΟΡΟΣ

(ἀντ) ἦ πολλάκις ἐννυχίαι–
1291   σι φροντίσι συγγεγένημαι,
καὶ διεζήτηχ' ὁπόθεν ποτὲ φαύλως
ἐσθίει Κλεώνυμος.
φασὶ μὲν γὰρ αὐτὸν ἐρεπτόμενον τὰ
1295   τῶν ἐχόντων ἀνέρων
οὐκ ἂν ἐξελθεῖν ἀπὸ τῆς σιπύης· τοὺς δ'
ἀντιβολεῖν ἂν ὅμως·
ἴθ', ὦ ἄνα, πρὸς γονάτων,
ἔξελθε καὶ σύγγνωθι τῇ τραπέζῃ.

ΚΟΡΥΦΑΙΟΣ

1300 φασὶν ἀλλήλαις ξυνελθεῖν τὰς τριήρεις εἰς λόγον,
καὶ μίαν λέξαι τιν' αὐτῶν, ἥτις ἦν γεραιτέρα·
"οὐδὲ πυνθάνεσθε ταῦτ', ὦ παρθένοι, τὰν τῇ πόλει;

111 Probably the character in a Socratic dialogue by Aeschines
of Sphettus who claimed to be a pupil of Anaxagoras (Athenaeus

similar character, Ariphrades the sleazy.[111] Yes, that's what he likes to be. But he's not merely sleazy, or I wouldn't even have noticed him, nor even utterly sleazy. The fact is, he's added a brand new meaning to the term. He pollutes his own tongue with disgraceful gratifications, licking the detestable dew in bawdyhouses, besmirching his beard, disturbing the ladies' hotpots, acting like Polymnestus[112] and on intimate terms with Oeonichus.[113] Anyone who doesn't loathe such a man will never drink from the same cup with me.

CHORUS

Oft in the dark of night
have I communed with my thoughts
and wondered where on earth Cleonymus
gets off eating so happy-go-luckily.
For they do say that he used to pig out
on the substance of rich men
and wouldn't leave the trough,
though they would all beg him,
"By your knees we implore you, sir,
have mercy on the table and leave!"

CHORUS LEADER

They say that the triremes got together for a conference, and one of them, a senior ship, said, "Young ladies, don't you even want to know about this business in the city?

5.220b-c); less likely the "ridiculer" of tragic diction criticized in Aristotle *Poetics* 1458b31. Aristophanes attacks him again in *Wasps* 1280-83 and *Peace* 883-85.

[112] A seventh-century lyric poet from Colophon.

[113] Mentioned in connection with music in an anonymous comic fragment (*adesp.* 396).

ARISTOPHANES

φασὶν αἰτεῖσθαί τιν' ἡμῶν ἑκατὸν εἰς Καρχηδόνα,
ἄνδρα μοχθηρὸν πολίτην, ὀξίνην Ὑπέρβολον·"
1305 ταῖς δὲ δόξαι δεινὸν εἶναι τοῦτο κοὐκ ἀνασχετόν,
καί τιν' εἰπεῖν, ἥτις ἀνδρῶν ἆσσον οὐκ ἐληλύθει·
"ἀποτρόπαι', οὐ δῆτ' ἐμοῦ γ' ἄρξει ποτ', ἀλλ' ἐάν
με χρῇ,
ὑπὸ τερηδόνων σαπεῖσ' ἐνταῦθα καταγηράσομαι."
"οὐδὲ Ναυφάντης γε τῆς Ναύσωνος, οὐ δῆτ', ὦ θεοί,
1310 εἴπερ ἐκ πεύκης γε κἀγὼ καὶ ξύλων ἐπηγνύμην.
ἢν δ' ἀρέσκῃ ταῦτ' Ἀθηναίοις, καθῆσθαί μοι δοκῶ
εἰς τὸ Θησεῖον πλεούσας ἢ 'πὶ τῶν σεμνῶν θεῶν.
οὐ γὰρ ἡμῶν γε στρατηγῶν ἐγχανεῖται τῇ πόλει·
ἀλλὰ πλείτω χωρὶς αὐτὸς ἐς κόρακας, εἰ βούλεται,
1315 τὰς σκάφας, ἐν αἷς ἐπώλει τοὺς λύχνους, καθελ-
κύσας."

ΑΛΛΑΝΤΟΠΩΛΗΣ
εὐφημεῖν χρὴ καὶ στόμα κλῄειν καὶ μαρτυριῶν
ἀπέχεσθαι,
καὶ τὰ δικαστήρια συγκλῄειν, οἷς ἡ πόλις ἥδε
γέγηθεν,
ἐπὶ καιναῖσιν δ' εὐτυχίαισιν παιωνίζειν τὸ θέατρον.

ΚΟΡΥΦΑΙΟΣ
ὦ ταῖς ἱεραῖς φέγγος Ἀθήναις καὶ ταῖς νήσοις ἐπί-
κουρε,
1320 τίν' ἔχων φήμην ἀγαθὴν ἥκεις, ἐφ' ὅτῳ κνισῶμεν
ἀγυιάς;

392

They're saying that somebody's requisitioning a hundred of us for an expedition to Carthage, a lowlife male citizen, that brackish Hyperbolus." They all agreed that this was awful and intolerable, and one of them spoke up, who'd never been boarded by men, "God forbid he should ever be my commander! If need be, I'd sooner grow dilapidated right here and be rotted by woodworms!" And another said, "Nor will he command Nauphante, daughter of Nauson,[114] heavens no, or I wasn't built of pine timbers! If that's what appeals to the Athenians, then I suggest we sail to the Theseum or the shrine of the Furies and sit in asylum. Never shall he make a fool of the city by being our commander. If he wants to go sailing, let him launch those trays where he used to display his lamps for sale, and sail off all by himself to hell!"

Enter SAUSAGE SELLER

SAUSAGE SELLER
Keep your language pure, everyone; close your mouths, call no more witnesses, shut up the lawcourts that this city's so fond of, and on the occasion of our revolutionary good luck, let the audience sing a paeon!

CHORUS LEADER
Light of holy Athens and protector of the islands, what glad tidings do you bring, that we should fill our boulevards with the aromas of sacrifice?

---

[114] Appropriately nautical names; Nauphante is otherwise unattested in Attica.

1303 Χαλκηδόνα v.l. Γ Σ

ARISTOPHANES

ΑΛΛΑΝΤΟΠΩΛΗΣ

τὸν Δῆμον ἀφεψήσας ὑμῖν καλὸν ἐξ αἰσχροῦ πε-
ποίηκα.

ΚΟΡΥΦΑΙΟΣ

καὶ ποῦ 'στιν νῦν, ὦ θαυμαστὰς ἐξευρίσκων ἐπι-
νοίας;

ΑΛΛΑΝΤΟΠΩΛΗΣ

ἐν ταῖσιν ἰοστεφάνοις οἰκεῖ ταῖς ἀρχαίαισιν
Ἀθήναις.

ΚΟΡΥΦΑΙΟΣ

πῶς ἂν ἴδοιμεν; ποίαν τιν' ἔχει σκευήν; ποῖος
γεγένηται;

ΑΛΛΑΝΤΟΠΩΛΗΣ

1325 οἷός περ Ἀριστήδῃ πρότερον καὶ Μιλτιάδῃ
ξυνεσίτει.
ὄψεσθε δέ· καὶ γὰρ ἀνοιγνυμένων ψόφος ἤδη τῶν
προπυλαίων·
ἀλλ' ὀλολύξατε φαινομέναισιν ταῖς ἀρχαίαισιν
Ἀθήναις
καὶ θαυμασταῖς καὶ πολυύμνοις, ἵν' ὁ κλεινὸς
Δῆμος ἐνοικεῖ.

ΚΟΡΥΦΑΙΟΣ

ὦ ταὶ λιπαραὶ καὶ ἰοστέφανοι καὶ ἀριζήλωτοι
Ἀθῆναι,
1330 δείξατε τὸν τῆς Ἑλλάδος ἡμῖν καὶ τῆς γῆς τῆσδε
μόναρχον.

394

SAUSAGE SELLER
I've boiled down Demos for you and transformed him from ugly to handsome.

CHORUS LEADER
And where is he now, you inventor of wondrous conceptions?

SAUSAGE SELLER
He lives in the violet-crowned Athens of old.

CHORUS LEADER
How can we see him? What sort of outfit is he wearing? What sort of man is he now?

SAUSAGE SELLER
He's as he was when his messmates were Aristides and Miltiades.[115] You'll soon see for yourselves: that's the sound of the Propylaea being opened. Now raise a cheer for the reappearance of the Athens of old, wonderful and celebrated in so many songs, home of the renowned Demos!

A facade is revealed, transforming the scene building into the Athens of Old.

CHORUS
Oh Athens the gleaming, the violet-crowned, the envy of all, show us the monarch of Greece and of this land!

Demos emerges from the gates, now young and handsome.

[115] Athenian heroes of the Persian War era.

ARISTOPHANES

ΑΛΛΑΝΤΟΠΩΛΗΣ

ὅδ' ἐκεῖνος ὁρᾶν τεττιγοφόρας, τἀρχαίῳ σχήματι
    λαμπρός·
οὐ χοιρινῶν ὄζων, ἀλλὰ σπονδῶν, σμύρνῃ κατά-
    λειπτος.

ΚΟΡΥΦΑΙΟΣ

χαῖρ', ὦ βασιλεῦ τῶν Ἑλλήνων· καί σοι ξυγχαί-
    ρομεν ἡμεῖς·
τῆς γὰρ πόλεως ἄξια πράττεις καὶ τοῦ Μαραθῶνι
    τροπαίου.

ΔΗΜΟΣ

1335   ὦ φίλτατ' ἀνδρῶν, ἐλθὲ δεῦρ', Ἀγοράκριτε.
ὅσα με δέδρακας ἀγάθ' ἀφεψήσας.

ΑΛΛΑΝΤΟΠΩΛΗΣ

                                        ἐγώ;
ἀλλ', ὦ μέλ', οὐκ οἶσθ' οἷος ἦσθ' αὐτὸς πάρος,
οὐδ' οἷ' ἔδρας· ἐμὲ γὰρ νομίζοις ἂν θεόν.

ΔΗΜΟΣ

τί δ' ἔδρων πρὸ τοῦ, κάτειπε, καὶ ποῖός τις ἦ;

ΑΛΛΑΝΤΟΠΩΛΗΣ

1340   πρῶτον μέν, ὁπότ' εἴποι τις ἐν τἠκκλησίᾳ·
"ὦ Δῆμ', ἐραστής εἰμι σὸς φιλῶ τέ σε
καὶ κήδομαί σου καὶ προβουλεύω μόνος",
τούτοις ὁπότε χρήσαιτό τις προοιμίοις,
ἀνωρτάλιζες κἀκερουτίας.

SAUSAGE SELLER

Here he is for all to see, wearing a golden cricket, resplendent in his old-time costume, smelling not of ballot shells but peace accords, and anointed with myrrh.

CHORUS

Hail, king of the Greeks! We too share your joy, for your condition is worthy of the city and the trophy at Marathon.

DEMOS

Agoracritus, dearest of men, come over here. Your boiling has done wonders for me!

SAUSAGE SELLER

Who, me? My dear fellow, if you only knew what you were like before and how you used to act, you'd worship me like a god!

DEMOS

Tell me, how did I used to act, and what was I like?

SAUSAGE SELLER

First of all, whenever somebody said in the Assembly, "Demos, I'm your lover and I cherish you, and I alone care for you and think for you," whenever anybody started a speech with that stuff, you'd flap your wings and toss your horns.

ARISTOPHANES

ΔΗΜΟΣ

ἐγώ;

ΑΛΛΑΝΤΟΠΩΛΗΣ

1345 εἶτ᾽ ἐξαπατήσας σ᾽ ἀντὶ τούτων ᾤχετο.

ΔΗΜΟΣ

τί φής; ταυτί μ᾽ ἔδρων, ἐγὼ δὲ τοῦτ᾽ οὐκ ᾐσθόμην;

ΑΛΛΑΝΤΟΠΩΛΗΣ

τὰ δ᾽ ὦτα γάρ σου νὴ Δί᾽ ἐξεπετάννυτο
ὥσπερ σκιάδειον καὶ πάλιν ξυνήγετο.

ΔΗΜΟΣ

οὕτως ἀνόητος ἐγεγενήμην καὶ γέρων;

ΑΛΛΑΝΤΟΠΩΛΗΣ

1350 καὶ νὴ Δί᾽ εἴ γε δύο λεγοίτην ῥήτορε,
ὁ μὲν ποιεῖσθαι ναῦς μακράς, ὁ δ᾽ ἕτερος αὖ
καταμισθοφορῆσαι τοῦθ᾽, ὁ τὸν μισθὸν λέγων
τὸν τὰς τριήρεις παραδραμὼν ἂν ᾤχετο.
οὗτος, τί κύπτεις; οὐχὶ κατὰ χώραν μενεῖς;

ΔΗΜΟΣ

1355 αἰσχύνομαί τοι ταῖς πρότερον ἁμαρτίαις.

ΑΛΛΑΝΤΟΠΩΛΗΣ

ἀλλ᾽ οὐ σὺ τούτων αἴτιος, μὴ φροντίσῃς,
ἀλλ᾽ οἵ σε ταῦτ᾽ ἐξηπάτων. νυνδὶ φράσον·
ἐάν τις εἴπῃ βωμολόχος ξυνήγορος·
"οὐκ ἔστιν ὑμῖν τοῖς δικασταῖς ἄλφιτα,
1360 εἰ μὴ καταγνώσεσθε ταύτην τὴν δίκην,"
τοῦτον τί δράσεις, εἰπέ, τὸν ξυνήγορον;

THE DEMOS

I did?

SAUSAGE SELLER

And then in return he got away with cheating you.

DEMOS

You don't say! They did that to me, and I didn't catch on?

SAUSAGE SELLER

They certainly did, because your ears would open up like a parasol and flap shut again.

DEMOS

Was I that mindless and senile?

SAUSAGE SELLER

You certainly were, and if two politicians were making proposals, one to build long ships and the other to spend the same sum on state pay, the pay man would walk all over the trireme man. Here, why are you hanging your head? Won't you stand your ground?

DEMOS

It's that I'm ashamed of my former mistakes.

SAUSAGE SELLER

But you aren't to blame for them, never think it! The blame's with those who deceived you this way. Tell me afresh: if some tomfool advocate says, "there's no grain for you jurymen unless you convict in this case," what will you do to that advocate, eh?

ΔΗΜΟΣ

ἄρας μετέωρον εἰς τὸ βάραθρον ἐμβαλῶ,
ἐκ τοῦ λάρυγγος ἐκκρεμάσας Ὑπέρβολον.

ΑΛΛΑΝΤΟΠΩΛΗΣ

τουτὶ μὲν ὀρθῶς καὶ φρονίμως ἤδη λέγεις·
1365 τὰ δ᾽ ἄλλα, φέρ᾽ ἴδω, πῶς πολιτεύσει; φράσον.

ΔΗΜΟΣ

πρῶτον μὲν ὁπόσοι ναῦς ἐλαύνουσιν μακράς,
καταγομένοις τὸν μισθὸν ἀποδώσω ᾽ντελῆ.

ΑΛΛΑΝΤΟΠΩΛΗΣ

πολλοῖς γ᾽ ὑπολίσποις πυγιδίοισιν ἐχαρίσω.

ΔΗΜΟΣ

ἔπειθ᾽ ὁπλίτης ἐντεθεὶς ἐν καταλόγῳ
1370 οὐδεὶς κατὰ σπουδὰς μετεγγραφήσεται,
ἀλλ᾽ οὗπερ ἦν τὸ πρῶτον ἐγγεγράψεται.

ΑΛΛΑΝΤΟΠΩΛΗΣ

τοῦτ᾽ ἔδακε τὸν πόρπακα τὸν Κλεωνύμου.

ΔΗΜΟΣ

οὐδ᾽ ἀγοράσει γ᾽ ἀγένειος οὐδεὶς ἐν ἀγορᾷ.

ΑΛΛΑΝΤΟΠΩΛΗΣ

ποῦ δῆτα Κλεισθένης ἀγοράσει καὶ Στράτων;

ΔΗΜΟΣ

1375 τὰ μειράκια ταυτὶ λέγω τἀν τῷ μύρῳ,
ἃ στωμυλεῖται τοιαδὶ καθήμενα·
σοφός γ᾽ ὁ Φαίαξ δεξιῶς τ᾽ οὐκ ἀπέθανεν.

DEMOS

I'll hoist him in the air and toss him into the death pit, with
Hyperbolus hung around his throat!

SAUSAGE SELLER

That's the way; now you're talking correctly and sensibly.
As for the rest of your policies, give me an idea how you'll
behave.

DEMOS

In the first place, to all the men who row long ships, as soon
as they make port, I'll pay in full what they're owed.

SAUSAGE SELLER

You're making a lot of half-flattened rear ends happy!

DEMOS

Furthermore, no man once entered on a muster roll for
infantry service is to be transferred to a different list by
using private influence; he will stay on his original list.

SAUSAGE SELLER

That bites Cleonymus right in the shield handle!

DEMOS

And no one without a beard will rendezvous in the market-
place.

SAUSAGE SELLER

Then where are Cleisthenes and Strato going to do their
rendezvousing?

DEMOS

I mean these teenagers in the scent shops, who sit around
chattering like this: "Oh, Phaeax is a sharp one, and how

ARISTOPHANES

συνερκτικὸς γάρ ἐστι καὶ περαντικός,
καὶ γνωμοτυπικὸς καὶ σαφὴς καὶ κρουστικός,
1380 καταληπτικός τ᾽ ἄριστα τοῦ θορυβητικοῦ.

ΑΛΛΑΝΤΟΠΩΛΗΣ
οὔκουν καταδακτυλικὸς σὺ τοῦ λαλητικοῦ;

ΔΗΜΟΣ
μὰ Δί᾽, ἀλλ᾽ ἀναγκάσω κυνηγετεῖν ἐγὼ
τούτους ἅπαντας, παυσαμένους ψηφισμάτων.

ΑΛΛΑΝΤΟΠΩΛΗΣ
ἔχε νυν ἐπὶ τούτοις τουτονὶ τὸν ὀκλαδίαν
1385 καὶ παῖδ᾽ ἐνόρχην, ὅσπερ οἴσει τόνδε σοι·
κἄν που δοκῇ σοι, τοῦτον ὀκλαδίαν ποίει.

ΔΗΜΟΣ
μακάριος εἰς τἀρχαῖα δὴ καθίσταμαι.

ΑΛΛΑΝΤΟΠΩΛΗΣ
φήσεις γ᾽, ἐπειδὰν τὰς τριακοντούτιδας
σπονδὰς παραδῶ σοι. δεῦρ᾽ ἴθ᾽, αἱ Σπονδαί, ταχύ.

ΔΗΜΟΣ
1390 ὦ Ζεῦ πολυτίμηθ᾽, ὡς καλαί. πρὸς τῶν θεῶν,
ἔξεστιν αὐτῶν κατατριακοντουτίσαι;
πῶς ἔλαβες αὐτὰς ἐτεόν;

1378 συνερτικὸς v.l. Σ

---

116 See [Andocides] 4.36-37. Phaeax would later make an important expedition to Sicily (Thucydides 5.4-5) and received votes in the ostracism of Hyperbolus c. 416.

resourceful in beating that capital charge![116] He's intimidative, penetrative, aphoristically originative, clear and aggressive, and superlatively terminative of the obstreperative."[117]

SAUSAGE SELLER

To the talkative you're not flippative of the finger, are you?

DEMOS

God no, I intend to put a stop to their decree mongering and force them all to go hunting!

Enter a Slave Boy with a chair at Sausage Seller's signal.

SAUSAGE SELLER

On that understanding, please accept this split-bottom chair and a well hung boy to carry it for you. And if you ever get the urge, use the boy as your split bottom too.

DEMOS

Happy me, I'm really starting to relive the good old days!

SAUSAGE SELLER

You'll certainly say so when I present you with the thirty-year peace treaties. Come out here on the double, you Treaties!

Enter two Treaties, costumed as girls.

DEMOS

Glory to Zeus, they're pretty! God love me, is it OK if I lay them down and ratify them? Where did you ever get hold of them?

[117] By contrast, Eupolis calls Phaeax a chatterer and an ineffective orator (fr. 116).

ARISTOPHANES

ΑΛΛΑΝΤΟΠΩΛΗΣ

οὐ γὰρ ὁ Παφλαγὼν
ἀπέκρυπτε ταύτας ἔνδον, ἵνα σὺ μὴ λάβῃς;
νῦν οὖν ἐγώ σοι παραδίδωμ᾽ εἰς τοὺς ἀγροὺς
αὐτὰς ἰέναι λαβόντα.

ΔΗΜΟΣ

1395   τὸν δὲ Παφλαγόνα,
ὃς ταῦτ᾽ ἔδρασεν, εἴφ᾽ ὅ τι ποιήσεις κακόν.

ΑΛΛΑΝΤΟΠΩΛΗΣ

οὐδὲν μέγ᾽ ἀλλ᾽ ἢ τὴν ἐμὴν ἕξει τέχνην·
ἐπὶ ταῖς πύλαις ἀλλαντοπωλήσει μόνος,
τὰ κύνεια μειγνὺς τοῖς ὀνείοις πράγμασιν,
1400   μεθύων τε ταῖς πόρναισι λοιδορήσεται,
κἀκ τῶν βαλανείων πίεται τὸ λούτριον.

ΔΗΜΟΣ

εὖ γ᾽ ἐπενόησας οὗπέρ ἐστιν ἄξιος,
πόρναισι καὶ βαλανεῦσι διακεκραγέναι.
καί σ᾽ ἀντὶ τούτων εἰς τὸ πρυτανεῖον καλῶ
1405   εἰς τὴν ἕδραν θ᾽, ἵν᾽ ἐκεῖνος ἦν ὁ φαρμακός.
ἕπου δὲ ταυτηνὶ λαβὼν τὴν βατραχίδα·
κἀκεῖνον ἐκφερέτω τις ὡς ἐπὶ τὴν τέχνην,
ἵν᾽ ἴδωσιν αὐτόν, οἷς ἐλωβᾶθ᾽, οἱ ξένοι.

404

KNIGHTS

SAUSAGE SELLER

Why, wasn't Paphlagon hiding these Treaties in the house all along, so you couldn't get at them? Now I'm presenting them to you to take back home to your farms.

DEMOS

And Paphlagon, who behaved this way, tell me how you'll punish him.

SAUSAGE SELLER

Nothing severe; he's merely going to take my old job. He'll have his own sausage stand at the city gates, hashing up dog and ass meat instead of politics, getting drunk and trading insults with the whores, and drinking the runoff from the public baths.

DEMOS

Well done! You've come up with just what he deserves, to have shouting matches with whores and bathmen. And as your reward, I invite you to the Prytaneum, to sit where that pariah used to be. Put on this emerald robe and follow me. And somebody escort that one to his new place of business, so that the foreigners he used to strongarm can have a look at him now!

DEMOS, SAUSAGE SELLER, Slave Boy, and Treaties lead the CHORUS off; PAPHLAGON, costumed and equipped as a sausage seller, is prodded out of the house by two slaves and marched off in the other direction.

INDEX OF PERSONAL NAMES

Reference is to play and line number. Italicized references are annotated.

406

INDEX

Dicaeopolis: A passim
Diocles: *A 774*
Diopeithes: *K 1085*
?Dracyllus: A 612

Erechtheus: *K 1015*, 1022, 1030
Euathlus (son of
    Cephisodemus): *A 703–12*
Eucrates: *K 129*, 254
Euphorides: *A 612*
Euripides: A 394–488, K 18;
    mother of, A 457, *478*
Euthymenes: A 67

Geres: A 605
Geryon: *A 1082*
Glanis: *K 1004*, 1036, 1097
?Grypus: *K 877*

Harmodius: *A 980*, 1093, *K 786*
Hieronymus (son of
    Xenophantus): *A 389*
Hipparchides: A 603
Hippias: *K 449*
Hippodamus: *K 327*
Hylas: K 67
Hyperbolus: *A 845–47*, K
    1302–4, 1363

Ino: *A 434*
Iolaus: A 868
Ismenias: A 861
Ismenichus: A 861

Lacrateides: *A 220*
Lamachus: A 270, 567–625,

722, 960–66, 1071–1141,
    1130, 1174
Lycinus: A 50
Lysicles: *K 132*, 765
Lysistratus: *A 855–59*, K 1267

Magnes: *K 520–25*
Marilades: *A 609*
Marpsias: *A 702*
Megacles (son of Coesyra): *A
    614*
Miltiades: *K 1325*
Morsimus: *K 401*
Morychus: *A 887*
?Moschus: *A 13*
Myrsine: see Byrsine

Nauphante: *K 1309*
Nauson: *K 1309*
Nicarchus: *A 908–58*
Nicias: K 358
Nicobulus: *K 615*

Oeneus: *A 418–20*
Oeonichus: *K 1287*
Olympus: *K 9*
Orestes (son of Timocrates): *A
    1166–73*

Panaetius: *K 243*
Paphlagon: K 2 and passim,
    fictive name for Cleon
Pauson: *A 854*
Pericles: *A 530–34*, K 283
Phaeax: *K 1377–80*
Phaenarete: *A 49*
Phaenippus: A 603

407

INDEX

*Composed in ZephGreek and ZephText by
Technologies 'N Typography, Merrimac, Massachusetts.
Printed in Great Britain by St Edmundsbury Press Ltd,
Bury St Edmunds, Suffolk, on acid-free paper.
Bound by Hunter & Foulis Ltd, Edinburgh, Scotland.*